P9-CQJ-105

Praise for *The Highlander's Heart*

"*The Highlander's Heart* is an engrossing, enthralling, and totally riveting read. Outstanding!"

—Jackie Ivie, national bestselling author of *A Knight And White Satin*

"Another vivid portrait of romance in fourteenth-century Scotland… the plot never falters, and fans of Highland romance will appreciate Forester's devotion to historical accuracy and effortless storytelling."

—*Publishers Weekly*

"A delightful romp. With its large and wonderfully crafted cast of characters, a triple romance, colorful historical details, and the mayhem and madness that ensues, the author entertains and amuses all."

—*RT Book Reviews*

Praise for *The Highlander's Sword*

"A masterful storyteller, Amanda Forester brings new excitement to Scottish medieval romance!"

—Gerri Russell, award-winning author of *To Tempt a Knight*

"A radiant gem… If you love stories of Highlanders, then you will most certainly love this… such a wonderful story that it invaded my dreams, making me long for a Highlander of my own."

—*Yankee Romance Reviews*

"I loved the richness of [Ms. Forester's] work... the lush and vividly created scenes added to the realism of the story... The narrative is fantastic."

—*Long and Short Reviews*

"Moody, atmospheric Scottish fiction at its best! Amanda Forester makes fourteenth-century Scotland jump off the page and into your imagination with her strong attention to detail and great characterization."

—*Queen of Happy Endings*

"If you love historical romance, you won't want to miss this one. It's amazing! Romance, humor, and a Highland mystery all rolled into one... Amanda Forester's writing just warms the soul."

—*Wendy's Minding Spot*

"Thrilling... Amanda Forester has a talent for incorporating intrigue and romance in equal measure into a plot. She has clearly done her research, as her language and descriptions of food, parties, beliefs, and holidays brim with credibility... Forester will capture the hearts of readers."

—*Romance Junkies*

PAPL
DISCARDED

TRUE
HIGHLAND
SPIRIT

Amanda Forester

sourcebooks
casablanca

Copyright © 2012 by Amanda Forester
Cover and internal design © 2012 by Sourcebooks, Inc.
Cover illustration by Anne Cain

Sourcebooks and the colophon are registered trademarks of Sourcebooks, Inc.

All rights reserved. No part of this book may be reproduced in any form or by any electronic or mechanical means including information storage and retrieval systems—except in the case of brief quotations embodied in critical articles or reviews—without permission in writing from its publisher, Sourcebooks, Inc.

The characters and events portrayed in this book are fictitious or are used fictitiously. Any similarity to real persons, living or dead, is purely coincidental and not intended by the author.

Published by Sourcebooks Casablanca, an imprint of Sourcebooks, Inc.
P.O. Box 4410, Naperville, Illinois 60567-4410
(630) 961-3900
FAX: (630) 961-2168
www.sourcebooks.com

Printed and bound in Canada
WC 10 9 8 7 6 5 4 3 2 1

To Squid-Man and Captain Kitty Pants, who give me such joy. And to Ed, my true hero.

One

MORRIGAN MCNAB SILENTLY DREW HER SHORT SWORD, careful to remain hidden from the road. She checked to ensure her black head-scarf was in place, concealing her nose and mouth. The target of today's villainy clopped toward them through the thick mud. Twelve men were in the mounted party, their rich robes identifying them as wealthy, above the common concerns of daily sustenance… in other words, perfect marks.

Concealed by the tree and thick foliage, Morrigan scanned the approaching party for weapons. It appeared to be a hunting party, since all had bows slung across their backs and long knives at their sides. The dead boar they carried strung between two riders was also a clear sign of a hunt. Despite their alarming arsenal, most looked complacent, paying more attention to the flask they were passing around as they laughed and joked among themselves. One man, the one carrying a metal-tipped pike, scanned the woods around him as if he sensed danger.

Morrigan glanced at her brother Archie, only his eyes visible over the mask he wore. He pointed to her, then to the man with the pike. Morrigan narrowed her eyes at her brother. He always gave her the hard ones. Morrigan gave a curt nod and turned her focus back to the pikeman. He looked fit and vigilant. She preferred fat and careless. The war horse was a fine specimen too, tall and strong, trained to stand his ground in battle. It would not be easy to take him down.

The hunting party clomped closer, and a man walking behind the riders came into view. Morrigan wondered why he was left to slog through the mud behind the hunting party. Many of the horses would carry two men with ease. The walking man was dressed in a worn traveling cloak and a brightly colored tunic with a lyre strapped to his back. He must be a minstrel. Those wealthy hunters probably considered him unworthy of a ride. Damn rich bastards.

Archie gave a bird call, the signal. Morrigan tensed in anticipation, coiled, ready to strike, and counted. The men jumped at twenty; she always leaped at nineteen.

Morrigan sprung onto the road and charged the man with the pike, screeching like some fey creature from hell. Archie and the men surged into the fray, the men's shouts blending with the surprised cries of the beset hunting party. The pikeman lowered his weapon toward her with a snarl, but Morrigan dropped to the ground and rolled under the nicely trained war horse, which was obliging enough not to move.

Regaining her feet on the other side of the horse, she pounded the hilt of her sword into the man's elbow that held the pike, which now was pointed the wrong direction. The man howled in pain, his black teeth showing, and swung to hit her. She anticipated the move, ducked out of the way, grabbed the pike, and flipped it out of his hand. She had her sword tip stuck under the edge of his hauberk before the pike sunk into the mud. She applied just enough pressure to give him pause.

Her fellow bandits had likewise subdued the rest of the party. It was quiet for a moment, an odd silence after the explosion of sounds a moment before, that terrified both man and beast into mute submission.

"Good afternoon, my fellow travelers." Archie McNab stood before the hunting party, a scarf covering his nose and mouth. He gave a practiced bow with an added flourish. Morrigan rolled her eyes. Her brother liked to think of himself as a gentleman thief. True, he was laird of his clan, but Morrigan had little tolerance for petty niceties. They were there to rob them. What was the point of being genteel about it?

"I see ye are burdened wi' the evils o' worldly possessions. But ne'er fear, my brethren, we have come to relieve ye o' yer burdens."

Morrigan held out her free hand, hoping the man would readily hand over his pouch of coins like the other wide-eyed members of his party. He did not comply and instead nudged his horse, causing it to step sideways.

"Grab the reins," Morrigan commanded a young accomplice. The lad took up the reins of the war horse and held the animal's head while Morrigan kept her eyes and her sword on the black-toothed man. He snarled at the lad, who balked and stepped back.

"Hold its head!" Morrigan snapped. The last thing she needed was this man making trouble.

"Now if ye fine gentlemen will make a small donation to the fund for wayward highwaymen, we shall set ye on yer way in a trifle," said Archie.

On foot, Morrigan mentally added. The warhorse Black Tooth sat upon was a fine specimen. She reckoned she would look better than he astride such a fine animal. The rest of the hunting party readily handed over their money pouches and weapons, but not Black Tooth. He glared a silent challenge. Morrigan sighed. For once, just for the novelty of it all, she'd like things to be easy. It was not to be on that day. Nor any day, truth be told.

Morrigan stabbed her mark harder, but other than a scowl, he made no move to comply. She could kill the man, but Archie was firm in his orders not to kill unless necessary, and Morrigan had to acknowledge the wisdom of it. Robbing folks was one thing, murder was another. The last thing they needed was a band of Highlanders come to rid the forest of murderous thieves.

The man still refused to hand over his money bag, so Morrigan grabbed the pommel of his saddle with her free hand and put her foot on his in the stirrup and hoisted herself up. It should have been a quick move. She grabbed his purse and pulled it free. Suddenly, he shouted and kicked the horse. The lad dropped the reins and the horse lunged forward, throwing Morrigan off balance. One punch from Black Tooth, and Morrigan fell back into the mud.

The black-toothed terror charged the horse in front

of him, causing the mount to spook and rear. The result was chaos, as the remaining horses broke free, urged on by the hunting party who sensed a chance to break free.

"Grab the horses, ye fools!" Morrigan jumped up shouting. "They be unarmed, get them ye bastards!"

But more than one thief, having secured the desired reward, melted back into the shrubbery rather than face the angry hunters. The hunting party broke free and galloped away down the path they had come.

"Damnation!" Morrigan yelled at her thieving brethren. "What is wrong wi' ye cowardly knaves?"

"We got the coin," grumbled one man in response.

"But not the horses, ye fool! Now they can ride for their friends and come back for us. And ye," Morrigan turned on the spindly legged lad who had dropped the leads of the warhorse she coveted. "Ye ought to be more afeared o' me than any bastard on a horse." Morrigan strode toward the boy with the intent of teaching a lesson that would be long remembered, but her brother caught her arm.

"Let him be, he's only a lad."

"I was younger than that when I joined this game," Morrigan shot back.

"Aye," Archie leaned to whisper in her ear. "But we all canna be heartless bitches like ye." With teasing eyes he straightened and said in a louder voice. "Besides, we have a guest."

Standing in the middle of the muddy road was the colorfully dressed man with a lyre slung on his back. Damn hunters had left him with a bunch of thieves. Morrigan cursed them once again along with their offspring and their poor mothers for general completeness. She was nothing if not thorough.

Despite being surrounded by thieves, the man appeared surprisingly calm, though perhaps after their pathetic display of incompetence he rightly felt he had nothing to fear.

"Allow me to introduce myself," the stranger said with a seductive French accent and an equally appealing smile. "I am Jacques, poor traveling minstrel. At your service." He gave a polished bow that put Archie's attempts at gallantry to shame. Morrigan caught her brother's eye to make sure he knew she had noted it.

"And what brings ye to be traveling with such cowardly companions that they would leave ye at the first sight of trouble?" Morrigan asked.

"The hunters I met on the road. They invited me to walk behind them to their hunting lodge." Jacques gave an impish grin. "I can only assume my services, they are no longer required."

"Ah, then they are doubly fools, for a minstrel is a rare prize indeed," said Archie.

"You mean for me to be ransomed?"

"Nay, nay, ye are our guest. We are but humble thieves, but we shall take ye to…" Archie swallowed what he was going to say and coughed. "We shall take ye to the doorstep o' the great Laird McNab. We dare no' cross the border o' his domain, for he has no tolerance for our kind, but I am sure he will welcome ye. And he can pay for yer services," said Archie McNab, jingling his ill-gotten gains.

"Archie," hissed Morrigan drawing him aside. "What are ye doing? We canna bring him back to our hall."

"Nay, we will drop him close and let him walk the rest," whispered Archie in response. "Then we will ride ahead and wait for his arrival. We are still masked, so he canna identify us as McNabs."

"But he has certainly heard us, Brother. Do ye no' ken he will recognize our voices?"

"Nay, nay, ye worrit yerself. Think, Morrigan. When was the last time we had a minstrel?" Archie's eyes gleamed above his mask.

Morrigan shook her head. It had been a long, long time. And for good reason. What minstrel in his right mind would travel into the Highlands to sing for the poorest clan west of Edinburgh? It was a tempting opportunity, and Morrigan knew all too well the devious gleam in Archie's eyes. They would soon be hosting the clan's first minstrel in twenty years.

Archie gave some rapid commands. The men, quick to see a potential reward, eagerly complied, gathering the weapons, money, and the dead boar. The minstrel appeared to be a pleasant sort of man, making no complaints and readily agreeing to the plan of taking him near the "great Laird McNab." Morrigan wondered at the shocking hubris that would lead to that bold lie. Her brother always dreamed big and generally settled for much less.

Morrigan jumped up on her own mount. They needed to make haste, before their hunting friends returned in greater numbers looking for the return of their property, and for a hanging as their supper amusement. Perhaps the hunters would have the minstrel play a lively tune, while Morrigan and her fellow thieves danced at the end of a rope. Aye, it was most assuredly time to leave.

"Here, my friend," said Archie leading the minstrel toward Morrigan. "Allow us to give ye a ride."

"Nay," said Morrigan, easily seeing Archie's intent. "Let him ride wi' someone else."

"But ye are the lightest among us."

"Nay, Toby over there is hardly seven stone."

Archie walked quickly toward her and hissed, "Toby is a young fool. Ye take the minstrel and dinna let him get away." Archie turned back to the minstrel saying, "So pleased ye could join us."

The minstrel smiled at Morrigan. "I am causing you inconvenience? I must apologize." His voice was smooth as velvet with his polished French accent. His eyes were a shocking, bright blue in contrast to his black hair, and even Morrigan had to admit that he was nice to look upon.

"No inconvenience, I assure ye," Morrigan found herself saying. Maybe inviting a minstrel back with them was not such a bad idea.

She reached out her hand to help him onto the horse and he took it, swinging himself up easily with little assistance. He positioned himself behind her, the thighs of his long legs touching hers. Suddenly Morrigan felt quite hot in her hauberk and she took a deep breath. Damn, but he smelled nice too.

Morrigan revised her opinion of the minstrel. He was trouble; and like most of Archie's plans, it would no doubt go horribly wrong.

Two

MORRIGAN DUNKED HER HEAD IN THE WATER BASIN again, trying to get the mud out of her ears. Rolling around in the muck, and other substances she would rather not consider, was hardly good for her general appeal. Her brother had dropped off the minstrel as close to their home as he dared and gave him strict instructions to follow the road to McNab Hall. They rode off in the opposite direction, then doubled back and raced to the hall.

Archie gave excited instructions to the cook and provided him the boar to roast. News of their minstrel's arrival spread like fever through the castle, infecting the generally glum residents with uncharacteristic anticipation. The news of their success on the road was relayed with more reservation, since the true nature of the McNabs' extracurricular revenue source was a well-known secret.

In appreciation of their guest's arrival, people broke out their Sunday clothes and did a cursory wash. Despite her fear that inviting the minstrel was a poor idea at best—for if he identified Archie as the leader of the band of thieves, he could spread that news far and wide—even Morrigan felt compelled to make herself presentable. Though if anyone asked, she would cite the mud as the reason, certainly not the warmth of the minstrel's smile. Other lasses would surely have swooned to be in close proximity to such an attractive man. Good thing she was immune to that sort of rot. She doubted he even knew she was a girl.

Morrigan donned her usual attire, a long, loose tunic belted at the waist, and trews over her long legs. Underneath she bound her chest with a wide strip of linen. She found the evidence of her womanhood cumbersome in her present occupation. Since she was doing a man's job, it was easier to look the part. Morrigan pulled on a pair of black leather boots and wrapped her one vanity, her long, brown hair, into a cap. She was thin and tall, standing at eye level or higher than most men in her clan. Only her brothers and a few others beat her height. Unless one knew otherwise, she looked to the world like a young lad. A young, thieving lad.

Ever since Morrigan took up the sword, she had dressed as a man. Archie had tolerated it when she was young, but in her teen years he had demanded she cease her militant ways and put on a skirt. She had replied that when he could best her at the lists, she would give up her sword. Morrigan absently traced the etched design on her scabbard with her left hand. Her sword was still at her side. Not that Archie was unskilled at the martial arts, but Morrigan could still best him, and every other McNab warrior for that matter.

Morrigan briefly considered putting on something feminine, in honor of their musical guest, and for the amusement of shocking her clan. She opened a trunk at the foot of her bed, but the only gown she could find was one she wore when she was ten, the year her mother died. Had it truly been so many years? Morrigan slammed the trunk shut. If she had been born a man, it would not have been so bad, but as a lass... Morrigan shook her head. Since she had been born a lady, her life by anyone's estimation was a pathetic travesty.

Morrigan stomped into the great hall, so named only because it was the largest room in the tower castle, not for any intrinsic greatness. A few faded tapestries hung on the walls, the ones of any value had long since been sold to support the clan. Rushes of undetermined age covered the floor. Since Morrigan could not recall the last time they were changed, it had undoubtedly been too long. The trick was not to let one's feet sink below the top layer to the slimy, stone floor underneath. The central hearth of the room was large, built in grander times. The small peat fire smoldering in the gaping hearth was a salient reminder of the unlucky clan's poverty.

Passing by the lower tables on her way to the head table, Morrigan was ignored by men and women alike. Since she was the sister of their laird, they could do little about her existence in the hall, but the clan made it clear they did not approve of her gender-confused attire. According to the clan, and particularly the women of the clan, she should remain a lady, even if the clan starved without her aid. They would eat the game she caught, spend the coin she stole, but even if her support was all that stood between them and starvation, they would never accept her.

Morrigan understood their rejection. Long ago she decided she would sacrifice herself to support the clan. As chatelaine of the castle, it was her job to do everything she could to protect and support the clan. For Morrigan, that meant utilizing her one true gift: skill with a sword. Yet taking up the sword meant being ostracized from the clan she supported. She hated it. But there was no other way.

Morrigan sat at the table, noting that someone had bothered to put on tablecloths. The rumor of a minstrel brought out the hopes, and generally disregarded table manners, of the McNabs.

The minstrel entered the hall shortly after Morrigan. Unlike his previous hosts, who granted him the dubious honor of trudging along behind their horses, the minstrel in McNab Hall was treated as an honored guest, sitting just off the high table itself. Men and women crowded around him asking questions and preventing him from eating one of the best meals McNab Hall had seen in a long time. The minstrel's fine features and easy smile may have played a role in the attraction. Serving wenches refilled his cup, leaning low on the table and spilling out more than just whiskey.

Morrigan considered leaving the spectacle, but the smell of roasting pig proved too tempting even for her to ignore. Cook had risen to new heights in the preparation of the meal. She suspected that there would be meager days ahead, since they were most likely eating all the food in their larder in just one day. Villagers had come in from the surrounding areas, and many freshly scrubbed faces could be seen around the full tables. Morrigan turned to her brother beside her, intending to voice her complaint, but Archie's eyes were glowing.

"'Tis wondrous, no?" he asked.

"Aye. 'Tis is the best night we e'er had!" replied her younger brother, Andrew, taking a healthy bite of roasted meat. Andrew had not been with them on the raiding party. It was one of the few things Archie and Morrigan agreed upon. They were sending Andrew to university in Edinburgh and would never allow him to join in their thieving ways. Their young brother was to be the salvation of their clan.

The great hall was filled with the unusual smell of delicious food and the utterly foreign sound of laughter. Before Morrigan's eyes, men brought logs to the fire and coaxed a blaze unseen for years. Memories of long ago flashed through her and formed a lump in her throat. It was different once, when her parents were alive. Music had filled the hall. It was before poverty had made them desperate, before her mother's death had killed every ounce of joy she had ever known.

Morrigan closed her eyes to dispel the ghosts, but the music continued to play. Opening her eyes, she saw that Jacques stood before the crowd, playing a familiar tune on his lyre. His hands swept skillfully over the instrument, producing a rich melody, pure and true. Never before had she heard anything more beautiful. He was a tall man, well proportioned and trim. Everything about him was smooth, from his fluid movements to his silky voice. The hall silenced to hear him, ensnared in the melodic web he spun.

The music was familiar; soothing ballads of lovers or rousing songs of Scottish victories over the evil English invaders. People cheered at the victories of the Scots, cried to the sorrowful ballads of unrequited love, and danced to the lively tunes. Morrigan listened with quiet enjoyment, appreciating the skill of the minstrel, until unwanted memories marred the beautiful melody like a dissonant chord.

Music sliced through her with sharp pleasure. The minstrel had chosen a painfully familiar tune. The haunting melody he strummed on the lyre touched her deeply, penetrating her carefully wrought barriers. Morrigan clenched her jaw, trying to keep the emotions at bay. She needed to escape before anyone noticed the bewitching effect the music had on her.

Morrigan stood from the table and made her way to the door. No one noticed. Morrigan, the lass who feared neither death nor pain, who never ran from a fight, who never looked at a man but to mock him, turned and fled up the tower stairs.

Morrigan chose the east tower because she wished to be alone. The top floor was dirty and damp, with the faint odor of mold. It was a perfect fit for her mood. One corner was drier than the rest, and Morrigan plunked herself down on a stool, leaning back against the wall and placing her candle on the alcove in the wall beside her. Something squeaked in the moldy rushes. With a healthy curse aimed at men and rodents (one being no better than the other), she put her booted feet up on a crate to avoid having them nibbled by hungry pests.

Taking perverse pleasure in teasing herself, she wondered which of the serving wenches the minstrel would bed tonight. From the way those lasses stared at him with hungry eyes, there might be a fight for him. Perhaps he would simply line them up and pleasure them in turn. Indeed, no doubt that would be how he would spend his night.

Morrigan tried to distract her thoughts from the melody he played, but the painful refrain sang softly in her mind. She fought valiantly against it, but the memory surfaced unbidden and unwanted. She was a little girl, and her father played the lyre as her mother sang. It was the same song, the same sad love story. Tears that threatened spilled down her cheeks. She wiped them away in frustration, but two more followed, and soon it was pointless to fight the flood. She missed her mother and her father, dead these twelve years. She missed what might have been. Had her mother been alive, Morrigan would be married with children of her own, not some wretched thief. More tears spilled over the life she could never have.

Morrigan gave herself a slap, wiped away her tears, and kicked a mouse, who had succumbed to the tempting smell of leather, off her boot. She pushed the emotions back down where they belonged, buried somewhere under her spleen. To cheer herself, she engaged in a rousing game of mentally listing her elder brother's many faults. His deficiencies being many in her estimation, she warmed to her task and successfully chased away any remnants of emotional vulnerability with the comforting chill of cynicism.

So wrapped in her internal musing, she failed to hear footsteps on the stair. The door swung open, and Morrigan vaulted to her feet, drawing her sword. She froze at the sight. In the doorway stood the minstrel, the tip of her sword at his throat.

"I beg your pardon, sir. I am disturbing you. I shall take my leave." The wide-eyed minstrel took a step away from her blade.

"What are ye doing here, minstrel?" Morrigan growled, but she lowered her sword as he posed no threat. "Are ye lost?"

"It is clear I must be, for I was told this tower was not in use."

"'Tis not. Why do ye seek it?"

"I wish only for a place to rest before I leave on the morrow."

"But why here? Did McNab no' offer ye a place to sleep by the fire? If that dinna suit ye, I am sure ye had no lack of offers for a warm bed."

The minstrel gave a slight smile and a shrug. "I confess I have received several of the offers most charming, but of some charms a little is more than enough. I found I wished to withdraw to a quiet place for some peace."

Morrigan snorted. "Tired of being haggled over like the last good mackerel at a fish market?"

The minstrel laughed. "It is true what you say. If you have decided not to run me through, I will indulge my most terrible curiosity and ask why you, too, are in this abandoned place."

Morrigan sheathed her sword and motioned to the pitch blackness of the open window. "I was enjoying the view."

"The view?" The minstrel strode to the window and gazed out into the inky darkness. "Ah yes, the view. It is an uncommon sight, no?"

Morrigan's lips twitched upward into a half smile, half smirk. The more she tried not to smile, the more she failed at the endeavor.

"Banished are you, or running away?" asked the minstrel with a smile.

"Something like that," said Morrigan.

"Should I take my leave? I saw you leave the great hall and thought perhaps you had an appointment of a charming nature."

Morrigan raised an eyebrow. He saw her leave? He was observant. Of course he assumed her to be a lad, so his eyes were not all that sharp. "Nay, I came to be alone."

"My choice of ballads was not to your liking?"

Morrigan shook her head and searched for a safer topic. "I enjoy a livelier tune."

The minstrel leaned against the wall and put up one foot against the stones. He swung around his lyre and plucked a jaunty tune, singing bawdy lyrics. Morrigan smiled in spite of herself. As long as he kept his musical selections to risqué tavern songs, she was on solid ground.

"Ye are skilled, minstrel. Where did ye learn?"

"The monastery where I was raised," said Jacques with a gleam in his eye.

"Yer French monasteries must take a more liberal

view toward their hymns. I have yet to hear an English monk perform a tune as ye just played."

"Perhaps I should not have left, but I have found an enlightening repertoire of musical delights in my travels."

Morrigan sat back down on her stool. "I am sure ye have." Her eyes ran down the polished wood lyre in his hands. It had clearly seen some travel, but underneath was a beautiful instrument, its tone clear and sure. "I used to play, years ago it was."

"Did you now? Here, let us see what you can do." Jacques handed over the instrument with a smile.

Though she wished to touch it, Morrigan accepted it slowly. She had played long ago, back when her father taught her. Back in a time best forgotten.

"I doubt I remember anything."

Jacques grabbed the crate and sat next to her. "Give it but a try," he encouraged.

Morrigan plucked each string, the notes clear and pure. It was indeed a fine instrument. Finding the position for her left hand was difficult. She had grown since the last time she held a lyre and the position she remembered was off. The note she played was flat and sour.

"Ugh. I dinna remember."

"Your fingering is off is all." Jacques reached around her with his left hand and demonstrated the correct fingering.

Morrigan flushed at the weight of his arm on her shoulders. He was warm and smelled of woodsmoke from standing near the hearth. She stole a glance at the minstrel who leaned close to her. His hair was black and straight, with a tendency to fall over one eye. He was clean shaven, and despite his itinerant lifestyle, he obviously took care of himself. His eyes were a clear, deep blue, so bright she had never seen the like.

"…and those are the main chords," Jacques finished.

Had he been talking? Heat raced up Morrigan's spine. What had he said? Something about chords?

"Try the first one," he prompted.

"Um…" Morrigan took a wild guess and grimaced at the sour tone.

"Here, let me show you again." The minstrel leaned closer, moving her fingers into the correct positions.

Morrigan ignored the tingling sensation his touch put on her hand and focused on the lyre. She would not make a fool of herself. Plucking the strings, she thrilled in having found the right note. Slowly the memories of her past lessons came back and she played a halting tune. She stopped the moment she realized what she was doing. It was the same damn love song.

"You are doing well," encouraged Jacques.

Morrigan turned her face toward him. He was close. So close she could see faint flecks of silver in his blue eyes. Her heart did an odd flutter and skipped along merrily. His lips were full and drew her closer. She leaned toward him without thinking.

"Ah, well…" Jacques stood abruptly and pushed his hair back out of his eyes. "I… you…" He narrowed his eyes and stared at her as if seeing her for the first time. "Who are you?"

Morrigan stood and took pity on him. She removed her cap, letting her dark brown hair fall down to her waist.

"*Mademoiselle!*" His eyes went wide, gleaming blue.

Morrigan simply nodded, her lips twitching at his reaction.

The minstrel looked up at the heavens. "*Merci!*" He shook his head and gave her a wry grin. "It becomes clear now to me. No lad could be so pretty."

Pretty? No man had ever called her pretty, at least none who had the courage to make it known to her. She was the laird's sister... who dressed as a man and carried a sword. People feared her. There was power in that.

This was a different kind of power. The air crackled around her; she was in control. She took a step toward him. He looked delicious and smelled intoxicating. She was light-headed, like she had hit the whiskey a bit too hard. Her heart pounded against her rib cage, demanding to be set free. She paused, unsure what to do next. Surely this moment called for bold action. But what?

He took a step toward her. His eyes seemed to glow brighter. He reached for the lyre she still held in her hand and took it from her, setting it on the crate. His eyes never left hers.

"Am I to know your name?" he asked, his voice soft.

"Morrigan, McNab's sister." She took another step toward him so that their boots touched at the toe. She was slightly surprised to find she had to look up at him. He was a tall man, this minstrel.

"Morrigan," Jacques repeated.

"I was named after a horrible warrior she-demon. My mother almost died in the birthing."

"Morrigan the warrior," he whispered.

They stood close, neither moving. Even the wind that whistled through the tower seemed to hold its breath.

Without thinking, she pounced on the minstrel like a bird of prey on a hapless rabbit. She jumped up on tiptoe and grabbed his face with both hands, planting a firm kiss on his full lips. He stood frozen for a moment, and then started to put his arms around her. Morrigan broke free and stepped back. Her mind spun. Her brain sizzled. What had she just done?

Morrigan bolted for the door, but Jacques caught her hand in the doorway.

"I… I have offended you?" His face was concerned.

"Ye—" Morrigan wanted to give him a scathing rebuke. The best defense against embarrassment and shame was to come out swinging. "I've ne'er enjoyed anything more." Morrigan ran down the stairs wondering why in the name of St. Andrew she had told him the truth. What power did he hold over her?

Beware minstrels.

Three

Six months later…

"Ye ne'er paid me, ye horse thief!"

"Ye gave me a lame horse, ye cheat!"

"Thief!"

"Swindler!"

Morrigan rolled her eyes at the bickering men before her. Since her brothers were away from the castle, she was left to lead the clan until their return. It was not an honor.

At least one role had been relieved from her. Archie had finally found a lass willing to marry him, so his bride, the cheerful Alys McNab, was the chatelaine of the castle. Not that it helped Morrigan with the matter at hand.

"Put 'im in chains fer stealing!" demanded one of the men, glaring at his adversary with his one good eye.

"Throw 'im in the dungeon fer being a damn cheat!" demanded the other, alternating between leaning on his walking stick and using it to point at his enemy.

It was the day when the laird, Morrigan because there was no other, settled disputes from amongst the clan. Judging from the line of angry people behind the squabbling men, the McNab clan was full of malcontents. Morrigan counted herself foremost among them.

"Give him back the horse and be done wi' it," Morrigan said, stating the obvious solution.

"Nay!" both men shouted. They agreed on that at least.

"He made the horse lame. I dinna want back a worthless nag," said One Eye.

"I already gave him my best hunter, and now me poor dog's done been killed," whined Stick Man.

Morrigan had always mocked how her elder brother Archie had resolved the clan's problems. She had laughed at the petty matters brought before him, and his often-imaginative solutions. She was not laughing now. For the first time in years she wished to see Archie walking through the main door.

At that moment a figure did run through the door. Could it be?

"Fire! Come quick, the fields are burning!" screamed a lad, covered black in soot.

The hall erupted into chaos. Some ran away from the door, some toward it. Mothers scrambled to pick up their children as men ran for the main door, heedless of those around them.

"Halt!" hollered Morrigan, standing on the seat of judgment. Almost to her surprise, her clansmen slowed down and turned toward her. "Mothers, take yer bairns to the side. All able-bodied folk follow the lad to the fields. Dinna trample each other to the door, ye daft fools. Bring yer cloaks!"

Once she had herded her clan outside without anyone killing each other, Morrigan broke into a run out the main gate. She did not need a guide, the rising smoke was clear enough. She ran toward the blaze, the smoke stinging her eyes as she drew closer. With a fluid motion, she unpinned her cloak and began beating at the flames, trying to smother and stomp it out. The men and women who had followed her did the same, whipping up a thick haze of smoke, dust, and ash.

"My child! My wee bairn is still in there!"

Morrigan turned toward the woman's frantic cry. A crofter's hut was almost fully engulfed in fire. Flames licked up the side and the thatch roof was ablaze. A few men were holding back the frantic woman, tears streaking paths down her soot-covered face.

Morrigan raced toward the hut, but it was too late; it was almost completely engulfed and would collapse any moment.

"My bairn!" the woman cried.

A baby. Everything Morrigan wanted but would never have. She threw her cloak around her head and dove inside. Even on her knees, smoke choked her lungs, her eyes watered at the stinging assault. She could see nothing but flaming bits of thatch falling from the roof. It could cave in any second. The heat was unbearable.

Forcing herself forward, Morrigan searched frantically for the child, her lungs screaming for air. Feeling with her hands in the hut filled with black smoke she found the wooden cradle. Morrigan grabbed the wrapped bundle from the cradle and ran for the door. Acrid smoke smothered her, as if it was physically pulling her back into the flames.

Morrigan stumbled outside as the thatch roof collapsed with a giant rush of scorching heat. She fell to the ground, her lungs burning for air, her arms still protecting the squirming bundle.

"My child! Och, my wee bairn!" The mother took the bundle from Morrigan's hands. Morrigan tried to witness the reunion, but her eyes could not find focus. Someone grabbed her shoulders and dragged her away from the blazing hut.

Coughing and sputtering for breath, Morrigan attempted to stand. She had to continue to help put out the flames. Their clan had precious little to begin with; if their fields were destroyed, they would starve.

"Ye well, McNab?" someone asked her.

Morrigan recognized the voice but when she turned toward her clansman everything was a hazy blur. "Aye," she rasped. "Put out the fields." She tried to yell but it came out in a hoarse whisper followed by rough coughing.

"You the laird of this clan?" asked an unfamiliar voice.

Morrigan turned toward the man but could see nothing but a hazy black blur.

"Aye."

"This is for ye." The man grabbed her hand and stuffed a piece of folded parchment in it.

Morrigan's hand clutched it compulsively. "Who are ye?" she rasped.

The cloaked man chuckled and walked away.

"Stop him," Morrigan shouted. It came out as a barely audible whisper. Coughing racked her frame. The edges of her impaired vision went gray, and then there was nothing.

❧

Morrigan woke to a burning in her throat. Water. She needed water.

"Drink this."

Morrigan took the offered cup and gulped down the cool water. It hurt to swallow, but the cold was soothing on her angry throat.

"The fields," Morrigan rasped.

"Rest now. The fire is out," said Alys, Archie's new wife. Alys put a cool, wet cloth on Morrigan's forehead. Morrigan despised being coddled or being thought weak, but at the moment she hated moving even more. She was sore all over.

Morrigan blinked several times and rubbed her eyes with the cloth. Alys came into view. Alys was a stout woman with a buxom figure and dark brown hair that fell in natural ringlets. She had a pleasing face with full, red lips that warmed easily into a smile.

Alys was of the Campbell clan and had wed Archie directly before he had left to rescue Andrew, who was arrested for crimes committed by Archie and Morrigan. After many sleepless nights, they finally got word that Andrew had been saved and was staying with the Campbells. What happened to Archie, however, remained a mystery. They received no word, and he had not returned. Why Alys continued to stay with the McNabs when she could return to the comfortable situation of the Campbells was beyond Morrigan's comprehension.

"Least I can see again," muttered Morrigan. "What happened?"

"What happened is ye saved that sweet bairn's life," said Alys with a wide smile.

"The child lives?" Her heart soared. It meant more to her than she would ever admit.

"Aye!" Alys beamed at Morrigan. "Ye did well, Morrigan McNab. Ye did yerself proud."

Morrigan lifted a hand to wave off the comment and realized it was wrapped with white gauze.

"Yer left hand was burned, so I applied a salve and the bandage," explained Alys. "It should heal fine in time."

Morrigan wondered when she had burned her hand. The events were a bit cloudy in her memory. "The fields…?"

"Aye, the lads put it out. Suffered some damage but we'll survive."

"How long have I been here?" Morrigan strained to speak but could barely manage more than a hoarse whisper.

"A couple o' hours, I warrant."

"How did the blaze start?" Morrigan struggled to sit up. Fields do not burst into flame without help.

"No one can say. They did find clumps of straw in different places in the field. Once those caught it made it more difficult to put out, but the lads managed."

Morrigan shook her sore head. "Someone set that field on fire."

Alys pulled a folded parchment from her pocket. "I found this in yer hand." Alys's eyes were questioning.

Morrigan sat up farther and swung her legs over the side of her pallet. "The man, now I remember. There was a man, dark, wearing black maybe. I coud'na see. Did the lads catch him?"

Alys frowned and shook her head. "What did he look like?"

"I canna say, my eyes were so clouded from the smoke." Morrigan snatched the parchment from Alys. One glance chilled her blood.

"What is it?" asked Alys.

"'Tis naught."

"But who is it from?"

"I said 'tis naught yer concern. Thank ye Alys for yer care, I can take care o' myself now."

"Morrigan." Alys used her patient voice. "With Archie and Andrew gone, we need to work together to help our clan. Please, let me help ye."

"This is not yer clan, Alys. Ye would go back to the Campbells if ye had any sense to ye."

Alys inhaled sharply and pursed her lips together, the tears in her eyes a clear indication that Morrigan's shaft had struck home. Alys stood and swept from the room without looking back.

Morrigan sighed. She was actually beginning to respect Alys for her competence and her hard work. The tower was considerably cleaner since she took on the role of chatelaine. But McNab was not her clan. Alys had a way out. She should go back home where she would be safe, protected, and fed. It was more than what she could expect from life with the McNabs.

Morrigan fingered the dangerous seal on the parchment. It was a picture of two knights on a single horse in red sealing wax. Morrigan saw it before when it was sent to Archie. It always contained instructions from the man who paid them to do certain tasks, generally of an illegal or immoral nature. Who sent the missives or why, Archie would not say.

Morrigan broke the seal and opened the missive.

Kill the bishop of Glasgow, or they all will die.

Morrigan stared hard at the words. She sounded them out carefully to ensure there was no mistake. She was not the most proficient reader, but she knew her letters well enough to be chilled by the missive's meaning.

Kill. It most definitely said kill.

"Damn ye, Archie," Morrigan rasped. "What the hell have ye gotten us into this time?"

◈

It took one week before the pain in Morrigan's throat subsided. It was another week after that before she could draw a full breath without wheezing. During that time Morrigan paced, fretted, and waited for her wayward brothers to return. She wished to see Andrew because she was secretly fond of her younger brother. She wanted to see Archie because only he knew who sent the missives and who was threatening the clan.

Archie and Morrigan followed the directions in the missives for the past several years. Generally the directions were to raid a particular clan's livestock or rob a certain group of travelers. Truth was, they did that anyway, so doing what the missives required for an extra reward was hardly a difficult decision. In return, they received small payments, sometimes some cloth or occasionally some livestock. The McNabs were raiders. Thieves. Nothing to be proud of, but it was the only way they had to provide for their clan, impoverished as it was. Raiding was the only thing she did well. Very well, though it was a shame to admit it.

It had not always been that way. Years ago, the stomachs of the McNab children did not rumble as much as today. They had never been a rich clan, but they had never been poor either. Morrigan's grandfather was to blame for their current distress. He had sided with the English when it was no longer fashionable to do so.

Grandfather McNab had made a promise to the English king, and he would keep his word. Most lairds had sworn allegiance to England, Robert the Bruce included. But the Bruce had no compunction in switching his allegiances when it was politically advantageous to do so. McNab had not, and when Bruce came into power, he revoked much of their land, took their cattle, and forced them to pay huge reparations. The clan never recovered.

So they stole when they were hungry. Morrigan had no ethical dilemma regarding her criminal activities. She knew whose bellies her stolen goods filled. Their neighboring clans had benefitted from their disgrace. Morrigan cared not if they stole back some of what used to be theirs.

"Rider approaching!" a watchman called from the wall.

Morrigan put her hand on her sword hilt and strode out of the main hall to the inner ward. She stepped lightly, a habit from her career choice, her boots making little sound on the stone passageway.

Outside, a rider had been let through the main gate, which was never fully repaired from the last time some invader had knocked it down. People in the courtyard gathered around; a visitor was unusual and cause for inspection.

"A message for the McNab," said the messenger.

"I'll take that," said Morrigan. "See to his horse and get the man a draft o' something wet."

"What news?" asked Alys, wiping her dirty hands on her apron. She had no doubt been working on a kitchen garden again. Morrigan was not sure if she appreciated the effort or resented her for making improvements some might say Morrigan should have considered years ago.

"'Tis from Andrew," said Morrigan. She could tell by the small, tight writing of her university-educated brother.

Alys followed Morrigan into the tower house and up to the family solar. "What does it say? Does he know where Archie is?"

Morrigan broke the seal and tried to read Andrew's proficient, tiny script. Perhaps sending him to university was not such a grand idea after all. She sat down on the stone seat cut into the wall by the window and focused on the smooth lettering. Alys hovered over her shoulder until Morrigan's glare got her to step back, but no farther than the end of the stone seat.

"Nay, it canna be!" exclaimed Morrigan.

"What is it?"

"Andrew has married Cait Campbell, Laird Campbell's own sister!"

"Nay!" Alys forgot herself and snatched the parchment from Morrigan's hand to read it herself.

"If ye dinna mind, Alys," snarled Morrigan and grabbed it back. "I wonder how on earth he managed it."

"I canna believe Cait be wed. I served her since she was a wee thing," mused Alys.

Morrigan grunted in return. She knew Alys had served as Cait's lady-in-waiting. What she did not understand was how Cait came to be married to her younger brother.

"'Tis a good match, Andrew is a fine lad and I've no doubt Cait will be verra pleased wi' him."

"I wonder why Campbell would allow such a son-in-law. I well know Andrew's finer qualities, but material wealth isna among them."

"There is more to life than money, Morrigan."

"Ha! The man who said that ne'er went to sleep wi' an empty stomach or watched his children beg for food."

Alys was silent, and Morrigan continued to read Andrew's missive, straining to make out the words, sounding out the more difficult ones. Andrew's prose was almost as expensive as his education. Morrigan preferred plain and simple.

"Andrew will continue to stay wi' the Campbells," said Morrigan. "He talks a bit about his love for Cait Campbell, what a waste of good parchment."

"But Archie…"

"I'm getting to it." Morrigan concentrated hard. "It says Andrew has not seen Archie and then it says something about the bishop o' Glasgow." A cold weight of apprehension formed in the pit of her stomach. What had Archie done with the bishop? She concentrated hard on the writing but the two sentences that discussed Archie had been hopelessly smudged.

"The bishop o' Glasgow?" asked Alys. "What is he to Archie?"

"I dinna ken," replied Morrigan. Except that perhaps Archie had been sent to kill him, but Morrigan was not inclined to share all her secrets with Alys. "Here, maybe ye can make it out." Morrigan handed over the smeared parchment to Alys's willing hand.

Alys focused intently on the parchment, her brows scrunched together in concentration. After a minute, she held it up to the light, frowned, and squinted at the words. "I canna read it," she finally admitted defeat. "What would Archie be doing wi' the bishop o' Glasgow?"

Morrigan did not answer, her mind examining the pieces of the deadly puzzle. In his letter, Andrew devoted many lines to describing his love for Cait, and his plans to seek the knighthood. If Archie had been arrested for killing the bishop, wouldn't Andrew's missive have taken a different tone?

"I know naught what Archie is doing," Morrigan replied.

"Do ye think he needs our help?"

Morrigan snorted in affirmation. "He is always in need o' help. Foolish bastard that he is."

Alys frowned.

"Ye of all people canna deny Archie is in desperate need o' sense. His daft plans are always ending poorly."

Alys lifted her chin and folded her arms across her chest. "I woud'na say so."

Morrigan sighed. Alys had been part of one of those daft plans and had no doubt taken offense. "Ye marrying him was more than he deserved."

"He needed me."

"I would ne'er deny that." Morrigan stared aimlessly out the window. She could wait for Archie no more. The warning from the man who burned her fields promised retribution against the clan if she failed to comply with his evil demand. They were too close to the edge of starvation to survive another attack. They needed that grain. The full harvest must come in, or many of her clan would not survive the winter.

It didn't matter that the thought of murder turned her sick; she must protect the clan. She would go to Glasgow and do what had to be done. There was no other choice.

"I need to go after him." Morrigan caught Alys's eye. "I need ye to look after the clan while we all are gone."

"Ye said I was no' part o' yer clan." Alys pinched her lips together, and Morrigan realized her careless barb still stung.

Morrigan shrugged. "Ye've been granted a demotion. Welcome to the McNabs."

Alys smiled brightly.

"I woud'na be so pleased. Ye've ne'er wintered wi' us before."

Alys sat beside her on the bench and took Morrigan's hand in hers. "I will care for them, my sister."

"I know ye will," said Morrigan softly, giving Alys's hand a squeeze.

Morrigan stood and strode from the room before Alys could say anything more. Emotions rose dangerously to the surface, and Morrigan could not afford to be anything but heartless.

She needed to begin her journey.

She needed to kill the bishop.

Four

MORRIGAN SLUNK THROUGH GLASGOW, JUST ONE shadow among many. She avoided the warm, delicious smells wafting from the Boar's Head Inn. She skirted around the raucous laughter and inviting orange glow of the Sword and Thistle. She did not wish to be remembered. Not when her visit to Glasgow may end in murder.

Morrigan had spent the past two days trying to ascertain the location of the bishop of Glasgow and her brother Archie McNab. Not wanting to call attention to herself by asking questions, she had shadowed the local populace, listening to their conversations. She had discovered the bishop was alive and well, but of Archie she heard nothing. Perhaps that was for the best. If he had been arrested for attempting to kill the bishop, she was sure she would have heard something in the fishmongers' gossip.

Trouble was, she had very few options. The bishop was alive. Archie was missing. And Morrigan was out of time. Her preference, if she had to kill someone, was to kill the author of the message demanding she kill the bishop. But who had sent the message? Only Archie knew the answer and he was annoyingly absent.

Morrigan skirted the town and slipped around to the back of Glasgow Cathedral toward the bishop's castle, which served as the residence for the bishop. Sneaking around the back, hidden from view by thick forest, she leaned against the cool stones of the outer wall surrounding the impressive, five-story castle. She paused to think, surely there must be a better way. To murder a bishop was unthinkable. And yet, if she did not, how many of her clan would die? The soot-streaked face of the baby returned to her. The babe would die without food, as would her mother and many others.

The bishop's life was the price for the survival of her clan. Her soul was also the price to be paid, for though her grasp on theology was weak, Morrigan knew that if she murdered a bishop, she would be damned to hell. One evil act would cost her more than he, for he would go on to his reward, while she would be doomed to burn in agony for all eternity.

Morrigan turned her face to the wall, the rough, damp stone chilling her heated skin. Was there any way to be forgiven for such an act? Morrigan considered what heroic act might undo a heinous murder, but she knew in her heart there was none. Once done, she could never be forgiven.

Morrigan climbed the back wall and crept through the darkness toward the bishop's castle. Her stomach churned and she tasted bile. She swallowed hard. She must think of nothing except the necessity of the task ahead. If she did not succeed, her people would be killed.

Light spilled from an open window, casting a rectangular block of light on the shrubs around the building. Morrigan avoided it and snuck to the stone wall of the castle fortress. She pressed her shoulder against the rough, stone wall and crept closer to the open window.

"Will ye be needing anything else tonight, Yer Grace?" spoke a female voice from inside the window.

"Nay, thank ye. I'll sit and read a while before I retire. Leave the candles, there's a good lass," replied an elderly, male voice.

Keeping to the side in the shadows to avoid being seen, Morrigan surveyed the room. An elderly man was sitting with his back to her, leaning slightly forward. The bishop made a perfect target. Could it really be so easy?

Slowly she pulled a bolt from her quiver and held her crossbow in place with her foot to draw the bow. She loaded the crossbow with a shaky hand and took aim at the bishop. She took a deep, silent breath of the cold, night air. One twitch of her finger would send her to hell eternal.

Morrigan hunched her shoulders and stared at the ground. She could not do it. And yet, her people would die if she did not act. The mothers, the children, the babe whose life she had so painfully saved. No, she could not let them die. The bishop was old. He had lived a good life, or at least a long one. It must be done. There was no other choice.

She held up the bow again. All she needed to do

was pull the trigger. She bit her lip and closed her eyes. She must do it. She must. Her eyes shut, she placed her finger on the trigger.

Suddenly, something hit her in the stomach, knocking the wind from her lungs. Her crossbow triggered, firing the blot harmlessly into the castle wall. She fell backward onto the ground, someone forcing her down, covering her mouth. Fighting for breath, she knocked the man hard on the side of his head and tried to wriggle free. He grabbed her wrist before she could grab her knife and held a blade of his own to her throat.

"Hello? Is someone there?" called the bishop.

Instinctively, Morrigan froze, as did the man who held her.

"Ye be needing me, Yer Grace?" asked a woman's voice.

"Och nay, sorry. I thought I heard something outside." The bishop's shadow loomed large in the window of light.

"Probably some animal," said the woman. "Here, let's close the shutters afore ye be hurt by some wild thing."

The light dimmed, but Morrigan remained still. She would toss off her attacker soon enough, but first she wanted to make sure the bishop had stepped away from the window.

Her attacker also seemed to be waiting. He smelled of woodsmoke and something familiar. She was engulfed by the vague memory of something pleasant.

Things were getting out of control. In a swift move, Morrigan reached up with her legs, grabbed the man's head between her ankles, and flung him and his knife from her. In a flash, she scrambled to her feet.

The man lunged forward, knife in hand, but stopped himself with a jerk. In the dim light his face became recognizable. "Morrigan," his lips spoke her name without sound.

It was Jacques the minstrel.

Morrigan dove for the crossbow and came up pointing it at the wayward minstrel. He dropped his knife and slowly raised his hands. Only then did Morrigan realize she was pointing an unloaded crossbow at him. Why did he not cry out or run away? She slung back her crossbow and drew her sword. Still he made no movement. Her mind was spinning. What was he doing there?

She blinked hard to dispel him, but he was no apparition. It was the minstrel. The first man she had kissed. The only man she had kissed. The man who had since warmed her dreams. The man who just saw her try to kill the bishop. What was she going to do with him now?

She gestured him back toward the gloom of the outer wall and followed him, making sure to retrieve his knife and the bolt that had bounced off the wall. They reached the far wall and stopped. What was she supposed to do? Jacques still made no move to escape and seemed content waiting for her to decide his fate, yet Morrigan was at a loss of what to do next. A true mercenary would kill the witness and return to finish the business with the bishop.

Her limbs were heavy and her heart pounded. She barely had the strength to raise her sword. She needed to get away and think it through.

"Climb over the wall," she hissed to the wayward

minstrel. "Dinna try to escape for I can load my crossbow faster than ye can run."

He nodded and easily pulled himself up and over the wall in one fluid motion. Morrigan scrambled after him, not easy with a sword in hand but she managed. On the other side he waited for her, making no attempt to run. She gestured toward the forest, and he obliged her by walking into the trees.

When his back was turned, she quickly sheathed her sword and loaded her crossbow, following after him into the forest. The minstrel made no attempt to escape, even when he walked through thick brush and she lost sight of him for a minute. She rushed after him, sure he would take the opportunity to flee, but she found him waiting for her on the other side, his face obscured in shadows.

After walking a good ways up a hill through the thick forest, Morrigan deemed it safe to stop. It was time to do what needed to be done. She must kill the minstrel and go back to finish off the bishop.

Ice flooded her veins, as if she had been plunged into a frozen loch. Morrigan shivered involuntarily in the silver moonlight.

"The night, it is cold. My cloak is yours." The minstrel slowly unpinned his brown cloak and held it out to her.

"Keep it," said Morrigan. She hardly wanted his kindness. She needed him dead. He had seen her; he knew she was going to kill the bishop.

The minstrel placed the cloak over a low-hanging branch and backed away. Morrigan took a few steps forward to ensure he did not get too far out of range,

catching sight of an ominous shape by his thigh—he
carried a sword!

"Yer sword, drop it!" She held the crossbow with
two hands, aiming carefully. Why had he not attacked
her with it? "Drop it!"

The minstrel complied without hesitation and
backed away from the sword. Morrigan approached
slowly and picked up the sword. It was cold and heavy
in her hand. A long sword, a warrior's sword. Why
would a minstrel carry that?

"What were ye doing outside the bishop's window?"
Morrigan barked.

The minstrel shrugged. "Enjoying the sights. The
bishop's castle is quite impressive, no?"

It was a lie, but said so boldly and with such confidence that she had to force herself not to be drawn
into merry conversation.

"Why do ye carry such a sword?"

"I am told the Highlands are a dangerous place, yet
I have found it quite hospitable. That is for most of
my visit."

Morrigan glared at him. She was getting nowhere.
Did he not understand she could kill him? "Why do
ye no' ask what I am doing here?"

"But I would never ask a lady impertinent questions, in particular when she is pointing a weapon at
my head."

"A common occurrence for ye?"

"I should hope not! But I feel I must learn from this
for my future edification."

"Yer future is quite uncertain, sir."

The minstrel's lips hinted at a smile. "Ah yes, that I

can see with much clarity. I fear you may seek retribution for my breaking a most important rule of conduct."

"And what would that be?"

"Never kiss the sister of your host."

The ice in Morrigan's veins melted instantly into fire. She gulped the cold night air, trying to cool herself down. It was good they were standing in near darkness because she had a horrible suspicion she would otherwise be caught blushing. Damn that minstrel. She needed to get away for a few minutes and clear her head.

"Sit down wi' yer back to that tree," Morrigan commanded.

The minstrel complied, casually reclining back against a tree. If he was concerned for his safety, he hid it well.

Morrigan stepped around him to the back of the tree. "Yer hands," she commanded, and he readily complied, placing his arms behind himself around the tree. It was almost irritating, his lack of fight. Why would a man carrying such a sword let her tie him to a tree without any resistance? And with what was she going to tie him?

"My bootstraps might work if there be nothing else."

Morrigan exhaled through gritted teeth. "Give them to me."

The minstrel did so quickly, which only added to Morrigan's frustration. She was supposed to be taking him captive, rendering him helpless. Why then did she feel he held the power?

She tied his hands behind the tree securely. If he thought she would be gentle or did not know how to tie a knot, he would soon learn his mistake. Morrigan stomped off without sparing him a glance, taking his sword and cloak with her. She tromped through the brush, not caring for her direction. She needed to get away from the mysterious minstrel and his confusing actions and befuddling words. Who was he?

Morrigan sat on a fallen tree trunk and tried to think. She had a mission. She had to kill the bishop. And she had to kill... the minstrel? She put her head in her hands. It was all starting to sound like some tragic ballad. How could she have possibly gotten herself into such a mess? The McNab curse. No matter what they did, it always came out wrong.

In the cold darkness, Morrigan realized nothing about her situation had changed. She still needed to kill the bishop, and if she left the minstrel alive he could tell everyone who did it, which could bring retribution onto her clan. Hellfire, how she hated her life.

One thing was for sure. The night would end in death.

Morrigan sat on the tree stump as the night air grew cold, and the silver moon rose above the trees. She considered many different options, but they all circled back into the same set of facts. The bishop must die to save the clan. The minstrel must die because he saw her. Morrigan pressed her head in her hands. Her damnation was complete; she was already in hell.

A soft rustle in the bushes caught her attention. Without making a sound she picked up her loaded crossbow. A deer, an old buck, ambled into view. She aimed and shot. Dinner was served.

Morrigan attempted to haul the carcass back to where she had left the minstrel tied to the tree but the animal was quite heavy. She strained but made little progress, cursing the deer, herself, the minstrel, and her general lot in life.

Digging down with her knees, Morrigan strained to pull the carcass. Suddenly her load became lighter and she stumbled forward, unprepared for the sudden shift in weight. Behind her, someone had lifted the backside of the carcass. Morrigan spun and gasped.

It was the shadowy form of the minstrel.

Five

"WHAT? HOW?" MORRIGAN SPUTTERED.

"I am at your service." The minstrel smiled as if he had offered to pick up a dropped handkerchief.

Morrigan dropped her end of the beast, causing the back end to be jerked from his hands. "I left ye tied to a tree. How are ye here?"

"Yes, my apologies for causing you any unwanted surprise. But see you?" He drew back his sleeve and revealed a sheath for a knife. "I could not remain comfortable while a lady was in need."

"I am no lady." Morrigan spat on the ground for emphasis. "Ye're free now. Ye can go and tell everyone I tried to kill the bishop."

"Ah, but then I would have to say why I, too, was in the garden, and I do not know what my reason might be."

"Why are ye still here? Ye could run away."

The minstrel gave a quick smile that did not reach his eyes. "Yes, perhaps I should go as you say. But then, I am not sure if the bishop is friend or foe. Can you say why you pointed at him the loaded crossbow?"

"I do not know what my reason might be," Morrigan repeated.

They looked at each other in the dim light of the moon. Morrigan considered drawing her sword or reaching for her crossbow, but her heart was not in it. Besides, she was not sure if she could best him, a chilling thought indeed.

"What will you do with it?" Jacques asked.

"Wi' what?"

"The deer."

"Eat it." Morrigan's stomach grumbled with emphasis. It had been a long while since she had eaten meat. Too long.

The minstrel began picking up pieces of wood and small sticks.

"What are ye doing?" asked Morrigan.

"Me, I like my meat cooked. And you?"

By unspoken consensus, Jacques started a fire while Morrigan prepared the meal. It was shoddy work at best, but she was able to carve out some steaks and soon they were both holding meat sizzling on sticks over the fire.

The dancing firelight and the welcoming smell of roasting meat enticed Morrigan to relax. She struggled to stay on guard. She did not know the man beside her. She clearly had underestimated his abilities. She did not attempt to disarm him, nor did he ask for the return of his sword. It was a tentative peace at best, forged over the prospect of a good meal. But something needed to be done. A quick glance at his sword in the firelight revealed intricate metalwork and a jeweled scabbard. Why would a minstrel carry such a sword?

"Who are ye?" she demanded. "Ye are not a traveling minstrel, are ye?"

The man shook his head. "I am Sir Dragonet, at your service."

"A French *knight*?"

"I serve the Duke of Argitaine."

"But why are ye here? And why disguise yerself as a minstrel? And why…" Morrigan broke off. She was going to ask about what happened in the tower, but she could not, would not speak of it.

The French knight sighed. "I most humbly ask your pardon for the deception. The Duke of Argitaine plans to make war on the English with the help of the Scots. The English have won much in France. We seek to attack them along their northern border—"

"And have the English make war against the Scots instead," Morrigan added, her eyes narrowing.

"And take the fight to the English," Dragonet continued. "The duke must know those clans who will support him and those who would betray, so he sent minstrels, such as myself, to determine without revealing themselves, if it might please the clan to join the campaign."

"Ye're a spy."

Dragonet ignored her. "By the singing of different ballads, even those songs which were critical of England, I could judge how it was received and discover their true feelings toward England."

"And you also took time to talk to the natives, earn their trust, and find out what information ye could." Morrigan flushed hot. The stick of meat in her hands drooped toward the flames, causing the fat to spit and pop.

Sir Dragonet avoided her eye and instead carefully turned his slab of meat on the stick. "Yes, it is as you say."

"So everything ye said and did was a lie." Morrigan's voice was cold.

The knight's head bowed slightly, as if her words had stung him. "I have deceived people, yes. But to you, Lady Morrigan, my words and actions have been true."

Morrigan sputtered and nearly lost her dinner to the flames. "Look at me, ye daft French knight. I am no lady! I have worked and fought and stole like a man ever since I first picked up a blade. Dinna mistake me for something I'm not. I have faults indeed, but at least I have never pretended to be someone I'm not."

Morrigan's words spilled out like a bubbling pot boiling over. She could tolerate people responding to her with rejection and fear. What she could not abide was a French knight with a polished manner and sweet words that bordered on… kindness.

The knight became fascinated with his meal, inspecting his roasting job, blowing on it, and taking a bite. The flickering light from the campfire cast him in a warm hue. He was handsome. Strikingly so. A day's stubble showed on his face, a contrast to his soft, full lips. He paused for a moment in his eating, staring into the fire, his black hair falling over one eye.

"Your roast, you like it well done?"

Her meat was on fire. "Oh!" She jerked it out of the flames but the stick was also ablaze. Her sudden movement caused the stick to break and her roast to fall into the fire. "Damn!" Morrigan scrambled up to find a new stick, something to rescue her meal.

In a flash, Dragonet stood and while she bent over to grab another stick, he deftly drew his own sword, belted at her side. He skewered the flaming meat with his sword, blew out the flames, and held it out to her.

"It is edible, I believe." Dragonet stood before her, pointing his sword at her heart.

Morrigan's gaze traveled down the sword to the man holding it. A single lunge would kill her. She waited, her eyes focused on his.

"Or you could have mine, if you prefer." Somehow he managed to say it with sincerity, not sarcasm.

With a slow, fluid movement Morrigan drew her knife and removed the meat. Instantly, he lowered the sword and wiped it clean on a handkerchief.

"What is it ye want from me?" Morrigan asked. No one showed mercy without wanting something in return.

The French knight sat back down, placed his sword on his far side, picked up his own meal, and began eating again. Morrigan gave up and sat a few feet away, taking on the challenge of eating her own charred meal. Their silence was only broken by the occasional pop from the fire, bursting orange sparks into the sky.

"Did he hurt you?" Dragonet asked softly.

"What do ye speak of?"

"The bishop. Would you tell me why you wish to kill him?"

Morrigan shook her head. She could not speak of it.

"If I can be of service to you, I will help you as I am able."

"Why would ye care?"

Dragonet finished his meal and tossed the stick into the waning flames. "The bishop, we must know if he can be trusted. Many lives hang in the balance. If he should betray us to the English…" Dragonet let his words hang a moment before continuing. "If you know a reason why he should not be trusted, I am eager in hearing you."

"Is that what ye were doing in the bushes? Spying on him?"

"But of course. Though if called to testify, I am compelled to warn you, I will disavow all recollection of this conversation."

"'Tis fair." Morrigan nodded. "I can speak no ill word against the bishop. In truth I have ne'er met him."

"I beg you would forgive my curiosity, but why hold a crossbow to his back?"

Morrigan shook her head. "I had my reasons."

"You decided to spare him?"

Morrigan frowned, but said nothing.

Dragonet slid closer to her. "Please tell me your reasons. You are not one to do anything without cause."

"How would ye ken anything about me? Maybe I simply enjoy watching a man die."

"If such was the case, you should have opened your eyes while you pointed the crossbow. No, you are no murderer. You must have a reason most desperate."

"My reasons are my own."

"Is it related to your brother being with the bishop?"

Morrigan's eyes flew open before she could check her response.

"You were not aware?" The French knight regarded her carefully.

It was pointless to lie. "Nay." Her brother no doubt received the same message—was he trying to kill the bishop too? Morrigan considered her words. "What were the circumstances of ye seeing him wi' the bishop."

"They appeared to be breaking bread together."

Morrigan applied herself once more to her charcoal dinner. It would never do to look too interested. One thing for certain was she needed to talk to Archie before trying to kill the bishop again. A sense of relief flooded Morrigan, a reprieve from the heavy burden she had dragged for the past month. The man beside her was the one loose end. She glanced sideways at the French knight. In the orange light of the fire he seemed to softly glow.

What was she to do with such a man?

"Will ye tell yer duke or anyone what ye saw o' me tonight?" Morrigan asked the knight beside her without giving him a glance. She instead focused on finding a bite of meat that was not charred, as if her dinner was her foremost concern.

"If I wished to sound the alarm, I would have done so the moment I saw you."

"Why dinna ye call out?"

"I also was in the bushes."

Morrigan nodded. "Ye dinna wish to get yerself caught."

"And…" Dragonet paused, picking up another stick and poking at the fire. "And I recognized you."

A strange sensation flooded through Morrigan. She shook it off. "Why should that matter?"

Dragonet shrugged. "It did." He poked another burning log. "It does."

Morrigan was flooded again with that rush of something warm and tingly. She decided it must be anger. With every word he reminded her of their kiss in the tower. Was he trying to manipulate her into talking more freely? Was he trying to suggest his emotions had been engaged after a brief encounter? It was nothing but lies.

"Dinna try to sweet-talk me, I'll have none o' it," growled Morrigan. "Save yer honey-dipped, forked tongue for someone more gullible. Yer latest conquest may swoon at yer feet, but I assure ye I am no' so easily fooled."

Dragonet did not look up from his fascinating work of randomly poking at the fire, but he appeared to decrease somewhat in size, as if her words had deflated him. "I beg your pardon, my lady, if my words give offense."

"I am no lady!" Morrigan's voice raised, her exasperation growing. He looked up at her, his eyes glinting in the firelight. She sputtered over her words. "Ye dinna ken who I am." She turned back to the fire. "Ye can ne'er ken what hides in the heart o' another. What secrets they may conceal."

The knight beside her took a sharp breath but said nothing. The leaves around them rustled in the unseen wind, causing the fire to heighten and pop flaming sparks into the air. She was too close to him, both of them sitting beside each other on the ground by the fire. She should pull away, but made no effort to move.

"You speak the truth." Dragonet's words finally broke the silence. "You never know the deceit that poisons the heart of man." His head was bowed toward the fire, his voice soft and low.

His words tugged at her like unshed tears. She shifted her position and her hand brushed against his. She was surprised at the contact with his warm hand, but did not move away. His dark eyes met hers. His lips parted with an unspoken question.

"I…" Morrigan bit her lip trying to think of some explanation. "Speaking o' deceit, show me the knife ye conceal."

He lifted his hand into hers and slowly rolled back his sleeve, revealing a small harness strapped to his wrist. His eyes never left hers, the question in them remaining.

Morrigan swallowed on a dry throat. With both hands, she explored the harness he wore and the blade it concealed.

"I have ne'er seen the like. Did ye make it yerself?" Morrigan tried to focus on the knife, but her hands ran over the leather harness, the steel and leather hilt, his warm hand with well-worn calluses on his palm and fingers. The marks of a swordsman.

"Y-yes." The French knight's voice wavered. His eyes were wide and black in the dim light.

"'Tis well done," she said softly. "But how do ye draw it?"

With a quick flick of his wrist the knife was in his hand.

Morrigan froze. The blade was pointed toward her. With cold insight she realized she had gotten too close. Her life may be the cost.

"Do ye mean to kill me, knight?" Morrigan quietly placed her hand on her sword hilt.

Dragonet frowned and shook his head, sheathing the knife with another flick. "Never would I harm you."

"But I saw ye in the courtyard o' the bishop. I could tell someone what I saw."

"Who would you tell? And if you did, I would deny it. A thousand pardons, my lady, but I doubt they would take your word over mine."

Morrigan flinched at the truth of his words. "'Tis the first time my bad reputation e'er kept me alive."

"No harm will come to you at my hand, Lady Morrigan." Dragonet's eyes pierced into hers. He spoke the words like a vow. "Not now. Not ever."

At the core of her being, Morrigan knew his words to be true. With cold dread she realized she trusted him, and trust was a dangerous emotion. She pushed it away like refuse and mentally scrambled for the guarded suspicion that kept her alive. "Do ye carry a blade on the other wrist as well?"

"*Oui.*" He held out his other hand, but he made no effort to roll back the sleeve, so she slowly rolled the fabric of his sleeve up, revealing the smooth, leather harness beneath. She ran her hands down the leather harness, admiring much more than the concealed knife.

Morrigan turned his hand over in the guise of inspecting the straps, but really to put her hand in his. His warm hand closed around her fingers gently, a friendly gesture and more. The other hand also held the smooth calluses of a swordsman. He used both hands in battle. What else could he do with those hands?

Desire swept through her, hot and powerful. All that she denied herself pounded through her veins. She chose the life of a warrior to help her clan, but the sweet pleasures of a mate, a husband, these she had forsaken. She fought against the powerful emotion with little success. She should not feel desire toward anyone, especially not some French minstrel, spy, knight… hell, she did not even know who he was.

Morrigan unstrapped the leather buckles, taking the dagger from his wrist. It was a nice piece, a good weight in her hand. On the handle of the dagger was a black circle with a white cross—a crest of some sort?

"Ye should no' let a lady disarm ye." She pointed the blade at his chest only a few inches away.

"But you assured me you were no lady." His voice was low and smooth. In one quick movement he grabbed her wrist and struck the blade into his own chest.

Morrigan cried out and pulled back the blade, surprised and shocked by the movement. He had stabbed himself in the chest, yet he appeared uninjured. Her fingers flew to his chest, exploring the smooth, hard surface. Too hard. She slipped a hand down his shirt.

"Leather armor," said Morrigan shaking her head. Who was he? "Ye came dressed for battle?"

Dragonet shrugged. "It is habit, I suppose."

"Do ye always dress this way? Were ye armed like this when we…"

"Yes." The answer was simple but the implications were large. He had held her, *kissed* her, with knives strapped to each wrist. He could have killed her.

"Are ye disarmed now?"

"No." A faint smile crept onto his face. "Are you?"

She tried to resist returning the smile and failed. "Nay."

"Let us start with the obvious." Dragonet assessed her person carefully, causing a wave of heat wherever he cast his eye. "You hold my knife in your hand, you have your table knife, the dagger you took from me earlier, a short sword by your side, and a crossbow within reach." He did a double take at the crossbow and raised his eyebrows. "When did you reload it? I amend myself. It is a *loaded* crossbow by your side."

Morrigan could not help but smile. "And ye, sir knight, have a sword by yer side, yer table knife, another knife strapped to yer wrist, and I would guess yet another in yer boot."

"But of course." Dragonet pulled a long, thin knife from his boot and tossed it in front of the fire.

"A *misericorde*, mercy giver." Morrigan was impressed. The blade could slip through the gaps in a man's armor to deliver the fatal blow.

"I would surmise it is the same for you?" said Dragonet.

Morrigan nodded and tossed the knife from her boot beside his, her blade a blunt instrument compared to his elegant weapon.

"And now, my lady, have you more weapons upon you?"

Morrigan nodded with a sly smile. They played an amusing game, one she knew she should not play, which made it all the more appealing.

"Ah, then let me take a guess. More knives?" Dragonet asked.

Morrigan shook her head.

Dragonet searched her with his eyes and shook his head. "Without a more thorough search of your person, I shall not discover your secrets."

Morrigan smiled and pulled out a small ax that was strapped to her outer thigh and concealed under her long tunic. She threw it beside the knives. "And ye, sir knight. Do I ken all yer secrets?"

Dragonet shook his head, the reflected flames of the fire dancing in his eyes. "I invite you to discover them as you may."

Morrigan looked him over but no additional weapons were in sight. Her pulse raced, and she wondered if she had the courage to act out the dreams that had plagued her since meeting her deceptive minstrel. She put her hand to his chest. She dared.

Morrigan ran her hands over his chest and frowned. Slowly pulling up his tunic, she found what she was looking for. Strapped to his leather armor in front and along the sides were a series of small throwing knives. These served a dual purpose of being a weapon and also additional steel plates to enhance his armor. She slowly pulled each one out, throwing them onto the growing pile of weapons.

When she finished she pushed him softly to the ground. He lay on his back without resistance, but she could see he caught his breath, his chest rising and falling rapidly beneath his armor.

Above him, Morrigan was in control. She moved

her hands over his shoulders and down his arms, making a show of searching for more weapons, but in truth delighting in the feel of him. He was a tall, lithe man, but his muscles were pronounced and solid.

"And now?" asked Morrigan. "Have I disarmed ye?"

Dragonet closed his eyes and shook his head no.

Morrigan's pulse quickened further, and she ran her hands down the outside of his far thigh. She found nothing, so she moved on to the thigh next to her, trying to keep her hands from trembling. Under his tunic, strapped to his outer thigh, was a rondel dagger. She added it to the pile.

He never moved, but his body drew her to him. She lay on her side beside him, unable to pull away. Without opening his eyes he wrapped one arm around her, and she snuggled closer, laying her head on his shoulder. It was wonderful and oh, so wrong. The air around them crackled with danger.

"And now do I ken all yer secrets?" she asked, her voice a hoarse whisper.

"No. But you have all my weapons." He reached his other arm around her. "And have I disarmed… what is this?" He pulled a small war hammer attached to her belt at her back. He tossed it on the pile with a flick of his hand. "In all my travels I have never met anyone like you, Lady Morrigan. And now, have I discovered all your weapons?"

"Nay."

Dragonet gave a soft growl and ran his hands over her back and neck and down both arms, sending happy shivers down her spine.

"I fear searching your person further," said Dragonet

with a slow smile. "For if I give offense, you may use this concealed weapon against me."

Morrigan reached up and unwound the leather rope with two wooden ends that bound her hair. Her long brown hair spilled over him, and she showed him what was in her hand.

"A *garotte*! To strangle impertinent men no doubt. Truth, but you do live up to your namesake."

Morrigan stiffened. She was not sure being called a demon warrior fell in the category of a compliment.

"A beautiful warrior." He amended, running his fingers through her hair, softly massaging her head and neck.

The sensations he produced were wickedly arousing. She wanted him. Right there on the forest floor. She knew she should not be anywhere near him, but her rational brain faded into irrelevance and raw desire took hold. She ran her hand over his chest, wishing she could feel more than the hardened leather of his armor.

She pressed herself closer until her cheek rested against his, the rough stubble stinging her skin. Turning her head, her lips touched his, soft and warm. He held her closer, and she kissed him, unsure at first, then bolder and harder. He pressed her to him, one arm around her waist, his other hand in her hair. Her world spun, and she broke the kiss, gulping the cool moist air.

"What is this?" Dragonet asked, finding something in her thick hair.

"No!" said Morrigan, but it was too late. He had found her hair pin and pulled out the small concealed dagger from its sheath. "Careful!"

"Is it poison?" he asked, holding the tiny blade no bigger than a pin.

Morrigan sat up and gingerly took the small dagger from him, replacing it into her larger hair ornament where it belonged. It was one weapon she had not wished to reveal. What was she doing kissing him?

"'Tis a powerful sleeping draft," she explained. "The hair clasp belonged to my mother. She said it had saved her life once and told me to wear it always." She looked away from him; she must break the spell.

The fire before them waned into embers. Despite being hot a moment ago, the night air cut the chill through to her bones. Dragonet sat up beside her. Glancing over at him she saw a stranger once more. Reason had taken hold.

"I should go see to my brother," said Morrigan, her voice flat. It was hardly her first choice of how to spend her evening.

Dragonet took a deep breath and let it out again. "Then all that remains is to wish you a good evening, Lady Morrigan, and thank you for not killing me."

"Dinna mention it. In truth," said Morrigan, busying herself by collecting her weapons and strapping them back into place, "I think it would be best if we pretended this night never happened."

"As you wish, my lady," said Dragonet without looking at her. He, too, collected his knives and replaced them with a deft hand.

Dragonet was first to his feet. He collected his sword and cloak, and bowed her a farewell.

"Wait," said Morrigan scrambling to stand up. "Here is yer wrist knife."

"Keep it," said Sir Dragonet and disappeared into the darkness.

Six

KNIFE IN HAND, SIR DRAGONET FASHIONED HIMSELF NEW bootstraps to replace the ones he had sliced to escape being bound to the tree. Morrigan was no fool when it came to a knot. It had been a long shuffle with loose boots through the woods back to his room at the inn. Fortunately, the inn's host was able to procure him some leather he could easily make into straps. Unfortunately, bootstraps were hardly his biggest concern.

Dragonet lay on his clean, straw pallet in the little room afforded by the inn and willed himself to sleep. Images of Morrigan were all he could see. He tried to clear his mind, think of something else, anything else, but the memory of her hands on his body seared paths of molten heat where she had touched him. No one had ever touched him like that before. He wanted more.

Dragonet jumped out of bed and splashed some cold water from a basin on his face. How could he let it happen? Avoiding feminine wiles had not been a problem while he lived in the monastery. It had been more difficult when he assumed the role of a minstrel, but he had been careful around members of the opposite sex, never to get too close, never to be alone with one. He had defenses against regular women, ladies, serving wenches, anything wearing a skirt. Yet Morrigan slipped past his defenses like his mercy giver blade sliced through gaps in armor, leaving a man dead.

It was hardly his fault. With Morrigan's height, thin build, and the loose men's clothing giving her an amorphous shape, she appeared to be nothing more than an ill-tempered lad. Too late, he discovered her baggy clothes hid a shapely body. When he wrapped her in his arms, he could feel the beautiful woman beneath the disguise.

Morrigan's hair was surprisingly soft and thick, and her large, dark eyes were framed by long eyelashes. She could be a beauty if she wished. So why did she chase people away with her sarcasm and militant ways? Whatever her reasons, he could accept it. She may scare away lesser men with her sharp tongue and walking arsenal, but beneath was a lady of infinite passion and seductive sorrow. Anger he understood. Pain he knew. He feared neither.

Morrigan was a rare treasure, one hiding in plain view, and he was the only one who could see her. She was a secret. His secret. And he was a master of secrets.

Heat flushed through him and his breath came faster, showing in the night chill of the room. Fiery tongues of desire lapped his skin. She was his alone. No one would ever know. She would be his. Except…

Morrigan could never be his.

Dragonet started to pace to clear his head. He was

on a mission. He could not be caught in an entanglement with a local girl. It was unthinkable. Not with so much riding on his actions. His father... his father had trusted him with the mission, and Dragonet would not fail him.

It had been almost a year since he last saw his father. Dragonet remembered the day in his native France when his father had honored him with a rare summons. Jacques Dragonet bowed and kissed the ring of his father, the bishop of Troyes. The bishop acknowledged him with a slight inclination of his head and continued his meal. Dragonet stood before the bishop, his stomach rumbling at the smell of the feast.

"Did you find the silver chest?" asked the bishop, taking another bite of the savory, meat-filled pastry before him. Dragonet knew better than to suppose the bishop would invite him to join the meal.

"No, Your Grace. I do not believe it is in the monastery."

"You believe it to be gone, or you know it," the bishop glanced over his pastry, his eyes glinting in the candlelight.

"I have spent the past two years working with the master of the treasury. I have taken inventory of the treasures and relics they hold; none fits of the description of the silver box you described." He had scoured the monastery belonging to the Hospitaller Knights, a warrior order of monks.

"Some treasures hold such value they are kept from the eyes of young monks."

"Yes, Your Grace. I have come to be on most friendly terms with the master of the treasury and have supplied him with enough wine on occasion as to help him be forthcoming. He shared with me his secret stash of goods, namely whiskey. He also spoke of a silver chest once when he was deep in drink, but he said it had been so precious it had disappeared. Carried off by angels was his report."

The bishop grunted and shook his head with disdain.

"He was heavily beset by drink at the time," explained Dragonet.

"It was carried off, I do not doubt it, but hardly by angels. No, it has been stolen from me." The irrelevant fact that the bishop had no right to the treasures held by the Hospitallers was not mentioned by either.

"I am sending you on a quest." The bishop's words struck deep and true. It was what Dragonet had been praying for, a chance to prove himself to his father.

"I am ready, Your Grace." Dragonet had trained hard, studied hard, prayed and fasted. He had joined the Hospitallers as his father had asked, and immersed himself in their rigorous training. Dragonet wished to prove to his father that he had been worthy of his notice, worthy of the opportunities that had been given him.

"You know of the Knights Templar?"

"Yes," replied Dragonet. Who did not know their sad history? "Their order was declared to be heretical and disbanded."

The bishop gazed slyly over the rim of his wine glass. "King Philip owed the Templars money, and a lot of it. The Templars main heretical act was in not forgiving it. King Philip pressured the pope, who also owed the Templars money. The pope agreed to disband the order on charges of heresy, giving to the Hospitallers their assets, minus of course a substantial contribution to the king's coffers."

"So you believe the silver chest to be part of the Templars' treasure?" Dragonet asked.

The bishop nodded and took a long drink of wine, draining the glass. He set the empty glass on the table and poured himself another. Dragonet wondered what he could do to warrant his father sharing a sip.

"Yes, it was found in Jerusalem and brought back to France. They were forced to hand it over to the Hospitallers locked in a silver chest. That much I have gathered from the records of the Inquisition."

Dragonet shuddered. To fall into the hands of the Inquisition and their torturous ways was the stuff of nightmares.

"What is this thing for which you search?" Dragonet could not help being curious. The least his father could do was let him know what was in the box. Unfortunately, his father was accustomed to doing less than the least for his unacknowledged son and dismissed the impertinent question with a flick of his hand.

"We need to find the missing chest without alerting the one who holds it to its value or to our interest. I recently heard the confession of a dying knight who spoke of a group of Templars who returned from exile after the persecution and stayed with the Hospitallers before returning to exile. The relic must have been removed at that time."

"Where is the treasure now?"

"Scotland."

"Scotland!" Dragonet could keep neither the surprise nor the dismay from his voice.

"Some Templars escaped to Scotland years ago, but I have heard nothing of this box or what it contains. There are whispers of a hidden Templar fortune, but what is mere gold?" The bishop took another hearty bite of his savory pastry.

Dragonet said nothing. Gold was only meaningless to those who had never known want.

"You will go and find this silver chest," the bishop commanded.

Dragonet again said nothing. *Scotland?* Did people actually live there? Wasn't it terribly cold and populated by barbarians? The thought of leaving France was an unwelcome one.

The bishop stopped eating and gave Dragonet an appraising glance, as if judging how much to offer in order to gain compliance.

"Inside the chest is a relic so powerful, there can be none beside it. The old Templars are the key, they are where you must begin." The bishop lowered his voice. "The Holy Grail itself is but nothing compared to this treasure."

Dragonet waited for him to reveal what was the treasure of the Templars but the bishop merely took another sip of wine, waiting for Dragonet's answer. The room was silent.

"I never wanted a child, but today I am glad to call you my son. Will you go on this quest, Sir Knight?" asked the bishop.

The corner of Dragonet's mouth twitched involuntarily. His father had asked him in a manner that made it impossible to refuse. He was being manipulated. It was nothing new. And yet it was also his best chance at proving himself to his father.

"Yes, Your Grace. I will go where you send me."

"Good. You will put aside your monk's robes and disguise yourself as a traveling knight and join with the Duke of Argitaine on his mission to Scotland."

"The Duke of Argitaine?"

"Yes, he goes to convince the Scots to make war against the English. You will travel with Argitaine. It will give you the perfect excuse to search the countryside for the Templars. I feel I must warn you that the previous monks I have sent looking for the relic have never returned. Some were killed, others..." The bishop shrugged. "The relic is not unprotected. Reveal to no one who you are." The bishop paused, his eyes narrowed into suspicious slits. "I hope my faith in you will not prove to be misplaced."

"I will bring you back the silver box, Father." Dragonet bowed and kissed his father's ring.

His father had asked him to find the silver chest, and he would. Finding the treasure was his purpose. His quest. Nothing must stand in his way.

Ah, but Morrigan... Dragonet flopped down on his pallet and pushed the traitorous thoughts aside. He was a monk. A monk! It did not matter he had taken those vows at such a tender age he had no idea what he was denying himself. It was done. He must banish the confusing feelings that emerged whenever he thought of her. His future was his mission. It could never be anything else.

He forced himself to evaluate the situation logically

and focus back on his mission. In his travels, he had learned that Templar knights had come to Scotland and joined Robert the Bruce in his war against England. But that had been years ago. He had discovered the names of several knights, but all had died. A grandson of one of the knights had been found, but he was living in a poor crofter's hut, drinking his way through day and night. Dragonet had searched the unassuming hut, and found nothing but squalor.

More Templar knights may have existed, but who and where he did not know. He did learn the office of the bishop of Glasgow had been traditionally sympathetic to the Scots' cause. Could the Templars have found in him an ally? The bishop's castle would make an excellent hiding place. What was the bishop's agenda? And why did Morrigan point a crossbow at his back?

Thoughts of Morrigan flooded back, unbidden and unwelcome. He closed his eyes, but he could still see hear her voice… what would she say to him? Even in his dreams she insulted him.

The darkness in his room turned a softer shade of gray. Dawn would be soon. It was time to go back to the castle and determine whether the bishop was friend or foe.

Seven

BY THE TIME MORRIGAN DRAGGED THE CARCASS OF THE deer back to the bishop's castle, the sun threatened to rise and her body threatened to collapse. Her back hurt, her arms hurt, her feet hurt, but she welcomed the pain that focused her thoughts on something other than a certain minstrel turned French knight.

Morrigan hoisted the carcass over her shoulders, ignoring the screaming blaze of pain spreading down her back. Focus on the pain. Better than thinking of Jacques or Dragonet or whatever his name was. Morrigan pounded on the door to the servants' entrance and dropped the beast at the feet of a surprised maid.

"I caught a bastard poaching deer on the bishop's land," lied Morrigan. "I scared him off but no' before he took down this buck. It belongs to the bishop. Is my brother McNab here? I need to speak to him. Where did ye say he was staying?"

The servant girl stared at the dead creature, then at Morrigan, then back at the carcass, but eventually led Morrigan down a narrow hallway. Morrigan was shown into a small room with a stone fireplace and two wooden benches. The fireplace was unlit, the walls were plain, and the only light came from a small window. The maid left without saying a word.

Morrigan sat heavily on a wooden bench. The room was so spare she guessed it was rarely used, probably reserved for guests of unknown class and origin, such as herself.

"Morrigan! By the saints, what happened to ye?" Archie McNab burst into the room with his long stride, but stopped short, his eyes widening. Morrigan glanced down at herself and noted with some disgust that the deer had bled down her side. She was not only dirty but half covered in blood and gore as well. She was surprised the wench let her in the castle at all.

"I am unhurt. I brought a deer for His Grace."

McNab opened his mouth as if to speak but only shook his head with a shrug. "Ye're daft. Always was."

"Nice to see ye too, Brother," Morrigan ground out.

"'Tis good to see ye, truly. But what are ye doing here? How is the clan?"

"Fine, no thanks to ye. Why have ye been gone so long? We took ye for dead." Morrigan was not sure if she should be joyful or furious to find Archie in such good health.

"Did ye no' receive the missive I sent? Sodden Sal promised to deliver it direct."

"Nay, we received naught." Morrigan stood and put her hands on her hips. "Let me understand, ye entrusted yer message to a knave named *Sodden Sal*?"

"I am short o' funds," Archie said with a shrug. "But how is the clan? Why are ye are here?"

Morrigan glanced around. "Are we alone? Can we talk?"

Archie shut the door and they both sat down on the bench. Morrigan noted he appeared to be well fed and adequately dressed. There was also something different about him, something she could not name.

"What is it? Tell me the whole," said Archie in a way Morrigan appreciated. Archie may have foolish notions, but when it came to the clan he took his leadership seriously. There was little he would not do for the clan. It was the one thing they had in common.

"The main fields were burned, we lost a third of the crop," Morrigan said bluntly.

"Nay!" Archie shook his head, the haunted look returning to his eye. "We need it for the winter. How did such a thing happen?"

"It was set purposely. I was given this." Morrigan reached down her shirt into the linen strips she used to bind her chest and produced the threatening missive with the odd seal.

McNab took the folded parchment and held it up to the gray light of dawn, but did not open it, a flicker of recognition crossing his face. "Please tell me ye did no' harm the bishop."

Morrigan shook her head. "What is happening, Brother? Who sent this? 'Tis time to tell me the truth."

"I ne'er meant it to come to this," Archie mumbled and closed his eyes for a moment, rubbing his face with his hands. "It started many years ago, before either o' us was born. Ye recall the stories o' Robert the Bruce fighting against the English?"

"Aye. What has that got to do wi' this?"

"Around that time the Church declared the Templar Knights to be heretics and persecuted their members. Many fled to Scotland for safety."

"I ken the history, what is yer point?"

"A group o' these Templars was traveling in winter and got caught in a blizzard. Our grandfather found them and offered them shelter. They had some things wi' them. Things they were anxious to hide. They paid Grandfather McNab handsomely for his charity and asked for something more, the ability to buy a portion of our land. The only condition was he could ne'er tell anyone he had sold the land."

"The farmland we are not allowed to use!" said Morrigan. She had always wondered why some of their best fields had been allowed to go fallow so long. It was all starting to make sense.

"Aye. A few years later, when the McNabs were punished by Bruce for choosing the wrong side of the conflict, the Templars advocated for leniency, ensuring we kept our land."

"But not our sheep or chickens or pigs," interrupted Morrigan, her bitterness seeping through.

"Aye. Though I doubt the Templars cared for us as much as they wished their treasure to remain safely hidden."

"Wait—treasure? Did you say they hid treasure on our land?"

"Their land actually…"

Morrigan waved a hand impatiently. "Do ye mean to tell me there is a treasure on our land and ye ne'er looked for it?"

"O' course I have, what do ye take me for?" Archie

scowled. "There is naught on the land they bought but a cave. And aye, I have searched it. 'Tis just an empty cave. Whatever they hid there must have been moved long ago."

"Which cave? Where is it?" Their problems were not so lofty a good amount of coin could not solve them.

"The one by Loch Pain."

Morrigan knew of the cave with all its creepy passages. She avoided it, but she knew others, including her brother, had explored it. It contained no treasure. She should have known better than to hope, if only for a moment, for a lost treasure to fall into her hands. "Perhaps our clan would have better luck if we renamed our topography wi' more happy names," she grumbled.

Archie smiled faintly. "Perhaps. Since they saved our land, the Templars determined we owed them allegiance and demanded we serve their cause or suffer the consequences. We were not bothered for a while, but recently the messages have gotten more frequent and more demanding, until this." Archie held up the missive Morrigan had given him.

"So this is from the Templars?" Morrigan glanced at the red, wax seal with two knights on a single horse.

"This is their seal. Father showed it to me afore he died. There is only one Templar left that I know. He was verra young when he first fought for Robert the Bruce, but he has grown into the devil. It is he who wants us to kill the bishop."

"But who is it?"

"'Tis the Abbot Barrick."

"The Abbot Barrick?" Morrigan repeated. "The *abbot* sent us that message?" Morrigan wished she had not stayed up all night, maybe then her brain could keep pace with the events before her. "But why would the abbot want us to kill the bishop?"

"I dinna ken."

Morrigan stood and paced the room, trying to clear her head and think through what needed to be done. "What are we to do now? Go after the abbot?"

"Nay, Morrigan. Leave that bastard alone. I have told the bishop the whole, and he is taking me to testify against the abbot in Rome." Archie gave a small smile, his eyes gleaming.

"Rome!" Morrigan stopped short and stared at her brother. "But that's so far... Rome?" Morrigan shook her head. The thought of her Highland brother traveling to some far off land was inconceivable. Rome was a place that lived in myth, not in reality. "But how? When?"

"The bishop has applied for permission to travel through England as pilgrims. We leave on the morrow. I am sorry ye are in this Morrigan. I must go, but I will return as soon as I can."

"But why are ye leaving?" Morrigan fought the urge to convince him not to go. Though she enjoyed mocking Archie and complaining about his poor leadership and ill-conceived schemes, the thought of trying to try to take his place was chilling.

"I can name Barrick as the one trying to have the bishop killed and this missive ye brought will help us." Archie held up the letter with the red seal. "I burnt all the ones I received."

"And what am I to do in the meantime? What is to keep the clan safe from Barrick while ye are gone?"

Archie rubbed the back of his neck and frowned, causing a deep worry line to form on his forehead. "With the bishop gone, ye canna be expected to try to have him killed. I hope to return soon, before the abbot can do any more mischief."

"But he could—"

"I understand, but we must no' work for the abbot. I will return with help as soon as I am able. It will work. It has to work." Archie appeared to be trying to convince himself.

Morrigan nodded. She knew she could not work for the abbot again. "I hope this bishop can be trusted."

"The bishop isna like Barrick. He is a good man." Archie's face relaxed in a way Morrigan had rarely seen. "He advocated for Andrew and not only saved him from the gallows, but encouraged Campbell to allow Andrew to marry Cait."

"I got the missive from Andrew, though I had a hard time believing it." Morrigan shrugged. "If the bishop can bend the Campbell to acknowledge a McNab as his brother-in-law then the bishop is truly a miracle worker."

"He is." Archie smiled faintly and his eyes went soft, an unusual look for him. "Even after he caught me trying to kill him, he dinna have me arrested and killed, so I am inclined to think positively toward him."

"With all due respect, Brother, the bishop has many more years and a few more pounds on him than ye. How was he able to stop ye?" Archie was a fool, but twenty years as a raider and highwayman had given him certain nefarious talents. Overpowering a fat old bishop should have been among them.

Archie motioned to her and Morrigan sat down on the bench beside him. He leaned forward, his voice lowered to a hush. "'Twas the strangest thing, Sister, but I coud'na raise a hand to him. I think *God* is on his side."

"I would hope so, him being a bishop and all."

"Truly, I found him alone, I had my knife, and suddenly the door slammed open and I broke my nose and I coud'na harm him."

A chill tickled the back of her neck. She had tried to kill the bishop too. It had been an easy shot, simple, no way to miss. Yet she had hesitated and was tackled to the ground. Had she also been thwarted by divine intervention? She had never been particularly religious, except to recognize she was on the list of the damned, but it was somehow important to her that God did stand beside the worthy. Not her, of course, but the chosen few.

"I hope this bishop o' yers will extend his protection to ye when ye travel," mumbled Morrigan.

McNab's eyebrows shot up, and Morrigan scowled. She had been tricked into showing uncharacteristic sisterly concern.

"Thank ye." Archie said softly. "Now tell me how is it wi' the clan. How much was destroyed? Can we survive the winter?"

Morrigan opened her mouth to tell him the truth but closed it again. Archie needed to go with the bishop and testify against Abbot Barrick or none of them would ever have any peace. "I have heard there are French soldiers trying to convince the clans to join them in fighting against the English," Morrigan said instead.

"Aye, and willing to pay for every clan that joins," added Archie.

"Pay?" Archie had her attention. Odd that her French knight had not mentioned anything about payment. "They are paying the clans who join them?"

"Dinna even think it, Morrigan. I dinna want ye fighting against the English. They will just slaughter us, and I dinna want ye anywhere near a camp o' soldiers."

"Ye doubt my ability to defend myself?" Morrigan gave him a cold stare.

"Nay, I trust ye would slaughter any man who came within arm's reach. And then ye'd face a hangman's noose. Tell me we are no' so desperate we need think o' joining a war party."

"It was a thought, that is all." Morrigan stared at the blank wall.

"Morrigan, tell me true. Can we survive the winter? I want to testify in Rome but not so much as to leave the clan to starve. The clan comes first. Always has. Always will."

Morrigan nodded. "I know it." And saying it she realized she did know it. He was not much of a leader perhaps, but he had always tried to support the clan. And now he had a chance to finally stop Barrick. "We will be fine," Morrigan lied. "Go to Rome. Stop Barrick. 'Tis the best ye can do now for the clan." That part was true at least.

"Thank ye. I am confident ye will do right by the clan."

Morrigan looked down at her hands. It was the best compliment her brother had ever paid her, and it touched her more than she wished to acknowledge.

She took a deep breath and searched for something to say to break the awkward silence that stretched between them. Brothers and sisters were not meant to be kind. "Yer new wife is a nuisance."

Archie frowned. "Ye best be treating her right. If I need to choose, yer arse will be banished."

"Banished from the poorest clan in the Highlands? Oh, how will I e'er survive the loss?" Morrigan mocked. She was feeling much better. Normal. Normal was good.

"Truly Morrigan. I want ye to make her welcome."

"I avoid her when possible. She's always up to something. First it was cleaning the tower, and then it was planting a kitchen garden. She made poor Kip clean out the cesspools, I tell ye it was something foul."

"The clansmen treat her well?" Archie could not hide the twinge of anxiety in his tone.

Alys had done more to make the tower habitable than the rest of the McNabs had in the past twelve years since their parents died. The clansmen adored Alys and fell over themselves to carry out her requests. Morrigan shrugged and glanced away. "She is tolerated."

"I think I love her."

Morrigan's head snapped back to Archie.

"Tell her that if I dinna return."

"Tell her yerself. I'm no messenger."

Archie gave a faint smile. "Aye, I hope to."

Another silence fell. The task before them was monstrous. Archie was headed for Rome. She needed to find a way to keep the clan alive until he returned.

"I best go before they realize it was I poaching on the bishop's land." Morrigan stood and took two steps toward the door. "Dinna die Archie. 'Tis yer responsibility to be laird, and I expect ye to come back."

"Morrie." Archie spoke the name he used when she was a child. He had taken over raising her and Andrew twelve years ago after their parents died of the fever. How she had looked up to him during that horrible time of loss. She had been only ten and had adored her older brother. The bitterness had grown over time.

Morrigan turned and found a different Archie McNab before her. He stood taller; his eyes were warmer, less haunted and desperate. He was changed, she could feel it.

"I apologize for not giving ye the life ye should have had," said Archie. "Ye should be a wife and mother now, not acting as laird in my absence, and certainly no' going wi' me on raids. I failed ye and I am sorry."

Morrigan opened her mouth to respond but said nothing. Archie never apologized. Never.

"'Twas my choice," Morrigan said, her voice oddly hoarse. "I dinna blame ye." But she had blamed him. She did not realize until that moment how much she needed to hear him say he was sorry.

"I want to make things right, ye ken?"

"Aye, Brother. And ye will." A lump formed in her throat. She feared this would be the last time she ever saw her elder brother.

"Thank ye, Morrigan."

Footsteps sounded outside in the hall.

"What is the punishment for poaching?" Morrigan asked.

"Why did ye bring the carcass here?"

"Ye would have me let that meat go to waste?"

The footsteps grew louder.

"Come quick." Archie removed the screen to the window that opened to the forest behind the castle.

Morrigan grasped Archie's offered hand and climbed through the window.

Archie held her hand with a firm grip. "I trust ye to do what is right."

Morrigan's eyes met his for a brief second and she nodded. He released her and she slipped through the garden without a sound.

Well concealed in the large, green summer leaves of a bush, Dragonet watched Morrigan creep through the garden and easily scale the castle wall. Dragonet smiled.

Merci, ma chérie, Dragonet silently mouthed the words. He now knew the possible location of the lost treasure and the name of the last Templar.

Eight

"You have served me well, Sir Dragonet."

Dragonet inclined his head, accepting the praise of the Duke of Argitaine. The duke sat at a table in a private sitting room of the inn, reviewing the map Dragonet had made, which indicated those clans who were likely join the French in fighting against the English and those clans who were more likely to side with the English. The news had spread that the duke was paying clans to join his cause, and clan representatives started to arrive to negotiate price.

"I understand your reticence in using these methods, but you must admit they produced results."

"Yes, Your Grace," replied Dragonet, standing at the duke's side. In truth he had not been enamored with the prospects of pretending to be a minstrel, but listening to the castle gossip and noting the reactions to patriotic Scottish songs were telling methods of finding a clan's true loyalty. It also provided him an excellent way to try to find the last Templars, not that the Duke of Argitaine had any idea of Dragonet's other mission.

"I am glad to have found favor in your eyes. If I have pleased you, I would ask to take your leave for a while, that I may visit the abbey of the Abbot Barrick."

"You wish to visit an abbey?" asked the duke.

"Some prayer it would do me good, Your Grace."

"I admire your discipline, sir knight, but we are here in Glasgow with their impressive cathedral. Surely there can be nothing in a remote abbey you cannot find here at the cathedral. You may have leave to do your prayers here, for I need you to help make decisions as to which clans to trust to join our cause."

"My full report has been given to you, Your Grace."

"And I appreciate it, but nothing can replace you by my side as I speak with different clans. I need not remind you that if I trust a clan loyal to the English crown with our battle plans, all will be lost."

Dragonet paused to consider. He did not wish to leave the duke, for he felt some loyalty to him. More importantly, however, Dragonet was on a mission for his father. He needed to find the silver chest and the treasure it contained. It was time to sever his ties to the duke.

The door opened, and in stepped a serving maid with a respectful bow to the duke. "Another man to see ye, Yer Grace."

"Before you see this next man—"

"In a moment, Dragonet." The duke raised his hand to silence him. "Which clan comes?" he asked the serving maid.

"Clan McNab," said the maid with another curtsey.

The duke glanced at Dragonet who remained silent. "Show him in."

Dragonet froze as Morrigan entered the room. She was cleaner than the last time they met, but she was still wearing the loose men's clothing that disguised her shape, and a long cap that hid her hair. She wore a long, black cape pinned to her shoulder and the unmistakable shape of a sword was at her side.

She glanced at him when she entered the room, their eyes meeting for the briefest of moments before she turned her full attention to the duke. It was the eyes that gave her away. How could those seductive, dark eyes belong to anyone other than a beautiful woman? Surely the duke must see through her disguise. Dragonet glanced at the duke, but he remained seated and calm. He only saw what he expected to see.

"Yer Grace," said Morrigan with a bow.

"McNab," acknowledged the duke, switching from his native French to the English he spoke but hated. "Why did you wish to see me?"

"I hear ye are paying clans to join yer fight against the English," said Morrigan.

"You are correct in your understanding," said the duke with his smooth French accent. "Do you wish to join the noble cause of defending the Scots against the English, your oppressor?"

"How much will ye pay?"

The duke turned his head to look at Dragonet. They'd reached the point at which Dragonet would either give a nod or shake his head, making the final judgment as to whether or not that clan should be trusted. Morrigan also turned toward Dragonet. Her eyes were wide and pleading.

Dragonet was torn. He did not wish Morrigan to

be caught up in the war that was coming. He wanted her far away from harm. And yet, he had overheard enough of her conversation with her brother to know her clan was in a desperate situation. What would happen to them if she was denied the coin to support them? And what would Morrigan do next to raise those funds?

Dragonet nodded his head.

"Good. Your payment will depend on how many warriors you can bring." The duke reviewed the many key elements to the contract, waxing elegant on his own remarkable contribution.

Morrigan again met Dragonet's eye and gave him a small nod, thanking him. Dragonet's heart soared even as his stomach churned. He hoped he had made the right decision.

Morrigan and the duke negotiated price until both were satisfied. Their business concluded, Morrigan gave a bow and exited the room without a backward glance.

"What did you wish to speak to me about?" asked the duke.

Dragonet paused. He needed to search the abbey. "I would be most pleased to stay with you and fight the English," Dragonet said, surprising himself.

"We are pleased to have you," replied the duke. "Perhaps we can visit this abbey of yours later."

"Yes, later," murmured Dragonet. He needed to find the relic in the abbey... but for the moment his attention was seized by a different kind of Highland treasure.

Morrigan marched her men toward the makeshift war camp, her mind focused on the wrong thing. She should have been considering the accommodations for the men, wondering if the meager tents and provisions they brought would be enough. She ought to have been considering battle strategies, and how to best train her men to fight effectively or, more importantly, stay alive. She should have been concerned about when the well-known secret of her gender would be revealed.

All these things were more important and more pressing than the one question that haunted her thoughts and dreams. Was *he* here?

He of course was the minstrel... knight... Frenchman, who went by the name Jacques or Dragonet or heaven only knew what else. Who that man truly was, she had no way of knowing. Yet he had taken up residence in her thoughts and refused to leave, despite Morrigan's best attempts to free herself from his ghost.

Morrigan's soldiers, who consisted mostly of temporarily reformed highwaymen and farmers with bad attitudes, reached a slight rise above the makeshift camp for the Scots' army. The Scots were amassing their forces for an assault on the English town of Nisbet. It was to be their first attack.

Tents littered the field before them, in a rather deranged arrangement with different banners representing different clans intermixed and confused. The grounds they had picked were hardly ideal, being low and boggy. Even on the rise above the camp, the smell of rotten food, unwashed clansmen, and human waste wafted up as an invisible warning to return from whence they came. Even her horse stopped short, unwilling to step into the camp.

"Well that's a sorry sight, I say," said Harry, one of the McNab raiders.

"Aye, it is at that," said Willy, a tough old Highlander of undetermined age.

"Hope ye like mud, lads, for we'll be living in it," said Morrigan with something she hoped was cheerful resolution. "What banners can ye make out?"

It was far from a passing question. She wanted to ascertain what type of reception she might get, for the McNab clan was not a favorite among the patriot crowd. There may be some clans who would praise the McNab history of loyalty to the successive kings of England, but she was not going to find them among an army roused against the English.

"Looks like we got the earls o' Douglas and March. I think there's Ramsey too," answered Willy. He had the best eyes of the lot.

"Anything that looks French?" asked Morrigan, trying to sound nonchalant. She reached in her sleeve and unbuckled and rebuckled the strap that held Jacques' knife to her wrist. She had worn it since he had given it to her. Because it was useful. No other reason.

Morrigan's stomach fluttered. What if he was there? What would he say to her? Would he talk to her at all or pretend not to know her? Would he reveal who she was? How did he feel about her? Did he think of her too?

Morrigan spat on the ground. She needed to get

control of herself and stop acting like a biddable
bar maid. She was there to do a job. She had taken
an initial payment in gold moutons from the Duke
of Argitaine. It had been enough to secure some
additional grain and some livestock. The coin was
supposed to outfit her men with weapons and gear.
Morrigan had decided that providing food for themselves and their families was more important. At least
they could face the winter without fear of starvation.
If they survived the war.

"Nay, I dinna see them Frenchies."

Morrigan nodded. It was for the best. He could
only bring trouble. Yes, she was certainly glad that
French bastard was nowhere in sight. Absolutely for
the best. Could not be happier. Truly, very happy.

"Ye coming?" asked Harry.

Morrigan realized Harry and Willy had started
riding off toward camp ahead of her. Morrigan clicked
and nudged the horse down the grassy hill and into the
stench of camp.

Ahead of her, Willy suddenly stopped with a curse.

"What is it?" asked Morrigan, riding forward.

"Look there to the right. Graham," said Willy, and
spat a large amount of brown liquid on the ground.

"Hell," muttered Morrigan. Of all the clans that
disliked them, Graham was foremost on the list, probably having something to do with Archie abducting
Graham's daughter a few years back. Not one of
Archie's better plans to be sure. The daughter had
been returned, or rather escaped and returned herself,
but the incident had done nothing to improve relations with their neighbor.

Morrigan briefly considered simply turning around and going back home. It was hardly the honorable response, but camping in a muddy pit surrounded by people who despised her more than the English was not an attractive prospect. They had enough to get them through the winter. If the duke wanted his money back, he could come to the Highlands and repossess the chickens.

"Look, there's the Campbell banner, too," said Harry.

Campbell? If Campbell's men were there that would mean Andrew was too.

"Ride into camp," commanded Morrigan.

❧

Dragonet heard the battle before he could see it. The shouts of men and clash of metal blended into an ominous roar, echoing through the rocks and trees of the rough terrain. Dragonet signaled his knights to follow him and nudged his horse into a gallop, a building sense of concern forming an unsettled pit in his stomach. Was she there?

Dragonet was conflicted about what to do regarding a certain sword-wielding Highland lass. A single word from him and she would be expelled from the force. But then what would she do? Her clan's situation was desperate; having spent a few days there he could easily attest to their poverty. If he prevented her from joining the force, would she go back to serving the abbot?

It was not his problem; heaven knew he had enough of his own, yet he could not get her out of his head. As he raced toward the battle at Nisbet, he wondered if she was there. Would she have the sense to stay clear of the fight? He already knew the answer to that question, and urged his mount faster.

Following the growing noise of war, Dragonet rounded a corner and found a few English foot soldiers in full retreat. He followed them, encouraging them to run faster or disappear into the brush. Foot soldiers were not who Dragonet had come to harass. Drawing his sword, he charged down the road until he found his target. The Governor of Nisbet was surrounded by his knights, who were putting up a fierce battle to protect their master. Douglas was pressing hard to capture his prize, sword in one hand, a shield in the other.

On the far side of the road, one foot soldier fought furiously to prevent the governor from escaping. He held a sword in one hand and a mace in the other. He took on two, three at a time. Skilled and quick, he prevented their escape. He was aided by some additional soldiers who blocked the sides of the road, but it was clear their role was primarily defensive, forming a barrier of shields, funneling the governor's personal guard toward their champion.

Dragonet commanded some of his men to help Douglas and took the rest to help the soldier prevent the governor's escape. If they could hold them a little longer, the governor could be captured. Due to the rough terrain on either side of the road, Dragonet and his knights were forced to dismount to push through and aid the rear flank. The champion could not hold out much longer.

Dragonet attacked the governor's rear guard just as a charging English guard with a spear caught the foot soldier on the shoulder, pushing him back into the forest. The governor's guard surged through the opening, but Dragonet and his men prevented the governor from escaping. The governor was theirs.

One of the guards howled in frustration and raced toward the Scot champion who was pinned to a tree by the spear. Dragonet bolted to assist the brave soldier and took down the Englishman with a single blow.

Dragonet stepped forward to help the Scot, who was desperately pulling at the spear that pinned him to the tree. Dropping his sword next to the weapon of the young soldier, Dragonet's heart stopped. He knew those weapons. With a rush of slick panic he pulled out the spear.

Morrigan.

Nine

It was true what they said. Your life does pass before you before you die. Morrigan watched the review of her life with decided displeasure. Most women her age were wives and mothers. Somehow her life had taken a most wretched wrong turn.

Morrigan grabbed at the spear, slick with her own blood, trying to pull it from her shoulder. It was no good, she was pinned to the tree. She watched an English soldier run at her, his actions strangely slowed, his sword leveled at her throat. This was it. This was how she was going to die.

The Scot army attacked Nisbet at dawn, then retreated, luring the governor to make chase. They ambushed him on the road, which Morrigan did considerably well, until, of course, she was pinned to a tree.

She took her last breath and watched the Englishman run toward her to finish the kill. With a sick thud the man slumped and fell to the ground. A French soldier stood behind him. He stepped forward and grabbed the spear, wrenching it out of Morrigan's shoulder.

Pain exploded through her. She cried out and collapsed, her knees refusing to hold. The world became fuzzy around the edges and she struggled to remain conscious.

"Morrigan!" The French knight lifted his visor, revealing the piercing blue eyes of Sir Dragonet.

Morrigan stared at her rescuer for a moment, the sounds of the battle fading away. Dragonet kneeled beside her and put his arm around her unhurt shoulder to prevent her from falling farther into the mud. He had saved her life.

"Ye are here," she murmured, pushing off her helm.

He gave her a slow smile, but the worry in her eyes remained. "Yes, I am here. You are injured?"

Morrigan returned his smile with a faint one of her own. He had saved her. She reached up to touch his check to see if he was real. Morrigan took a deep breath—what was she doing? She needed to get control of herself.

"I am well," she said, trying to sit up on her own. "A scratch. Nothing more."

Movement behind Dragonet caught her eye. Another knight approached, his bloody sword in hand. In an instant, Morrigan flicked the knife Dragonet had given her into her hand and threw it at the throat of their attacker.

The knight lifted his shield in time and the knife stuck into the wood.

"Hello now. That could have killed me," said the knight with a slight French accent.

Had she tried to kill a Frenchman? No, the colors on his hauberk were wrong. It was the clan of... Graham.

Morrigan groaned, of all the bad luck. She had tried to murder one of Graham's men. That was hardly going to improve clan relations.

"Sorry about that," mumbled Morrigan.

"No harm done," said the knight cheerily. "I am Chaumont, and who might you be?"

"McNab," said Morrigan in a voice hardly above a whisper. She glanced up to see his reaction but he merely bowed.

"This soldier needs a surgeon," said Dragonet, easily lifting Morrigan in his arms, armor and all. At least he had not revealed her gender.

"I am fine," Morrigan lied. "No surgeon necessary. Put me down!"

"Jacques?" asked Chaumont, ignoring Morrigan's protests and addressing Dragonet. "Am I confused or did I know you as a minstrel?"

"*Oui*, I am Jacques. I am also Sir Dragonet, a knight for the duke."

"Ah," said Chaumont with a devilish grin. He looked at Dragonet and then at Morrigan. "I see."

"I can walk," demanded Morrigan, pushing herself out of Dragonet's arms. Her legs were not as strong as she wanted, but she gritted her teeth and willed herself to stay upright. The pain in her shoulder was burning, blood trickling down the inside of her hauberk.

"This is a nice piece," said Chaumont pulling the knife out of his shield. "Wherever did you get it?" he asked Morrigan, turning the knife Dragonet gave her over in his hands and rubbing his thumb over the symbol of the white cross.

"Dragonet," muttered Morrigan without thinking. Damn but her shoulder was starting to throb.

Chaumont looked at her with bright eyes then again at Dragonet. "I see." He stepped close and held out the knife to return it to her. He was older than she, but undeniably handsome. "I saw what you did, taking on three Englishmen at a time. I decided you must be very brave, very skilled, or very foolhardy."

"I am a McNab. Foolhardy is our family creed."

Chaumont laughed, a great merry sound. He placed the knife in her palm, then turned it over to kiss the back of her hand. "Until we meet again, *mademoiselle*."

Chaumont strode away, leaving Morrigan gaping in his wake. Mademoiselle?

"How did he know?" She eyed Dragonet with suspicion.

"I do not know." Dragonet met her eyes directly. "I have said nothing to anyone."

Morrigan nodded. She believed him. Perhaps it was the look of truth in his eye, perhaps it was the screaming pain that dulled her mental faculties, but she believed him.

"Come, let us get you stitched," said Dragonet.

Morrigan followed, or more precisely was discretely assisted back to the road where she was accosted by the hulking form of Lord Douglas. Douglas was a large man, with bushy black eyebrows and bushier beard. If he was impressive in person, he was doubly so with armor adding to his considerable size.

"Well done, well done, my lad," Douglas praised, giving Morrigan a hearty slap on the back which sent waves of pain clear down to her toes. Dragonet tightened his hold around her waist and prevented her from falling when her knees buckled. Morrigan's jaw clenched in pain, silencing a scathing insult regarding Douglas's mother.

"We have captured the governor." Douglas rubbed his hands together. "Ah, now that will be a pretty ransom for sure. Ye did well my lad to prevent him from escaping. If ye were not a McNab I'd knight ye!"

"I am sure their share of the ransom will be sufficient," said Dragonet smoothly, preventing Morrigan from voicing something which probably would have required the Douglas to demand a duel.

"Well, well now," sputtered Douglas.

"And ours as well. Later we will meet to discuss the details," added Dragonet.

"Yes, yes of course." Douglas turned and left, less happily than he arrived.

Despite the pain, Morrigan smiled. "Thank ye, I am feeling much improved. My men can help me from here."

Dragonet paused but handed Morrigan over to one of her men. "I wish you a most speedy recovery." He removed his helm and pushed back the padded cap, revealing his face. His expression was unreadable. He paused again as if he wished to say more, but Morrigan's men were gathering and Dragonet's men were watching.

Dragonet bowed and was gone.

Morrigan's men helped her back to camp where she could wash her wound and find a surgeon. She knew that meant finding the clansman who was the least drunk to stitch the wound closed. Safe for the moment in her tent, she evaluated her wound. The spear had sliced through the top of her left shoulder. She had been pinned to the tree, but mostly by her clothes. It hurt and bled, but had not cut anything of importance and should soon heal.

Her stomach only rebelled once during the process of cleaning the wound so she considered the day a success. None of her men had been killed, they had earned a portion of a ransom, and she, thanks to the timely arrival of her minstrel, was still alive.

Not that he was *her* minstrel.

He wasn't even a minstrel anymore. Not that she cared in the slightest.

Morrigan reached for the bottle. After a liberal dose of medicinal whiskey both outside to cleanse the wound and inside her to dull the pain, she called upon Willy to put in the stitches. Like everyone in the camp, he was drinking to celebrate their victory, but Willy held his liquor better than most so he was elected to stitch.

"Are ye hurt?" Andrew ran into her tent and stopped short at the sight of the gaping wound on her shoulder. He went pale and sank to his knees beside her as she sat on a bench. "Oh, Morrigan. Oh no."

"It will be fine. It just needs some stitching," said Morrigan, trying not to be shaken by her brother's reaction. She glanced over at Willy, who was still trying to get the needle threaded. Not a good sign.

"Is it bad?" called a voice from outside the tent.

"Och aye, 'tis horrid. Come see," called Andrew, jumping up to meet his friend.

"What? Nay!" said Morrigan but it was too late. In

walked a young man, who appeared to be in his late teens. She quickly tried to cover herself up a bit more. True she had merely untied the top of her shirt and slid it down over her shoulder to reveal the wound, but it was hardly the way she met visitors.

"Morrigan, this is Gavin Patrick. He's the nephew o' the MacLaren," said Andrew calmly, oblivious to her concerns.

"MacLaren!" Morrigan stared at Gavin. There was no clan who hated the McNabs more than the MacLarens. Except perhaps the Grahams.

"Gavin, this is my sister Morrigan," continued Andrew.

"Andrew! Ye daft fool!" snapped Morrigan. "We are not on friendly terms wi' the MacLarens, and I am not heralding that I am yer *sister*!"

"Och, true, sorry," said Andrew, running his fingers through his hair, giving himself a rumpled schoolboy appearance. "But Gavin and I are friends now. He saved my life from hanging."

"And he saved me from matrimony." Gavin slapped Andrew's back in a friendly manner.

Andrew gave him a foolish smile. "Ye dinna ken what ye are missing."

Morrigan glared at the jovial lads. At least Andrew was well fed and happy. He had been outfitted in Campbell colors, complete with good armor and new boots. It was more than she had ever been able to give him.

"Ye finished threading that needle yet?" Morrigan asked Willy, who was lifting a bottle instead of a needle.

"No' yet. Just another drink to steady me nerves."

Andrew stepped closer. "I dinna think he is sober enough to thread a needle, let alone stitch yer shoulder."

"Do ye care to try?" Morrigan asked her brother. Andrew blanched in reply.

"My stepfather, Chaumont, has experience with these things. I'll get him." Gavin dashed out of the tent before Morrigan could stop him.

"Now see what ye've done!" chastised Morrigan. "He will probably get MacLaren and we'll all be in trouble."

"Nay, MacLaren isna here. Gavin came wi' Chaumont and the Grahams. According to Gavin, MacLaren said invading the English was a damn fool business and he would have naught to do wi' it."

Morrigan snorted. "He's right."

"Now, how is the patient," said Chaumont, stepping into the tent, followed by Gavin and Dragonet.

"W-what? Nay!" yelled Morrigan. This was spinning out of control.

"You know my friend Dragon, *n'est-ce pas*? He was asking about your health, so I told him to come on in," said Chaumont with a wink.

Morrigan cursed and spit on the ground. "I am fine. My man is about to put in a few stitches. There is naught to see here. Ye may all go now."

Willy responded by passing out drunk. The tent was silent for a moment as everyone stared at the unconscious Highlander on the ground. So much for holding his whiskey. Willy began to snore.

"Allow me to offer my assistance," said Chaumont with an artful bow. He picked up the needle and thread from the table and quickly threaded the needle.

"I also have some experience in the treatment of wounds, my lady," said Dragonet, dropping all pretense of pretending she was a lad. "I am yours to command."

"Gavin and Andrew, why do you not take our snoring friend here out to his friends? We would not want to trip over him on accident," said Chaumont.

"Do ye wish me to stay, Morrie?" asked Andrew, his eyes large as he stared at the needle in Chaumont's hands.

Morrigan sighed. She did want him to stay, but he was squeamish around wounds. She wished Archie was there. He was a fool, but he would not faint at the sight of blood.

"Nay, ye and Gavin go and take Willy wi' ye. And remember, the wenches ye find at a camp like this are to be avoided, ye ken?"

Chaumont arched a brow at her.

"Myself included," muttered Morrigan.

"Ye sure ye'll be alright?" asked Andrew. He was a good lad.

"Aye. I have two French nursemaids to see to me."

They waited as Gavin and Andrew lifted Willy off the ground and dragged him out of the tent.

"One of us should hold the lantern while the other places the stitches. Which one o' us would you like do the deed?" asked Chaumont in a flirtatious manner.

Morrigan blushed in spite of herself. "Have ye both had experience wi' stitching before?"

"I spent time with the Hospitallers, learning their trade," said Dragonet. "If you please to hold this to your shoulder. It will stop the bleeding." He handed her a clean, white handkerchief, and she complied.

"I have done my share of stitching," boasted Chaumont. "You may have noticed how I stitched MacLaren's face back together."

"I have heard of his ugly scar. Ye will do the

stitching." Morrigan pointed to Dragonet. "Ye can hold the light." She nodded to Chaumont.

Chaumont laughed. "A wise choice, my lady. A very wise choice indeed."

"How did ye ken I was a lass?" she asked.

"Ah, the evidence of my misspent youth, I fear. Your appearance does not betray you, but, you must forgive me, I have a true gift for noticing a pretty female face, no matter how she disguises herself."

"Ye boast at being a veritable knave?"

"Reformed, I assure you. Now let us see to your wound." Chaumont held up the lantern.

Heat rushed through her when Dragonet brushed aside her shirt to reveal her naked shoulder. It was hardly a romantic gesture, but her response was unconscious and immediate. He examined the wound with gentle hands.

"This will pain you, I am sorry to say," said Dragonet, his eyes large and dark in the deepening gloom of the tent. Night shrouded the camp, though from the shouts and cheers of the soldiers it had only increased the revelry.

"Aye," said Morrigan. "Whatever I say next, I do want to thank ye for ye troubles."

Dragonet poured whiskey on her wound and Morrigan cursed him, his manhood, and his mother with abandon.

"Your creativity is without rival, my dear," laughed Chaumont. "Did I ever tell you how MacLaren got his wicked scar?" He proceeded to tell the story of MacLaren's time in France and his marriage to Aila Graham. He even had the audacity to tell how Archie had kidnapped Aila and tried to force her to marry him. It was not a story Morrigan wished to be remembered, but Chaumont gave the tale a humorous turn and had both Morrigan and Dragonet laughing.

In the warm light of the lantern, Morrigan was increasingly aware of the attractiveness of both French knights. In truth, they were both remarkably handsome, their faces close to hers as they focused on their work. Chaumont was older, perhaps by ten years or more, but was still handsome with his laughing eyes and long, thin nose. Dragonet was younger, probably around her age, and his striking blue eyes often seemed to hide more than they revealed.

"And that is how I met my Mary," said Chaumont with a warm glow to his eyes. He may have been strikingly attractive, he may have flirted shamelessly, but he was not available. Even Morrigan could see he was hopelessly in love with his wife. "We have four little ones now, along with Gavin. We've been blessed, very blessed. How do you feel now, my lady?"

Morrigan realized Dragonet had completed his task and was binding the wound. Chaumont had done an admirable job distracting her through the pain.

"Thank ye both," said Morrigan in a soft voice. Things had gone much better and considerably less painfully than she had expected with Willy wielding the needle.

"I see my work here is done." Chaumont stood and placed the lantern back on the table. "I best be after Gavin. This is his first celebration of victory, my lady, and I fear he may not have heeded your sage advice. Best find him and knock some sense into him."

"If ye woud'na mind doing the same for Andrew if ye see him. I believe the lads are together," said Morrigan.

"It would be my pleasure. I know how I was at that age, and if Gavin is half of it he is bound for trouble."

"Ye are reformed now, are ye?" asked Morrigan.

"Oh yes, quite domesticated. I have daughters now, you see, and I live in fear they may someday run across a scoundrel like me." Chaumont shuddered. "That is why I keep this on hand." He patted his sword hilt. "When you feel better, my lady, I would invite you to come and train my daughters to use a sword. Not for war mind you, but I would like them to defend themselves if need be."

Morrigan smiled at him. Somehow Chaumont made her feel more like a lady and less like an abomination.

"Nice work tonight, Dragon," said Chaumont, pinning on his cloak. "The scar will be small indeed."

"Dragon?" asked Morrigan.

"A name some call me." Dragonet shrugged and looked away.

"It does not seem to fit ye," said Morrigan.

"Then you have not seen him with a sword in his hand," said Chaumont. "We had a friendly competition earlier today. Truly I have never seen such fine sword work in all my days. None can best him."

"Ye fought?" Morrigan asked. "But why?"

"A friendly competition I assure you. He offered his share in the ransom if he lost. How could I refuse such temptation?" asked Chaumont with an impish grin.

"Ye offered your share o' the ransom?" Morrigan asked Dragonet. Her head hurt trying to understand why the two Frenchman had fought.

Dragonet busied himself cleaning up the bloody rags and said nothing.

Morrigan glared at Chaumont. "Why did ye fight?" she demanded.

"He was most determined to win my silence on a certain matter. You have yourself a defender, my lady."

Morrigan's jaw went slack. "Ye fought to keep my secret?"

"I assure you, your identity as McNab's sister will not be revealed by my lips, nor Gavin's either," said Chaumont. "Though unless I very much mistake myself, I warrant Dragonet will recommend you leave now for home. I suggest you follow that advice. *Mademoiselle*." Chaumont bowed with a brilliant smile and left the tent.

Morrigan turned to Dragonet and realized they were very much alone. It was dark in the tent, the only light coming from the glowing lantern. "Why would ye fight for me?"

"How does your shoulder feel, my lady?" asked Dragonet, ignoring her question. He was straddling the bench beside her. It was a better position for his ministrations, but Morrigan felt awkwardly close to him. Memories of their last kiss flooded her.

"Fine." Morrigan coughed. Her throat was rough and dry. "Ye did well." A different emotion and new question emerged with every beat of her racing heart. What was she to say to him?

Dragonet handed her a flask and she drank deep. If ever there was a time to drink it was then. She handed it to Dragonet, but he merely put the cap back on without taking a sip.

"Ye fought to protect me."

He looked away. "Yes."

"Why?"

"I feared something in my manner may have betrayed you. I would not wish you any harm because of me."

"Ye dinna need to fight for me. I can take care o' myself."

He turned back to her, the flickering lamplight dancing in his eyes. "It is done."

She reached out her hand to his. "Then I thank ye."

He put his other hand on top of hers, warm and protective. "I have something for you." Dragonet reached into the pocket of his cloak and pulled out a jingling velvet pouch. "Your share of the ransom."

"The governor made ransom already?"

"No, but he will soon. I talked to the Douglas about the price. This is your share."

"But if he has not yet paid the ransom, then where did this…" Morrigan peered into his dark eyes. They merely reflected her face back to her. "This is from you." She picked up the bag. It was heavy and jangled deliciously with coins.

Dragonet paused. "Yes."

A ripple of excitement coursed through her at his simple reply. "I canna accept this."

"It is yours. I am giving to you an advance. I will accept your portion when the ransom is paid."

"I have no need of an advance. I can collect from Graham when the time comes."

"You do not trust me? You think I am trying to rob you? Count it if you wish." Dragonet sat up straight and leaned away from her, offended.

"Nay, I did no' say that. I'm sure 'tis the correct amount."

"Then accept it!" Dragonet challenged.

"Fine, I will!" shouted Morrigan.

"Good," said Dragonet with a warm smile.

Morrigan frowned. What just happened?

"And now I would like for you to leave," said Dragonet, the smile disappearing from his face.

Morrigan inhaled sharply. The force of his rejection stung worse than her shoulder.

"What I mean is, I do not wish you to get hurt." He motioned toward her shoulder. "Again."

"I have given my word to stay and fight." The McNabs had been branded cowards by many. They were many things, but cowards they were not, and Morrigan intended to prove it.

"Go home, Morrigan."

Morrigan shook her head. "Everyone expects us to turn tail and run. I winna bring shame to my clan."

"You have proven to all you are no coward. Now it is time to return to your home."

Morrigan shook her head. "I have no reason to return."

"You are injured." With a hesitant hand Dragonet touched her bare shoulder, slowly tracing around the bandage. Her skin burned beneath his gentle caress.

Morrigan's lips parted to speak, but no words came to mind.

"You must heal," whispered Dragonet. The wound was deep, and the risk it would fester was real.

"I will be well." Morrigan reached for his hand and it trembled in her fingers. "Are ye cold?"

Dragonet shook his head, and indeed his hand was warm.

"Then why do you tremble?"

Dragonet looked down and said nothing.

Morrigan leaned forward, unsure what to say but certain she needed to be closer.

His eyes found hers. "Today when I saw you pinned to the tree, but a moment from death, I felt—how do you say? I felt a fear, a sickness. I do not ever wish to feel that way again. If you please go home, it would be to me a great comfort."

Something inside Morrigan's chest cracked open, painful, but sweet. This man spoke words of kindness as she had never heard before. With horror she feared the waves of emotion churning inside her might leak out in tears. Something must be done and quick!

And so she kissed him. He did not move at first, but his hand holding hers tightened. His lips were warm and soft, yet shot slivers of lightning through her at their touch. Slowly he encircled her with his arms and drew her into his embrace. Her shoulder stung but it was nothing compared to the raw pleasure his lips offered. She moved back to catch her breath, her heart galloping hard. He also was breathing shallow and fast.

She had never before desired a man—she thought herself immune to it—but she was surely afflicted now with a fever from which she had no wish to recover. The sensations he roused in her with a single touch were confusing, intoxicating, and dangerous.

She leaned in again, but he pulled back and shook his head. "You are hurt. I would not take the advantage."

"I am no' hurt, I assure ye. Naught but a scratch."

"I am glad of it." He kissed one cheek, then the other, resting his cheek against hers for a moment before he whispered in her ear, "Go home, Morrigan. Please."

Before she could think of a response, Dragonet stood and strode out of the tent, leaving her with an open mouth and a bag full of coins.

Ten

SHE SHOULD HAVE GONE HOME. ANYONE WITH ANY sense would have. But she, along with a long line of McNabs before her, had no sense. Besides, Andrew was still among the war party, and Morrigan was not about to let him march off to war without being there to protect him.

Morrigan marched her men into the main camp, her mind focused once again on the wrong thing. After their success at Nisbet, they were joining a larger force to prepare for the assault on Berwick. Despite the pressing concerns of war, she knew Dragonet would be in the camp, and his reaction at seeing her comprised the majority of her thoughts.

Dragonet had occupied her thoughts so frequently he had become a sort of mental companion. She remembered their kisses more than was healthy. As unlikely as it seemed, he wished to protect her. It appeared he may even care for her. The feelings this reflection arose were conflicting, alternating between wanting to throw herself into his arms and vowing to never see him again. One thing was for sure, he was good to his word and did not reveal her identity. The secret could not stay hidden forever, but before she was discovered, she hoped she would have a head start out of camp away from the angry mob.

The weather had grown cold as it was late fall. The sky was low with heavy clouds, threatening snow, an improvement from the freezing rain. Given the cold and the damp, everyone was starting to look the same, bundled in multiple layers of clothing. She was currently wearing most of what she owned, nor was she the only one, given the amorphous shapes of the men surrounding her. It may be better for her disguise, but she wished she could feel her toes.

The camp itself was a sprawling expanse of a field, which had either not been planted or had been ruined by the tramping soldiers. The clans and the French knights each had their own section identified by their own banner.

Setting up camp was exhausting, and nobody was happy with the close quarters. Morrigan hoped for a rest, but was informed that there would be a meeting to discuss invasion strategy. Each clan was expected to be represented.

"State yer clan!" demanded a gruff, well-fed man at the entrance to the main tent, clearly chosen for the duty for his size rather than his disposition.

"McNab," answered Morrigan. If she expected a poor reception she was not disappointed. Carriers of the black death would have been given a cheerier reception.

"McNab, is it? We dinna want yer kind round 'ere."

Morrigan pressed her lips together, preventing a blistering retort from escaping her lips. "Yer opinion means little. So unless ye'd like to explain to the duke why ye prevented one of his guests from attending, move aside."

"Get lost, I tell ye, before I run ye through!"

Morrigan blinked. His response was more hostile than she expected. They just helped the Scots claim an important victory. Did that not afford them any good will? Morrigan sized up her opponent until the pieces of the unfortunate puzzle came into place.

"McGregor," said Morrigan.

"Aye," said the large man with a malicious wink. "Now bugger off."

Morrigan sighed. Perhaps they should not have raided the McGregors quite so often nor quite so effectively. Honestly, if the man wanted to keep his sheep, he should have kept better watch over them. Morrigan took a quick step to the left as if to go around. He countered and she spun back around to the right and slipped past.

"Damn yer eyes, McNab. My brothers are all in there, ye hear me!" called the man, but he did not pursue.

Morrigan slipped her way through the throng until she was in the middle of the group of standing people. The air was hot and stale in the tent; the odor of men who traveled long in the same clothes permeated the air. The ground was covered with straw, muddy, and wet. Morrigan did not mind, the smell of rotting rushes was nothing new.

She was late to the gathering, and a man with a French accent had already begun to speak. It was hard to see him clearly, but it appeared to be Chaumont, dressed in a fine embroidered cloak. Seated at either side on the raised dais were Laird James Douglas and the steward of Scotland. It was an impressive array of prestigious persons.

"I thank you for coming to join forces against the tyranny of the English." Chaumont said with more authority and less humor in his voice than she remembered. Of course she had been hitting the whiskey a bit hard that night. "Together we will put an end to the oppressor who takes the very food from our table and seeks to bend us to the will of England. Though these be dark days, we will stand victorious in the battle against the malice of our common foe!"

The crowd cheered, perhaps enhanced by the serving wenches who appeared at that moment to bring each man a tankard of ale. Morrigan declined. This was a time to stay sober. She squinted through the haze of the tent. Was the Frenchman truly Chaumont, or somebody else?

"Who is the man speaking?" she asked a man standing next to her.

"The Duke of Argitaine."

And so it was. "Those Frenchies look alike," she muttered to herself.

Several notable personages got up to speak along the same predictable vein while her comrades drank themselves into a greater appreciation for the speeches. Douglas stood along with the steward of Scotland, who was ruling in King David's stead. Scotland's king was still sitting in an English prison since the last time Scotland tried to invade. Morrigan wondered about the steward's endorsement of the invasion. With the king of Scotland being held for ransom in

England, invading could hardly improve the king's tenuous situation. The steward was also King David's nephew and currently his heir. Morrigan smiled. If the king never returned, the steward would become the king of Scotland. Ah yes, his motivation for war was clear enough.

Morrigan wanted to know the details of the plan. No Scottish invasion had ever been successful. What made them think that they could win? Finally James Douglas took the floor for a discussion on strategy. Douglas was not as tall as the duke or some of the others, but he was a hulking man and commanded many soldiers' respect and unabashed fear.

The Douglas started to speak and a hush fell over the crowd. "As you ken, the English are attacking our French brethren. They are like the locust, which destroys all it sees. I need not remind ye o' the massacre at Neville's Cross or Hallidon Hill. We must stand now with our French brothers in their time of need. The English king has declared himself the king of France—what say ye to that?" The crowd obligingly hissed.

"Make no mistake, if the Sassenach king ever defeats France, he will not hesitate to use his power to dominate all o' Scotland! King Edward will finally succeed in his goal to put himself on the throne of Scotland. What say ye to that?" The crowd booed loudly.

Morrigan waited for the actual battle plan to be revealed. Simply marching into England would end the way it always did—defeat for the Scots. One thing she did believe; Scotland would not long stand if England conquered France.

Movement from the side caught her eye. Sir Dragonet came into view and spoke quietly to the Duke of Argitaine. Dragonet stood behind the assembled titled personages, as should any good knight. He was tall, wearing armor under his surcoat. Morrigan swallowed hard and wished she had not passed the chance for a draft of ale. He was the perfect picture of a knight. Tall, straight, alert. He barely resembled the easy-moving minstrel who had played for them months ago. What would he do when he discovered she had not returned home as he asked?

"...and that is how we will begin our invasion," said Douglas.

Morrigan snapped her attention away from the attractive young knight back to Douglas. The invasion plans. What had he said?

"So our plan is Berwick?" asked one man.

"Aye. We will take Berwick and hold it to use as a base to invade Newcastle and then York. Once we control the port o' York, we can help ourselves to its wealth."

"And use the money to help our brothers in France to repel King Edward," Argitaine added.

"And what of us? If we take the riches of York, will we no' share in the reward?" asked Morrigan, her thoughts falling from her lips as spoken words. Dragonet spotted her in the crowd. He opened his mouth slightly then shut it again, the only visible sign that he had seen her.

"And who is this young sir?" asked the Duke of Argitaine, with all the false politeness of the aristocracy.

"I am..." Morrigan hesitated. Her family name

was not likely to engender a positive response. "I represent McNab." The temperature in the room increased exponentially as the eyes of the men turned toward her.

"McNab. We are joined together in the common purpose of fighting King Edward and our English enemy. A victory against King Edward in France is a victory for the Scots as well," said Argitaine.

"That be well and good, but it winna put bread on the table," answered Morrigan.

"And what do ye ken about battle, McNab?" jeered a man in front of her. "Is yer clan no' the one that refused to go to war against the English?"

"I ken that to attack England is naught but folly. Is that no' what we did when King David invaded and got himself captured? How will we prevent the same thing from happening again?" asked Morrigan. All sets of eyes turned hostile. Men grumbled in opposition.

"What would be your plan?" Dragonet's voice rang over the growling men.

Morrigan searched Dragonet's face, but he revealed no emotion.

"I would attack but no' hold. I would plunder towns, take what we want, then leave. Give King Edward a headache wondering where or when we will attack again. Keep him on the defensive and us out of a direct fight with the English soldiers, for if we face them on the field, we will most likely lose."

The men around Morrigan stepped back, not wanting to sully their own reputations by standing in her proximity. They circled around her like wolves.

"Coward!" cried one man.

"This strategy gave us success in Nisbet," said Morrigan.

"You speak the truth McNab," said Chaumont, Gavin at his side. "And one thing I can surely attest, this McNab is no coward."

Morrigan glanced at Dragonet, who was whispering to the duke.

"Are ye afeared of an honest man, Yer Grace?" Morrigan shouted over the rumbling crowd. "It worked in Nisbet. Did it no', Laird Douglas?"

The room hushed and all eyes turned to Douglas, who shifted his weight in his seat with some discomfort. "It was successful in Nisbet, but it was never our aim to hold that town. Berwick and the castle must be taken."

"To fight the English on the open field is folly. We shall lose," declared Morrigan.

"Traitor!" cried a man in the crowd.

"Knave!" called another. The crowd was getting murderous.

"Please, gentlemen." The duke raised his hands to quiet the crowd. "This man has spoken his mind. He is incorrect, but I wish him no ill will. Since you have no faith in our plans, I invite you to leave the camp and return the coin ye were given to arrive here tonight."

Morrigan bowed without saying a word. She had said enough. The fact that the duke would never see those coins again was not a discussion she chose to have at that time. Or ever. Men glared at her and began to close in. Morrigan turned toward the door and fingered her sword hilt.

"I shall see that McNab leaves camp," said Dragonet, his voice stern. In a moment he was behind her, his hand on her shoulder, guiding her out of the tent. The men stepped back, allowing them to pass. They exited the tent, and Morrigan breathed deep of the cool night air, a refreshing change from the hot, stifling air in the tent.

Dragonet continued to walk beside her, saying nothing. Morrigan was not sure what to think of his silence. They tramped through the large camp until the tents were not quite so crowded and they drew nearer to the outskirts, where the McNabs had been assigned a small bit of land. She had to tell the men to stop unpacking and start packing. By the saints they were going to hate her.

"Are you healed?" asked Dragonet in an undertone.

"Aye, 'tis well." Truth was her shoulder was still healing and it pained her to move her left arm. Fortunately her left arm was not as necessary as her right, given her current occupation.

Dragonet stopped in a small, open space between the clan camps. He frowned down at her, tall and serious. "Why are you here? Why did you not go home? Do you not have all you need for your clan?"

"Aye, we are no longer in a desperate position, thanks to the ransom and the duke's coin, which, by the way, he's going to have a hard time ever seeing again."

Dragonet shrugged. "So why not go home?"

"I made an oath. Perhaps you noticed that the McNabs are no' well thought o' in these parts. The least I can do is keep my word. I wanted to regain some honor for my clan." Morrigan looked away into the dark gloom of the night.

"By getting yourself killed tonight?" he asked, a mischievous light in his eye.

Morrigan's lips twitched up in spite of herself. "I suppose ye're going to tell me ye saved me back in that tent."

"No, no. A knight never boasts of his accomplishment. However, as an accomplished minstrel I may put the adventure into a ballad." Dragonet smiled and his form relaxed, like the easy minstrel he once was. Morrigan returned his grin before recalling that she never smiled, unless it was to mock one of her hapless brothers.

"You told the duke to send me home."

"But of course," replied Dragonet without a hint of apology.

Morrigan shrugged. Perhaps it was better that way. She had offered to fight, they had refused her. She could leave with her honor intact, at least in her mind if not in those of others.

"Was I incorrect in my assessment of their invasion plans? Do I lack understanding of the finer points of war?" asked Morrigan.

Dragonet looked up at the clear night sky. Stars were in abundance, scattered across the sky like lost jewels. The silver moon cast the landscape in shades of gray. "Your conclusions, they are correct."

"Then why was I thrown out o' the meeting?"

"You say the things nobody wishes to hear. The English are strong, well trained, and well equipped. To have a hope of success, you must believe it is possible to win. You robbed people of this belief."

"But going out wi' a poor strategy is daft!"

"War is daft. A sensible person would not do it."

Morrigan paused. It was not the answer she

expected. She had been raised on the stories of glorious battles, of brave heroes and valiant warriors. "Ye are a knight. Are ye not?"

Dragonet turned back to her, his face in shadow, his eyes black. "I am many things."

A cold wind blew against her, and she wrapped her cloak closer. "What happened to glory and honor and valor and all that rot?"

"I have known many brave men. Most lie in their graves."

A shiver slid up her spine as the wind snaked through the sea of tents, rustling the flaps. It was the only sound. The men had retreated away from the cold into their tents, leaving them quite alone. She took a step closer.

"So why are ye here? Why no' return to France?" she asked.

He shrugged. "To be fed and housed in the winter, it is a significant improvement over being hungry and cold."

Morrigan nodded. "Yet surely this canna be the only way ye can provide for yerself. Why no' go back to being a minstrel?"

Dragonet gave a lopsided smile that reminded her greatly of his more casual minstrel days. "I was never truly a minstrel, I confess. I was on the orders from the duke."

"Aye, but what keeps ye from becoming a minstrel in truth?"

"Ah, the worn-out excuse: glory and honor and valor and all that rot."

Morrigan smiled back into his dark eyes. "Ye are pitiful."

Dragonet inclined his head and leaned toward her, speaking in a low tone. "Most men are, my lady."

Despite the cold wind, Morrigan was surprisingly warm. And growing warmer with every inch she leaned closer to Dragonet.

"I, well, I should go." Morrigan's feet made no attempt at movement. Instead she leaned closer. Dragonet remained still, his face unreadable in the darkness.

Morrigan's heart pounded, drawing her toward him, drowning out all rational thought. This is where she wanted to be, close to him. In vain she tried to remind herself of all the reasons she distrusted people in general, and men in particular. This man was different. He slid past her defenses. He saw her, the real lass beneath the bitter disguise, and he did something no man ever did, he accepted her. Maybe he even liked her a little, or at least he was not repulsed by her, and that was good enough.

Without stopping to think, Morrigan wrapped her arms around his neck and kissed him hard on the mouth. At first he did not move, then he returned her embrace and held her tight. Morrigan relaxed into him, warm and happy. Yet it was dangerous to kiss him in open camp. If they were caught...

A small noise caused them both to jump apart. Morrigan glanced around, but no one was in sight. Morrigan took several large steps back. Had she gone daft? What was wrong with her?

"I must go. I must!" Morrigan turned and stomped away.

"Wait!" Dragonet caught her hand and spun her back into his embrace. "Promise me you will leave this place. Promise me you will go home now." His words were raw, his grip was tight. He was no longer holding back.

"I… Andrew is still here, I canna leave him."

"Campbell will look after him. He was nowhere near the heat of the battle last time." Dragonet leaned close, his lips a whisper away from hers. "Unlike you."

Morrigan's heart thumped hard against her hauberk. She slowly wrapped her arms around his neck but as much as she wanted to feel his lips against hers, she refused to close the gap.

"I will watch out for him too, as I am able," added Dragonet.

"Thank ye," whispered Morrigan. "Dragon." Heat surged through her clear down to her frozen toes. "Perhaps the name does suit ye."

Dragonet touched his lips gently to hers but did not kiss. "Promise to me you will leave." He spoke the words on her lips.

It was impossible to think clearly with his arms around her and his lips touching hers. He was warm and strong and speaking some nonsense about something in the future, when all she cared about was happening right now.

"Promise," he whispered again, his soft lips moving on hers. She longed to press herself into him, but waited, taking pleasure in the sweet torture.

"I promise," she said, licking her bottom lip and his as well.

His kiss was hard and urgent, nothing like what they had shared before. Morrigan held him tighter, eager for more. He grabbed her tightly and lifted her closer so that the toes of her boots barely touched the ground. His kiss invaded her mouth in a manner new and shocking, his touch a steamy contrast to the night's chill.

Suddenly he stepped back, removing her hands from around his neck. "Forgive me. I forget myself." His voice was shaky, his hand in hers trembled. It appeared their kiss had affected him as powerfully as it had her. So why was he pulling away?

Still dazed, Morrigan said nothing, hoping the sweeping dizziness she was experiencing would not lead her to do something as embarrassing as falling at his feet.

"Farewell, my friend." Dragonet squeezed her hand, then released her and placed his hand over his heart. "I will never forget you." He bowed and turned back into the dark camp and was gone.

Confusion and disappointment cut through her cloak, yet deep within a spark had lit her soul.

Eleven

DRAGONET HUDDLED WITH HIS FELLOW FRENCH knights around a central hearth in a garrison commandeered by the French. The Scot and French army had taken the town of Berwick but could not capture the castle. They settled into a siege, but the castle was well stocked to ride out the winter, and the attackers were the ones running out of supplies. The English army would be coming soon. If they could not take the castle before the English arrived, they would be pinned between two enemy armies and forced to march against the English on the open field.

The first day of winter came with an ice storm pelting the invaders with frozen slivers of despair. Dragonet's compatriots were unaccustomed to the cold weather. They were also unappreciative of the Scots' rustic charm. Their initial whispers of discontent had grown into a roar of protest. The French knights wanted to go home.

The duke sat apart from the rest, warmed by a mug

of wassail and the weight of the decision before him. With a sigh he stood before his knights, the elite of his force. The room silenced before his grim face.

"We have done what we could. We will now return to France. Spread the word to begin the packing."

A cheer rose from some of the weary French knights. Dragonet did not join them. The Duke of Argitaine walked slowly back to the corner of the room. Dragonet followed him.

"Your Grace, please reconsider," said Dragonet. "We asked these clans to join our fight. We cannot leave them to their fate now."

"They knew the risks." The duke ran his hand over his forehead in a single worried gesture.

"They believed we would be with them."

"They were paid for their service," mumbled the duke.

"Is that what you think of them? They are nothing to you but mercenaries?" A cold chill wrapped itself around Dragonet's chest and squeezed. It was an odd feeling; he guessed it must be worry or anger or something in between.

In the waning fire's flickering light, the duke's face was gray and haggard. "What would you have me do? If we stay we will lose to the English."

"Morrigan," mumbled Dragonet. He could hear Morrigan's words echoed in the duke's statement of futility.

"Pardon?"

"You ignored or rejected those who warned of the dangers of this path. It was you who encouraged the Scots to invade. You who promised the prosperous alliance between our two countries would last forever."

The duke rose as did his voice. "You would give the command to send your fellow soldiers into certain death? If we stay it will mean French blood spilled, French lives lost."

"If we leave we are condemning the Scots to death. It is acceptable to you to spill Scot blood and lose Scot lives?"

The duke threw up his hands and began to pace. "I do not expect you to understand."

"I understand perfectly."

"If I march into a battle I know I cannot win, our people back home will be left undefended. It is well and good to try to be honorable but not at the expense of the mission."

"But if you sacrifice your honor to win, what do you have?"

"You have victory. Do you think the wives of the men you would send into battle would be comforted knowing your sense of honor proved fatal?"

"I am not saying this is a battle we must fight, but let us draw back into Scotland instead. Let us not abandon them."

The duke shook his head. "Our mission was to distract the English from France. We have accomplished our mission. We must now return to France and press the English to our advantage."

Dragonet clenched his jaw and shook his head. He was disappointed in the man he had respected.

"You are a young man, Dragonet. Someday you will learn that sometimes the mission must come first."

"Despite my youth I can see that winning at the price of one's honor is a hollow victory at best. No man can truly be a knight without his honor."

"Enough! You go too far!"

Dragonet realized the other knights had taken keen notice of their heated discussion and had gathered at a respectable distance, their eyes wide.

"I apologize, Your Grace," said Dragonet with a small bow.

The duke stared at him with weary eyes. "You choose to stay here?"

"Yes, Your Grace."

"I envy your convictions, but not your decision. I give you leave to stay and wish you the best." The duke stood and held out his hand, which Dragonet grasped. "Godspeed, my friend. I doubt I will ever see you again."

The next morning, Dragonet watched as the Duke of Argitaine and his knights rode out of Berwick, quiet as ghosts on the fresh fallen snow. Dragonet pulled his cloak tighter around himself against the cold and nudged his mount, moving noiselessly through town on the blanket of snow. He would join the Scots. His honor demanded he not abandon those he had encouraged to join the ill-fated invasion.

Yet Dragonet was torn in his allegiances. He, too, was on a mission. He was also honor bound to serve his father, so which claim on his honor held precedence?

On an abandoned street Dragonet met some familiar faces.

"Greetings Dragonet," called Chaumont, bundled against the chill. "I thought you had all left." Chaumont turned back to Gavin. They were attempting to rig a pallet, with a large bundle tied to it, between their horses.

"The duke, he has left. I decided to stay a while. What is it you are doing? Looting the town?"

"You find us on a mission of mercy. Andrew has taken an arrow, and it has started to fester. We must get him to Mother Enid as quickly as possible."

Dragonet dismounted at once to peer at the pale face of Morrigan's brother Andrew. She would be distressed by the sight. Dragonet recalled his promise to Morrigan and it suddenly became clear whom he was honor bound to serve.

"Please allow me to help you," said Dragonet, assisting Chaumont and Gavin in their task. "Where is Mother Enid? Close, I pray?"

"Unfortunately not," replied Chaumont. "She is at St. Margaret's Convent, a long journey into Scotland I fear. Yet Mother Enid has medicine we can find nowhere else."

"St. Margaret's—that is under the Abbot Barrick, is it not?" asked Dragonet.

"Yes," answered Chaumont. "I thank you for your help with the litter, but I fear we would be imposing to ask your help on such a long journey."

"I will help see Andrew safely to St. Margaret's. It is the least I can do." Dragonet had two reasons to go to St. Margaret's. His path was clear.

❧

McNab Hall, Scotland

She was warm. She was fed. Her clan was happy. Things were not normal. Morrigan was on edge, waiting for everything to go horribly wrong.

"Good morn to ye, Morrigan," said Alys, bustling into the family solar carrying a large basket. "Here, let me build up that fire for ye."

Morrigan wanted to chastise Alys for waste, but she could not. The fuel supply had been checked. For once, they had enough. Morrigan glared at Alys. All the rampant happiness was her fault.

"How do ye like yer eggs?" asked Alys.

"The hens are still laying?"

"Aye. We built a new coop attached to the kitchen. I think they'll be warm enough to produce through the winter."

Morrigan scowled. The new chickens had been a gift from Campbell, thanks to his sister marrying Andrew. Morrigan wanted to return the hens when they arrived, but her clan turned murderous at the idea. Even she was not brave enough to stand between a hungry McNab and his supper, so the chickens stayed. And now they were having eggs for breakfast. When would the madness end?

"I was thinking on the holidays this year. I wish to make it special, give the folks here some joy." Alys continued to putter around the room, picking things up and setting them down in the same places, wiping away imaginary dust. She was hatching some daft plan no doubt.

"That's the third time ye've dusted that candlestick

in the past five minutes," commented Morrigan, leaning back in her chair by the fire.

Alys stopped and turned to Morrigan, a hint of blush to her cheeks. "Is it? How careless o' me."

"What do ye want, Alys?" Morrigan folded her arms across her chest, prepared for battle.

"Want? Me?"

"Ye're a horrible liar, Alys."

Alys sighed and took a gown out of the basket. She held it up for Morrigan to see. It was a dark blue silk with fine, gold embroidery through the bodice. Ribbons dressed the neckline and sleeves. It was a fine gown. Too fine.

"How much did ye pay for that?" Morrigan stood and fingered it with resentment. "Ye ken we canna afford finery as this. What could ye be thinking?"

"I dinna pay for it. 'Twas a castoff from Cait. I added the embroidery and the ribbons to give it a fresh look. Do ye like it?"

Morrigan sat down. Cait's castoffs were better than any gown ever worn by a McNab. Not even her mother had worn that quality. Morrigan could never afford such a gown for herself, not that she would ever wear a gown. She was aware of her own perplexing jealousy and pushed it aside. She did not mind being irritable, but she drew the line at petty. "'Tis fine work, Alys. Though I dinna ken when ye would wear such a gown."

"I have more here that are designed for everyday wearing. A red linen and a green wool." Alys pulled the gowns from her basket and looked at Morrigan with expectation.

"Verra serviceable," said Morrigan. Why was Alys showing her gowns?

"Ye like them?"

"I'm sure ye'll look fine in them." Morrigan guessed at what Alys wanted her to say. She stared into the fire and hoped if she ignored her, Alys might find another confidant for the perplexing talk of gowns and ribbons.

"Oh, they woud'na fit me. They are for ye."

Morrigan turned toward Alys so fast her head spun. She opened her mouth but no words emerged. She was so utterly surprised she could not say how she felt. Should she be upset? Insulted? Pleased?

"Why dinna ye try one on?"

Morrigan shook her head, still unable to speak. How could Alys see her as anything other than an overbearing harpy, hopelessly ruined? If Morrigan admitted she wanted to be a lady, to get married, to have a normal life, it meant acknowledging how truly miserable she was. It was better to stay angry, and in denial than open that pretty box of grief.

"I could do yer hair too. Ye've got lovely hair."

Morrigan shook her head more vigorously. Her hair was her one feminine vanity. Alys was treading on sensitive ground.

Alys sat on a bench next to her and sighed, fingering the beautiful, blue silk. "Please will ye tell me why ye winna consider wearing a gown."

"It is too late for me." Morrigan swallowed a large lump forming in her throat. "With what I have done, the things I have seen, I can never be a lady now."

"'Tis ne'er too late to change, Morrigan."

Morrigan shook her head. "Everyone knows what I've done."

"What ye've done is provide for yer clan. Ye should be proud o' yerself. I heard how ye fought off five English at once and captured the governor o' Nisbet. And did ye keep yer share fer yerself? Nay, ye gave every last coin to see to the comfort o' yer clan."

Morrigan grabbed a poker and thrust it ruthlessly at the fire. "I hardly fought five at once, three at the most."

"Quite so!" exclaimed Alys warming to her topic. "I see all ye do for the clan, Morrigan. Ye should be proud o' yerself. Ye deserve a good husband, to be mistress o' yer own home."

Morrigan put up her hands, signaling Alys to slow down. "First ye want me to put on a gown, and now ye wish me married?"

"And why not?"

"I've been a raider, an outlaw since I was old enough to wield a sword. No self-respecting man would wed a lass who wears breeches and can best him with a sword."

"So marry someone from a different clan. Ye could go somewhere else, start over. No one would e'er have to know. Look at me. I was a ladies' maid and companion to Lady Cait for many years. I was ne'er given the opportunity to marry, and no one e'er thought o' me as anything but a lady-in-waiting. By running away wi' yer brother I became mistress o' my own home."

"No decent man would marry me!" Morrigan stood and started to pace. Alys was determined to bring it all out into the light. "Understand this, Alys. I am not a Campbell like ye. I am a McNab. A clan disliked from one side o' this country to the other. I have no dowry. Nothing to tempt a man's interest. Even if I ne'er dressed as a man and stole for my supper, there isna a man from here to Hadrian's Wall who would take me. Never was. Never will be."

"Then go beyond the wall," Alys stated, utterly unfazed by Morrigan's outburst. "Marry an Englishman."

"*Alys!*"

"Alright, ne'er mind that. Bad idea. How about a Frenchman? Did ye meet any in yer travels?"

"A Frenchman," murmured Morrigan. She brushed her fingertips over the smooth blue silk.

Twelve

THE GOOD NEWS WAS ANDREW WAS STARTING TO recover. The bad news was Dragonet was no closer to finding the silver box his father wanted. They had been at St. Margaret's a week, and thanks to the skilled hands and potent potions of Mother Enid, Andrew's fever broke and the wound was looking less red and angry. Dragonet had called on all the lessons he learned from the Hospitallers to keep Andrew alive until they reached Mother Enid. Fortunately, she knew what to do from there.

Attending a wounded soldier had also given Dragonet the excuse to prowl the convent and the nearby abbey. Using a stolen key, he had searched the abbot's personal apartments both in the abbey and at the convent, but found nothing of significance. There was considerable correspondence in which the abbot had requested permission to build a large cathedral, but his requests had been repeatedly denied. Nothing in his papers led Dragonet to the location of the silver box.

The abbot himself was a gruff man with a hostile

demeanor. Dragonet supped with him once and decided one ruined meal was enough for a lifetime. The abbot was not one to share his secrets willingly; there would be no dropping of information at his silent table.

The Templar chest was out there somewhere, and he had one more place to look. Dragonet prayed long into the night, waiting for the elderly nun keeping vigil in the chapel to fall asleep. When she began to quietly snore, he knew the time was right.

On silent feet, Dragonet slid from the pew and snuck to the front of the chapel to begin his search. His searched behind the altar and around the pulpit. To the side he found a small door in the wall, no bigger than a barrel, which led to catacombs below. It looked promising.

"I'll save you the trouble and tell you I have already searched there," said Chaumont.

Dragonet whirled around to find the tall knight sitting in the front pew, his long legs stretched out before him. Dragonet bowed. "I am much obliged to you, sir. What is it I am looking for?"

Chaumont smiled and held out a knife. "Same thing as I, unless I mistake myself."

Dragonet glanced over at the still-sleeping nun and sat down beside Chaumont. On the knife handle was a familiar marking, a black circle with a white cross. "You were a Hospitaller monk?"

Chaumont laughed softly. "Never a monk, no, but I was born in a hospital run by the Hospitallers, and after my mother died, I was raised by the monks there. I heard of the treasure that was taken by the

Templars and have been determined to find it and return it if I can."

"That is why you came to Scotland?"

"One of many reasons. It was not, however, why I stayed."

Dragonet nodded. He had listened to many stories about Mary, Chaumont's wife, in their travels. He tried not to be jealous. A loving wife may be his desire, but it was not his future.

"Are you certain Barrick is or was a Templar?" asked Dragonet.

"Yes, of that I am certain. The Templars came several times to the monastery. I was young, but I remember him. I have searched this place, the abbey, everywhere I could think of, but I have not found anything that might be called a treasure. I begin to believe Barrick does not have it after all."

"Who does?"

"I am not certain, but Barrick has never been what you might call sociable. Perhaps the other Templars did not trust him and hid it."

"Are there any other Templars left?"

"None that I know."

The two men were silent in the dimly lit chapel. There was much Dragonet wished to say but could not. "Thank you for confiding in me," he said instead.

"You seem an honest man," said Chaumont.

"I am sorry to disappoint you then," said Dragonet.

"I think not. I have learned to trust my judge of character. I believe you will do what is right when the time comes."

Dragonet swallowed a lump in his throat. Chaumont

believed him to be a Hospitaller, seeking the return of their property, but he was not. He would give the treasure to his father instead.

Dragonet pushed aside guilty thoughts. He must get back to his quest. Nothing, not even his honor, must stand in the way. With a sudden flash of irony he realized he had criticized the duke for putting the mission before honor. Dragonet realized he was no better.

Dragonet stood. He suddenly felt unworthy to be in the chapel. He made his bow of respect and left, Chaumont following behind.

"Do not be discouraged, my friend. I am sure you can succeed where I have failed," said Chaumont cheerily.

Dragonet stopped in the courtyard, the moon struggling to be visible through the thick fog. Chaumont was a good man, honest and open. And trusting. Too bad Dragonet was unworthy of it. He wanted to please his father, but he was beginning to hate the man he was becoming to win his father's approval.

"Is there no one else?" Dragonet asked. "None that came from France that may know Barrick or the other Templars?"

Chaumont pondered for a moment. "Mother Enid came from France. She has been here a long time and knows Barrick. I do not know if she can help, but we can ask."

"Ask me what?" asked a voice from the fog.

"Mother Superior," said Dragonet with a bow. "You are awake late."

The frail figure of Mother Enid appeared out of the dense mist. "I am awake early. Have you two not yet taken your rest?" She shook her head and made a tsking sound. "Enjoy your youth whilst you can, my lads, for it is fleeting."

"Since we are all awake, is there somewhere we could go to talk in private?" asked Dragonet.

"Well now," said Mother Enid with a mischievous smile. "I have not had an offer like that from two handsome knights in many a year. Nice to know I still have some appeal."

Chaumont laughed heartily and followed the slow-moving Mother Enid to the library. He coaxed the embers of the fire into a fresh blaze, and they all sat around the hearth warming themselves from the night chill.

"Now what is it you two wanted to know?" asked Mother Enid.

"I seek information about the Abbot Barrick and how he came here from France," said Dragonet.

The smile left Mother Enid's bright blue eyes. "And why do you ask me about Barrick?"

Dragonet took a breath. "I believe he was a Templar and may have taken something from France that I have been sent to return."

Mother Enid stared into the fire without speaking. The silence grew so long Dragonet glanced at Chaumont, who shrugged.

"He was and he did," Mother Enid finally spoke.

"I beg your pardon?" asked Dragonet.

"I knew someday I would be called to give an account," said Mother Enid, still staring into the fire. "I decided I would tell the truth to any who asked. In all these years, you are the first who did."

Mother Enid took a deep breath. "I was treated

by the Hospitallers. It was toward the end of my
pregnancy, and no, I had no husband. I became
quite ill; the delivery was very difficult. At the time I
believed I was being punished for my sins. Afterwards
I was gravely ill. I burned with fever, and I have
little memory of that time. At one point I remember
waking up on a boat. I was lying on a special pallet and
was told not to try to move.

"From there I remember traveling overland in a
wagon, still lying on the pallet. At one point, one of
the men who were with me took something out from
under my pallet. He told me to forget it. I believe it
was a silver chest."

Dragonet sat up straighter. "Do you know where
this chest is now?"

"No. There were other things too. I believe I was
used by these men, former Templars, to smuggle
treasure out of France that they believed to be theirs.
Perhaps they were right; I cannot judge."

"How did you come here?" asked Chaumont.

Mother Enid smiled slowly. "I made a deal with
God in my travails that I would become a nun if I
survived. I do not think the men believed I would
live. Indeed, they appeared to be surprised that I
survived the journey. In the end they offered to send
me back to France, but I declined. I felt starting over
in Scotland may be the best for me."

"This treasure, where is it now?" asked Dragonet.

"I do not know. In truth I never spoke about the
things under my pallet with them. I was feverish for
much of my journey, I do not think they knew that I
was aware of these items. I feared if I mentioned it…"

Mother Enid shrugged. "I do not think they valued my life as much as I did."

"Who were these men?" asked Dragonet.

"I knew them as Michael, Claude, Stephan, and Barrick."

"Those must be the same men who came to the Hospitaller monastery in which I was raised," said Chaumont. "I remember them from when I was young, Barrick in particular. I was told they made several trips to the monastery over the years. I believe they lightened the storerooms of the Hospitallers every time."

Mother Enid smiled with a glint in her eye. "I do not doubt it. I believe they felt it was very much their own, since the pope gave the Templar treasure over to the Hospitallers when the order was disbanded."

"Other than Barrick, are any of the men still alive?" asked Dragonet.

"No. I believe Stephan may have had a son, but there are no other descendents I know."

Dragonet nodded. He had found the grandson of Stephan alive and drinking himself into an early grave. "Did ever you meet or see any of them again?"

Mother Enid nodded. "Michael. I cared for him as he lay dying." Mother Enid paused for a moment. "He kept repeating 'pray the hours for the treasure.' He said it many times. I thought he was speaking of prayer leading to a heavenly reward, but I cannot say for sure."

"'Pray the hours'?" Dragonet leaned closer. "Other than monastic prayer, do you know what he meant?"

"I am sorry, I cannot help you."

"I thank you, you have been helpful indeed," said Dragonet, standing. "Please forgive us for trespassing on your privacy so early in the morning. I am sincerely grateful for your candor. Please be assured of my discretion."

"And mine," said Chaumont, also rising. When they reached the door, Chaumont turned and asked, "Out of curiosity, whatever happened to the child?"

"My son," said Mother Enid in a faraway voice. "I was told he died."

"I am sorry," said Chaumont.

Mother Enid turned away. "So am I."

Thirteen

"Ow! THAT HURTS!" COMPLAINED MORRIGAN.

"'Tis supposed to, Sister dear," replied Alys and pulled Morrigan's hair even harder.

"Ye are going to leave me bald!"

"Nay, I'll leave ye a few strands left, I promise. Now sit still. I have done my mistress's hair since I was eight years old. I ken what I am doing. Dinna worrit yerself."

"I canna believe I let ye talk me into this," grumbled Morrigan.

Alys began to hum a happy tune.

"Ye're enjoying this, dinna deny it!" challenged Morrigan.

"Aye, I have wanted to do this for a long time." Alys styled Morrigan's freshly washed hair into the latest fashion. Apparently, female fashion was painful. "Ye have the best hair I've e'er seen. 'Tis such a rich color, like chestnuts, and thick like a rope but shiny like silk. None o' the Campbell lasses have hair like yers."

Morrigan reveled in the compliment without a word. She had always thought her long, straight hair was simply brown. *Chestnuts*. That was something special. It did occur to Morrigan that Alys may be flattering her to keep her still while her hair was styled. If that was the case, it worked. Morrigan offered no more complaint to the procedure.

"Have ye thought who will be the first-foot this eve?" asked Alys.

It was New Year's Eve, or Hogmanay, as it was known in Scotland, and tradition dictated that the first visitor, or first-foot, of the New Year must be someone special.

Morrigan shrugged. "We had Harry do it last year."

"Harry!" Alys did not sound pleased. She stepped around from her work to confront Morrigan, her hands on her ample hips. "The first-foot determines the luck for the entire year. No wonder ye all are in the state ye're in."

"Well, Harry is tall," said Morrigan apologetically. The first-foot was supposed to be tall, dark, and handsome, if you could get it. He was also supposed to bear gifts symbolizing good luck for the New Year. Last year Harry had stumbled in at midnight drunk, the bottle of whiskey he was supposed to gift the clan having been consumed while he waited outside for his cue to enter.

Alys went back to her work with a few extra tugs on Morrigan's head. "Harry indeed," she muttered.

Morrigan started mentally going through the list of tall, dark, and handsome Highlanders who could serve as first-footers. It was a short list. In truth, she could not think of one.

"Have ye any thoughts on the matter?" asked Morrigan. Alys was sure to have a better plan than hers. Alys had been the one to organize all of the Christmastide celebrations. They were in the midst of the twelve days of Christmas, and never before had the McNabs been so merry.

Alys mumbled in reply. There was no obvious candidate, but Morrigan was certain Alys would sort it out. Alys was, after all, the one who decorated the castle with holly and ivy. It was she who directed the play of Adam and Eve on Christmas Eve, and she who found a Yule log big enough to last all twelve days of Christmas. Dear to Morrigan's heart, or more accurately her stomach, Alys had also instructed the cook how to prepare feasts, including boar's head, mincemeat pies, puddings, stews, and mouthwatering gingerbread.

Initially Morrigan objected to the Christmastide feast, expressing concerns that they would run out of food before they ran out of winter and demanded the plans be changed. The McNabs had not celebrated with anything more than an extra dose of hearty wassail in years. But Alys calmly explained how Morrigan's ransom prize, in combination with some well-timed gifts from the Campbells and careful economy, made it all possible. Alys may have been barely literate, but when it came to household accounts, she was the mistress of her domain.

Morrigan never ran from a fight, but after hours of ledgers and patient explanations, she sounded her retreat. She would take care before challenging her sister-in-law's household management again. Besides, Alys had her own recipe for baking gingerbread, one to which Morrigan was becoming quite partial.

As much as Morrigan was uncomfortable and slightly confused by the infusion of celebratory spirit in the McNab household, she could not deny that her people were cheerier than they had been in a long time. Although Archie McNab was not there to witness it, marrying Alys was the one thing he finally got right.

"There now," said Alys walking around Morrigan to examine her handiwork. "Ye look verra well, if I do say so myself."

"What have ye done? It feels odd," said Morrigan reaching for the headdress Alys had pinned to her head.

"Dinna touch it!" scolded Alys. "Yer hair is so thick I was able to do several tiny plaits to make a pattern on yer head, can ye see?" Alys held up a polished, copper mirror and Morrigan tried to see her new style.

"I canna see anything beyond this daft headdress," complained Morrigan. The headdress itself was quite pretty, made of a gauzy material and gold ribbons. At the nape of her neck, Morrigan's thick hair was divided to form twó plaits entwined with more gold ribbons. Even with the plaits, Morrigan's hair reached her waist.

"Now for the gown," said Alys.

Morrigan opened her mouth to protest.

"Have some gingerbread," said Alys handing her a large piece.

"Buying my compliance with baked goods?" Morrigan grumbled, but took a bite of the special treat.

"Aye and I'm no' ashamed to say it. Now stand up and stay still. I'll do all the work, ye just eat and think on the feast we'll have tonight."

"I'm no' a child," mumbled Morrigan, standing up and taking another bite. She was defeated by her love of gingerbread.

Alys had Morrigan step carefully into the blue silk gown. Alys fastened the tiny buttons at the wrists of the sleeves with nimble fingers. Next she began tightening the ties in the front and back to create a formfitting look through the bodice.

"Is breathing important?" asked Morrigan, her mouth full of gingerbread.

"Nay," answered Alys cheerily. "Try bending over."

Morrigan bent over at the waist and Alys cinched her in tighter. "Ow! What are ye doing?"

"Giving ye a wee bit o' lift."

"Lift? Lift o' what?" Morrigan glanced down and answered her own question. The gown was low cut, at least to her standards, and squeezing out of the top was a considerable bit of cleavage that had never before seen the light of day. For Morrigan, who was accustomed to keeping herself bound as flat as possible with linen strips, the sight of her own well-proportioned bosom was a step too far.

"Alys, what are ye going to put here?" Morrigan gestured at her chest.

"Do ye have any jewels? A necklace perhaps? Something from yer mother?"

"Hang that! I canna walk out o' the solar looking like this. Tell me true, how are ye going to cover my... my..."

"Ye could try for a maidenly blush."

"Alys!"

"Dinna get yerself in a state; ye look lovely."

"This isna fair. Ye are wearing a gorget." Morrigan pointed to the part of Alys's veil that wrapped under her chin and covered her neck and chest.

"Aye, but I am a married lady, I am expected to dress wi' more modesty. Ye are verra fashionable. 'Tis what all the Campbell sisters wear."

"So an unmarried lass is supposed to flaunt her wares like a fishmonger?"

"I woud'na quite put it like that, but aye, a lass should dress to catch a man's eye."

"Nay. I winna go down looking like this. They will laugh at me!"

"Nay. None of our lads values his life so cheaply." Alys gave her a smile.

Morrigan shook her head. In her men's clothing, she was protected. She knew who she was, and while she may not have been accepted, she was never mocked. Dressing as a lady, she was lost.

"I dinna ken why I let ye talk me into this." Morrigan began to pace, a simple task she found more difficult in skirts. "No amount o' gingerbread is worth this."

"Morrigan, Sister," said Alys gently. "There can be no future for ye dressing as a man and going to war. Like it or no', ye are a lady. 'Tis yer birthright. 'Tis time ye claimed it."

Morrigan shook her head. Not much in the world scared her, but opening herself to ridicule, that put the fear in her.

"'Tis Hogmanay, the beginning of a new year," continued Alys. "Ye can choose a new path. Ye can be the lady ye were always meant to be. Besides, think o' what a shock it will be for the clan. Ye should do it to amuse yerself with their surprise if naught else."

"What is for supper?" asked Morrigan, weighing her options.

"Boar's head and goose and mincemeat pies and frumenty, oh lots of things."

"Are ye serving my favorite sauce wi' the goose?"

"Aye."

Morrigan narrowed her eyes at Alys. "What is my favorite sauce?

Alys sighed and shrugged. "Please, Morrigan, please come down to the great hall wi' me. Let this be a new beginning for ye. A fresh start. Besides, I need ye. Like it or no', ye are the only family I have here. Please come down wi' me."

Morrigan sighed. She kicked off the pretty little slippers and tugged her leather boots on under the gown. Around her waist she strapped her short sword. Morrigan glared a challenge to Alys.

"Ye look lovely... and a little frightening," declared Alys.

Morrigan smiled. It was the best compliment she had ever received. "Let's be done wi' it."

Morrigan stomped out of the room, defiance blazing in her eyes. She was determined to kill any man who insulted her by staring at her... and any man who insulted her by not staring at her. It was bound to be a bloodbath—no different from any other New Year's with the McNabs.

❧

Wearing a skirt holds a power of its own. Morrigan had always believed she must bully others into doing what she wanted. Apparently, she could gain the same effect by merely flashing a little cleavage.

Walking into the great hall arm in arm with Alys

caused such a stir it was comical. Men stared. Women stared. Even the dogs stared. The room was silenced. It was the best entrance she had ever experienced. From that point forward, men she had known for years rushed to bring her a mug of wassail or a joint of meat. When she expressed a desire for whiskey, five men ran to her with their flasks.

She was not without detractors, however. One man made a rude comment and was escorted out of the hall by Harry and Willy. If his yelps outside the door were any indication, he was sent on his way with a bit of rough treatment. The women's gossip was another hurdle, but Alys excused herself at one point and said something to a group of whispering women that made their faces burn. Morrigan smiled in spite of herself. She had never before had a female friend, but in Alys she had a powerful ally.

After supper, Alys organized mummers and some entertainment. Though nothing in the world could convince Morrigan to sing or dance, she did enjoy the festivities, much as she was loathe to admit it. Before her a juggler was trying to perform his act. Actually it was a page named Kip, and he could not juggle at all, but his comic attempts had the hall roaring in laughter. And the more they drank, the more amusing the act became.

"Och, Morrigan, help me," whispered Alys at Morrigan's shoulder. Alys had disappeared ten minutes ago and returned looking harried, a strand of hair falling free from her generally tidy veil.

"What's the matter?" asked Morrigan, following her out the side door and into a small passageway beside the hall.

"Look, 'tis the blacksmith's son, Liam. I canna raise him." Alys pointed at the young man in a heap on the floor.

Morrigan rushed to the lad's side and blew a sigh of relief when she found him breathing. "By the saints, he reeks o' whiskey and beer," said Morrigan. "He's fine where he is; let him sleep off his drink. He'll learn a lesson about moderation in the morn, I wager."

"Nay, we must get him to his feet. He is the first-foot!"

Morrigan evaluated the lad where he lay. Alys had done an admirable job of finding a tall, dark, and handsome Highlander, albeit a bit young and passed-out drunk. "He would make a good first-foot, but he's drunk as sin."

"Help me get him to his feet. Maybe if we walk him around a bit," said Alys, her brows knit together in worry. This was important to her.

"Alright, up wi' ye," said Morrigan wrapping the lad's arm around her shoulder and hauling him off the floor. For a thin lad, he was a heavy one, as if his father had fashioned him steel bones from his blacksmith shop.

Liam's head lolled to one side as Morrigan and Alys struggled to get him upright. Finally they succeeded in lifting the lad to his unstable feet. Liam opened his eyes and looked at his rescuers, one on each arm.

"Bonwie lasses. Look, I gots me two o' em!" Liam grinned and retched on the floor. Morrigan dropped him and stood back to protect the gown. She was still not sure how she felt wearing gowns, but she was certain it was not going to be ruined by a green lad who couldn't hold his liquor.

"Oh hell!" exclaimed Alys, watching Liam slump back down to the floor.

"Alys McNab!" chastised Morrigan in mock horror. "Such language! I'm ashamed o' ye. Ye must change the company ye keep."

Alys flashed Morrigan a wry smile. "Sorry to offend yer delicate ears, but this was my first-foot. Who do we get now?"

"Rider's approaching!" came the cry from the hall. Both Morrigan and Alys left the snoring lad and hustled toward the main entrance of the great hall.

Someone knocked on the door three times. The raucous laughter of the McNab clan grew quiet as they strained to see who would be the first-foot.

"Did ye get a first-foot?" hissed Alys.

"Nay, did ye?" whispered Morrigan.

Alys shook her head. "So if neither of us arranged for a first-foot, who's at the door?"

"Only one way to find out." Morrigan put her hand to her sword hilt. "Open the door," she commanded.

The large, wooden double doors were unbolted and swung open with a mournful creak. With a rush of frozen air, snowflakes swirled around the cloaked figure of a man. Into the hall stepped a tall man, dark and handsome. Morrigan gasped.

It was Dragonet.

Fourteen

"Ye knock on the door," said Andrew, stepping back to let Dragonet go first. "'Tis Hogmanay and ye can be the first-foot."

"I hope your fever has not returned, for I have no idea what you are saying." Dragonet looked Andrew up and down. He was on his feet at least, though his arm was still in a sling, and Dragonet knew his wound was far from fully healed.

"'Tis the eve o' the New Year. The first visitor is the first-foot. Go on wi' ye, knock quick. I am mighty cold." Andrew smiled through chattering teeth. He had lost a lot of weight during his convalescence.

Dragonet wondered if the cold had made Andrew delirious, but he obligingly knocked. He waited, a nervous buzz humming in his stomach. She would be there. Morrigan. The one person he should not see. Ever. She made him forget everything, his mission, his vows, his next breath. She was dangerous, and he would not have come, except that she was the last lead he had to find the silver chest.

Morrigan was the only person he knew who could

tell him the location of the cave where the Templars had hidden their treasure so many years ago. He did not know if it was still there, but he had to find out. Dragonet had tried getting the information from Andrew, but other than to say he had heard of a cave he was not allowed to enter, Andrew knew nothing of it. Morrigan was Dragonet's last chance.

After a pause, the door to the great hall was opened with a loud creak, and Dragonet stepped into the room filled with people. The hall was more festive than he remembered it, with fresh rushes on the floor and boughs of holly and ivy decorating the walls. The air was smoky but warm, a welcome relief from the bitter cold.

Two women stood to greet him. One had a shorter figure with a pleasant smile and rosy cheeks. The other was a tall, handsome woman who gaped at him like he was an apparition. He tried not to stare in return. She was dressed in a beautiful blue silk with gold embroidery. Dragonet was no expert in fashion, but even he could see the gown was a fine piece and no doubt quite dear. He decided the woman must be a stranger, because no McNab could afford such a fine piece.

The tall woman had large, dark eyes and long lashes. Her hair was dressed in lace and two long plaits that fell to her waist. Her gown clung nicely, revealing a small waist and shapely figure. He tore his gaze away from her to avoid gawking at her cleavage. She was striking and oddly familiar, but he was certain they had never met. A lady of her stature could not be forgotten.

Despite the number of people in the room, all

conversations hushed and everyone focused on him. Was that what Andrew meant by being a first-foot?

"A happy New Year to you ladies," said Dragonet with a graceful bow. *When in doubt, charm with politeness.*

"Welcome to McNab Hall, sir," said the shorter, cheerful woman. "Here, come by the fire and warm yerself. 'Tis not often we get visitors this time o' year."

"I come with a gift I believe belongs to you." Dragonet motioned to Andrew, who emerged from the shadows.

"Andrew!" shrieked the tall woman and ran to hug the shivering lad. "Why are ye here? Och, Alys, he's been hurt, bring him to the fire."

"Morrigan, I am well. Alys need no' fuss over me," Andrew protested.

Morrigan? Dragonet staggered back to catch his balance as if he had been physically struck.

"Wheesht!" Morrigan silenced all protests. "Sit in this chair by the fire and mind me proper. I'm no' surprised ye got yerself hurt, going off wi' those Campbells like a damn fool. I told ye naught would come o' hanging after that Cait lass, but ye ne'er listen the way ye ought. I blame Archie for sending ye to university. Put daft notions in yer head."

Yes, it was the same Morrigan. His beautiful Morrigan. For a few beats of his heart, everything was silent. He watched people crowd around the injured lad and jump to obey Morrigan's commands. All eyes were on Andrew. All Dragonet could see was Morrigan.

The last time Dragonet saw Morrigan, she wore so many layers against the bitter chill she was little more than an amorphous blob. She could have been a woman, a man, or a bear for all the bundles showed of her shape. Tonight, Morrigan was a lady. Her waist was small and shapely, her figure trim, her hips rounded nicely, and her bosom... Dragonet tried to avoid staring at her luscious curves. Could it truly be Morrigan?

"Bring Andrew some food and hot wassail, now! Dinna talk to him; can ye no' see he's tired? Now eat this, ye ken? Ye look like death, and I canna say ye dinna deserve it!" Morrigan stood with one hand on her hip and the other on her sword hilt. It was indeed Morrigan.

The transformation was remarkable. Her thick hair was plaited down to her waist. Her gown was of fine silk. All worthy things to catch his eye, and yet his gaze wandered once more to her décolletage. Despite the importance of his quest, Dragonet decided what he truly needed to know was where she had been hiding those breasts. Morrigan turned to him, her eyes narrowing. Had she caught him gawking?

"What are ye standing there for? Come sit. Drink. Ye must be froze to the bone. Dinna ye have enough sense no' to be traipsing about in the snow after dark? Bring a chair for Sir Dragonet, now, dammit!"

Dragonet complied with her orders, as did everyone else. She fussed over Andrew and hid her good intentions with criticism and complaint. Andrew began to look harried, but Dragonet was bemused. It was not her words but the meaning behind them that mattered.

Alys pressed a mug of hot wassail into his hand. "Thank ye for bringing our lad Andrew back home. My good sister will thank ye too when she finishes wi' her fit. 'Tis her way o' showing she cares, ye ken."

Dragonet nodded. "I did not know Lady Morrigan had a sister."

"I am lately married to Laird McNab."

Dragonet inclined his head toward her. "Lady McNab." She smiled and proceeded to quietly organize the festivities. Dragonet sipped the warm, soothing wassail, the cup thawing his frozen hands. Feeling returned to his fingers with a dull ache. He took another swig against the pain.

Andrew's greeting was warm and long. It was clear he was well liked in the castle, and soon he was called upon to tell his harrowing tales of war and how he was injured. Andrew's tale was a modest, sanitized version of the reality of the siege to take Berwick. He was trying to protect his clan from the ugliness of war. The unfortunate truth was the invasion had ended in defeat, and the sleeping giant of England had been awakened. Many in the hall recognized Dragonet as the minstrel and asked him to play, but Morrigan chastised her clansmen, commenting on how dreadfully fatigued he appeared to be. It was not a compliment, but Dragonet was relieved not to be called upon to perform. After an hour of greeting, followed by drinking, followed by stories, followed by more drinking, Dragonet was feeling warm and cozy and quite tired. Andrew's eyes were half open, if they were open at all.

"Time for bed," Morrigan said in her direct manner. "Alys, have ye prepared his room?"

"Aye, the rooms are prepared for both our surprise visitors. Come now, Andrew my lad, ye look mighty tired." Alys gently helped Andrew from the chair and led him to his chamber.

Morrigan glanced at Dragonet, as if he was nothing but an afterthought. "Come, I'll show ye the room if ye care to have it." Morrigan stomped off and Dragonet jumped up to follow her.

Unfortunately, his presence had been marked by several lasses in the castle who had been flirting shamelessly and chose that moment for a drunken pounce.

"Dinna follow her," said one flame-haired wench, grabbing his arm. "All she has is a bed; she'll no' give ye what I can offer." She squeezed her breasts and licked her lips.

"Thank you for that kindly offer but…"

"Nay, he dinna want yer ill-used arse," squawked a black-haired wench who had long since lost her head covering. "Come wi' me, sugar. I ken what a knight like ye wants."

"Thank you, but no. All I want is to sleep." Dragonet disengaged himself from the clutches of the amorous drunk and hustled after Morrigan, worried he had lost her. He need not have been concerned, since the sounds of cursing led him to her directly.

"Damn, stupid thing. How do people walk in this fool gown?" Morrigan was doubled over on the castle stairs, trying to disentangle the hem of her gown from her feet.

"I believe you must lift your skirts when walking up stairs to avoid treading on the hem of your gown," said Dragonet, leaning against the stone wall behind her.

Morrigan straightened and whirled around to face him. "Ye wear gowns much do ye? Perhaps tomorrow ye can wear one to supper and show me how it's done."

Dragonet merely smiled. He had learned from

wearing his monk's robes, but that was not a topic open for conversation. Morrigan glared at him, but her cheeks were rosy.

"Well ye offered yer advice, now what do ye want?" demanded Morrigan.

"You mentioned a room?"

"So ye dinna wish to bed one o' those wenches?"

"I am greatly tired. All I want is to sleep."

"Have them come for ye in the morn. They can service ye after ye're rested."

"I do not wish to be... serviced."

Morrigan shrugged and continued up the stairs, skirts in hand. "'Tis no concern o' mine. I dinna ken why ye should tell me about it."

Dragonet followed her up four flights of the winding staircase to the floor where the family lived. Torches flickered in their iron holders, leaving long, black trails of smoke on the walls. They passed an open door to a solar, and a few doors farther, Morrigan stopped at another open door.

"Here is yer room." She stopped at the threshold as if wary to enter, even for a moment.

Dragonet walked past her into the room. It was in deep shadow, the only light coming from the flickering torches in the hall. "The room is very nice. I thank you."

"Thank Alys."

"I will do as you suggest. She is a new addition to your family?"

"Aye, Archie wed her several months ago. One o' the few things he got right."

"She seems a kind woman."

Morrigan nodded but remained in the doorway, leaning her shoulder against the door frame. Dragonet waited for her to speak.

"I want to thank ye for bringing Andrew home. It is a kindness I…" Morrigan's voice trailed off and she looked down, wiping the palms of her hands on her silk gown. "But why?" Her gaze reached him again, her eyes large and black in the dimly lit room. "Why would ye leave yer fellow knights to bring him all the way back to the Highlands?"

Dragonet had anticipated that question and gave a ready answer. "The town of Berwick, it was taken, but not the castle. We planned a siege, but they were well equipped and could have lasted through the winter. We learned King Edward had amassed an army to march against us, eighty thousand men, experienced soldiers all. To stand against them, it would be folly."

"So ye left?"

"I fear they all did. The Duke of Argitaine decided to withdraw once the hope of success had waned. After that the clans, they slipped away one by one."

"Like rats leaving a sinking ship." Morrigan crossed her arms over her chest, temporarily blocking his view from the one thing he should not be looking at. "Did I no' warn that would happen? But would anyone listen to me?"

"Your judgments have been proven correct, my lady."

"Lot o' good that does anyone now. But why are ye here? Why no' return to France wi' yer fellow knights?"

"I promised to you I would look after Andrew."

"Ye certainly took yer promise seriously."

"He is a good lad. It was not difficult to want to

help." His promise to Morrigan was not the only reason he was there, but he was accustomed to revealing only half-truths, though it never made him as uncomfortable as it did then. Dragonet looked down, avoiding her eye. "I felt it wrong to leave, after I had encouraged the clans to go to war."

Morrigan snorted and began to pace out into the hall and back to the doorway, still never crossing the threshold. "What do those arrogant Frenchies care if they cause pain and suffering for us? Why be concerned about people they feel are infinitely below their notice? Damn nobility, they care naught for the lives they destroy."

"I cannot defend the duke's decision, but I will offer my apologies most sincere."

Morrigan stopped, her eyes locked on his. "Why are ye here Dragonet? Why care for my brother and travel all this way?"

Again Dragonet was uncomfortable but not unprepared in his answer. "I found Chaumont and Gavin taking Andrew to see the Mother Enid. Naturally, I accompanied them to lend my assistance to his care."

"I still canna believe Chaumont and Gavin would help us. The MacLarens have always hated the McNabs."

"It does not appear Gavin realizes he is a MacLaren, nor Andrew a McNab."

"They did forge an ill-conceived friendship," Morrigan conceded.

"Ill-conceived or no, Gavin helped take Andrew to the Mother Enid for the medicine that could save him. I think also Chaumont was desirous to take Gavin away from the war going poorly. He discharged the

Graham soldiers and helped Gavin take Andrew away from danger."

"I ne'er thought I would be beholden to a MacLaren." Morrigan scowled at the prospect. "But that still does not explain why ye brought Andrew here from the convent."

Dragonet again avoided her eye. "Andrew wished to be home, and I thought it right to oblige him. I did not wish for him to travel alone. I gave you my word I would look out for him, so of course I provided my aid. Or do you think it is only the Scots who know how to keep their word?"

"N-no, I ne'er meant to say that," said Morrigan.

"You have a low opinion of Frenchmen, I understand, but there are a poor few who have some regard for their honor."

"I ne'er meant to question yer word," said Morrigan, flustered.

His calculated attack had worked to throw her off the offensive, though he did not gain much satisfaction from the ruse. In one glorious, dreadful moment he had the impulse to tell her everything and beg for her assistance in finding the cave and the treasure he sought. The difficulties such a confession would bring crashed down on him, silencing his rash impulse.

Morrigan averted her gaze and fiddled with the laces on the sleeves of her gown. "I am in yer debt. If ever there is anything I can do for ye…" Morrigan stepped closer and looked up at him, her brown eyes large in the gloom. Dragonet's heart skipped a beat. What was she offering?

Morrigan cleared her throat and stepped back,

changing the subject. "Ye dinna recognize me tonight, I warrant."

"No, I confess at first I did not."

"'Twas Alys's fault. She pestered me until I conceded. What... um... what do ye think o' her work?"

"Beautiful." Dragonet answered her question with the truth.

Morrigan glanced down and smoothed away invisible wrinkles. "The gown is verra fine."

"The gown, it is beautiful too."

Color sprung to Morrigan's cheeks, even the dim light could not hide her blush. It was quite charming. She could fight like a warrior, but still blushed like a maiden at a compliment. Dragonet was flooded with the desire to take her in his arms, to kiss her once more and not let her go.

"Was there any other reason ye came here?" Morrigan's voice was uncharacteristically soft.

"Yes." Dragonet's heart beat fast. It was the truth, more than the truth. The other truth was he had come to see her. Morrigan. His lady. He took a step toward her, but could not reach her. The unspoken truth of who he was and why he had come posed an insurmountable barrier, separating them forever.

"My chamber is next door." Morrigan inclined her head to the right. "If ye need anything..." Morrigan gave him a small smile, honest and trusting.

He wished to be worthy of that trust, but how could he tell her the truth? The monks who had searched for the treasure before him had been killed. If Morrigan realized something of value was in that cave, her life could be in danger too. It would be best to get the information without arousing her suspicion. Trouble was, she was already arousing something in him.

"I… I would like…" Dragonet was generally not at a loss for words, but then usually his heart was not beating so hard he feared it would crack a rib. "If you please to come in?"

"If ye wish." Morrigan slowly stepped over the threshold into the sparse room. She began to bite a fingernail, glanced up at him with sudden consciousness of what she was doing, and whipped her hands behind her back.

Dragonet took a quick breath. "Have you been well? Has your shoulder healed?"

"Aye. See for yerself." Morrigan slid down her gown to reveal her wounded shoulder, graced with a red scar.

Dragonet stepped to her on shaky legs and traced the scar with a fingertip. "It has healed well." It was sweet torture to touch her. He wanted more.

"Thanks to ye. I shudder to think o' what Willy would have done to me."

Dragonet smiled. "Comparing my work to Willy, I could hardly fail to impress."

"You did have the benefit o' being sober."

"And conscious."

The corners of Morrigan's mouth twitched. "Yes, I decided it helps. From now on I will demand any who put stitches in me be at least able to stand unaided."

"A wise decision, my lady."

Morrigan treated him to a rare smile and sat down on the bed. "And ye? What did ye learn from the campaign?"

Dragonet ignored his internal warnings and sat beside her. "War is a poor way to settle a disagreement."

"But ye knew that already."

"I learned that snow is cold. And rain here is cold. And I learned my fingers and toes, they do not care for it overmuch."

"Yer blood is too thin, my poor French friend." Morrigan took his hands in hers, sending ripples of excitement through him. "Ye need to stay a few more winters, and ye will toughen up."

"Toughen me or mark my end?"

Morrigan cocked her head and leveled an appraising glance. "I do not ken what to make o' ye, Dragon. I do know ye have no' shared wi' me much o' yer life or yer reasons for being here."

"My reasons…"

Morrigan squeezed his hand to stop him. "Yer reasons are yer own… for now," she added with a sly glance. "I am happy to have my brother returned to me, and I am pleased to see ye."

"I am well pleased to see you, my lady. I must say, I do appreciate your new look."

"Ye look nice too," she said without looking at him. Once again she fussed with the ties on her sleeves. "I dinna ken what to say now." Her eyes flashed with accusation.

Taken aback, Dragonet scrambled to ascertain how he had offended her. "You need not say anything. You are a most lovely hostess."

"I'm no' yer hostess, Alys is," grumbled Morrigan. "I'm yer… yer… what am I to ye?"

A shock of warning pulsed through Dragonet.

He must tread carefully. "I find you a most pleasing companion."

"Ye'd be the only one."

"I am pleased to hear it."

"Look now, are ye going to kiss me or no'? We kiss every time we meet, and now ye're here, but I dinna ken how to get to the kissing part."

Dragonet could not help but smile. She frowned at him and he succumbed to laughter, her forthright manner breaking through the tension.

"Are ye laughing at me?"

"Never have I met anyone like you, so completely without falsehood or pretense."

"Or shame."

Dragonet smiled at her in the dim light of the torchlight flickering from the hall. She was utterly unique and was surprisingly becoming in a gown. His attention had been captured earlier by her cleavage, but it was her eyes that held him in her power.

Before he arrived that night, he had every intention of avoiding physical contact. He should not toy with the affections of a lady, especially since it was not in his power to marry. Yet one look at her in the new gown, and the battle was lost. Besides, he doubted her emotions were engaged, as his were. She was a tough one, Morrigan McNab. Her heart was not likely to be easily touched.

The torchlight danced in her black eyes. She was his one desire, more than the silver box, more than proving himself to his father. She was all he could see. He leaned closer to her as she leaned in to him. They met with a kiss, sweet and tasting of wassail.

He moved slowly, wrapping his arms around her and pulling her closer even as she deepened the kiss. She was indeed willing, sliding onto his lap with ease. She fit nicely in his arms, like she belonged there.

"Close the door and let us go to bed," she murmured. "And ye can tell me all yer secrets."

"And will you tell me yours?" he whispered.

"Aye, I will tell ye anything."

This was everything he wanted. Everything he needed. He could get the information while taking the woman who set him ablaze to bed. It was perfect. His rational mind screamed in warning, but he was no longer thinking with his brain. He stood to shut the door.

"Ye can start wi' the beginning," said Morrigan. "Tell me about yer mother and father. Are they living? Is yer father a knight like ye?"

His father. Jumping into a frozen lake naked could not have shocked him with such searing cold. His father would take advantage of her offer. It was everything he wanted, and yet even his passion-drenched mind he knew sleeping with her could cause her trouble. He would not leave Morrigan the way his father had left his mother. Dragonet opened the door and turned slowly to her.

Morrigan's smile faded in the emptiness of his silence. "Is something the matter?"

"The journey, it has been long. I am greatly tired. I beg your forgiveness, for nothing would give me greater pleasure than spending more time with you, but I fear tonight I would be poor company."

Her jaw hardened and her eyes grew black and

cold. She put her hand on the hilt of her sword and
Dragonet instinctively took a step back.

"Now that you mention it, I am also quite
fatigued," said Morrigan, her voice flat. "'Tis been a
long night, and we all need sleep. I have no candle for
ye, I fear. I do hope Alys changed the ticking, for last
time I checked that mattress was filled wi' bed bugs.
Good night to ye then."

Morrigan swept past him and slammed the door
closed, leaving him alone in his room of utter darkness. Dragonet collapsed on the pallet and hoped for
the best. Instead of a lady for a bed partner he had
chosen bedbugs.

Fifteen

"ALYS, WHERE DID YE PUT MY BREECHES?"

"I tossed them in the wash."

"What?! What am I supposed to wear now?" Morrigan stood in her chemise, her hands on her hips. After her disastrous attempt at flirtation, she was not about to embarrass herself further. It was time to go back to a wardrobe that was comfortable, albeit wrong for a lady of her standing. She cared not. It was better than being rejected.

"I thought this might suit ye." Alys held out a wine-red gown. "Look, 'tis wool, verra practical."

"Dinna try to win me over wi' practicality. No gown could ever be practical."

"I am sorry, but yer other clothes I gave to the washerwoman this morning; they will be soaked by now. 'Tis winter too, so they may take a few days to dry."

"Let me know when they are ready," Morrigan sulked and pulled her chair closer to the smoldering fire. It was a cold morning.

"Come now, dinna take on so. Try the gown, it

will keep ye warmer than that chemise. Do I need to fetch more gingerbread?"

"Some things gingerbread canna fix," grumbled Morrigan, staring into the pitiful fire.

"What happened?" asked Alys, sitting in a chair next to Morrigan. "Forgive me, but last night I heard voices and saw ye speaking with Sir Dragonet." Alys's eyes were wide and hopeful.

"Ye were eavesdropping on us?"

"Aye, but I coud'na hear much and remain hidden," Alys confessed, a gleam of mischief in her eye.

Morrigan glared at Alys, but she was hardly one to criticize another for lack of etiquette. "Nothing much happened, Alys. Nothing, ye ken? Dinna labor under a false assumption; Dragonet has no interest in me."

"I spoke a bit to Andrew last night before he fell asleep. He told me how many times Dragonet has helped ye."

Morrigan wrapped her arms around herself against the chill and said nothing.

"Did Dragonet no' save yer life in battle?"

"Aye," said Morrigan with reluctance.

"And was he the one who stitched yer wound?"

"Aye."

"Which, by the way, ye never mentioned, and I only found out about it through Andrew," Alys chastised.

Morrigan shrugged.

"And did Dragonet no' save ye from an angry mob?"

"I could have handled it."

"And did he no' help save Andrew's life and bring yer brother all the way home?"

"Is there a point to all these questions?" Morrigan scowled at her sister, who smiled deviously in return.

"Simply making sure I have the truth. It all looks verra promising." Alys rubbed her hands together.

"Dinna try yer hand at matchmaking. He's not interested."

"Nonsense. Ye must make some allowances for fatigue. Andrew may sleep all day; the poor lad is exhausted."

Morrigan sat up in her chair, a glimmer of hope rekindled in her heart. Dragonet did come a long way to keep his promise to her. He must have been extremely tired from the journey. His kiss certainly spoke of his interest.

"Come now," said Alys standing up, her eyes shining. "Let us get ye in yer gown."

"Bring the gingerbread."

⁓

Morrigan walked to the solar and paused at the door. He was in there, she knew it. What was he thinking? She was inexperienced in trying to ascertain what a man was thinking or feeling, particularly in regard to romance. It had never been part of her life. Never wanted it. Never had it. Now she was at a distinct disadvantage.

One thing for sure, she was not going to make a fool out of herself again. She would not be asking for more kisses, only to be rebuffed. If he was interested in her, he was going to have to prove it.

Morrigan put her hand on the door latch but did not enter. She never ran from battle, but these feelings threatened to hurt her in ways she had no way to treat. In truth, her stomach was doing more unhappy flips standing outside the solar than when preparing for battle. At least in war she knew what to expect. This was uncharted territory.

"Ye going to open that door? This tray is getting mighty heavy."

Morrigan spun around to find Alys holding a large tray laden with breakfast.

"Aye, sorry," mumbled Morrigan, opening the door and helping her sister-in-law with the tray.

Dragonet was indeed in the room, standing by the window. He bowed when the ladies entered, a practiced art, smooth and graceful. He wore a linen shirt under a linen surcoat of bright blue with patterns embroidered along the edges with yellow thread. Under that he wore snug-fitting woolen hose and black leather boots. His clothes fit him well, hugging his tall, trim frame.

Morrigan tripped over the hem of her gown and fell to the floor in an ungraceful heap. Dragonet leapt to her side and caught the tray before it fell, helping Alys to put it on the table.

"My sir, ye are quick and I thank ye. Well now, some o' the cider has spilled, but that is all." Alys bustled around the table setting places and sopping up the mess.

"Are you hurt?" Dragonet asked Morrigan, who was sitting on the floor.

Morrigan was hoping she would open her eyes and find she had not fallen to the floor like a drunken whore at the feet of the man who made her heart skip a beat. Or perhaps she would die of mortification and thus be spared this awkward moment. She opened her eyes, but she was still on the floor, Dragonet offering a hand to help her up. She was not even wearing her sword to fall on.

Morrigan sighed and accepted his offered hand. He helped her to her feet with a smile. She felt tingly at his touch and grimaced in return. How could she recover her dignity after that shocking display?

"Yer hands are cold," Morrigan muttered. "Ye should put on yer woolens."

"I fear I lack a proper wardrobe. In France the climate is much more temperate."

"Och, ye poor dear," cried Alys, grasping both his hands. "Ye are near froze to death." She felt up his arms and reached up to cup his face. Morrigan sat at the table, trying not to be jealous of her sister. "Ye need a proper plaid, ye do. 'Tis the least we can do." Alys hustled out of the room, leaving Morrigan and Dragonet at the table.

"I did not mean to suggest she should clothe me," said Dragonet, apologetically.

Morrigan shrugged. "Alys lives to dress the unsuspecting and needful. She will be greatly disappointed if ye refuse her."

"Then I shall accept with grace. I am guessing you also were the recipient of her attentions this morning."

Morrigan looked down at her red woolen kirtle. "Aye. She put my regular clothes in the wash. It was this or run around in my chemise."

"A wise choice." Dragonet broke a round loaf of bread in half and offered her some. Morrigan accepted, wondering about its meaning. Then she wondered at what point she had become a simpering lass, looking for deeper meaning in every action of a man. She of all people should know most of men's actions had no deeper meaning whatsoever. Morrigan focused back on her porridge. Nothing could squelch amour like a bowl of oats.

"Here now, this will keep ye warm, I warrant." Alys bustled back into the solar and wrapped one of Archie's plaids, a large blanket made of thick woven wool, around Dragonet and pinned it at the shoulder. It hung around him like a cloak of red and black and green plaid.

Alys sat down to her breakfast and ate fast, all the while looking cheerfully at both Morrigan and Dragonet. Morrigan, being accustomed to Alys's usual cheerful self, could plainly see Alys was more than just happy, she was positively giddy, in a calculating sort of way.

"Well now, much to do today. May I take the tray back down to the kitchen?" Alys stood and took the tray with her. Morrigan was only half finished with her porridge but let it go.

"Morrigan dear, I know ye be verra busy today, but could ye stay and keep Sir Dragonet company? I have much to do today, what wi' it being the eighth day of Christmas and the first day of the New Year. The feast must be prepared, ye ken. I hope it is no' too much of an imposition, but we owe Sir Dragonet so much, what wi' his saving our dear Andrew's life."

Morrigan smiled in spite of herself. "As ye wish." It was nicely played. Alys had given neither of them the option of escaping each other's company.

"Verra good. I will send for ye when the midday meal is ready, but I fear I may no' be able to see ye at all this morning, for I am quite overcome wi' work."

Morrigan stood and called her bluff. "Perhaps I should help ye if ye are so burdened."

"Och, nay! Stay and keep our guest company. It would set my heart at ease. Good morn to ye sir." Alys spun out the door of the solar with the large tray on her shoulder and a dazzling smile on her lips.

Morrigan turned back to Dragonet and inhaled sharply, unprepared for the sudden wave of desire that rushed through her. If she thought he was handsome before, he was doubly so with her brother's plaid pinned at his shoulder. He looked better in plaid than any clansman she knew. He wore the colors like he belonged there. Like he belonged to her.

"I hope I am not keeping you from your duties," said Dragonet.

Morrigan shook her head, her mouth too dry to speak.

"This is a pleasant room."

Morrigan glanced around. It was nothing more than a simple room.

Dragonet looked around too, as if searching for something to break the awkward silence. "You must get quite a bit of snow in the winter."

Morrigan nodded. She had become mute. She struggled for something to say to fill the gaping maw of silence, but her brain disappointed her by only thinking of how attractive his eyes were and how kissable were his full lips. Since both of these topics were exactly the type of conversation she was determined to avoid, she struggled to find safe ground. What did a lass talk about with a lad? Having not been a lass very long, she had no answer, and the dreadful silence continued.

Morrigan strained to think of something intelligent to say. Had wearing a gown made her soft in the head? What did practitioners of polite conversation say? Having never asked herself that question, she struggled with the answer. She must say something!

"How is yer mother?" Morrigan asked, relieved to have said anything. There! That was polite.

"Deceased," said Dragonet.

Morrigan slumped into a chair by the fire. She might as well go back to bed. Nothing she could say could recover from that.

"Backgammon or chess?" asked Dragonet, motioning toward two boxes on a side table.

"I despise backgammon."

"Chess it is! Do you enjoy playing?" asked Dragonet, dragging the side table to where Morrigan sat by the fire. The table had a chessboard pattern worked into squares of stained wood. Dragonet began putting the pieces onto the board.

"I play rarely."

"Good, then we should be evenly matched."

"Perhaps then we should play for stakes?"

Dragonet paused and met her eyes.

"I may not play often," explained Morrigan, a smile playing on her lips, "but I play verra well."

"As you wish," said Dragonet slowly. "I have but little coin on me."

"Nay, I'll no' take yer money. What else could we play for?"

Dragonet stared at her for a moment in silence, his face impassive. "Truth."

"Truth?"

"Whoever wins, the other must answer truthfully any question they pose. I would like to get to know you better."

"Playing for the truth. An interesting choice. I agree to yer stakes, though I confess I thought ye'd ask for something a little less academic, like articles of clothing."

Dragonet blinked. "Is that an option?"

Morrigan scrunched up her nose. "'Tis a cold day, we best not."

Dragonet sat in the chair opposite hers. "I confess I am quite warm now." He shook his head and took a deep breath. "Very, very warm."

"Need to go roll in the snow?"

"You are wicked when you jest, my lady."

"I am wicked all the time."

Morrigan turned her attention to the game, at least that is what she tried to do. In truth she was too busy trying to determine whether she would rather win or lose to put much effort into the game. What question would he ask her? What question would she ask him? She knew what she wanted to know, but could she ask it directly?

Morrigan played poorly, her mind otherwise engaged. Dragonet also appeared to be distracted or a poor player.

"Ye were no' fibbing. Ye do play poorly," said Morrigan. "Check."

"I must be distracted by my worthy opponent." Dragonet moved his king out of check.

Distracted? What did that mean? Morrigan moved a piece at random.

"Checkmate," said Dragonet.

Morrigan blinked at the board. She did not see that coming, although she barely noted the board the entire game. Her heart beat a little faster. What would his question be? Dragonet leaned back in his chair and pursed his lips.

"Well? Do ye have a question for me?" asked Morrigan, more excited about his question than she had been about the game.

"Why did you start dressing like a man and going raiding with your brother?"

Morrigan let out a great whoosh of air as if she had been punched in the gut. "What makes ye think I was a raider?"

"I was traveling with the hunting party you attacked, do you not remember? You have surprised me a few times, I confess, but I am not so blind I did not recognize my captors as my host."

"I knew Archie was a fool to bring ye back here," muttered Morrigan.

"I was glad to be here."

Morrigan scowled and said nothing.

"Come now, it is the time for the truth. We made a wager. Your honor is at stake, my lady."

"Little value in that." Morrigan took a deep breath. How to begin? "I took up a wooden sword for play as a child. I only had the two brothers, ye ken, so if I wanted to play, I had to join their games. At first it was all a jest, but I enjoyed the exercise and found I was good at it. Verra good. My mother kept me in hand until she died in my tenth year."

Morrigan shifted in her chair. She did not speak of her mother often. "My father passed also, so a few years later Archie tried to do right by me and arranged a marriage for me to a rich landowner. A McGregor. He came to claim his bride, but when I saw him…" Morrigan gestured in the air. "He was old and fat and had a bushy moustache that collected food when he ate. I doubt he ever cleaned it."

"Dreadful," commented Dragonet.

"Aye, he was. He stood in the great hall, falling down drunk, and boasted how I was going to have such a big shock on our wedding night because he was such a great man. He then offered to expose his greatness to one of the serving wenches so she could be the judge of his manliness."

Dragonet frowned. "Your brother, what did he do?"

Morrigan shrugged. "I dinna give him time to figure it out. I got my sword, a real one mind ye, and charged the fat bastard, chasing him out o' the castle. I yelled that my sword was even bigger than his, and he would get a big shock on our wedding night because I would make sure he would no' live to see the morn."

Dragonet pressed his lips together in a vain attempt not to laugh.

"Ye find my poor manners amusing."

Dragonet chuckled. "Poor manners. I suppose that is one way to describe it. Good for you. If more women were like you, the men would be better behaved."

"If more women were like me, there would be fewer men to trouble with."

Dragonet laughed again. "Do continue, what happened next?"

"McGregor decided he would not like so much to marry me. The wedding was canceled and the story spread. Even ten years later there is no' a man from here to England who would take a chance on marriage wi' me."

The smile faded from Dragonet's face. "I see."

"Archie was disappointed. He ne'er chastised me for what I had done, but he did explain that the clan was in a bad situation. We were verra poor, and it was going to be a hungry winter. My marriage would have helped the clan. It was my duty to wed him."

"No." Dragonet shook his head.

"Aye, it was. Many a lass finds herself married at twelve to a man she would no' choose, but she does it. It was my duty to marry that bastard and I should have done so. But…" Morrigan sat back in her chair. It was tiring telling the tale. She had never spoken about it to anyone. There had never been a need, everyone knew what she was and what she had done.

"I was determined to pay back my clan for shirking my responsibility, so I dressed as a lad, strapped on a sword, and…" Morrigan pressed her lips together trying to avoid a smile. "I snuck onto the McGregors' land and stole fifty head o' sheep."

"By yourself?"

"Aye. After that I declared I would join Archie to

do whatever I could to serve my clan with a sword in my hand. Archie was no' pleased, though he took the mutton wi'out question. I got him to agree that I could do as I please until he could best me wi' a sword. We had a huge fight in the courtyard. In the end, he got eight stitches and I got to keep my sword."

Dragonet raised his eyebrows. "You bested your elder brother?"

"I was mighty full o' myself at the time, but I can see now it wasna a fair fight. I attacked him with abandon. He tried to disarm me wi'out hurting me. He held back. I did not. He could have bested me that day if he had been willing to do me harm."

"And now?"

Morrigan stood by the smoldering fire. "Now I can hold my own."

"I can bear witness to the truth of that assertion. But what now for you? Will you continue with the sword or…" Dragonet gestured at her new gown.

Morrigan turned toward the fire and rested her arms on the mantel. "I dinna ken what to do now. Going on raids was bad enough, but leading my clan to war? How can I ever go back to being a lady now? 'Tis a pity actions so honored in a man are so shameful in a lass."

Dragonet stood and moved beside her. "Your actions, they have no shame, my lady." Dragonet put his hand on her shoulder, warm even through her clothes. Morrigan turned and looked up at him, so unusual a position she caught her breath. She rarely needed to gaze up to see into a man's eye.

"Ye dinna know me," whispered Morrigan.

"I see no shame in you." Dragonet's words were a soothing balm on an old and painful wound.

"What would ye have me do?"

"You must improve your chess game to win my answer," said Dragonet with smiling eyes.

Sixteen

AFTER SPENDING A FEW DAYS IN HER COMPANY, Dragonet knew exactly what he wanted in life. She wielded a sword, wore a gown, had a heavenly body, and a vulgar tongue. No matter, he wanted her for his wife. In truth, he wanted to take her to bed.

"Shall we play another game of chess?" Dragonet asked instead. Taking a vow of chastity had not seemed a burden when he was twelve and women were unappealing. Insight into what he was missing was not helpful to his cause. He needed to be ruthless, get the information he needed, and leave.

From the conversation he overheard between Morrigan and Archie that night in Glasgow, he knew the cave was somewhere near Loch Pain. He had passed Loch Pain in his travels and found it was a rather large body of water, and none of the locals he had spoken to knew of a cave. Morrigan was the only one who knew the cave's location. He had tried asking benign questions about the landscape in the area, hoping she would volunteer information about a cave. She had not.

"What for? Ye lied to me," accused Morrigan.

"What did I say that was untrue?" Dragonet held his breath. What had she discovered?

"Ye said yer play was no' good—liar!"

"I was attempting the modesty." Dragonet exhaled in relief.

"There is a penalty for yer falsehood," said Morrigan gravely.

"There is?" asked Dragonet, wishing he was not excited at the prospect. What was wrong with him?

"I get to ask ye a question and get a truthful answer."

Dragonet inclined his head. "I accept my punishment. What is your question?"

"Who are ye truly? What is yer real name? Why did ye bring Andrew back here? And how did ye get so damn good at chess? I'm no' usually such a bad player!"

"You are a good player," Dragonet soothed. "But I have the advantage of spending several years playing with a Hospitaller chess grand master."

"A Hospitaller monk?"

"Yes."

"Are those no' a warrior order?"

"Yes. They trained me as a knight as well." Dragonet avoided her eye and instead set up the chess pieces. He was dangerously close to saying too much.

"So what were ye doing at a monastery?"

"Too many questions. You need to win for me to answer more."

Morrigan put one finger on the plate of delicious gingerbread Alys brought them. The gingerbread was fresh from the oven, warm and soft, filling the room with the smell of sweet spices. Morrigan slid the plate across the table toward herself.

Dragonet stopped what he was doing "You would deny to me the gingerbread?"

"You would deny me the truth?"

"Cruel woman. The inquisition, they could take lessons from you. No man could withstand such torture."

Morrigan took a bite of the warm gingerbread, letting it melt in her mouth. "Mmmmmm…"

"My mother named me Jacques," Dragonet began to speak in a rush, all the things he wanted to tell her bubbling to the surface. "Dragonet was the name given me when I was elevated to the knighthood. I was given to the care of the Hospitaller Knights after my mother died." Dragonet paused and took a gulp of mead to swallow down the emotion that always came when he thought of how his beautiful mother died. "It was the plague. Everyone in the household perished. I was given to the Hospitallers afterwards. Their order also had been much afflicted. I was trained to fight, to play chess, to play the lyre by masters in their fields. I think they wanted to pass on their skill before the death struck again."

"Did they die?"

"Many did." He rearranged the pieces on the board, making minute adjustments to their already perfect position.

"Ye dinna care to speak of it."

"No."

"I am sorry I teased ye."

Dragonet shrugged. It was more than he had revealed to anyone in a long time.

"The plague struck this region many years ago, but we were spared in part due to our remoteness," said

Morrigan. "It was the one time being ostracized was a blessing. It struck some of the towns, but no one in the castle fell ill."

"You were very lucky to be spared. I was living in a town when it struck. My family fell ill. There was nothing I could do." Dragonet stared at the chess pieces with unseeing eyes. "So many sick and dying. So much fear. Even the priests would not come in the end. My mother... there was no one left to bury her... so I had to..."

Morrigan reached out and took Dragonet's hand. He struggled against the tears that sprung to his eyes.

"Forgive me for asking, I did no' wish to cause ye pain," said Morrigan gently.

"Even after all these years, to speak of that time is difficult." He wrapped his fingers around her hand, warm and comforting.

"I am sorry for yer loss."

"And I for yours." Dragonet remembered Morrigan had also lost her mother at a young age.

"How old were you when she died?" Morrigan asked.

"I was ten years."

"I was also ten when my mother passed away." Her voice was soft.

"It is a hard age for such a loss."

Morrigan turned toward the window and nodded. He took her other hand in his, and they sat together in the fading light of dusk, holding hands. They were silent, but it was comfortable, as if he was finally where he belonged. He belonged with her.

"I miss her," whispered Morrigan.

"Me too. I often wish..."

"Me too."

They lapsed again into companionable silence until Morrigan took a deep breath. "Such maudlin topics of conversation, I am sure Alys would not approve."

"I should say prayers before the evening meal." Dragonet squeezed her hands and stood. "Good evening, my lady."

"Ye always say yer prayers, sir knight?" asked Morrigan as Dragonet walked to the door. "Must be the monk in ye."

Dragonet stopped short and turned to face her, his stomach dropping to his feet. Had she discovered the truth? "I beg your pardon?"

"Being raised by monks, I warrant they instructed ye to pray."

"Ah, yes." Dragonet exhaled a held breath. "They were most insistent I do so. Shall I see you later in the great hall?"

"Indeed."

"Would you give me the honor of escorting you to the meal?"

A slow smile spread across her face that sent tingles up his spine. She cleared her throat and almost managed to chase the smile from her face. "'Tis no need, but I will accept yer company if ye so wish."

Dragonet bowed and was unable to suppress a true smile in return.

❦

"How are ye feeling?" Morrigan asked Andrew. It was late in the day and he was just waking. He lay on his bed, Morrigan sat on a chair at his side. In truth she did not like the way he looked. He was pale and thin. The wound was still swollen and red.

Andrew smiled. "Good to be home."

"Ye should have stayed at the convent; ye were in no condition to travel."

"I am only tired, and I can rest better here."

"Dragonet should ne'er have brought ye."

"I wanted to come home. 'Twas my choice. Dragonet offered to see me safely home. I think he was concerned for my well-being."

"Why, er…" Morrigan flicked imaginary crumbs from her gown. "Why did Dragonet help ye?"

Andrew shrugged. "I dinna ken. But I can tell ye it was a good thing he did. I was not as strong as I thought." Andrew gave a sheepish grin.

"But why Dragonet? Why did he no' return wi' the French soldiers?"

"I thought…" Andrew shrugged. "He had been so helpful, so attentive to ye, I thought maybe ye had an understanding."

Morrigan shook her head. "The one thing we dinna have is an understanding. I am at a loss to explain his presence here."

"He's a good man, Morrigan. If ye fancy him for a husband, I would wish ye verra well."

"First Alys, now ye. I wish ye woud'na make me a match. I have no word from Dragonet that his interest leans in that direction." Morrigan took a deep breath and changed the subject. "How do ye like marriage?"

"Cait." Andrew's eyes turned wistful and he gave a lopsided smile. "She is wonderful."

"That's no' how I remember her." Morrigan muttered.

"Ye never got to know her. She is beautiful."

"I am glad ye are happy. 'Tis a goodly marriage. I will admit she has been kind to us."

"I knew she would be. If the Campbells were no' so far away I would have gone there first. I hope to rest here a few weeks and then continue on to her." Andrew shifted a bit in his bed and looked away in a shy manner. "When I left, I believe she was increasing."

"Ye got her breeding? Well, Andrew. Good for ye, lad. Though I think ye are a mite young to be having children."

"Old enough, it seems," he said with a wide grin. "Cait and I were talking, and we agreed that what ye need is… err…" Andrew stuttered and cleared his throat. "What ye need is a good husband. Might do ye good."

"That is quite enough o' that, Andrew my lad." Morrigan stood up and tucked him tightly beneath the covers the way she did after their mother died and she had taken care of him. "Ye sleep now."

"I love ye, Morrigan. I know ye tried to protect me, ye and Archie both, and I thank ye for it. If I dinna get another chance, I wanted to let ye know."

Her younger brother had lost weight, lying wan and weak in the bed. A lump formed in her throat. "Ye will be fine. Get some rest now; I'll check in on ye later." She walked to the door and turned back to him. "I… I love ye too."

❧

Etiquette books were of no use whatsoever. Morrigan rummaged through her mother's things trying to find something useful. She had spent the past two hours struggling to read a book that purported to be a guide for ladies but it was no help.

For several days Morrigan had spent most of her waking hours with Dragonet and most of her sleeping hours thinking about him. He was a favorite of the castle, singing and playing his lyre at mealtimes. He taught Morrigan to play a new song. They chatted long hours by the fire and played countless games of chess. But while her skin burned for his touch, he remained distant, careful not to touch her, or to kiss her, or to hold her, or to do any of the things Morrigan wanted. Yet he remained at the castle and spent all his time with her, so what did he want?

"Morrigan? Are ye… reading?" asked Alys. Morrigan realized her mother's room was where Alys slept, awaiting Archie's return.

"I think I might show my earlobes."

"Pardon?"

"This book is no' verra helpful, but it did warn showing the earlobe may send a man into an uncontrolled, lustful frenzy."

"Ye canna show yer earlobes. 'Tis no' proper."

"Hang proper. I'm looking for uncontrolled, lustful frenzy."

"Dragonet?"

Morrigan sat on a bench with a sigh. "I dinna understand what he is about. We talk and talk and he seems to want to spend all his time wi' me, but then he shows no interest in me. And even when I think he is attracted to me, he ne'er acts on it. I dinna ken what to do. I must make a verra poor lass."

"Nay, ye are a fine lady." Alys sat next to her on the bench. "What do ye talk about with him?"

Morrigan shrugged. "Nothing. Anything. We talk of my family; he doesna like to speak of his. He asks about the castle, the grounds, our clan and our land, people who visited, nothing of importance."

"Give him some time. I think he is shy."

Morrigan shook her head. "Nay. Something is going on, but I canna make out what."

Later that afternoon Morrigan and Dragonet were alone in the solar together. It was most likely not proper, but unfortunately nothing untoward was occurring. Dragonet remained the height of politeness and respectability. Morrigan mentally cursed his propriety.

What did a lass need to do to get a little ravishment? At Morrigan's request Alys had squeezed her into a kirtle and laced the surcoat up tight, revealing more cleavage than ever before. On the matter of the earlobes Alys refused to budge, hiding them respectably behind a veil, but the veil itself was made of fine lace. Alys reluctantly agreed to allow her hair to flow freely down her back.

Morrigan pushed back a strand of hair as she studied the chessboard. They were playing again, and she was tired of losing.

"Check," she said slowly, considering her options. It appeared Dragonet was in a bad position, but then it often seemed that way right before he won.

He moved his king out of check. Morrigan considered her next move with increasing excitement. Could it be?

Morrigan made one final move. "Checkmate."

Startled, Dragonet stared at the board like he was seeing it for the first time. He gave her a wry smile and knocked over his king. "Well played."

"I won!" Morrigan smiled. "I have ne'er seen ye play so poorly. I hope ye are no' falling ill."

"No, not ill. Forgive me, but I was distracted by your new look today."

Heat ran up the back of her neck and flushed her cheeks. "I needed to do something to gain an advantage over ye."

"Well played indeed!" Dragonet laughed.

"Do I win a boon?"

"Yes, I am yours to command."

Ravish me!

Morrigan blushed again at her own thoughts. Did she dare ask once again for a kiss? Across the small table, Dragonet's blue eyes blazed. He brushed back his straight, black hair that fell across his left eye. His full lips drew her. She wanted his kiss more than she had ever wanted anything.

"Teach me a new song?" asked Morrigan sweetly.

"But of course!" Dragonet went to fetch his lyre, and Morrigan cursed her stupid self for being so craven.

Dragonet sat on the stone bench carved into the wall by the window. The light was better there so Morrigan could find her fingering. He had taught her several songs, and she enjoyed playing the lyre again. His in particular was a fine instrument. And sitting next to him was a fine thing, too.

Morrigan sat next to Dragonet, wondering how she might entice him to kiss her. A practiced flirt could no doubt achieve her object readily, but she was not practiced in such arts.

"Which song would you like for me to play?" asked Dragonet, handing her the instrument.

Kiss me, ye fool.

"I dinna ken. Something romantic."

"Romantic." Dragonet said the word slowly, causing more heat to crawl up her back. "There is the ballad of Tristan and Isolde."

"Did that not end poorly for the lovers? She was wed to King Mark, was she not?"

"Yes."

"Do ye ken any ballads o' love where the lovers have a happy ending?"

Dragonet thought a moment. "Well, there is King Arthur and... no that did not end well. How about..." Dragonet shook his head. "In truth I can think of none."

"There should be at least one ballad where the lovers were allowed to wed and live together in happiness."

"According to the French court, true love can only exist outside of marriage."

"That is stupid," said Morrigan in her ever-so-tactful manner.

"Indeed."

"Why can lovers no' marry and be happy?"

"I wish it could be so." Dragonet turned to look out the window, but Morrigan had glimpsed the look of despair. Why was he so unhappy?

"It is snowing again," commented Dragonet. "Do you ever go out in it?"

"Not if I dinna have to."

"When I was young we got very little snow. The few times it fell it was like a holiday. We all ran out to play in it and throw the snowballs. We would gather it up and eat it like a treat."

"'Tis wet, cold, and abundant in the Highlands. But when I was verra young, I do remember playing in the first snowfall. After a while it gets tiresome. And cold."

Dragonet turned back to her with a smile, cocking his head to one side. "I am trying to picture you as the young girl having fun."

"Dinna strain yerself."

Dragonet laughed. "Forgive me, but you do not play much now."

"I play! Did I not play a hundred games of chess wi' ye?"

"And you enjoyed it so much you complained though every game."

"Ye are one to accuse me!" declared Morrigan, going on the offensive. "Name one thing ye do for your own amusement, no' for the entertainment o' others, no' to be polite, but simply because ye enjoy it."

"I enjoy playing the lyre, even when there is no one but me to hear it. I enjoy speaking with you, even when you look like you want to hurt me."

"Verra predictable answers. Debatable and dull. I pray ye would say something to astonish me."

"Astonish you? Let me think. When I was a child, I would go into the hills behind my town in search of caves. I had been told the story of large, black bats that lived in the caves, and I wanted to see them. I searched and searched and finally found a cave, but alas, no bats. My cave, it was actually more of an indentation, hardly a cave at all, but I returned there many times, just in case a wayward bat decided to move in." Dragonet brushed his hair from his eyes. "There now, have I astonished you?"

"Mildly amused perhaps."

"Do you have any natural caves in these parts?"

"Aye there is one, a large cave wi' many tunnels. We were no' allowed to go in it when we were children, lest we get lost."

"Sounds intriguing; maybe you could show it to me." Dragonet leaned toward her, giving her his full attention. Her heart skipped along merrily.

"Nay, too cold this time o' year."

"Was it St. Jerome who translated the Bible while living in a cave?"

"St. Jerome dinna live in the Highlands."

Dragonet laughed. "Dare I ask if there are bats in your cave?"

"I dinna ken. I am no' fond o' caves overmuch. Or bats."

"Is this cave nearby?" Dragonet's eyes were shining. This was the most excited she had seen him in a while. He must really like bats.

"Nay. 'Tis near the village of Kimlet on the shores of Loch Pain, by where the river empties into the loch."

"I would like to see it."

"Nay. 'Tis a creepy old cave wi' many tunnels. I've heard o' folk getting lost in that cave, some ne'er returned. Dinna go there, ye ken?"

Dragonet gave her a broad smile. "Thank you."

"For what?"

"For your concern. And now I believe I am to play a song for you." Dragonet plucked out a jaunty tune on the lyre that had Morrigan smiling and tapping her toe.

"Could ye teach me that one?" asked Morrigan when he was finished.

"Certainly." He handed the lyre to her and put his left arm around her to show her the fingering. She liked that part the best and was often a slow learner, so he had to show her several times.

Dragonet showed her the fingering, and she purposely botched it. "Could ye show me again?" she asked, looking up at him through her lashes. He leaned closer and complied. Her heart was pounding so loud she could not hear anything he did. His arm was warm around her shoulders, his side pressed close to her. When she turned to him, their faces were dangerously close.

The air crackled between them, and Morrigan leaned closer, unable to resist. His breathing was shallow and rapid. However distant he may act, he was not unaffected. He reached up and touched her hair, twisting a thick strand around one of his long fingers. Morrigan inhaled sharply at the intimacy of the gesture. In one bold move, Morrigan removed her veil.

"*Ma chérie*. You are so beautiful." For the first time in her life, Morrigan felt it was true. Dragonet threaded both his hands in her hair, massaging her head. She closed her eyes and arched her back, trying not to groan in delight. He pulled her closer, one hand moving to her back, the other still wrapped in her hair. She pulled him tight with one hand, the other still holding the lyre.

When she opened her eyes again he was very close, his full lips begging to be kissed. She wanted him but paused, waiting for him. She did not wish to always be the one to initiate. Would he kiss her?

He moved slowly forward until his cheek touched hers. Just as she was swallowing her disappointment, he turned and kissed her cheek, then her jaw, then her earlobe. He kissed her softly then drew her earlobe into his mouth and gently suckled, sending waves of pleasure coursing through her.

"Oh!" she breathed.

He pulled back, his eyes wide. "Bad?"

"Good!" She pulled him back, but he resisted.

"I am sorry, but I want to… to…" Suddenly he pulled her close, crashing his mouth into hers. He was not gentle or slow, but passionate and urgent. He plundered her mouth with his as if he could not get close enough. She opened herself to him and gave as good as she got.

"Well now, I thought a spot of something hot might be nice on a cold day like this," said Alys, entering the room with a tray of food and drink before her.

Dragonet jumped away from Morrigan as if she was on fire. Truth be told, she almost was.

Alys placed the tray on the table and looked up at them, her naturally rosy cheeks growing redder. "Ah, well. I see. Verra good. Much too busy to stay. Carry on wi' whatever ye were doing. Canna stay. Winna be back for a long time." Alys turned and hustled from the room. Despite her embarrassment, she could not help turning at the door and giving Morrigan a wink before shutting the door behind her.

Dragonet stood and pushed his hair from his eyes with both hands, muttering something in French. He turned back at her, his eyes desolate. "I am sorry. I am so sorry. I beg your forgiveness."

"Nay, 'tis naught to forgive." Morrigan's body trembled from the shock of intimacy and its sudden removal. She remained seated on the bench, her legs too unsteady to rise.

"I beg your pardon, my lady." He bowed and fled for the door.

Morrigan stared at the open doorway wondering what had happened and how it had gone from so good to so wrong. She put her head in her hands. One thing was clear. She was again alone.

Seventeen

DRAGONET SMACKED HIS HEAD WITH THE PALM OF HIS hand. How could he be so colossally stupid? Just as he found the information he needed, he fell victim to his own carnal desires and kissed her. No, not a kiss. What he did couldn't be considered a kiss. He had mauled her, desperately trying to pull her closer. He was not sure if he was trying to kiss her or consume her.

It was bad enough that he had kissed her again. But to kiss badly? It was inexcusable. What must she think of him? Was she laughing at him? She must be telling Alys how he had lost control and tried to eat her.

Dragonet groaned and collapsed on his bed. He should leave. Maybe if he snuck out at first light, he could avoid the inevitable confrontation. And laughter, as she would no doubt mock his futile, immature, pathetic, adolescent, attempts at passion.

The only alternative was even worse. If she actually welcomed his inexperienced attentions, then he should offer marriage immediately. Any true knight would go to her brother and arrange terms. But of

course he was no ordinary knight, and marriage was
the one thing he could not offer.

If her heart was engaged even a fraction as much as
his, he was going to hurt her. It would hurt to leave,
but he must. He knew he would live the rest of his life
in love with her, grieving the loss of her company. He
did not wish her to suffer the same.

He must leave on the morrow and hope for her
mockery. Could he ever make it right? He sighed and
put his hands over his eyes. It could never be made
right. He was wrong to tarry so long. He must return
to his quest.

⁓

Morrigan paced in the solar, waiting for Dragonet.
They had shared the feast of Epiphany together with
her clansmen, but in the crowded hall one could not
say anything of importance. She had spent the meal
trying to guess at his feelings toward her, and her
emotions were raw from the effort. Did he dislike her
kissing? Was he not attracted to her? Was he merely
shy? She did not know whether to act cool and distant
or warm and encouraging. Her heart was on the verge
of elation or heartbreak. If only she knew which one.

Dragonet entered the room slowly, his eyes lingering
on the sword she decided to strap on after the meal.
She did not know how the conversation would
proceed, and she wanted to be prepared for all options.

"Enjoy yerself tonight?" Morrigan asked. It was a
cautious beginning.

"It was a fine meal."

His answer told her nothing. She wanted to ask

why he had run from the room earlier, but could not find the words. *How does one ask about that?*

"Here. This is for ye." Morrigan held out a small, wrapped parcel, rather crumpled from being gripped in her hand. Dragonet eyed her with reserve. She realized that, while she had one hand extended, the other was on her sword hilt. She forced herself to move her hand from her sword to her hip. Dragonet stepped forward and gingerly took the parcel from her hand.

"Open it. 'Tis for Twelfth Night." It was tradition to exchange gifts on Epiphany, the last day of the twelve days of Christmas.

"Thank you," Dragonet murmured and opened the paper package. Inside was a linen handkerchief, poorly embroidered.

"I made it myself. 'Tis verra bad because I rarely take up a needle."

"I will cherish it." Dragonet clutched it to his chest. He did not look well. His face was drawn and gray; his eyes were dull and tired. The room was silent as death.

Morrigan searched for something to say, something to bridge the ever-increasing chasm between them, but her mind was blank.

"I have something for you too." Dragonet walked over to where his lyre had been left on the window seat.

"A song for me?" asked Morrigan. Perhaps in song he could reveal what the hell was going on with him.

Dragonet held out his lyre to her.

"Ye want me to play a song?" asked Morrigan, taking the offered instrument.

"I want for you to keep it."

"Yer lyre? But why? I could no' accept such a gift."

"Please take it. I cannot play anymore. There is no song in me."

"Why? Tell me the meaning o' this!" Morrigan demanded. Anger flashed through her. She was tired of guessing; she wanted the truth from him.

"I must leave now."

Morrigan froze. Something inside her chest cracked open. She clutched the instrument to her breast, fighting against the growing pain. He had broken her. "Ye are leaving?"

"I am sorry, but I must go."

"Go where? Why must ye leave?" Had he found her lacking?

"I am sorry. I cannot stay. I am but a poor bastard, not worthy of your notice. I humbly beg your pardon for any of my actions that may have offended. Please give my apologies to Lady McNab. I will leave at first light on the morrow."

Morrigan opened her mouth to say something, anything. "Have a good journey. Good evening to ye." Morrigan swooped from the room in a proud manner, though it did her no good.

She stood in the hallway, fighting back tears, unsure where to go or what to do. Footsteps told her Dragonet was entering the hall, and she rushed into Andrew's room to avoid the man.

Andrew had not recovered his strength as she had hoped. He was lying in bed, looking if anything a little thinner and weaker than before.

"Sister." Andrew held out his hand.

Morrigan stepped forward quickly to take it. "Ye should be resting."

"I am. I canna be in bed all day; ye must let me out." Andrew smiled, but dark circles had formed under his eyes, and he made no attempt to move.

"Rest a while longer, and ye'll be up and bothering us in no time."

"Maybe another week, and then I can travel back to the Campbells."

Morrigan nodded. "I am sure Cait will be glad to see ye." Andrew would be going nowhere next week or for several weeks to come, but Morrigan said nothing.

"Cait." Andrew smiled. "I hope ye can be as happy as we are. How goes it with Dragonet?"

Morrigan took a deep breath. "He's leaving tomorrow."

"Leaving? Where?"

"I dinna ken."

"Why is he going? Ye dinna scare him away did ye?"

"Nay. At least I dinna mean to. I dinna ken why he is leaving." Morrigan rubbed the ache that formed on her forehead.

"Talk to him. Be nice. I was so hoping…"

"Dinna worrit yerself. I will speak wi' him."

"Promise me?"

"I dinna think he is interested…"

"Promise me!"

Morrigan sighed. "Aye, I promise. Now rest so ye can get yer strength back. Ye'll have bairns to raise soon enough, so sleep while ye may."

"I think we'll have a boy." Andrew smiled even as eyes drooped and closed. Morrigan sat next to him, her hand in his until he slept peacefully.

Morrigan felt Andrew's forehead for fever and was

relieved to find it cool. Still, he was not recovering the way she had hoped. Morrigan shook off such traitorous thoughts and stood up, taking a deep breath. Andrew would be fine; he was simply tired, which was understandable from his long ordeal. He was a hearty lad. He would recover soon.

Morrigan began to pace the room, harried by the thoughts that crowded around in her mind, pushing and shoving at each other, demanding her full attention and concern. She must figure a way to speak to Dragonet, a task she would rather avoid. Yet she promised Andrew she would speak to him, and she was not about to deny Andrew anything. But how to approach her confusing knight, and what to say?

An ill-advised plot came to mind. Morrigan turned it around in her head. It was a bad idea. The chance for success was slim, the odds of disastrous failure were great. She should clearly reject such an ill-conceived scheme.

Except she was a McNab, so she liked it instantly. Yes, tonight would be the night.

❧

Cold. It did not matter how many blankets he piled on, he was still cold. Dragonet stared unseeing into the utter blackness of his room. He had found the information he wanted so he should be happy. Why then did he feel dead inside?

A small knock at the door got his attention. Before he could say anything, Morrigan slipped inside his room, holding a single candle. She wore her plaid wrapped around her, which she clutched to her chest with one hand. She shut the door behind her, and the plaid slipped a little, revealing a naked shoulder.

Dragonet sat up, the vision of Morrigan commanding his full attention. In truth, much of him was up and at attention. He opened his mouth to speak but said nothing.

"I… I…" Morrigan stammered and gulped air. "I brought ye a candle." She walked toward him and put the candle on a small table by his bed.

"Thank you," he whispered, trying to think of something else to say.

"Are ye cold?" She motioned to the pile of blankets on top of him.

"No, not anymore." Dragonet realized he was hot, burning so that he was even perspiring.

"I had thought to warm ye tonight."

Done. Morrigan was offering herself to him? Despite his rejection, Morrigan, the temptress of his dreams, was there, tonight, offering herself to him. He took a deep breath and tried to slow his heartbeat, which pounded so fast he thought he might collapse from the shock.

"Well, do ye want to or no'?" demanded Morrigan.

"Yes! Yes, very much I want to. Yes." He was babbling and saying things that he knew he should not. His rational brain screamed a warning, but it was steadily drowned out by the throbbing of his… heart.

Morrigan sat on the edge of his bed. "I dinna ken what ye are about, Dragonet, but I will show ye what I want. After the kiss we shared today, I dinna think ye are indifferent toward me."

"You… you liked the kiss? I did not think it was very good."

"Oh, well then." Morrigan clutched her plaid close to her chest.

"I mean *I* liked it, but I thought you would not. I lost control. I do not know why I was so overcome."

"It was the earlobes." Morrigan nodded sagely.

"Earlobes?"

"I read it in a book. The sight of earlobes can cause fervent, lustful frenzy." She tucked her hair behind her ears, revealing the suspect body part. "How are ye feeling now?" she said, turning her head to the side to make sure he got a good look.

Dragonet smiled. "I feel the frenzy, yes." It was the truth, too.

"Verra good. Ye may ravish me now."

"R-ravish?"

"Aye. Ye do know how to ravish?"

Dragonet blinked. In truth, he had never ravished anything in his life. Though with a naked Morrigan, he was more than willing to give it a try. And yet his rational brain screamed at him to take care. He could not act honorably toward her and offer marriage. He must still leave. This was not right, but turning her away? That would only be worse.

"Morrigan, I..." What could he say? "Are you sure you want to do this?"

Morrigan nodded; her large brown eyes caught the flickering light of the candle. "I want ye close to me. I have wanted it a long time. I have never felt this way about anyone, and I dinna think I will ever feel this way again. I wish for one night. One night to pretend I am no' so repulsive to men. There is no man who would ever wed me unless ye..." Morrigan pulled her plaid tighter and looked at him with sad eyes. "I will spend the rest of my days and nights alone. So I ask ye for one night."

Dragonet wrapped his arms around her and held her close, resting his chin on the top of her head. "You must not say such things. You are most desirable to men. You are every man's dream."

"Nightmare ye mean." Morrigan's voice was muffled from being pressed into his chest. She opened her plaid and returned his embrace, pressing her naked chest into him. He cursed the misfortune he was wearing his tunic.

Any man who could draw breath would take her immediately to bed. Any of his fellow knights would. Several monks he knew would. Even his father the bishop would. But then... he would be no better than his father. Could he leave her the way his father had abandoned his mother?

"Morrigan. Please do not throw yourself away on me. I am sure you will find a good man to marry you."

"I want ye to be my husband." Morrigan's voice was so soft he could barely make out the words. Perhaps she had not meant for him to hear it.

He held her tight, trying to ease the growing ache in his heart. "I wish I could pledge my troth to you. In truth, there is no other lady I would wish to marry if the choice, it was mine, but I am... I am..."

"Married?" She pulled back from him and wrapped her plaid around herself tight.

"No. I am not married, but—"

"Ye are promised?"

Dragonet drew a breath of freezing air. The room

had grown suddenly cold. "Yes." He was promised in a manner of speaking, to the church.

"Why did ye no' say something to me? Why keep it a secret?"

"I am sorry. I ought to have said something."

"Aye, ye damn well should have!" Morrigan stood and glared at him. "Why no' mention it when we kissed the first time, or the second, or perhaps the third? If ye wanted to keep it a secret to trick me into yer bed, why tell me now when I am ready to give ye all? Why come all the way back to the Highlands just to make me miserable!"

"I am so sorry," Dragonet repeated. "I never wanted to hurt you."

"Too late for that now." Morrigan's eyes burned into him, causing physical pain. "I wish I had ne'er laid eyes on ye, ye lying maggot. Make sure yer sorry arse is gone by morning." Morrigan stomped out of his chamber and slammed the heavy wooden door shut.

Dragonet shivered under the blankets. He doubted he would ever be warm again. He had never before been that cold. So terribly cold.

He hated himself. He hated his father. He hated his quest. He thought himself on a noble journey, but he was consumed with deceit. He now knew his feelings for Morrigan were shared, but the realization only caused him pain. Marriage, the only decent option, could never be.

Dragonet sat on the bed suffocated by the silent blackness of his room. Tears he had not shed in so many years fell unchecked to the floor. There was no escape from the truth. He was going to hurt the one person he loved.

❦

Morrigan rose the next morning after a sleepless night. She went to Dragonet's room, but he was gone, as she knew he would be. She was empty, a gaping hole where her heart used to be. Yet most people thought her heartless to begin with, so it could be no great loss.

She wandered into the solar, struggling to move her arms and legs, which were strangely heavy. The solar was gray in the muted light of dawn. The banked fire smoldered, emitting a thin, gray ribbon of smoke.

Morrigan sat down at the table and stared at the beautiful instrument, Dragonet's lyre, which mocked her with happy memories. She remembered the first time he played in the hall. She remembered how he played it for her in the tower, leading to their first kiss. She remembered how he played it for her yesterday, which led to their last kiss.

"Damn ye, Dragonet," she whispered, running a finger along the smooth surface of the glowing instrument. Why would he leave her such a beautiful prize? Why reject her and then give her the only object in his possession of any worth?

She was tired. Tired of his lies, tired of his games, tired of him. It was time to make him go away forever. She took the lyre in hand and walked over to the fireplace. She kicked the banked fire with the toe of her leather boot, knocking off the ashes and encouraging a flame to appear.

She stared at the beautiful instrument in her hand, a

single tear streaming down her face. She wiped it away impatiently. She was heartless, cold, and brutal. People could not hurt her. Objects meant nothing to her. She was the destroyer of beauty and love. She felt nothing.

Morrigan held the instrument over the flames. It was time to say good-bye.

"Morrigan, nay!" Alys snatched the lyre from her hand. "What are ye doing?"

"Dragonet left. He is betrothed to another, and he left. He gave that to me, and I will see it burnt to ashes."

Alys's shoulders slumped. "I see."

Morrigan said nothing but held out her hand for the return of the instrument. Time for a funeral pyre.

"Nay. We may need the coin this instrument can bring." Alys's usually rosy cheeks were pale. "'Tis Andrew; his fever has returned."

Eighteen

MORRIGAN URGED HER MOUNT FORWARD, SQUINTING into the driving snow. Instead of soft flakes, the snow fell in small ice pellets that stung her eyes in the bitter cold; still, she pressed on. Andrew's life hung in the balance, and she would never give up.

Alys's warning echoed in her head. Andrew needed a special medicine if he had any chance for survival. The only one who made such a potion was Mother Enid at St. Margaret's Convent, a good day's ride from McNab Hall. In bad weather, which Morrigan was forced to concede it was, it could take longer. Morrigan had not waited to take volunteers for the trip. This journey meant the difference between life and death for Andrew, and she would see it done.

She had passed through the village of Kimlet many hours before, stopping only for a change of horses and a warm meal to keep her going. It was getting darker by the minute, and she held up a lantern to see her way in the driving sleet. The snow on the road was deep and the going was slow. Too slow for Andrew. Too slow for her too, for she knew being caught long in the elements would be fatal to both herself and to her horse. She pushed on.

Near the road was a stream, which led to the convent. Taking a chance, Morrigan led her mount down to the stream bed. The stream was shallow and had frozen. Would it hold her? She slowly guided her horse onto the frozen stream bed. Despite an occasional crack, the ice held. The snow was less deep than on the road and the path was better marked by the sides of the stream so it would be more difficult to get lost. She kicked her mount into a faster pace. They needed to find St. Margaret's fast. Neither she nor Andrew had much time left.

Hours passed and Morrigan pushed on through the night. She was worried for Andrew, but her growing concern was surviving the night. Her horse was showing grave signs of fatigue. If he went down, she would not survive. Desperation welled up inside her like a breached dam. She must not fail.

Please, she prayed. *Please let me reach St. Margaret's. Please let me get the medicine back to Andrew in time.* Morrigan shook her head. She must be desperate indeed if she was turning to prayer. She knew full well God could not hear a sinner's prayers.

She closed her eyes, too frozen for tears. When she opened her eyes again, a single light shone in the distance. Her heart leapt at the sight, and she guided her weary mount toward the light. It grew brighter until there was no more doubt. She had reached St. Margaret's.

No one was fool enough to be outside on a night like that, but she was able to rouse a stable lad sleeping in the stables to care for her horse and stumbled to the nuns' sleeping quarters in the driving snow. She knocked on the door and was relieved when at length it was opened. She stated her business and struggled to retain consciousness until she found Mother Enid's sleeping quarters. Ignoring the protests of the nuns around her, Morrigan entered the room without knocking.

"Forgive me, Mother Superior, for waking ye like this. I am Morrigan McNab, and I need medicine for my brother Andrew. His fever has returned."

Mother Enid moved slowly from her cot, but her eyes blazed a bright blue. "Andrew's fever has returned? That is not a good sign, but I will do what I can." Mother Enid wrapped a blanket around her shoulders against the chill and spoke to several other nuns who had been awakened by Morrigan in her haste to find Mother Enid. "Bring this lass some mead and bread, she is half-froze."

"I need the medicine and a fresh mount, then I'll be on my way." Morrigan's words may have been more convincing had she not swayed as she spoke.

"Sit down," Mother Enid suggested, and Morrigan complied, or possibly fell into the chair. "Did you come all this way through this storm?"

"Aye, he needs the medicine now."

"You are lucky to be alive, my dear. God must be watching over you."

Morrigan sat back, too tired to argue. She had never known God to take much interest in her life. But then again, perhaps the Almighty liked Andrew better than her.

"Please, the medicine. I can pay if ye wish."

"What I have I give to those who are in need. Sister Joanna, please fetch one of the green bottles from behind the flour bins in the pantry."

Morrigan closed her eyes. She was so tired even her bones ached with weariness. She would rest just a moment until they could bring the medicine.

"Can you feel your fingers, Morrigan? They are completely white."

Morrigan shook her head without opening her eyes. She had long since lost the ability to feel her fingers and toes. She hoped they would not freeze such that she would lose them, but Andrew was more important right now.

"Mother Enid, I canna find any bottles where ye say."

Morrigan's eyes flew open to Mother Enid's frowning face.

"I had two dozen bottles stashed there," said Mother Enid.

"Mother Enid?" said a young blond nun, who had not taken the time to put on her veil. "Abbot Barrick came yesterday and asked for the fever medicine that ye keep in the apothecary so I gave it to him. He asked if ye had any more and I said yes and he said to give him all of it, so I did."

Mother Enid put a bony hand over her eyes. "Oh, child."

"Did I do wrong?" asked the blond nun, her blue eyes watery. "I am sorry if I did."

"Do not fret, my child. You meant well; now go back to bed." Mother Enid ushered all of the nuns out of her small quarters and shut the door.

"Please say ye have more medicine somewhere," begged Morrigan.

"I fear I do not. Barrick had been taking more and more, so I hid a stash in the pantry. If that is gone, I have none other."

Morrigan inhaled sharply, fighting a growing sense of panic. "But ye can make more, right?"

"I can, but the brew takes a special herb and I have none left. Lady MacLaren may have some, but the roads to where she lives in the mountains may be difficult to traverse until the thaw."

"Nay! Andrew needs the medicine now. What does Barrick want with all that medicine?"

"He says he needs it to provide care for the wounded returned back from the battle with England."

Morrigan stared at the nun, a cold reality infusing her veins. "He is selling it for profit."

Mother Enid nodded. "I fear so."

"Damn that bastard! Och, forgive me, Mother Superior, I forget myself." Morrigan tried to stand on shaky legs. "I will go ask him the price."

"Sleep first," said Mother Enid firmly. "Barrick is asleep at the abbey now, there is naught you can do until dawn."

"I care no' for his sleep; I'll rouse him."

"You may not care, but he would. Do not give him an excuse to deny you the medicine."

"I must go," said Morrigan, even as Mother Enid was gently leading her to the bed. "I canna stay," argued Morrigan, though the slightest nudge from Mother Enid made Morrigan collapse on the pallet.

"Sleep now," said Mother Enid.

Morrigan closed her eyes and knew nothing.

∾

Morrigan woke to a bright sunlit room. She sat bolt upright. Had she slept through the day?

"'Tis the dawn; do not fear, my child."

"I must go—ow!" Morrigan clenched her fist and wished she had not. Pain shot through her fingers and up her arm.

"We have been slowly warming your hands and feet as you slept," said Mother Enid, pointing to rags and bins of water. "I believe you will keep all your fingers and toes for now, though the rewarming process can be painful."

"Thank ye, Mother Enid. There are few who would have taken the time to care for me. I fear I am unworthy of yer attentions." Morrigan figured that if Mother Enid knew more about her, the good nun would not have bothered trying to help her.

"I care for all God's children, as the Good Lord instructed me."

Morrigan struggled to put her boots back on, ignoring the dull ache in her joints. "Thank ye," she mumbled, unaccustomed to kindness. "I will see Barrick for the medicine. He must give it to me."

"I wish there was more I could offer you." Mother Enid shook her head. "I do not like sending you to that man. Take care, for the abbot is not as his title would suggest."

Morrigan nodded. "I ken he is no' to be trusted." She knew it well. He was the one who demanded her brother kill the bishop. He also was the one who had ordered her fields burned.

"Stay safe, my child."

Morrigan was given a fresh mount and a bundle of food for her journey. Unlike the day before, the sun shone bright in a blue sky, reflecting off the sparkling white snow. Morrigan held her reins in one hand and used the other to shield her eyes against the glare. The abbey was not far from the convent, and despite the snow she made it there within an hour.

The abbey consisted of several outbuildings and one tall tower. No one was outside or in the stable, so she tended to her mount herself and then went to the tall tower to look for Barrick. Inside the tower was a great room in which several monks dressed in black robes were sitting at a meal. At her entrance they turned to look at her. No one said a word. No one rose to ask her business or help her. The large room was eerily silent and smelled of fear.

A chill crawled up Morrigan's spine. "I am looking for Abbot Barrick," she announced, her voice echoing off the bare walls.

Still no one said a word.

"'Tis a matter most urgent; can you say where he is?" asked Morrigan. These men were like the walking dead. Finally, one rose like a specter and pointed to a staircase.

Morrigan bounded up the spiral staircase, trying to ignore a growing sense of foreboding that she was walking deeper into the demon's lair. On the top floor, she found a closed door being guarded by two hooded monks. The hair on the back of her neck stood up in warning. This was not a place she wanted to be, but for Andrew... "I need to see Abbot Barrick on an urgent matter."

The guards looked at her and said nothing. Had everyone taken a vow of silence?

Morrigan sighed and ran between them for the door. It pushed open to her touch and she stumbled into the room.

"Hey, ye canna go there!" shouted one of the guards.

Morrigan smiled. He was not so mute after all. She ran into the comfortable room, richly furnished. Beautiful tapestries hung on the walls, and an ornate wooden screen stood in one corner. The abbot was sitting before a roaring fire, a glass of wine in his hand. On the table beside him was a veritable feast of appetizing dishes. The savory pastries alone beckoned her. She blinked at the stark contrast.

Abbot Barrick eyed her suspiciously. "Remove her!" he commanded.

"Nay! I have come for medicine for my brother, Andrew McNab. I will pay you."

A slow smile spread across Barrick's face. With a wave of his hand he dismissed his monk guards. "You are Archie's sister. The one who took command when both your brothers left you. How are you today, Morrigan?"

Morrigan was taken aback. How did he know so much about her? She doubted she wanted to know. "I need medicine for Andrew," she repeated. "Mother Enid said you had the medicine I need."

"I am sure that is true. Mother Enid likes to be right in all things."

Morrigan waited for him to say more, but Barrick turned his attention back to his meal. His fare was quite a bit better than the porridge being consumed downstairs by his fellow monks.

"May I have some of the medicine?" asked Morrigan, trying to be patient. She did not wish to antagonize him.

"No," was the curt reply.

Morrigan waited for more, but the abbot continued to eat his food. He was a solid man, square-shouldered and barrel-chested. His face was weathered and wrinkled, but he was still quite in command of himself and those around him. Morrigan did not like the way he held his knife as if he was going to plunge it in her at any time.

"I can pay ye for it," repeated Morrigan.

"You could not pay my price."

"Name it."

Barrick glared at her, his eyes as sharp as the dagger he held. "You know what I want you to do. You ignored my command."

"What command?"

"Come, let us not play coy, Lady Morrigan. If you think you will find allowances from me for your sex, you are mistaken. I commanded you to kill the bishop. Archie failed me, then you. Why should I reward those who disobey me?"

Morrigan was speechless. She had not thought he would so openly admit to demanding they kill the bishop of Glasgow. There was no mercy or shame in the Abbot Barrick, but she still needed the medicine. "The bishop is gone now. How else may I earn the medicine?"

Barrick took a bite of pastry and chewed slowly as Morrigan waited. "There is one small thing. You know of a cave that was bought from your grandfather many years ago?"

"Aye," said Morrigan, thankful that Archie had confided in her.

"There is something in that cave, a silver box. I wish for you to bring it to me. Do that and you may have the medicine."

"My brother said there was nothing in that cave."

"Your brother lied."

"Where is it? There are many tunnels."

Barrick waved his hand in a regal gesture. "That is not my concern."

"Give me some medicine first, for my brother will no' last long."

Barrick laughed a humorless growl. "The box first, then the medicine."

Morrigan shook her head. "I need to care for him first. If ye will no' give me the medicine now, I will seek it elsewhere. I will no' serve ye if it means my brother's life."

Barrick gave her a piercing stare, as if sizing up her resolve.

"Guards!" he commanded, and the two men entered. "Retrieve the medicine we took from the convent yesterday, and measure out enough for three days. Take it to Andrew McNab at McNab Hall."

"Nay!" interrupted Morrigan. "I will take it."

"You will not touch it," growled Barrick. He dismissed the guards with a curt nod. "You have bought your brother three days."

"'Tis no' enough."

"When you bring the box, I will give you the rest of the bottle. I am being very generous."

Morrigan fancied the contents of the silver box would be worth hundreds of bottles of medicine, but the life of her younger brother could not be measured in gold.

"I will do it," said Morrigan, and she quit the room without looking back.

Barrick watched her leave with a small smile on his face. How obliging it was of Andrew to be dying at that moment.

"I trust you heard that," said Barrick.

"Aye," said a rough lad emerging from behind the screen.

"Follow her to that cave, and see if she is able to find the box."

"I've looked there. The cave is naught but a stinking hole," whined the lad.

Barrick smiled in his cruel way. "Your grandfather was a great Templar knight. How his seed could ever have produced such a worthless piece of dung as you, Mal, I will never comprehend. Then again, your grandfather was not known as the brightest of men."

"Smart enough no' to trust the likes o' ye," grumbled Mal.

"Insolence in a fool is hardly becoming."

"Why do ye want to find it now? I thought ye said ye wanted it to remain hidden until ye became the bishop of Glasgow?"

"I fear the bishop may be attempting to make trouble for me. I will need to hold a strong hand in order to prevail against him. It is time. I need the relic now."

"What should I do if she finds it?"

"Kill her and bring me the box." Barrick spoke as if the conclusion was obvious.

"And what if she doesna find the box?"

"Kill her anyway. I do not wish to see her again." Barrick turned his attention back to his wine. "And tell the brothers not to bother sending the medicine to that worthless McNab. We would not wish to waste it."

Mal walked toward the door but turned back before opening it. "What is in the box?"

Barrick smiled slowly and dismissed Mal with a wave of his hand. "'Tis not your concern. Now go!"

Nineteen

DRAGONET RESIGNED HIMSELF TO ANOTHER DAY'S HARD search. When Morrigan told him the cave was on the banks of Loch Pain near the river, he believed it to be a relatively simple matter to find. He was wrong. He had spent all day yesterday searching in the driving snow until the cold forced him to take shelter in the village of Kimlet for the night.

He resumed his search at daybreak. Fortunately the day was as bright and sunny as the previous one was stormy. He hoped he could find it, but the piles of snow rounded all the shapes in the landscape beneath a thick, white blanket and hid all clues to the location of the cave. After several hours, Dragonet knew it was going to be another long, cold day.

Despite the sun, the wind blew hard and the temperature was noticeably colder than the day before. Not that he cared much. He had lost interest in finding the relic. It seemed a grand adventure at one time, but now he simply wanted to be done with it. Yet the mission was all he had. He had to find the relic to return to France—back where it was warm, back where he could hide in a monastery away from temptation. He would find the relic, if it took him until spring to do it.

At the end of a fruitless day, he stopped to sit on a rounded mound of snow he guessed to be a tree trunk in a copse of scraggly trees. The loch was not far from Kimlet, so he had walked the distance to begin his search. The sun was getting low on the horizon, and it was near time to start walking back.

On the road above him, a figure trotted by on horseback. He strained to see around the tree trunks at the figure bundled in several cloaks. Where was that man going? Could he show him the way to the cave?

Dragonet could not think of why the man would be going to the cave, but he had little to lose. Taking care to remain hidden in the brush, he began his pursuit.

∽

There were many things in the world that Morrigan hated. The English figured prominently on that list, along with wealthy barons and conceited aristocrats. She did not like days of fasting, cold porridge was not appetizing, and she despised turnips of any temperature. Added to her growing list were women's clothing, minstrels, and evil abbots.

Though she hated many things, there were only a few she actually feared. She could leap at an armed man from a tree without a second thought. She could tame a wild horse without concern. She had marched into war with few qualms for her personal safety. But caves… caves were different.

When she was young, she was warned not to go

in that cave. She was warned not to do many things which she eventually ended up doing anyway, but not the cave. Nothing terrified her as much as the suffocating darkness of a cave.

Morrigan clicked her horse to a trot, the fastest speed she could manage in the snow, and passed by the hills and trees with unseeing eyes. How was she to get the box Barrick wanted? If Archie believed there was treasure inside, he would have explored the cave thoroughly. If he could not find any treasure, how would she be able to?

Morrigan slowed as she approached the mouth of the cave. The snow covered all of the natural land-marks to find the entrance, which was difficult to find on a clear day. With all the snow, it was going to be a challenge.

Morrigan guided her mount along the shore of the loch, looking for the mouth of the river that would lead her to the entrance of the cave. The sun shone brilliantly over the sparkling, white, snow-covered loch. The wind gusted, and freezing cold slithered its icy fingers down the back of her neck. Morrigan adjusted her outer cloak higher around herself. Despite the bright sun, the temperature was crackling cold and the wind was frigid. Dark gray clouds on the horizon told her another storm would soon be upon her.

Morrigan squinted against the blinding sun reflected off the glistening snow, trying to see what was ahead of her. A short distance up the river she found the white lump she was searching for. She dismounted slowly, her joints complaining in the cold. Morrigan crouched down and brushed the snow from the rounded form. Beneath was a narrow plank bridge covered in snow and ice. Morrigan eyed the makeshift bridge with suspicion. It was no more than a few planks tossed across the river.

On the other side of the river, in the hillside concealed behind scrubby brush, was the entrance to the cave. It would be unrecognizable except for the plank bridge that crossed the frozen river.

"Can ye make it o'er that bridge wi'out breaking it through?" Morrigan asked her mount. The horse hung his head in silence. He was cold. She was cold. They both needed to get to the relative shelter of the cave before night came and the temperatures dropped further.

"Ye best tread lightly, ye ken?"

Her horse snorted in response.

Morrigan stepped onto the narrow plank bridge, her boot crunching down into the deep snow. The top of the river beneath was frozen, but she suspected under the thin layer of ice, frigid water still ran deep. Falling into the icy water would be a death sentence.

Morrigan slid her feet along the plank, cautiously finding ice beneath the layer of snow. She clicked her tongue, and the horse stepped onto the plank. "Easy now, easy."

Slowly she backed onto the bridge, leading her horse across the narrow, icy passage. She froze once at the sound of a loud crack, but the boards held, so she continued carefully guiding her mount. Finally across, she breathed a sigh of relief. Now all she needed was to find a treasure that not even her greedy brother had been able to find. Her shoulders slumped, but she continued to tramp through the snow to the cave.

Morrigan reached up to pat her horse's neck. He had done a good job. Over her mount's withers she caught a glimpse of a black form on the other side of the river. Was someone following her?

Morrigan ducked herself and her horse out of sight behind a large, snow-covered bush and wrapped the reins around a branch. Making her way around the other side, she concealed herself behind the snow-laden brush, slowly making her way back to the bridge. When she was close, she hid behind a large white lump that must have been a boulder and waited. She crouched in the snow as the cold seeped through her boots and her thick woolen mittens. Still she waited for her quarry.

A dark-clad figure emerged from behind some trees and made his way forward following her footsteps. She did not know who he was, but following her might be the last thing he ever did. He came to the icy bridge and paused for a moment. Morrigan gripped her sword and made ready to strike. The man crossed over the bridge quick as a cat, but it was Morrigan who was ready to pounce.

Morrigan leapt before the man, drawing her sword as she sprung, the ringing of steel slicing through the muffled, snow-coated landscape. He drew his sword instantly, and Morrigan attacked in one fluid movement, determined to disarm him quick. It was a move she had perfected, and it rarely failed her. It failed her today.

The man was clothed in multiple cloaks and had a

muffler wrapped around his mouth and nose, much like herself. Whoever he was, he was no stranger to sword play. He attacked with precision, skilled and sure. She took one step back then another, trying to find a weakness in his attack. She defended herself, searching for the opportunity to strike, but found none. She tried to note the pattern of his attack, but he varied his approach, keeping her off balance. He was in control.

"Drop your sword, knave, or I'll drop you," commanded Dragonet.

Morrigan's jaw dropped. The man was Dragonet? Was it Dragonet who always treated her with such respect, consideration, and downright timidity? Her sword wavered and he attacked. Morrigan dove out of the way of his blade and rolled to the side. He raised his sword to strike.

"Dragonet!"

The man stopped mid swing and staggered back as if struck. "Morrigan? Is it you?"

Morrigan stood, lowering her scarf. He did the same. It was indeed her French knight. The last man on earth she wanted to see.

"What are ye doing here?" Morrigan asked. Where was his horse? Was he *walking* home to France?

"I... I... did not expect to see you," stammered Dragonet.

"Why are ye still in McNab territory?" asked Morrigan, growing suspicious. "Tell me yer business here."

The French knight said nothing, silent as the snow-flakes beginning to fall.

Morrigan's mind whirled until pieces of the puzzle

began to fit together. Was it any coincidence that he was near the cave that supposedly held the treasure?

"I dinna think ye came here to look for bats." Her voice was flat.

"I am sorry," said Dragonet. Three little words that cut her broken heart to shards.

"Ye are here to find the treasure, no? The Templar treasure! Dinna dare lie to me!"

Dragonet's face was impassive. "I came for the treasure."

"All this time I thought ye cared for Andrew, for me, but nay, ye were only using our friendship to find out where the cave was. Ye used me. Ye used Andrew and put his life at risk by bringing him home."

"He wanted to—"

"Silence!" Blood was pounding in her ears in a deafening roar. Her vision narrowed, with Dragonet in the center like a target. Never had she wanted to kill a man more than that moment. "I'll hear no more o' yer lies. How could I have been so stupid? Damn ye Dragonet. Damn ye to hell!"

Morrigan attacked with everything she had, driving him backwards. She swung to kill, attacking his legs, slicing at his neck. He no longer attacked but defended her blows with speed and skill. She lunged forward again, and he deflected with precision. He was good. Irritatingly good. Impressively good. And it only made her hate him more.

She charged him, and he backed onto the bridge. She followed, her footing unsure on the icy wooden plank.

"Andrew's fever has returned." She shouted. "He will probably die because o' ye."

"I am sorry to hear it. I swear to you he was leaving

to go to McNab Hall. I thought I could be of help if I went with him."

"And find the location of the Templar treasure."

"Yes, but never did I intend to hurt anyone."

"Well, ye did. Now silence yer treacherous words and repent yer sins, for I will see ye dead!"

They clashed swords, bringing them close for a breathless moment. She pushed him back with all her might and lost her footing on the slick wooden bridge. Tangled sword to sword, she suddenly went down, one foot sliding sideways, the other sliding back. The sudden loss of resistance toppled him forward. He tried to catch himself, but his feet also slid out behind him, and they both fell over the edge of the bridge.

Morrigan and Dragonet crashed through the river ice to the frigid water below. The cold hit Morrigan with physical force. For an agonizing moment she was shocked into frozen oblivion. She could not move. Fighting to retain consciousness, she struggled to prevent herself from being entirely submerged and pulled herself up onto the ice toward the shore.

She was soaked through, frozen to her very core. Every muscle in her body screamed in pain and then went silent as numbness spread. Her many cloaks were so heavy with the weight of the water she could barely move. Dragonet slowly pulled himself onto shore and reached out his hand to her. She accepted the offered hand and allowed him to haul her to the bank. It did not matter. She looked him dead in the eye.

"We are both going to die."

Twenty

DRAGONET AND MORRIGAN STRUGGLED TO STAND, helping each other up as they went. The wind cut through their clothes like knives. Dragonet began to shiver uncontrollably. Morrigan was likewise afflicted.

"C-come," said Morrigan through chattering teeth. The freezing temperatures had effectively chilled her anger. It did not matter anymore.

Dragonet followed her as she stumbled forward. She struggled to move through the snow. After a few feet she grabbed her horse, which was waiting for her behind a large snow-covered bush. She did not bother to mount but pulled the beast forward to the hillside. She reached some white mounds and disappeared behind them.

Dragonet followed, and behind the snowy boulders and thick brush was the entrance to the cave. He was so cold he was finding it difficult to think, but it was clear he would have never found the entrance to the cave. Morrigan may have shared some details, but she had not given away all.

He ducked his head to enter. The cave opened

up into a large cavern with a sandy, frozen floor. Morrigan was struggling to open the satchel on her saddle. Dragonet moved to help her but he, too, found it difficult to move his fingers. He tugged and opened the satchel with brute force. Inside was some food and two precious, dry blankets.

"W-we must get out of these w-wet clothes," said Morrigan starting to remove her cloaks.

Dragonet nodded and began to do the same. He wished to say something to her, but he had no words and was not sure he could speak with his teeth chattering with such ferocity. He focused on removing his clothing, a difficult task with hands that were stiff and clumsy, but he knew remaining in wet clothes was a death sentence. Metal clanked as Morrigan tossed down her weapons. He did the same. He removed his leather boots, which were starting to freeze, his multiple cloaks, his hose, and his tunic. Down to his wet breeches, he paused. What was he to do?

Morrigan was also down to her breeches and a wide linen strip of cloth that she had wrapped around her chest. She tugged at the cloth but he could see that it had frozen in place. He moved to help her, pulling at the fabric until it began to give way. The cloth began to unwrap, and Morrigan turned in circles until it dropped to the floor.

Her naked back was to him. Despite the freezing cold, he stopped shivering for a moment, his heart pounding inside his chest. Her muscular back tapered into a small waist, revealing both her strength and her femininity. Never before had he desired a woman more.

She grabbed a wool blanket and wrapped it

around her, bending over for a moment to remove her breeches. She turned to him, still shivering but wrapped in a blanket.

"T-take the other blanket."

He wanted to, desperately. He had never been so cold. His body and mind moved slowly as if in a fog. And yet he did not wish to take from her. "B-both blankets are yours. T-take it and be warm."

Morrigan glared at him. "T-take everything off. Ye canna warm yerself if ye are wearing wet clothing."

Dragonet knew she spoke the truth, but still he hesitated. A faint glimmer of vanity warned him that freezing temperatures were not kind to the male physique. He pushed the fear aside and his breeches down. Morrigan looked him up and down; her face revealed no emotion, but her eyes gleamed. He wished for instant death. It was not granted.

"W-willing to take the blanket now?" she taunted.

He grabbed the extra blanket and wrapped it around himself. He was still cold. Very cold. They needed to get warm and fast or they would freeze to death. No wood was in the cave, eliminating the possibility of starting a fire.

"I-I must get something from this cave to exchange it for medicine for A-Andrew, ye ken? If I die, so also will he."

Dragonet tried to figure how a relic could be related to medicine, but his brain was not up to the task.

Morrigan stared at the floor. "There is only one way I k-ken to warm ourselves so far from a fire and a mug o' hot brew. 'T-tis for my brother's life, no' yers nor mine."

"I-I will do as ye command."

"I have heard two people together can..."
Morrigan faltered and shivered more violently.
"D-damn I'm c-cold."

Dragonet knew what she needed. He too had heard
that two people together could generate body heat.
Heat they desperately needed. Yet it was the one thing
he could not give her. His vows. His honor. He would
die for it. She shivered beside him, staring at the floor.
He would die for it, but he would not kill for it.

"P-please, let me warm you if I am able." Dragonet
stepped toward her, but she did not look up.

"Ye d-did not want me when I offered."

"I-I did want you. V-very much. I did not wish to
hurt you."

"Ye did hurt me."

"I b-beg your forgiveness. To save your life I would
d-do anything."

"And Andrew?"

"Andrew is a f-fine lad, but for you I care a good
deal more."

Morrigan's head snapped up, her eyes wide.
"Y-ye do?"

What had he said? Stupid brain, it was moving
slowly and forgot some things he said out loud and
others he kept to himself. He closed his eyes and
nodded. She pushed at his arms, and he opened his
arms and the blanket, his eyes still closed. She pressed
her naked body to his and wrapped her blanket and
arms around him as he did the same with his. He
wished she were warmer. More than that, he wished
his skin was less numb so he could feel her better.

Ironic that for the first time in his life he had a naked woman pressed against him, and yet he could barely feel it.

"H-how is this supposed to help?" asked Morrigan.

"I believe we are supposed to generate our own heat."

"I am n-not experienced wi' men. Ye must show me. And hurry, I'm f-freezing."

"I-I fear I have no experience either."

Morrigan pulled back enough to look up at him, startled. "Are y-ye saying yer a virgin?"

Dragonet nodded, his heart starting to pound.

"I dinna ken what to believe wi' ye."

"It is not the thing a man would lie about."

"Nay," said Morrigan thoughtfully. "Kiss me like ye did before. That made me hot."

Did it? Her blunt praise sprung life back to parts of him he feared had fallen off with cold. He leaned down and kissed her, putting his frozen lips to hers. He felt nothing. He opened her mouth with his tongue and deepened the kiss, searching for warmth. Together they found it, their lips locked in a desperate need for heat.

With Morrigan in his arms everything else slid away. Nothing else mattered. With her touch, life swirled within him again. The fire within her, the fire she kindled in him, it was their only chance to survive the night. And even if he should die, holding the woman he adored was how he chose to face his death.

Morrigan clutched him tight, pressing herself against him. He broke the kiss for air and, catching his breath, turned his attentions to her breasts. They were generous in proportion and tweaked with cold. His heart pounded with anticipation. He brushed a clumsy hand over one, but could feel little with his numb fingers.

With sudden insight, he kissed down her neck to her chest. Feeling his way with lips and tongue, he finally kissed what had so tempted him from the moment he saw her exposed cleavage in a gown. Swirling his tongue, he tasted heaven. Ah, she was so sweet. He suckled more, and she threw her head back and went limp in his arms. He smiled and moved his attentions to her other breast.

Breaking contact he said, "Morrigan, I—"

"I swear if ye stop now, I'll gut ye and use yer entrails to keep me warm!"

"Uh…"

She glared at him with such malice he believed she would make good her threat. He was not generally afraid of her, but there were times she could give him pause.

"I was going to suggest that we lie down."

"Truly?" Her eyes narrowed in suspicion.

"Truly." It was the truth. And if it had not been, he would have lied.

"'Tis a goodly idea." She smiled.

He smiled back. Cheating death was exhilarating.

She took her blanket and triple-folded it to create a cushion between them and the frozen ground. He indulged in frank admiration of her naked body. She bent over arranging the blankets, and he saw stars, which meant he was either dying of the cold or overcome by the magnificence of her perfect white *derrière*.

He only hoped he would live long enough to make good on the prospect her rounded backside offered.

She turned as she sat on the blanket, stretching out her long legs before her. She was perfect.

"Let down your hair." He kneeled before her and threaded his hands in her hair to release her beautiful locks. Fortunately, she had not submerged entirely and her hair was still dry. It meant she had a chance to survive.

"Careful!" she chided, batting away his hands and removing the pins herself. "If ye prick yer finger on this one, ye will sleep for hours."

Dragonet smiled and wrapped his hand in her thick hair, helping to set it free with clumsy fingers. None could take her against her will, of that he was certain. Her hair unbound, it fell down around her long and thick. His breath caught in his chest. She was everything he imagined, and better. Her large, brown eyes raked over him as he kneeled before her. Emboldened by the spark of desire in her eye, he let her have a good look.

"I speak to you the truth, you are most beautiful," he said.

"I like the way the muscles in yer stomach ripple."

He let her praise wash over him, warm and inviting. He knew she would not speak the words unless they were true, giving power to her praise. He gently lay down on top of her, pulling the blanket over them. He snuggled as close as he could without crushing her and wondered what to do next. After spending many years defending his celibacy, he wished he was not so inexperienced at that crucial moment. He knew in general terms what should happen next, but how did one get there? Besides, despite his interest he had another problem.

"I–I fear I am too cold," he admitted.

"Aye, ye're cold; hurry and warm me."

"I… I am not sure that I can. Things are really cold." His first time, and it was going to end in failure. He might as well jump back in the lake.

"What do ye mean cold? Ye mean ye're no' interested?"

"No! I am very interested. It is when a man, he is cold, he gets…" He was not going to say "small." Nothing in the world could force him to finish that sentence.

"I want to be on top," demanded Morrigan. He complied instantly, rolling them around. Maybe she knew what to do.

Morrigan put her hands against his chest, feeling her way down. He sucked in air.

"No' good?" she asked.

"Your hands are cold, but do not stop, I beg you." The fact that he noticed her cold hands meant he was warming.

She replaced her hands with her mouth and he gasped again. This time she did not stop. She worked her way down; his heart pounded harder with every inch lower she traveled. She kissed the muscles of his abdomen, his navel, and kept going lower. He grabbed the blanket in his hands to keep himself still. It was sweet torture.

Moving farther down, she kissed the inside of his thigh. His breathing came in short gasps, his body tingling in anticipation. She turned and kissed… him. He groaned uncontrollably, and he felt himself growing with her exquisite touch until he throbbed with need. The blood was probably leaving vital organs he needed to survive, but he cared not a whit. He would happily die for that pleasure.

She returned to him, and he spun her underneath him again, primal need drowning out fear, inexperience, and all rational thought. Pain throbbed in his fingers and toes as they slowly thawed back to life. He did not care, he only wanted one thing, and he did not care if it killed him to get it.

He thrust wildly and completely ineffectively until she slowed his movements by putting her hands on his hips and wrapped her legs around him. He touched his cheek to hers, shaking with cold and need.

"I do not know how..." he confessed.

"Slowly now, it will be well."

Dragonet took a deep breath and looked down at the woman he loved. The woman he would love for as long as he could still draw breath. He could look into her eyes forever. Slowly he began to rock forward and back, moving in concert with the beating of her heart.

She smoothed her cold hands over his back and backside, encouraging, accepting. He took a deep breath and moved forward, drawn by desire and her heat. She shifted beneath him, and moving forward again, he was drawn into pure bliss. He groaned and collapsed on top of her. Sweet heaven, she was so hot.

"Ow!" cried Morrigan, her face twisted in pain.

He struggled to take some of his weight off her. "Am I hurting you?"

"Aye. And my fingers hurt like hell."

"Do you want I should stop?" He started to withdraw.

Her eyes flew open, her lips twisted in a snarl. "Do ye want I should kill ye?"

He moved forward again and discovered what intense pleasure he had denied himself. It was good, very, very good. Oh, what a loving God who created this.

He continued along, allowing her to adjust the position of his hips until she closed her eyes and sighed happily. He had not seen her so enthralled since the time she snuck gingerbread fresh from the oven. He was glad to elicit the same ecstatic response.

He moved with increasing speed, a building desire sweeping through him like fire. He moved faster, yearning for release. The pleasure of his growing need mixed with the pain of his thawing fingers. Every movement made him hurt more, but oh, he had never felt anything so good. "*Ma chérie. Mon petit trésor.*"

She arched her back and cried out, clutching his back with her fingernails. He could not stop. Suddenly the growing wave of pleasure crashed, sending spasms of joy through him. "*Je t'adore. Je t'aime!*" He cried out, uncontrollably expressing his adoration and love.

The edges of his vision grew fuzzy, and he collapsed beside her. "*Je ne peux pas vivre sans toi.*" He gave in to the darkness and knew nothing.

Twenty-One

MORRIGAN WOKE UP WARM AND CONTENT IN THE
arms of her lover... an occurrence so unprecedented
it took her several minutes to remember all that had
happened. Icy river. Freezing to death. Cuddling to
keep warm. And then... well, she did not even have
words for it. If she knew what she had been missing
all these years, she would have abandoned her sword
and signed on as a tavern wench.

Except she didn't want *that* from any man. Just one.
The one who was softly snoring next to her. The one
who opened a world of unknown pleasure. The one
who used her to find the cave that held the treasure.

She elbowed him in the side and was rewarded by
a snort and louder snoring. She elbowed him harder.
He started and awoke. His eyes went wide.

"Morrigan!" He jerked his arm from around her as
if she was poison. "I... we..."

"I have a problem."

"I am so sorry." Dragonet pressed his head into the
blankets beside her. "It was the only way to save you
from the freezing to death."

"Ye regret it?"

"Never!"

"Neither do I. Now back to my problem. I need to find something in this cave. Andrew's life is at stake. I need to know if ye will help me or if I need to kill ye, for as much as I appreciate our... er... ye saving my life. I still need to save his."

"I will help you as I am able." Dragonet's eyes were solemn, as if he were speaking a vow. Her instinct told her to trust him. Of course, last time her instinct had been dead wrong.

Morrigan nodded and sat up. Dragonet did too, taking his blanket and his heat with him. She inhaled sharply at the shock of the freezing air hitting her naked body. Scrambling up quickly, she wrapped one of the blankets around her. She was cold again, but not dangerously so.

Her clothes were still soaking wet and half-frozen, discarded on the floor of the cave. Putting them on was not a possibility. Outside the mouth of the cave darkness had fallen, a single shaft of light from the rising moon illuminated the cavern. Her shoulders sagged. She could barely keep herself alive, let alone find some hidden treasure and save Andrew.

"May I cut a strip from this blanket to fashion shoes for you and me? Now that feeling has returned to my feet, they are quite cold," said Dragonet.

Morrigan nodded. She needed to start thinking smart. Grabbing her belt, she wrapped it around her blanket at her waist, gathering her blanket around herself and pinning it at her shoulders the way the men in her clan wore their plaids as a great kilt. The belt was still wet, but it kept her wool blanket around her and provided for more overall warmth.

"Here," said Dragonet, kneeling at her feet. She lifted up one very cold foot, and he wrapped a strip of wool around it as protection from the freezing temperatures. It worked well, or at least much better than nothing, and she willingly held up her other foot.

So many questions rattled around in her head it hurt. What did he think of her? Why had he misled her before? Why was he searching the cave?

"Ye spoke many words in a foreign tongue at the end when we..." Morrigan cleared her throat. "Were ye calling out the name o' yer betrothed?"

Dragonet hung his head and finished with her foot. He sat on a rock and began to fashion shoes for himself.

"I think ye owe me some answers," said Morrigan.

Dragonet nodded, but did not look up from his work. "In my life there is no lady but you. I told you I was raised by the Hospitallers. What I did not say is that I am a Hospitaller Knight."

"A knight? But I thought the Hospitallers were all monks."

"They are."

"But ye are not a—"

Dragonet looked up at her, her eyes large and mournful in the dim light.

Morrigan gasped and put her hands over her mouth. The truth sank cold and heavy in her gut. "Ye're a monk?"

Dragonet's eyes met hers, holding them as she held her breath waiting for his reply.

"Yes."

Morrigan staggered from the shock of his confession and sat down hard on a rock. "A *monk*? But why did ye…?" A fresh wave of anger rippled through her, familiar and warm. "Why lie to me?"

"An important relic was taken by the Templars and hidden in Scotland. I was sent on a quest to find it."

"But why lie to everyone? Why not say ye were a Hospitaller?"

"Several men came before me, trying to find the relic. They were all killed. I was sent in disguise with the Duke of Argitaine. We hoped that if no one knew I was looking for it, I could have better success."

"I dinna ken anything about ye," she murmured. She had been completely and utterly misled.

Dragonet sighed, worry lines etching on his forehead. "I never meant to hurt you."

Morrigan picked up a rock and threw it at him.

"Ow!" said Dragonet, rubbing his shoulder.

"Oh, did I hurt ye? Maybe if I said I dinna mean to, it would make it better." She picked up another rock and Dragonet backed away from her. She followed.

"If ye were a monk, why kiss me? Why feign interest?" Morrigan threw hard and was rewarded by a loud thud as it bounced off his chest. "Was it all a ruse to find the location of the cave?" Morrigan set her jaw and grabbed another rock. Maybe she was going to kill him after all.

"I was interested! I am! How can I explain it?" He continued to back away, running his fingers through his hair and making it stick out at odd angles. "I took my vows when I was twelve. The Hospitallers had lost many of their brethren and were willing to let me continue to stay with them, but only if I took orders. My family all died in the great death and I had nowhere else to go. Taking a vow of celibacy was nothing to me. What did I know of women at that age? It was not until I met you that I knew true temptation."

"Should I be flattered?" She let another rock fly.

"Ow! I beg your forgiveness. Everything I did with you, every time I touched you, was wrong. But it was not false. Ow! It was true to my heart. If I were free to marry you, I would."

Morrigan stopped short. Something inside her crunched in pain. She fell back on a boulder and put her head in her hands. Finally a man who wished to marry her, and he was a monk. That was the ol' McNab luck at work. "Ow," she said softly.

"If the circumstances, they were different…"

"If ye are trying to make me feel better, ye have missed yer mark."

"I am sorry…"

"For the love o' the saints, stop saying that! It does not help."

"Oh, I am…"

Morrigan shot him a glare.

"Right. Sorry." He cringed.

"Ye canna help yerself." Morrigan shook her head. She did not know what to feel any more. Strong emotions were so jumbled inside she went numb. She took a deep breath. Whatever he was or whatever they had done, it was not relevant to her current situation. What truly mattered was she was still alive, and Andrew would not be if she did not meet the abbot's demands to get the medicine.

Morrigan stood and gestured wildly in the air as if to banish the conversation and its confusing emotions. "I dinna have time for this. I concede ye played me well. But I still need to find something in this cave to save Andrew's life." She stood with a large, jagged rock in hand. "Are ye going to help or do I need to kill ye now?"

"I am at your service."

Morrigan nodded. She could not begin to discern her feelings for him, but she did know she could use some help. "I propose we work together to find it. We can fight over it later." It was time to get back to the problem at hand. She needed to save Andrew.

"How is anything in this cave going to save Andrew?" asked Dragonet.

"Mother Enid's medicine at St. Margaret's was stolen by Abbot Barrick. He is demanding I bring him something he believes is here before he will give me any more medicine. Andrew wanes; he has a fever. He needs it."

Dragonet nodded. "What did he tell you to retrieve?"

"A silver box."

Dragonet's eyes flashed, but he said nothing.

"That is what ye are seeking too?" asked Morrigan.

"Yes," acknowledged Dragonet softly. "Barrick must never be allowed to have it. He may be the one who killed the monks who came before me."

"I dinna doubt it, but Andrew must not be allowed to die." Their eyes met across the dimly lit cave. So close, and yet a barrier loomed between them. Lovers and enemies. For once in her life she knew exactly what she wanted, and it could never, ever be hers.

The moon was rising, and soon the angle would block its light from the cave. She needed to push aside the remnants of her heart, her dreams, and her dignity, and get to work before they were in complete darkness.

"Truce for now?" she asked, belting on her sword.

"Agreed."

"I believe I have a candle in my saddlebag," said Morrigan, searching for the precious item. She held out a tallow candle in success. "Now to light it before we lose the moonlight."

They had no flame or kindling, but Morrigan scraped off some cloth fibers from her blanket, which Dragonet lit with his flint, and from that tiny spark, she lit the candle.

Morrigan was pleased with their success but not with the prospect of going farther into the cave. She liked staying where she could still see the sky. The back of the cave stretched out before them like a gaping hole of doom. She did not wish to enter.

Dragonet belted a knife around his waist and made a clumsy attempt to copy her method of wearing a blanket.

"Och, let me," said Morrigan, turning to help Dragonet arrange his blanket.

"I can manage."

"Nonsense, ye're making a mess of it." Morrigan took the ends of the blanket from his hands and peeled it down to reveal his waist in order to pleat the garment correctly. She worked quickly, her mind abandoning its needful focus on her quest to admire the muscular physique before her. Dragonet was a tall, trim man. She bit her lip and resisted running her hand over his rippling stomach muscles.

Morrigan stepped around to his back to finish her work and get her mind off his chest, and froze at what she saw.

"I can take it from here," said Dragonet trying to cover his back.

Morrigan stepped back and allowed him to cover the deep, ugly scars searing tracks down his backs. "What are those scars?" she asked, trying not to wince.

"It is nothing. Let us continue our quest."

"Are those burns?"

"I was an awkward child." He took the candle and walked into the darkness of the cave.

Like a moth to the flame, Morrigan followed. "No one is that clumsy. Tell me the truth."

Dragonet turned, the candle's orange light flickering on his face. "To find this box, we must focus most diligently. Do you know where it is located, did Barrick give you any clues?"

Morrigan gave Dragonet a hard look. She did not like to have her questions ignored.

"Please, Morrigan." He spoke softly.

Morrigan sighed. She wanted to understand him, to know if he could be trusted. Yet what she really wanted was forever beyond her grasp. She needed to let him go.

"I dinna ken there is any treasure here," said Morrigan, allowing her question to drop. "Archie said he searched but found nothing."

"That does not bode well." Dragonet continued down the passageway of the cave, which became narrower with every step.

The walls were closing in on her, suffocating her.

Morrigan worked on controlling her breathing. She must not let the cave get to her. She must not let him see weakness. "Do ye ken where it is hidden?"

"I am sorry, but no."

"What have I told ye about apologizing?" asked Morrigan with a sharp edge. Her anxiety was turning her usually sunny disposition into something less than hospitable.

"As you wish."

They walked on a little farther, utter blackness stretching on ahead and behind her like an abyss. All she could see were the cave walls around her, illuminated by the dim light of a single candle. Morrigan's heart pounded, throbbing in her ears. She wanted out.

"Here, what is this?" Dragonet ducked his head to fit through a narrow gap and disappeared. Morrigan rushed after the light and stumbled into a large cavern. Gleaming crystals on the walls and ceiling reflected the light of the candle, dazzling the eye with its brilliance. Morrigan squinted at the sudden light and turned a circle awed by the sparkling crystals.

"Which path?" asked Dragonet.

Morrigan realized that multiple passages led from the dazzling room. "I know not," said Morrigan. She turned back the passages she came from and drew her sword to make a mark on the floor before the tunnel they had come from. She did not wish to be lost there.

"What is it you are doing?" asked Dragonet.

"Marking the tunnel we came from so we can get out of here."

"Good idea." Dragonet began looking around the

entrances of the other tunnels. "I would wager the Templars did the same thing."

They searched the entrances to the tunnels leading from the crystal room. The dirt floor of the crystal cave was frozen and the crystals themselves were like chunks of ice. Still, Morrigan searched around the tunnel entrance, feeling the cold, rough cave walls for any clues.

"What kind of marking would they leave?" asked Morrigan.

"I know not," answered Dragonet, standing on a rock to look up at the top of a long, narrow tunnel entrance. "Anything that looks man-made."

Morrigan grunted a response and went on to search the next tunnel. This one was small, a round hole barely large enough for a person to fit through, and a trim person at that. She brushed aside some debris on the floor and searched along the outside of the tunnel but found nothing. With considerable reluctance, Morrigan went down on hands and knees and put her head in the tunnel to inspect the inside. It was black and damp. Resisting the urge to crawl out, Morrigan felt around the inside of the tunnel, freezing slime oozing through her fingers. She shuddered, the inky blackness of the tunnel closing in on her.

She couldn't breathe. She needed air. Backing out of the tunnel in a mad scramble she scraped her knees and hit her head on the top of the tunnel.

"Ow! Hell and damnation!"

"What is wrong?" Dragonet was immediately at her side.

Morrigan grabbed the back of her head with one

hand and a rock on the top of the tunnel with the other, and heaved herself to her feet. The rock came off in her hand, causing her to stumble, but she was caught in the strong arms of Dragonet.

"Stupid cave! It's too dark and too small and too repulsive. I canna do this."

Dragonet pulled her close in embrace. She opened her mouth to complain, but sighed instead. Fool she was, but everything seemed better when she was in the warm arms of her lover... monk... enemy. Damn, she hated her life.

Morrigan tipped up her head, instinctively hoping for a kiss, but he was looking at something over her shoulder. "What are ye looking at?"

"Look, you uncovered a mark."

Above the tunnel where the rock had broken off in her hand was indeed a small mark carved into the stone. They both drew closer and inspected the mark, Dragonet holding up the candle to see it clearly. It was made by human hands, engraved into the stone in the shape of a *V*.

"What does it mean?" asked Morrigan.

"Maybe there are more," said Dragonet. He moved to the next tunnel entrance and pulled at the stones above the entrance. One came off easily. They converged on the space, putting their heads together and inspecting it with the candle. With growing excitement, Morrigan saw there was another mark, this one a letter *L*.

In unspoken agreement, they went around the glimmering room and pulled rocks from the top of each tunnel. Each tunnel had a letter. There were five tunnels leading away from the room, with the letters, *V, L, T, P,* and *S*.

"Vltps? What is that?" asked Morrigan.

"Lptvs?" Dragonet pushed his hair out of his eyes with a dirty hand.

"Stplv? I am no' the best with my letters, but do we no' need a vowel?"

"Pray the hours," murmured Dragonet. He turned toward her with a flash of a smile. "Pray the hours!"

"What are ye saying? Have ye gone daft?"

"The last words of the dying Templar to the Mother Enid were, 'Pray the hours.'"

"And?" Morrigan shrugged.

"The hours for prayer are Vigils, Lauds, Prime, Terce, Sext, None, Vespers, and Compline. I suppose they did not have enough tunnels for all of them but see—*VLPTS*—Vigils, Lauds, Prime, Terce, and Sext!"

Morrigan's pulse quickened. "So which tunnel do we want?"

"We should start with the first hour of the day, Vigils."

Naturally it was the small, grimy, panic-inducing tunnel. Morrigan stood in front of the passage, peering down into the dark, dank hole.

"Do you wish for me to go first?" asked Dragonet.

"Nay, I am taking mental accounts of my brother and deciding if he is worth this bother."

Dragonet raised an eyebrow.

"Give the candle, I'll go," groused Morrigan. The last thing in the world she wanted to do was crawl down a cold, slime-filled passage, leading deeper into the bowels of the cave. She gritted her teeth, kneeled down, and did it anyway.

She expected it to be unpleasant. It was that and more. The cold, the walls rubbing against her shoulders, the freezing slime she crawled through, any of it alone she could have handled, but in combination with the suffocating, trapped feeling of being in a small tunnel, it was too much. Her breath came in rapid gulps, her heart pounded until she feared it would explode and she would die in that squalid tunnel.

"Panting for me, my love?" teased Dragonet behind her.

"Wh-what?" Morrigan tried to turn to confront him, but was unable due to the confines of the tunnel. "Ye fool bastard. I coud'na care less about yer sorry self." Morrigan crawled faster through the tunnel, determined to find a larger space where she could confront the conceited Frenchman. Did he believe her thoughts contained nothing but him?

After crawling over several large rocks, the tunnel opened into another room-like space in the cave. This cavern was not so brilliant, just dark and damp, with large stalagmites and stalactites. Morrigan whirled around to face Dragonet, her hand on the hilt of her sword.

"You are out of the tunnel, Morrigan," noted Dragonet calmly as he stepped into the cavern.

Morrigan opened her mouth to berate him, then closed it again. "Ye did that on purpose to distract me."

Dragonet gave a half smile. "I noticed you are not overly fond of caves."

"That is one way to put it." Truth was she was terrified. She knew in her core she could not do it without him. "Which way now?"

This cavern had four tunnels leading from it, but once again they found, beneath easily removable rocks, letters above the tunnels and chose the one marked *L* for Lauds. This tunnel proved short, only a few feet, opening into another cavern. The cavern was not of even footing, having large slabs of crumbling rock dividing the cave into several levels.

They repeated the same process, but this time there were only three tunnels marked *S, T,* and *V.*

Dragonet shook his head. "Prime should be next."

"Well it is not here. Let's go to the next one, there is a *T* for Terce."

Dragonet remained unmoved. "We must be missing something. The monks would not forget Prime. The prayer is for early morning, before the first meal of the day. Many monks confessed the sins committed during the night before joining their brothers in the communal meal."

Morrigan walked around the walls of the cave, climbing up and down rocks to do so, but no other opening was found. "There is no other tunnel."

"We are missing something," repeated Dragonet.

Morrigan bit back a caustic remark. What she was missing was fresh air and the immeasurable joy of not being in a cave. "So what would you do for this prayer?" she asked, trying to stay focused.

Dragonet lay on his stomach on the floor of the cave, spreading his arms wide.

"I canna see how this is going to help us." Morrigan crossed her arms.

"This is how we would pray," said Dragonet, turning his head to see her. "We would…"

"Ye would what?" asked Morrigan, wondering why he had stopped talking.

He jumped up and ran to a slab of rock. "Here, look." Carved into the rock by the floor, only visible if one laid one's head on the ground, was the letter *P*.

Morrigan smiled. "Good one. But where is the tunnel?"

Dragonet felt around the base of the crumbling rock and discovered a small hole.

"Well I'm no' going in there!"

Dragonet reached his hand in the hole and frowned. All was silent in the cave except for the occasional drip of water from the stalactites. A slow smile warmed his face and he drew back his hand. He opened his fist to reveal a rusted iron object.

"A key!" exclaimed Morrigan. It was large and old and smelled like treasure, if such a thing was possible. Her pulse quickened once again, but this time it was more excitement than fear. She met Dragonet's gleaming eyes.

They were on the hunt.

Twenty-Two

"COME, LET'S FIND WHAT THIS KEY OPENS!" SAID Morrigan, scrambling to her feet. Dragonet stood up beside her, a smile on his dirty face. His appearance was a mite rough, with nothing but a blanket wrapped around him like a great kilt and a day's stubble on his chin.

Except for the facial hair, Morrigan was in much the same condition. It was barely enough to keep from freezing, yet with the find of a key, she was too excited to shiver.

Dragonet's eyes danced in the candlelight. They were going to find the treasure. He held out his hand to her. She hesitated for a moment. They were rivals for the prize they both sought. A wise person would keep her distance. Morrigan took his hand. The McNabs were rarely accused of being wise.

They walked to the tunnel marked *T* for Terce and entered together. The tunnel was comparatively wide, and they were able to walk two abreast. The tunnel twisted and turned a few times, and they had to go one at a time to pass through, but they continued to hold hands.

Morrigan searched for something to say, though she did not feel awkward with him in the silent cave, she thought she really ought to be. "So what is Terce?"

"Terce is the midmorning prayer done at the third hour after dawn."

"What would ye do at these prayers?"

"We would either stop our work and pray alone or gather in the chapel if we were able and chant some psalms and pray together in spoken word and in silence. That is how I started singing, through the chants. It can be very beautiful." Dragonet gave a wistful smile.

"Ye must be anxious to return," commented Morrigan, wishing she was less interested in his response to her statement.

"Sometimes, but..."

"But what?" asked Morrigan, looking ahead to where he had disappeared around a tight corner.

"This cave, it is familiar."

Morrigan followed him out into the crystal room, the sparkling minerals reflecting and magnifying the light of the candle.

"'Tis the same cavern! I canna believe we went through all that for naught."

"Not for naught," said Dragonet, holding up the key.

"We could have gotten the key by going through this tunnel," said Morrigan gesturing toward the tunnel they had just traversed. "Not that awful, slimy, tiny one."

Dragonet appeared unconcerned, walking toward the tunnel with the S without releasing her hand. "Sext is the midday prayer, set at the sixth hour after dawn," said Dragonet in a friendly tone. "We usually chanted more psalms, prayed, and then ate our midday meal together."

Morrigan thought "Sext" sounded a lot like "sex," and despite the cold, her cheeks burned at the memory of their time together. She kept her adolescent musings to herself. They had done what they needed to do to survive. It was no more than that.

Except that was a lie. It had meant everything to her.

Except he was still a monk, so it would be better if she could convince herself it meant nothing.

"Getting a little cramped here," said Dragonet, ahead of her in the tunnel. He bent down to avoid hitting his head on the rock, and soon they were both crawling on hands and knees. It was at least not wet, but very cold. The tunnel closed in, until Morrigan shook with the restraint it took her to avoid calling out for help. Her mind focused on one thing, her need to escape.

Suddenly, she ran into Dragonet's backside. He had stopped in the tunnel.

"Move!" she shouted, on the verge of panic.

"I have nowhere to go. Dead end."

"Nay, there must be a way, there must." Morrigan pushed him down flat and squirmed her way over him. Despite the fear that drove her, she was painfully conscious of all the parts of her body that touched his.

She also reached a dead end, but began to scratch and push on the stone walls until she pushed herself up. "The tunnel goes up," she said in amazement.

Dragonet stood next to her in the small space, his

body hugging hers. He reached for her hand, but she wrapped her arms around his tall shoulders instead.

"Rest easy, we will find a way out," reassured Dragonet.

Morrigan took a deep breath, mentally cursing her weakness when it came to caves.

"I am sorry," mumbled Morrigan, trying to pull away, but having nowhere to go. "Which way now?"

"Only one way to go," said Dragonet looking up.

"Aye." Morrigan took the candle with one hand, and with Dragonet's help she climbed up and stood on his shoulders. "Ah, here! There is another tunnel wi' an N. If I can get a little higher, I can reach it."

Dragonet pressed up her feet in his hands from his shoulders. Morrigan scrambled inside the tunnel, wondering how Dragonet would manage. She need not have worried. In a moment he appeared, shimmying up the rock.

"Clever," said Morrigan with a rare smile. The tunnel she was in was larger than the previous one, and it was a relief to let go of some of the panic. They followed that tunnel out into another, larger cavern.

"Look, I can see a gate!" Morrigan sprinted across the cavern toward the mouth of a tunnel that clearly opened to an iron gate.

"No, wait!" exclaimed Dragonet, catching her before she could run more than a few steps. "Let us check the hours to see if that is the correct passage."

They quickly took inventory of the room, aided by a torch they found hanging on the wall, which they lit with the candle. The cave flickered with orange light that revealed only one other tunnel leading from that room, and it had a small carved *V* above it, the next letter in the liturgy of the hours.

"This is the way we should go," said Dragonet, pointing at the next letter. "*V* for Vespers."

"Nay, I dinna want to go on some roundabout way just so we can do all the hours. Look, from this angle ye can see a bit of an iron gate through the passageway."

Dragonet shook his head. "I say we go to the correct tunnel."

"How do ye ken this isna the right way?" asked Morrigan, walking toward the short passage with the visible gate. "I'll go this way, ye can go the other, and we'll see who gets there first." Morrigan stepped into the tunnel.

"Morrigan, wait—" Dragonet grasped her hand just as the floor beneath her collapsed. Morrigan plummeted down, scrambling for something solid to hold onto, as the rock floor beneath her broke into shale. Dragonet's firm hand held hers tightly, and she clutched at him for safety.

Dragonet caught her at the edge of the gaping hole in the floor of the cave. He fell to his stomach on the solid rock, holding her hand as she dangled over the edge. Small rocks slipped over the edge of the precipice, taking a goodly long time before a muted splash was heard at the bottom. Dragonet reached to grab her with his other hand for better support.

"Dinna drop the key!" shouted Morrigan.

Dragonet stopped, stunned. "You are dangling over the cliff, and you are worried about the key?"

"I can climb up myself." Morrigan pulled herself up

his arm to reach the edge of the hole. "I dinna crawl through slime for naught, so dinna drop that key."

Dragonet helped haul her up to safety with the one hand not holding the key. "Your concern was that I would drop the key?"

Morrigan sat on the cold, stone floor next to Dragonet. She was breathing hard, her heart pounding in her chest. Almost dying was hard on a body. She met Dragonet's intense gaze. "Would ye have?"

"Yes."

Morrigan inhaled sharply. The shivers that ran down her spine were from much more than the cold. "That would be a foolish thing to do."

Dragonet leaned close and kissed her gently at first, then wrapping one arm around her waist and the other hand on the back of her neck, he deepened the kiss. By the time he finally pulled away, Morrigan's mind was spinning, and she forgot all about the cold.

Dragonet shook his head. "With you I am always doing the foolish things." He put his hand over his eyes. "I would beg your forgiveness—I should not have done that."

"We are beyond apologies now. I fear we must acknowledge the attraction between us."

Dragonet did not look up but nodded his head vigorously.

"It doesna change anything between us, does it?" Morrigan watched him closely, hoping somehow he would say yes, it changed everything.

Dragonet slowly shook his head no.

Morrigan struggled to her feet and off the cold ground, leaving her heart behind. The important thing was she had not lost her sword still strapped to her side. Once they found the silver box, she could take it from him by force. *Yes, brilliant plan.* She walked toward the *V* tunnel, her feet dragging like lead.

They walked through the tunnel together yet apart, not touching or looking at each other. The tunnel itself proved not to be too strenuous; there were a few large boulders to scramble over, but nothing overly challenging. Soon they emerged into the room with the iron gate Morrigan had glimpsed before. The cave had another torch on the wall, which they lit.

The gate itself was fashioned of thick, iron bars and fastened on either side with metal stakes bored into the rock. It was an odd size, spanning from the floor to the ceiling, but very narrow in width. Morrigan was a trim person, but even she judged she would need to turn sideways to pass through.

Dragonet examined the gate closely. "*Quam angusta porta et arta via quae ducit ad vitam et pauci sunt qui inveniunt eam.*"

"What are ye mumbling about?"

"It is from the Gospel of St. Matthew. 'But small is the gate and narrow the road that leads to life, and only a few find it.' The Templars went to a good deal of trouble to hide this and still demonstrate its importance. Using the hours of prayer, putting an iron gate here at the smallest width, it is all leading us in reverence and prayer for what it beyond."

"So what is it? What is this treasure?"

"I do not know, but it must be a relic of vast importance."

"Could it be the… the *holy grail*? The thing that Sir Lancelot went to find?"

Dragonet smiled, his eye sparkling. "I have always thought that naught but a story, but I am willing to be wrong."

"Open the gate!"

Dragonet fit the key into the lock with some difficulty due to the rust that had formed on the key. He turned the key and the lock clicked. With a tremendous squawk of disapproval, the metal gate swung open.

Morrigan darted through the gate, eager to find what was inside. The narrow gate opened into a sealed cavern. It had several large boulders in the room, but no way in or out besides the iron gate. On one boulder was a large, wooden chest.

Morrigan stopped a few feet away from the chest, recalling her fall and wondering if this one was likewise protected. Morrigan turned to express her concern, but Dragonet lifted up a large rock. He hurled it onto the ground next to the chest. Nothing untoward occurred.

They both cautiously stepped forward until they stood before the large, cedar chest. No lock prevented them from opening the chest, yet they paused.

"Maybe ye should pray or something," suggested Morrigan. It was an unusual request for her, and she was not sure why the words sprang to her lips, but it felt the right thing to do. She did not wish to be smote for coming into contact with something holy, something she was unworthy to touch.

Dragonet made the sign of the cross and took her

hand. "Lord, in all reverence we humbly come before you and beseech you to guide us to find what you wish, and do with it what you will."

Morrigan slowly unlatched one of the leather straps. Dragonet did the other. They looked at each other, much shared within a single glance. They would do this together. It was time to open the lid.

Twenty-Three

MORRIGAN TOOK A DEEP BREATH. ANTICIPATION crackled in the air. Dragonet's eyes mirrored her excitement and perhaps a little fear. What could possibly be so important?

The top of the chest was heavy, and they both pulled hard, lifting it open. The hinges on the back groaned softly at being disturbed after so long. A plume of dust rose when the lid was opened, assailing her nose with an old, musty smell. She batted at the air, trying to wave aside the dust to see within the dark chest. Inside the chest were several old books with ancient scrolls laying across the top.

"Books?" Morrigan crinkled her nose at the musty smell and the disappointment. She was hoping for something that glittered more.

Dragonet gingerly lifted one of the scrolls. "Augustine," he murmured reverently.

"Is it only books?"

"Only books? These are precious beyond words!" Dragonet's eyes gleamed with excitement as he carefully lifted and inspected each scroll.

"Are they worth anything? Could we sell them?"

"Sell them? No! These need to be given to a university or an abbey, where they can be studied."

"Are ye sure there is naught else?" asked Morrigan, losing interest in the project.

Dragonet lifted out more scrolls and a book. "Ah!" Underneath was an ornately engraved silver box, blackened with age. With a grunt, he lifted the heavy box placed it on the ground. Both he and Morrigan leaned in to examine their prize.

Despite the tarnish, it was a beautiful box, finely crafted. Whatever was in the box must be incredibly important. The hair on her arms stood up on end. What was in the box? What could be so prized by the Templars and still sought by monks? It must be holy.

"Ye do it," said Morrigan, not wanting to touch it lest she bring judgment down against her.

Slowly Dragonet lifted the lid to the box. Heaped inside were gold coins, diamonds, rubies, and other precious stones. The light from the torches reflected from the riches, dazzling her eyes. A ripple of sheer energy coursed through her. It was more wealth than she had ever seen or even imagined. It could save her clan. She could buy more farmland and grow crops. She could wear gowns that made even the Campbell ladies envious and have real wood fires in the winter and eat all the gingerbread she wanted. Oh, sweet gingerbread, she was rich!

Dragonet cautiously pawed through the contents, finding more jewels, necklaces, and coins. "I cannot believe this is all there is," he said in obvious disappointment.

"All there is? Have ye gone daft? This is a fortune!"

Morrigan thrust her hands into the treasure, relishing in the sheer weight of gold. It was heavy with possibilities. It was her salvation. And Andrew's too.

"Yes, but why would I be sent to find it? What makes this special?"

"'Tis a fortune in gold and jewels! What could be more precious?" Morrigan looked carefully at Dragonet. Had he hit his head when she fell? Was the poor lad concussed?

"These scrolls are of more importance."

"Ye are daft." *Head injury. Must be.*

Dragonet stepped back and brushed his hair from his eyes. "It does not make sense. If he meant a book or a scroll, why did he not say so?"

"Who?"

"No one," said Dragonet with a wave of his hand.

Morrigan did not believe that for a second, but she was too busy creating a mental list of all she would buy to give Dragonet much thought.

"Shall we carry it out together? Let us fight over it after we get it out. Unless ye are not interested and would like to give it to me. Ye can keep the books," said Morrigan with a magnanimous sweep of her hand.

"Much obliged," said Dragonet with a wry smile. "Indeed the scrolls hold for me more interest."

Morrigan shook her head but knew when to hold her tongue. If he did not want to fight for the silver box, the better for her. Her interest in Dragonet did not lean toward fighting—she would hate to accidentally cut off a part of his body of which she was particularly fond. Besides, she knew how well he could fight.

Morrigan closed the lid to the silver box and lifted it

up with a tremendous heave. It was quite heavy. With considerable effort she lugged the box to the narrow gate. She had to turn it sideways and push it out before her to get it through the gate.

"Dragonet? Are ye coming?" called Morrigan.

"There must be something more," said Dragonet, searching the cave. Morrigan wandered back toward him. The cave had several large boulders and a bunch of rocks and debris at the far side of the cave, as if at one point there had been a cave-in.

"What more could it be? Ye have riches, ye have books and scrolls, what else?"

"I do not know, but I have come a long way to miss something important."

The iron gate squeaked painfully and slammed shut. Morrigan and Dragonet ran to the gate in time to see a man take the key and pull the silver box away from their reach. Morrigan pushed on the gate. It did not move. She shook it furiously, the clanging of metal echoing through the cavern, but the gate would not budge. They were locked inside!

"Mal?" asked Dragonet. "What are you doing?"

The man in a black cloak looked up with a smirk. "What are ye wearing lad? And ye dressed a bit o' company the same, eh? Odd ducks them French t'be sure."

Even from a distance Morrigan could smell his whiskey-infused presence. "Who are ye?" demanded Morrigan, swallowing down sheer panic at being trapped.

"He is Mal, grandson of one of the Templars who hid this treasure," said Dragonet without betraying an ounce of emotion.

"Aye, ye know me then. Ye're right. The treasure should be mine. I am the last descendent."

"There is Barrick," commented Dragonet.

"Ah, Barrick. He wants this too, sent me to kill ye and fetch it for him. But he isna here, is he."

"Barrick sent ye here?" gasped Morrigan.

"Aye. Is that McNab? Thought ye were a goner when last we met."

"Ye were the man working for Barrick? Ye set the fields on fire!" accused Morrigan, rattling the iron gate once more.

Mal gave a clumsy bow. "Nice to have my work recognized."

"Ye bastard!" cried Morrigan, the edges of her vision were getting cloudy. She could not be stuck in this cave. She could not!

Dragonet elbowed her hard in the ribs. His face was a calm mask. "We also have no love for Barrick and do not mind acknowledging you as the rightful heir, but do not leave without claiming your inheritance to the full. There is yet another chest here. Let us out, and we can all three split it."

Mal edged closer, his eyes narrowed. He was a young man, but he appeared older at first glance. Morrigan suspected hard living, not age, had etched those lines on his face.

"Show me! What treasure?" Mal's eyes darted between Morrigan and Dragonet.

"See here. Come closer. There is a wooden chest," said Dragonet as if he was inviting a friend for supper.

Morrigan and Dragonet stepped aside so Mal could see the cedar chest. Dragonet caught her eye. He looked at her sword, then at Mal, then back to her. She grasped the hilt of her sword. She understood the message. They needed to lure Mal close enough to the bars of the gate so she could stab him with her sword and they could retrieve the key.

Otherwise they would slowly starve to death in this cave. Morrigan pushed the fear aside. She needed to be sharp if they were going to stay alive.

"What is in it?" asked Mal as he took two steps forward, but was not close enough to reach.

"I tell you the truth. The items in the chest, they are worth much more than the contents of the silver box," said Dragonet.

"I like me some gold. I dinna wish to be greedy," said Mal, taking another step closer and licking his chapped lips. "Open the lid, show me what's in it."

Dragonet opened the lid. Morrigan stood to the side, ready to strike.

"I canna see, lift it up to show me," said Mal.

"Come closer, it is heavy."

Mal edged closer, casting a wary eye at Morrigan, who tried to look bored and nonthreatening. He was almost within striking range.

"What is it?" he asked again.

"Come and see for yourself."

But Mal moved no farther forward. "Show me!"

"It is better seen than explained."

"I dinna trust ye. Keep whatever it is." He turned to walk away.

"Wait, here, I'll show you this." Dragonet lifted one of the scrolls from the trunk.

Mal turned back. "What is it?"

"An ancient scroll, brought from the Holy Land. The value of this scroll, it is immeasurable."

"A scroll? What the hell do I want wi' a scroll?"

"Ye can get a high price for that scroll," Morrigan added.

"And how do I explain hows I got it? Ye all enjoy the rest o' yer short life." He turned to leave.

"Nay!" shouted Morrigan.

Dragonet threw his knife at Mal, through the iron gate, catching him in the thigh. Mal howled in pain and cursed violently.

"Damn ye. Damn ye to hell!" he screamed as he pulled out the knife. He grabbed the box and heaved it up, carrying it out with him as he limped out of sight.

Dragonet bowed his head and leaned against the cave wall. "I hoped to bring him down so we might somehow retrieve the key."

Morrigan leaned her head against the cold iron bars and grasped one bar in each hand. "Ye tried. Ye did what ye could. Wi' any luck he'll die before he can leave the cave."

"Little good it will do us."

Morrigan slumped down and put her head in her hands. It was all over. She would die in the cave with him. Andrew would die too. She was a fool to have trusted Barrick to keep his word. He had sent Mal to kill her. Even if she had brought him back the treasure, she doubted Andrew would have ever seen more medicine, if he had seen the first dose at all.

Dragonet slid down beside her. He offered his hand, and she took it. He stared straight ahead with unseeing eyes.

"I failed you," he said softly. She was not certain he was talking to her.

Morrigan watched the torch flicker. Soon it would die out, and she would die a slow, painful death in the utter darkness of a forgotten cave.

"God must hate me," said Morrigan.

Dragonet squeezed her hand but said nothing.

"I failed ye too," said Morrigan.

"No, you never failed me. But I have failed my…" Dragonet's voice trailed off into the shadows of the cave.

"Failed yer what?" asked Morrigan.

Dragonet paused and took a deep breath. "I suppose it cannot matter now. My father, he is the bishop of Troyes. It is he who sent me on this quest."

"Yer father is a bishop?"

Dragonet nodded. "I have never before spoken these words. My mother told me the name of my true father on her deathbed. After she died, there was no one left. I was hungry, slowly starving to death. In desperation I went to my father. He saved my life, but he made me promise I would never reveal him as my father. He said I was to blame for the plague coming to our house. I was evil, born in sin, the result of my mother's seduction."

"What?!"

"He swore that if I ever revealed to anyone who was my true sire, I would burn forever in the fires of hell. He gave me a taste of what it would be like, the burns you saw on my back."

"That bastard!"

"I was young. His words, they had a lasting impression on me. He also said I could redeem myself in his eyes and God's, if I would serve him well. He sent me to the Hospitallers to search for this silver box, which I did for years before finally coming to the conclusion it was gone."

"He used ye! What a horrid man!"

"I thought if I could bring back this box to him, I could finally be right in his eyes. I could prove my worth. Maybe earn the right to be called his son."

"So that is why ye lied to me."

"Yes. I never meant to hurt you. I am truly very sorry."

"Enough. No more apologies. Ye do ken yer father was a coldhearted manipulative bastard, dinna ye?"

Dragonet shrugged.

"I thought my family was bad. Ye make us look like we overflow wi' loving kindness. My father was a tough, old man, but he loved me and wanted what was best for me. Archie is a fool and a failure, but even he tried to look out for me in his own way. 'Tis what family does."

"You have a good family."

"Ye'd be the first to say it, but compared to what ye survived…" Morrigan choked back sudden tears at the recognition of all she had and all she was going to lose. "I do have a good family," she said softly, squeezing his hand. It was a rotten way to die, but at least she was not alone.

They sat there together. Quiet, but comfortable. Of all the family she was going to miss, Dragonet counted among them.

Morrigan stared at the wooden chest. It was a large chest, and she wondered idly how the Templars had moved such a chest through all the passages.

"How did they get that chest in here?" asked Morrigan. "It winna fit through the gate."

Dragonet turned to look at the gate and back at the chest. "You are right," he said slowly. He stood up and offered her a hand up as well. "I was wondering why the torchlight will sometimes flicker, as if it is moved by the faintest wind."

Excitement grew like a wave. "Do ye think there is another way out?" asked Morrigan.

"I intend to find one."

Morrigan smiled. She liked fighting much better than despair. She looked around, trying to find a small passage. Dragonet lay on the floor and looked around the bottom of the cave, while she scanned the top.

"Look there!" she called eagerly. "It looks like a small *C* carved above those rocks."

"Compline!" shouted Dragonet. "How could I forget? The last prayer is compline."

Morrigan crawled over the rocks under the *C* but could find no passage. "There is nothing here."

Dragonet picked up a large rock and tossed it behind him. "So we make a way."

Morrigan smiled again. She liked this man.

Twenty-Four

HOW LONG THEY WORKED MOVING ROCKS AND STONES, Morrigan could not guess. Her shoulders ached, her back screamed, the muscles in her arms shook with fatigue, but she kept going. Every time she felt she must rest, she found Dragonet had doubled his efforts. He was determined and strong and persistent and all sorts of other lovely qualities. She liked the way his muscles rippled when he heaved a stone. She liked that he never once complained. She liked… him.

Dragonet heaved a large rock away from the top of the heap. "Rock!" he called as it rolled down the pile. The waning torch flickered. They both saw it and turned to each other, their eyes meeting.

"Did ye break through?" Morrigan scrambled up to the top of the pile where Dragonet stood.

Dragonet reached with his hand. "Yes, I think I did!"

Morrigan whooped with delight and began throwing rocks aside, heedless of her aching back. Dragonet was beside her, pulling and scraping with everything he had. Soon they uncovered a small hole. It was impossible to see the other side, but the air was colder and fresher, which gave them hope. Dragonet heaved away one more large rock, and the hole was large enough to fit through.

Morrigan fetched the torch and tried to see what was on the other side. "No good. I canna see. The angle is wrong. Well, one way to find out." Morrigan gave the torch to Dragonet and turned around to go through the space, legs first.

"I can go first if you wish," said Dragonet.

"No, I want out!"

"Careful," he said holding the torch in one hand and her hand in the other. He slowly helped to lower her down.

Morrigan found that squeezing through the small space backward was not particularly helpful for keeping her blanket covering what it ought. A cold wind across her backside was evidence of it. She sincerely hoped no one was on the other side watching her inelegant egress.

She dangled for a moment, then with Dragonet's help lowered herself down until her feet found purchase and she was able to scramble down. She landed in some sort of cave or passage, which she could barely see, the orange glow from the cave she just left the only light.

"I dinna ken where I am, but it is safe," called Morrigan.

She peered into the inky darkness trying to see where she was, a process made easier when Dragonet slipped down, somehow managing to carry the lit torch with him. It was clear they were in a tunnel.

"We go this way," said Dragonet, pointing in one direction.

"How do ye know?" asked Morrigan.

"Look at the torch flicker. Wind is coming from this direction."

They both headed down the passage until the wind blew harder and colder. In the distance Morrigan saw white. She walked faster, and then ran.

"Snow!" She ran to it, grabbing it with both hands. Their clothes were still laid out on the boulders. "We found the entrance to the cave!" She jumped on him in her excitement. She was free. She was out of the cave! He wrapped his free arm around her and pulled her close. They stood there for a moment, holding each other tight. They had escaped.

"Hey!" cried Morrigan, breaking free and looking around the mouth of the cave. "My horse is gone!"

"Mal made his way out. Look, fresh blood in the snow." Dragonet held up the torch, and she could see it was true.

"Bastard stole my horse." She neglected to mention that the horse in question had been procured through less than righteous means.

"More blood on the floor of the cave," said Dragonet, inspecting with his torch.

"Fool will bleed to death if he doesna wrap his wound. Doubt anyone will miss him."

"We need that silver chest," said Dragonet.

"And I still need medicine for Andrew."

Dragonet nodded. "About the things I told you when I thought we were trapped forever." Dragonet brushed the hair back from his face and stared out the mouth of the cave. "I ask for your discretion."

"Mayhap it would be best if we never speak o' what happened in this cave."

"Agreed."

They struggled around a large boulder partially blocking the entrance of the cave and through some frozen bushes to the outside. Blizzard-force wind struck them hard with ice pellets and snow. Morrigan raised her arm to shield her face and struggled a few steps into the deep drifts of snow, the icy wind freezing her bare skin.

Dragonet tugged at her arm and shook his head. They both went back into the relative protection of the cave.

"We canna make it in that blizzard," said Morrigan. "No' dressed like this. We'll freeze. Damn him for taking my horse."

"Even with the horse it would be difficult," said Dragonet. "We need to dry our clothes and let the storm pass before we can make it out."

"I have an idea!" Morrigan grabbed her war ax from the frozen floor and tramped back into the darkness of the cave. "Come, I will need yer help for this! If we move some rocks and a few o' these boulders..." her voice trailed off into the quiet of the stone cave.

Confused, Dragonet followed her.

A little while later Morrigan and Dragonet sat on rocks beside a crackling fire, holding their garments in front of the flames to dry. Morrigan's idea indeed had been brilliant. The lid of the cedar chest had been broken apart to make an excellent fire.

"Now if only we had something to eat. I had food in the saddlebags," Morrigan grumbled.

"More hot brew?" asked Dragonet. He had found a ceramic cup in the pocket of his cloak, and they packed it with snow and melted it over the fire to form a hot drink. Hot water, actually, but "brew" sounded less like deprivation.

"Nay. I'll get more wood for the fire."

Morrigan returned a short time later, her arms filled with scrolls.

"Do not even think it," said Dragonet, standing up, his eyes narrowed into glittering slits.

"We need to dry our clothes and be gone from here."

"No!" Dragonet stepped toward her with murder in his eye.

Morrigan took a step back before she remembered she never backed down. "We need to stay warm," she said, but with less confidence.

Dragonet wrapped his arms around her waist and drew her to him, the scrolls forming an uncomfortable barrier between them. "If you need warming, I will see it done."

"I… I…" Morrigan's mouth went dry, and her breath came fast. Heat flushed through her and settled in her core.

He took the scrolls from her limp arms. "You cold now?"

She shook her head. She was many things, but cold? No, not cold in the least.

"Go get something else to burn."

"Aye," answered Morrigan. She was prying off one of the wooden sides to the cedar chest before she remembered no one ordered her about. What was she thinking?

When she returned to the fire, it was with the determination to give him a good dose of her mind. He was standing in front of the fire wearing naught but a pair of breeches. The scars on his back were clearly visible, which made her ache with sympathy. His muscles glowed in the orange light of the fire, which made her ache with something else.

"I believe your breeches and linen tunic they are dry enough to wear," he said, holding them out to her.

"Thank ye. I brought more wood for the fire."

"Thank you. More brew?"

"Yes, please."

Dragonet averted his eyes, and Morrigan slipped into warm clothes, then sat on a rock near the fire and sipped her tea. She was vaguely aware she was going to say something to him, but she could not recall what it was, so it must not have been important.

She smiled. He smiled back. If only her brother's life was not on the line, she would be happy to stay.

She drank her "brew" and knew the magic could not last.

⤚⤙

Dragonet stacked the books neatly on the flat boulder in the gutting light of the torch, his hand lingering on them in a loving manner. The books were the real treasure, though he doubted his father would have sent him to Scotland to retrieve books and scrolls. He had examined them all, but other than the wonderful writings of Plato, Socrates, St.

Augustine, and a beautiful, illuminated Bible in four volumes, along with other magnificent works, there was nothing about the books or scrolls that would be particularly significant to his father. No, his father spoke of a silver box, but that held nothing but gold and jewels. As much as his father wanted riches, going to Scotland was hardly the most convenient way to collect them. So why was Dragonet sent on his quest?

Dragonet was warmer, wearing several layers of tunics, his breeches, woolen hose, and his warm, leather boots. Their cloaks still needed to dry, but that was all that remained before venturing outside. They had been drying their clothes for hours, sometimes catching a bit of sleep. They had taken turns going back for more firewood, and Dragonet was to haul the last piece, the bottom of the wooden chest.

Dragonet lifted it, but it was heavier and thicker than he anticipated. He had always been relatively strong for his size, so he heaved and lifted the wood in his hands. It was quite thick for a bottom, and something was strange about the sides. Was the piece hollow?

Dragonet turned to look just as the torch died, casting him in utter darkness. He stumbled forward, groping with his hands and pulling along the bottom of the chest as he went. After some searching, he found the hole out of the cave and tried to ease the wooden piece out but lost hold, and it crashed to the cave floor below.

Dragonet hoisted himself down and felt for the broken pieces of the chest.

"Dragonet? Did ye fall?"

"Bring a light!" he called back. There was definitely a hidden compartment in the chest.

Morrigan arrived, torch in hand. "What happened? Are ye hurt?"

Even with his excitement over the chest he still looked up at her and smiled. She had been able to dress in her men's clothing and was wearing several tunics, two pairs of breeches, woolen hose and her leather boots. It effectively hid her shape, but she was still beautiful in his eyes. Better yet, she was concerned for his welfare. It was wrong, no doubt, but very nice.

"The bottom of the chest, it had a false bottom. Something is inside."

"What?" Morrigan's eyes flew open wide. "Let me see." She crouched down beside him with the torch.

Dragonet gently pried back the boards and revealed a purple velvet bag, tied with a braided gold rope. He swallowed hard. This was it. This must have been what his father had sought for all these years.

"What is inside?" asked Morrigan, impatient.

Dragonet opened the bag with trembling hands. He prayed silently to be worthy to receive the gift.

"Come on!" urged Morrigan. She was always one to leap and then look where she was going as she fell. She was a good match for his more cautious nature.

Dragonet reached in and touched something that felt like fabric. The hairs on the back of his neck stood on end, and he pulled back his hand, unsure what had just happened.

"Go on then," said Morrigan.

Dragonet took a breath. He must be letting his imagination get the better of him. He reached in once more and pulled out a square of folded linen. He unfolded it a few times, but nothing was inside it, so he folded it back. He reached into the bag again, but there was nothing else inside.

"Is that it?" Morrigan asked. "What is it? A linen sheet?"

Dragonet himself was confused. "Let us gather these pieces and inspect them by the fire."

Morrigan stood up with her hands on her hips. "It doesna look like a holy grail to me," she grumbled, but she helped him pick up the pieces and together they carried all the bits to the fire pit where they had set up rocks for sitting and drying clothes.

Dragonet inspected all the bits of wood from the false bottom of the chest, but there were no clues there. It must be something in the purple bag. Why else create a secret hiding place for it? The jewels in the silver case were meant as a distraction from the true treasure. But where was it?

"Maybe something was wrapped in that cloth that has been since removed," suggested Morrigan.

Dragonet nodded. He had to admit it was a possibility. "Let's take a look at the cloth." He took it out from the velvet bag and again felt a tremor of excitement and fear. What was it? He started to unfold it and found it was quite large. He motioned to Morrigan to help, and she held one end while he held the other. Together they carefully held it out to its full length, about fourteen feet long and four feet wide.

"What is it?" asked Morrigan. "What is on it?"

The first thing he noted were some triangular markings that were repeated four times down the sheet, forming two lines on either side of the cloth.

But there was something else, markings in between the patterns.

"Odd shape," said Morrigan. "Like a winding sheet."

"A burial cloth," he murmured, trying to discern the markings. "Look, it is the image of a man, front and back, his arms crossed in front of him." A tingling shock ran though him.

"I see it! But it is oddly painted; why the colors are all backwards. Whoever made it did a poor job."

"Is that blood on the cloth?" asked Dragonet.

"Could be," said Morrigan slowly. "Looks like this man has suffered. Is that blood on his head, his side, and his arms? Are those holes in his wrist and his feet?" She looked up at him, her eyes wide. "What is this?"

"I do not know," said Dragonet. "But I think I know what the Templars thought it was. The burial cloth of—"

"Take it!" demanded Morrigan. "I should no' be holding it. Take it away from me!"

They quickly but carefully folded it the way it was and placed it back into the velvet bag. Morrigan sat back on a rock. She was noticeably shaking.

"So ye truly believe…" Morrigan lowered her voice as if not to be overheard by the stones. "Do ye think that is the burial cloth of… of… *Jesus*?" she whispered the name.

"I do not know. But I think the Templars believed it was. Little wonder they went back to France to retrieve it." He had done it. He had found the relic his father had wanted, but somehow he was more confused than ever. Should his father have possession of such a cloth?

"I never thought… that is, I have heard of Jesus

dying on the cross, but I never thought of him as being a real man. It must have been horrible."

Dragonet stared at the purple velvet bag. He had never thought that way either.

"How come God dinna like him? Why did he make him suffer?"

"Suffering is not a sign of God's displeasure with you."

"Truly? I always thought it explained the basic course of my life. Why then would he suffer like that?" Morrigan gestured toward the cloth.

"'*Ipse autem vulneratus est propter iniquitates nostras adtritus est propter scelera nostra disciplina pacis nostrae super eum et livore eius sanati sumus,*'" quoted Dragonet.

"Pardon?"

"It is from the prophet Isaiah. It says that he was pierced for our transgressions, he was crushed for our iniquities, and by his wounds we are healed."

"Healed o' what?"

"Our sins. Christ took the punishment for our wrongdoing so we can be forgiven."

"But why?"

"'*Sic enim dilexit Deus mundum ut Filium suum unigenitum daret ut omnis qui credit in eum non pereat sed habeat vitam aeternam.*'"

"Ye do realize quoting Latin to me is no' particularly helpful."

"I beg your pardon. It is from the gospel of St. John. It says God loved the world so much he sent his son to save the world, that those who believe in him may have eternal life."

"So because I did what was wrong, Jesus took my punishment, and now I can be right with God?"

"That is the essence of the Gospel." Dragonet had studied hard and learned well. His theology was sound, even if his practice was weak.

"Do ye truly believe that?"

Did he? Dragonet stopped and thought a moment. He reviewed his life, the things he experienced, the mistakes he had made, the times he had prayed. He had taken his vows to be a monk because his father told him to, and because he had little other chance of getting fed.

No one had ever asked him what he believed. And yet… he did believe it. He believed. For one moment of crystal clarity he saw the lies his father had told him for what they were, and the power his father held over him began to crack.

"I do believe," said Dragonet. He sat up taller; his shoulders felt lighter. "Do you?"

"I ne'er thought about it. I always figured I was damned, so what was the point. I ne'er thought someone else would take my place in the punishment. Ye truly believe I could be forgiven?"

"Yes. I know you can."

"I have been a liar and a thief, and I even tried to take the life of a bishop."

"God can forgive all. Even the greatest of sinners. Even you."

"Ye are charity itself." Morrigan said with an arch of one eyebrow. "Maybe. I dinna ken. I must think on it."

They both stared at the velvet bag, but it simply lay there. "What shall we do wi' it?" asked Morrigan. "And why do yer father and Abbot Barrick want it so badly?"

"This shroud, if deemed authentic, it would be an important relic, perhaps greater than any other. Whoever controls it would become powerful. Pilgrims would come see it. Wealthy patrons would pay to see it displayed. The Church might even build a cathedral to house it."

"So that is why Barrick petitioned the Church for a cathedral to be built."

"He must not get control of it."

"Aye, and yer father neither."

Dragonet paused. He held the one thing that could prove his worth to his father. Could he really let it slip away? "Then what is to be done? I have devoted years to this quest."

"Ye could make a living as a minstrel."

Dragonet shook his head. "My instrument I gave to a girl of my fancy."

"That was a mite shortsighted," said Morrigan, trying to hide a smile.

A man in love does foolish things. Dragonet smiled in return. There were still so many things he knew he should not say.

Silence permeated the cave, the velvet bag and its mysterious contents lying on a rock between them, small, and yet an impenetrable wall.

"The cloaks must be dry enough to travel," said Morrigan, staring straight ahead, the light from the fire casting a warm glow on her face. She was beautiful. "Shall we fight for the cloth now or later?" And deadly.

"Later. Let us see if we can get the medicine for Andrew without resorting to doing each other bodily harm. Besides, Barrick said he wanted the box, not the cloth."

"True. Ye agree to come wi' me? Until we get this matter resolved, I dinna wish to have that bag out o' my sight."

"Agreed," said Dragonet. He did not wish to let either the bag or the girl sitting next to him out of his sight. But of course keeping both of them would never be possible. Eventually he would have to choose.

Twenty-Five

"I WILL COME BACK FOR YOU." DRAGONET TURNED toward the cave to give a final farewell.

"Ye do know ye are talking to books." Morrigan raised an eyebrow at him.

"They have always spoken to me."

"That's more than I wanted to know." Morrigan continued to struggle through the deep snow.

The blizzard had mostly passed, though the sky remained gray and the hour was difficult to determine. Dragonet had put the books and scrolls back into the secret cave. Though the hole to the secret cave remained, it would be difficult to find unless one knew where to look.

Dragonet hid the purple velvet pouch holding the Templar relic in an interior pocket of his cloak. Morrigan did not wish to touch it, for she swore the cloth had burned her fingers once she realized what it was, or could be. She did not know what to make of it.

Her stomach growled with determined menace. She had ignored it too long. Maybe after a good meal they could determine what to do next.

The small village of Kimlet was an energetic hike from the cave. They arrived in time for the midday meal, and both Morrigan and Dragonet ate until their stomachs groaned for quite the opposite reason.

"I have eaten myself sick. Feels great," said Morrigan. "Now what?"

"Ask around. See what we can discover of our friend Mal. We must find the silver box."

"Aye," said Morrigan, though in truth she would have been quite content with a warm bath and a nap. Or even better, a warm bath, gingerbread, and a nap. Dragonet stood up from the table and stretched lazily. Morrigan's mind went rogue. Best of all would be a warm bath with Dragonet, slow sex all afternoon, and then a good, long sleep.

Morrigan stood and shook her head to dispel the fantasy. That man had ruined her. He had made her forget the gingerbread.

"Morrigan?" asked Dragonet. He was looking at her oddly. She guessed that was not the first time he had said her name.

"Aye? What? Let's move!" She bustled ahead, leaving him in her inarticulate wake.

Mal's location was surprisingly easy to ascertain. According to the innkeeper, he had checked in yesterday and had been feeling poorly. He paid to have a dispatch sent to the abbey. That morning a monk arrived and spent a short time with Mal. When the monk left, he told the host that the man was sick and needed to be left alone to rest, which the good innkeeper had done, not disturbing the man.

"Was this monk an elderly man, but sturdy built with square shoulders and a mean look?" asked Morrigan.

The innkeeper was slightly taken aback. "I dinna wish to speak unkindly about a monk, but… yes, he was as ye described."

"Which room is he in?" asked Dragonet. "Do not fear; we shall not disturb him."

"I warrant no one can disturb him now," muttered Morrigan to Dragonet, who nodded in agreement.

They went up to Mal's room and Dragonet paused outside the door. "Best let me go in first."

"Nonsense!"

They entered the room and found what they both expected, Mal dead on the bed.

"Is he?" asked Morrigan.

Dragonet briefly inspected the body. "Yes, quite. I can still smell the poison on his lips."

"You think it was Barrick?"

"Very likely. I would suppose Mal found he could not go on, sent to Barrick for help, and got this instead."

Morrigan nodded. "I dinna suppose there would be any point in looking for the silver box."

"Barrick, he must have it now," said Dragonet, but they made a search of the room for the sake of completeness. It was a small room, serviceable, but not many places for an injured man to hide a silver box, which was indeed gone.

"What now?" asked Morrigan. "I still need to get the medicine for Andrew."

"Let us go to the abbey. Maybe we could find a way to steal the medicine. No matter what we gave

Barrick, I would not trust him to give us the right bottle, as our friend Mal discovered too late."

"Agreed." Morrigan worried for a moment that Barrick sent poison to Andrew instead of medicine, if he sent anything at all. Morrigan sighed and forced herself to follow Dragonet back downstairs. She could do nothing about it now. The best she could do was to find the medicine and return to Andrew as soon as possible.

Dragonet calmly explained to the Innkeeper that Mal was doing quite poorly indeed and an undertaker might best serve him. Before they left Kimlet, Dragonet collected a few personal effects he had left at the inn, paid the innkeeper, and retrieved his horse. Morrigan also found her mount in the stables, and they were quickly on their way.

They were allies, but how long could it last?

⁂

Dragonet drew his cloaks closer against the biting wind. It was cold, but the snow had stopped, making travel slightly easier. They should reach St. Margaret's before nightfall, but then what? They must get the medicine for Andrew, and Morrigan would need to race back home to save her brother. Once he helped her find the medicine, there was nothing else to keep him in Scotland. He was still a monk. He was still on a mission. It was time to go home.

He had the relic his father had desired for years. He would finally prove to the old man he was not useless, unworthy of his notice. He would earn his father's respect, perhaps even make the old man proud. He would… Dragonet paused in his familiar rendition of how he could finally prove his worthiness to his father. What would his father really do?

"What are ye going to do wi' the shroud?" asked Morrigan, as if she could read his thoughts.

Dragonet considered the question for a moment, rocking gently in the saddle as his horse plodded through the snow. "Give it to my father, unless… in truth I do not know."

"I still need to get the medicine for Andrew."

"Even if you gave the abbot this relic, he may not give to you the medicine."

"So ye're going to give it to yer bastard father?"

"I am the bastard, I fear."

"Not in anything that counts."

Dragonet smiled. "Thank you.

"Ye canna give him this relic!"

"Many years have I sought to prove my worthiness to my father. This relic, it would redeem me in his eyes."

"I thought 'twas God who did the redeeming." Morrigan gave him a hard look.

She was right. He had fought so long against his father's disdain, trying to prove his worth, he had never stopped to consider why he struggled so hard to win the respect of a man he could not like. So what to do with the relic? Dare he give the shroud to another? Dragonet shuddered from more than the freezing wind. His father's rage would know no bounds.

"Hold there!" Four large, mounted men in black cloaks rode into view, their hoods and mufflers disguising much of their faces. Dragonet stopped short and scanned for weapons or signs of threat. He found none visible, but experience had made him cautious. "Who are you? Identify yourself!" called Dragonet.

"Are ye Sir Dragonet and Morrigan McNab?" asked a cloaked rider who blocked their path.

Dragonet glanced at Morrigan, but she gave a barely perceivable shrug. These were not friends of hers.

"Who wants to know?" demanded Morrigan, her hand on the hilt of her sword.

"We are friends. Mother Enid sent us to find ye and give ye the medicine ye requested."

"Mother Enid found more medicine? Where is she?" asked Morrigan.

"Follow me," said the cloaked man.

He turned his horse, and they followed him down the road and off onto a side path, and wound uphill through snow-covered trees and shrubs. The path narrowed so they could only ride single file; two cloaked men went first, followed by Morrigan and Dragonet, followed by two more cloaked men.

The men stopped at a cozy cottage, built on the side of the forested hill. Dragonet guessed it was a hunting box of some sort, but why Mother Enid, who did not appear to him to be the traveling sort, would be in a hunting box, he could not say. Four more cloaked men were outside the cottage.

Dragonet was suspicious. He dismounted with the others and drew close to Morrigan. "Be wary."

"Always," she whispered in return.

One of the men pointed at the hunting box. It was a snug little cottage, smoke rising from the stone chimney with the promise of warmth. The sun shone brightly on the pristine snow, giving the landscape a shimmering glow. His fingered the hilt of his sword. It might be a trap, but if there was any chance the medicine they needed to save Andrew was inside, Morrigan would be going in. And so he would too.

"No weapons," said the man, standing by the door.

"Mother Enid can tell me that herself," said Morrigan, brushing past him into the hut.

Dragonet followed her into the small one-room cottage. The little house was sparsely furnished and dark compared to the blinding sun outside. A small table was at one side of the room near a window, shuttered against the cold. The cloaked men remained outside in the snow. They must have been soldiers.

A figure was seated beside the fire. He turned and gave them a cold smile. It was Abbot Barrick.

"How nice of you to see me," said the abbot.

"How kind o' ye to send one o' yer lackeys to kill me," retorted Morrigan, drawing her sword.

"Now let us be civil," chided Barrick. "I have something you want, and if I not mistaken, you have something I want."

"What do ye want? I trust ye already have the silver box. That was the deal. Now give me the medicine!" demanded Morrigan.

Barrick shook his head. "So impulsive. So aggressive. It is not seemly in a lady. But then, you were never that."

"Enough, Barrick," said Dragonet. "What do you want?"

"You know exactly what I want. I want the shroud. 'Tis mine and I shall have it."

"You have everything that was in the box," said Morrigan. "We took naught from it. Not one coin."

"Who cares about a few measly coins," sneered Barrick.

"I do! If ye care naught for it, I'd be most obliged if ye give it back," said Morrigan.

"Where is it, *Brother Dragonet*?" Barrick ignored Morrigan and glared at Dragonet. "Do you think I do not know what you are? You are a Hospitaller knight sent to find the shroud!"

Dragonet internally recoiled at his words, but experience kept his face without expression. How could Barrick possibly know who he was? "I am a knight, yes. But who says I am a monk?"

"You did. I heard you pray with us before the meal."

"Many knights pray."

"You prayed as a French monk."

"I am French, yes. As are you."

"*Oui*. A French monk. There are prayers only a French monk would know."

"The good monks helped to raise me. I am not the only orphan for whom that is true."

"Yes, in truth I was suspicious about you from the moment you came onto the abbey grounds, but I was not sure. I'll admit you kept your cover better than the others who came before you. It was the only reason I let you leave the abbey alive. But now I find you searching for the relic, so I know the truth. Denials at this late point in the game are futile. Now where is it, Brother?"

Silence permeated the cottage. Dragonet tried to form the words to deny he was a Hospitaller monk, but could not. He was tired of lying.

"Where is the medicine?" asked Morrigan.

"I have it."

"Show me."

Barrick withdrew his left hand from his robes, revealing a small bottle. His right hand, Dragonet noted, he kept hidden in his robes.

"And how do I know if that bottle is Mother Enid's medicine or the same poison ye used to kill Mal?" asked Morrigan.

"Ah, you found our poor Mal. He was dying anyway... probably." Barrick shrugged. "I merely hastened his death along. He was of no use to me as a cripple. Here, see for yourself. The bottle is sealed with Enid's own stamp. It has not been touched." Barrick held up the bottle, and Morrigan stepped closer to inspect the seal, remaining out of arm's reach. She was still too close for Dragonet's liking.

"Now, Sir Dragonet. Give me the shroud. It is mine; I will have it," demanded Barrick.

"We told you, the silver box, it held coins and jewels, not a shroud as you say," said Dragonet. He tried to get Morrigan's attention. She was much too close to the bastard.

"If it is yers, why no' get it yerself?" asked Morrigan.

"Because he does not know where it is," answered Dragonet. "You told me about my life, now I will tell you about yours. You were a Templar when they fled to Scotland to escape persecution, but young then, merely a boy. Later, the Templars went back to France to retrieve certain items that had been given to the Hospitallers. The Templars hid them in the cave on McNab land, but they did not tell you where they hid them. Perhaps they thought you too young. More likely they did not trust you."

"My superiors in the order could not see the potential for the shroud. I always knew it was only a matter of time before I obtained it."

"You have long known the shroud was in the cave, but you feared if you revealed it too soon, the church would merely take it away from you, so you sought to gain power in the church. You requested permission to build a cathedral, but it was denied. You even tried to have the McNabs kill the bishop of Glasgow so you could take his position, but fortunately that failed too." Dragonet stepped closer to Barrick. "Now you have learned that the bishop has gone to the pope. You are desperate. You must get the shroud now to try to hold on to your position. You are afraid."

Barrick narrowed his eyes and revealed his right hand, which held a loaded crossbow. "I can see you need some added incentive." Barrick leveled his weapon at Morrigan. "Give me the shroud. Since you know me so well, you understand without me needing to make any vulgar threats that I will not hesitate to kill her, nor will I miss."

Dragonet's heart pounded in his ears. He struggled to remain calm. He needed to do something quickly before Morrigan was dead. Barrick would think nothing of killing her.

"I know where it is," said Dragonet. "Let her go. I will take you there."

"Where. Tell me."

"I left the true treasure in the cave," said Dragonet. "I can show you."

Barrick shook his head. "Why would you leave it in the cave?" He aimed at Morrigan. "Do not lie to me. You have it. You must. Guards! Have you searched their horses?" Barrick shouted.

"Aye!" came the answer from outside. "'Tis naught here."

"I tire of this game." Barrick stood with a menacing glare. "Perhaps you need to be shown the depth of my commitment to finding the shroud. Or perhaps you do not care for her overmuch. Either way, her time is gone."

"No!" shouted Dragonet. "I have it here. And I swear if you kill her you will shortly join her in death."

"Show me!" demanded Barrick, glancing between her and him.

Dragonet needed to give Morrigan a chance. A minute of distraction would be all she would need, and hopefully she would seize the opportunity.

"It is very fragile," said Dragonet. "It must be done carefully." He searched the interior pockets of his cloak.

"I should not have to tell you, if you pull a weapon, she is dead," commented Barrick.

Dragonet moved slowly to the side of the room, away from Morrigan, making it more difficult for Barrick to look at both of them at the same time.

"This is what you have been waiting to see," said Dragonet, producing the velvet pouch and placing it on the table. He did not open it but let Barrick see it clearly.

"Yes!" Barrick hissed, his eyes on the pouch.

Morrigan charged forward, pushing the crossbow up. The shot fired into the ceiling.

"Guards!" shouted Barrick.

Dragonet drew his sword and rushed to Morrigan, who had a sword in one hand, her battle-ax in the other. Six guards streamed into the room, swords drawn. Dragonet ran to the far window and kicked out the shutters.

"Go!" Dragonet pushed Morrigan to the window and she jumped through it. Dragonet engaged the first soldier, blocking his attack and knocking him back into his comrades, giving Dragonet time to escape out the window.

Dragonet ran around the cottage to the horse and found Morrigan engaged with two guards. He helped decide the contest, and they mounted quickly and galloped down the path, the six remaining soldiers following behind.

"Follow me!" shouted Morrigan and spurred her horse straight down the side of the hill, rejecting the safer trail.

Dragonet inhaled sharply, his lungs burning with the cold. She was either going to save them or get them both killed. Dragonet urged his mount forward and went over the edge onto the steep hillside. He followed Morrigan's descent, though he was certain his horse was slipping helplessly past the trees and rocks. Snow and ice pellets sprayed up at him, blinding him, branches of trees whipped him as he flew by. He sincerely hoped she knew what she was doing.

"Turn! Turn right now!" screamed Morrigan from somewhere in the trees.

Turn? She must be mad. Still Dragonet pulled up

on the reins and leaned hard to the right. His horse struggled and slipped farther down.

"Turn now or ye'll fall!"

Ahead Dragonet saw nothing but bright blue sky. He pulled back hard to the right and swung his body into the hillside. His mount scrambled and labored but found footing and turned right onto a small ledge. His horse stopped and Dragonet leaned forward, trying to catch his breath. Both horse and rider were breathing hard.

"Oh, thank heaven ye're not dead!" exclaimed Morrigan, appearing through the trees.

"Are you trying to kill me?" The words slipped out before he could arrest them. Blind panic can do that to a man.

"It was a shortcut."

"It was daft!"

"We got away. I doubt they will follow us."

Dragonet took a deep breath, his lungs burning from the effort and the cold. Several retorts flitted through his mind, which he rejected. Before him was a spectacular vantage of the valley, sparkling white in the brilliant January sun. His mount shuddered and grunted, pawing the ground near the cliff from which they had nearly fallen to their deaths.

"You are right. Thank you for helping us escape, but I fear my horse will never forgive you for the fright you gave us."

Morrigan's face warmed with a half smile, the one she used when she did not wish to admit she found him amusing.

"The shroud, did ye give it to him?" asked Morrigan.

"Yes."

"Why did ye no' toss a knife in him?"

"I would have had to kill him instantly to prevent him from taking a shot at you. Even in death his hand may have twitched and the bolt would have flown. I had to distract him so you could attack."

"But the relic… we worked so hard to get it."

"You are to me more precious." Until the words left his mouth, he did not know how much they were true. From the moment Barrick had a crossbow to Morrigan's head, her life was all that mattered. The relic was nothing to him compared to her.

Morrigan surveyed the crystalline landscape. "Thank ye." Her cheeks were flushed red from the cold and the exertion. Her hair was completely wrapped in a long, brown stocking cap. It could be an attractive look for no one, but still… he only had eyes for her.

Which, considering he was still a monk and had a relic to steal back, was a bit of a problem.

Twenty-Six

MORRIGAN AND DRAGONET RODE HARD FOR SEVERAL hours to reach St. Margaret's Convent. They needed a place to regroup before trying to regain the medicine and the shroud. How they were going to manage such a feat, Morrigan had no idea. She should be thinking strategies; instead she pondered Dragonet's actions.

He had given away the relic for her. He must love her more. He *loved* her? Her heart soared far into the bright blue sky.

But he was still a monk. Her heart plummeted down to the dirty snow, chopped and tossed about by the laboring horses. There would be no happy ending for her and none for Andrew either if she did not find a way to get the medicine. She needed to focus on getting the medicine.

They came over a rise where St. Margaret's Convent was situated in the valley below. Morrigan stopped short, staring at the scene below.

"What is all this?" asked Dragonet, reining in next to her.

"I dinna ken."

Below them were myriad tents and banners littering the valley around the convent. Hundreds of people milled about, horses and livestock corralled into several makeshift pens, and small, smoldering fires rose thin ribbons of smoke into the cloudless sky. The colors were bright and vibrant against the background of the white snow.

"How long were we in that cave?" asked Morrigan.

With an exchanged glance they spurred their horses onward and raced down the hill toward St. Margaret's. Hopefully Mother Enid could enlighten them as to her sudden increase in visitors.

After some difficulty finding a place to house their mounts and getting the attention of a flustered nun managing multiple guests' demands, Morrigan and Dragonet were shown to a private sitting area where a small group of people huddled around a fire.

"Morrigan, Sir Dragonet, come join us by the fire, you must be cold," said Mother Enid, calling them over. Mother Enid sat beside another woman, with red curls peeking from beneath her wimple and dressed in a fur-trimmed, wool gown. Standing next to her was a large, broad-shouldered man with a wicked scar carved from his left eye to his chin. Beside him was the tall, impeccably dressed figure of Chaumont.

Morrigan approached the party with some reservations. These were well-dressed, high-class people. These were the kind she would rob, not sit with by the fire on a cold winter's day. The large man turned toward her, giving her a hard look. No, she amended herself. That man she would let ride by unmolested.

"Lady MacLaren," said Mother Enid, speaking to

the seated lady beside her. "Allow me to present Lady Morrigan McNab and Sir Dragonet."

"Pleased to meet ye both," said Lady MacLaren with a pretty smile.

Morrigan stopped dead, her heart dropping beneath the floorboards. MacLaren? This was Lady MacLaren? The MacLarens hated, despised, and loathed the McNabs.

"You are acquainted with Sir Chaumont, I believe," continued Mother Enid, looking at Morrigan.

"Yes, I have had the pleasure of meeting the *mademoiselle* many times," Chaumont gave her a winning smile. "Dragonet, good to see you again, *mon ami.*"

"Have you then also met Laird MacLaren?" asked Mother Enid.

Morrigan took a breath and glanced at the door. Was he going to attack her now or wait for fewer witnesses?

"We have not met." MacLaren's voice was authoritative. Final.

Morrigan took a step back. She had no business being there.

"We were surprised to find you have so many visitors, Mother Enid," said Dragonet, oblivious to the danger. "Can you tell us the reason?"

"Yes, of course, though I believe MacLaren or Chaumont could do a better job than I. Apparently, the war goes ill and the clans have been called to meet here to plan their final stand against the English."

"The town of Berwick fell?" asked Dragonet.

"Berwick was abandoned after we left. The English took it without a fight," said Chaumont.

"It would have been an ugly fight," commented Dragonet.

"Trouble is, there was no one to prevent the English from invading north," said MacLaren in a deep voice. "King Edward has claimed the throne of Scotland and means to take possession of this country."

"We have been invaded by England?" asked Morrigan, alarmed.

"More conquered than invaded, I'd say," said Chaumont.

"Thought ye of all people would be pleased by that." MacLaren gave her a hard stare, his arms folded over his broad chest. He was a monster of a man.

"Lady Morrigan has fought against the English with distinction. She helped to take the Governor of Nisbet hostage and was wounded in the process." Dragonet stepped forward, as if to put himself between her and MacLaren. Foolish man.

"Yes, I can attest to that as well," said Chaumont. "Though I still am hurt you chose another to stitch your wound."

"Shows she has good sense," commented Lady MacLaren. "See the scar on my dear husband's face? 'Twas Chaumont's handiwork. The mere thought o' him wi' a needle makes me tremble wi' fear." She smiled, and everyone relaxed in the warmth of her eyes. Chaumont laughed outright, and even MacLaren smiled in return.

"I sent word to Lady MacLaren about your need for medicine for Andrew," said Mother Enid.

"Aye, I was distressed to learn that Barrick had stolen all Mother Enid's store o' medicine, especially when it is so desperately needed to treat the wounded," said Lady MacLaren. "Fortunately she taught me how to make it as well, and I brought what I had wi' me. I am afraid we arrived after ye left the convent a few days ago. Mother Enid told me o' yer great need so I sent a bottle on to McNab Hall. I hope yer brother will be well soon."

Morrigan stared at the woman, unable to speak. "Ye... ye sent Andrew the medicine?"

"Aye."

Dragonet brushed his hand against hers and smiled. He was happy for her, she knew. Morrigan glanced at Laird MacLaren. He stood as if ready for battle, his feet in a wide stance, his arms folded over his chest.

"Why?" asked Morrigan in honest confusion. "Why would ye o' all people help a McNab?"

"Mother Enid spoke o' yer need."

"But... but..." Morrigan could not form words. Her brother Archie had abducted Lady MacLaren years ago and tried to force her to marry him. How could she forgive their clan for that insult? "I thought ye hated us for what Archie..."

The fine lady shook her head. "Nay. 'Tis forgot. I carry no grudge against ye."

"Ye have forgiven us?" Morrigan's voice cracked. It was inconceivable. No one could forgive them.

"Aye. I forgave yer brother long ago. And against ye I have never felt any ill will."

Morrigan went down on a knee before Lady MacLaren. "Thank ye, my lady. This means more to me than I can say." Emotion formed a lump in her throat. She had almost killed herself trying to find Andrew a cure, and Lady MacLaren had given it freely.

The lady took her hand. "Please, will ye no' call me Aila?"

MacLaren cleared his throat, and Morrigan realized she had touched the Lady Aila, which must not be allowed. She jumped to her feet and stepped back.

"Ye have no' forgiven us." Morrigan spoke to the intimidating Laird MacLaren.

"My wife has virtues I do no' pretend to possess."

"I am glad of it," said Morrigan.

Laird MacLaren glanced down at his wife, who smiled up at him. "So am I," he said softly. The room grew quiet, and MacLaren cleared his throat. "Sir Dragonet, Chaumont has told me much about how ye helped him and Gavin. I am obliged to ye."

Dragonet bowed. "I am happy to be of service."

"We are meeting after supper this eve to discuss military plans to send King Edward back to England. Ye are welcome to join us if ye will," said MacLaren.

"Thank you, but I have other business to which I must attend."

His words struck Morrigan deep. This was the end. She had the medicine; he still needed the relic. He would go on without her. There was no reason for her to continue to stay with him. He would somehow retrieve the relic and return to France. His path was to a French monastery. Hers was back to McNab Hall. Alone.

"Thank ye, Mother Enid. Thank ye, Lady MacLaren. I canna tell ye how greatly I am in yer debt." With that pretty speech, Morrigan turned and strode from the room. She must get out to the fresh, cold air. Dragonet followed her into the frozen courtyard. She knew it without looking.

"I will help ye retrieve what was taken from us," said Morrigan, her back still to him.

"No," said Dragonet, just as she knew he would.

"I can help ye."

"I lost it today because I could not see you hurt. If I have to choose, I will choose you every time. If I want to retrieve the relic, I must go alone."

Morrigan took a ragged breath, as if ice water had flooded the cracks in her heart. He was saying good-bye. He was leaving her. She understood, but anger flooded through her in all its illogical power. She hated him for leaving her. She loved him for protecting her. She despised him for mending her heart, only to break it once more.

Morrigan whirled around to face the man who would abandon her. "Go! I have no need for ye and yer treasure hunts. Leave me be!"

Dragonet's eyes widened, like a trusting puppy who had been struck. They were not alone in the courtyard overflowing with soldiers, nuns, and camp followers. Several stopped to see what she was yelling about.

"Morrigan…" said Dragonet softly.

"Go about yer business, and I will go about mine. Ye need to leave, and I canna…" Morrigan looked away from the hurt in his eyes. "Just go." She turned and tramped through the dirty snow, her cold feet warm in comparison to her frozen heart.

A hand caught hers, and Dragonet pulled her into a small passage between two tents. It was a small space where they could talk unseen.

"What now?" demanded Morrigan.

"I cannot leave you angry. I will give to you a proper farewell."

"And what is a—"

Dragonet silenced her by kissing one of her cheeks, then the other. He then placed his hands on her cheeks and kissed her until her knees buckled.

"That is a proper farewell," he said.

"Ye monks are a friendly sort." Morrigan's head spun in a giddy sort of way.

"I am still a Frenchman, no?"

"Aye. 'Tis one of yer best features."

"*Au revoir, mon coeur.*"

"And the same to ye, whatever ye said. I'll be around all day if ye wish to come say good-bye again."

Dragonet left her with a smile.

✍

Dragonet wandered through the sea of tents, trying to devise a plan to retake the shroud, but instead he thought of Morrigan's lips on his and wondered if he would rather go say good-bye once more.

"Sir Dragonet!"

Dragonet turned toward the man and stepped back in shock. "Your Grace!" It was none other than the Duke of Argitaine. "I thought you had returned to France."

"Come into the tent; the wind blows fierce in these parts," said the duke. "We have found him, lads. I knew he would continue to fight with the Scots."

Dragonet followed the duke into the tent. Inside were three knights from the duke's personal guard, huddled around a brazier of coals. They acknowledged his entrance with small waves and nods.

"There is the man responsible for us freezing," said Sir Geoffrey. "I say we bury him in the snow for causing us woe." The smile he gave Dragonet was warmer than his words.

"But how are you here?" asked Dragonet.

"'Tis true, you are to blame," replied the duke. "Your words haunted me after we left. I needed to send the majority of the knights back to defend our country, but when the time came to board the ship myself, I found I could not leave with your words imputing my honor. I resolved to return and see this war through to the end." The duke gestured toward his three knights. "These poor souls volunteered to stay with me. Could not get rid of them, to be honest."

The three knights by the brazier waved and nodded once again.

"They are the bravest men of my company," said the duke with clear pride.

"Exchange 'brave' for 'foolish' and you speak the truth, Your Grace," said Geoffrey.

"I did not intend for my words to have this effect on you, Your Grace. My words, in hindsight, were foolish and rash. I beg your pardon for speaking them," said Dragonet.

The Duke of Argitaine smiled. "And yet you are still here."

"Yes, I… I helped take an injured man back home."

"Always an honorable man," said the duke, his smile returning. "You will join me tonight when we meet to discuss strategy. I fear there may be little we can do to prevent Scotland from falling to England, but I will at least be able to say I did not abandon the Scots before the war ended, even if it is not in their favor."

Dragonet sat on the offered bench by the brazier, his brain as numb as his toes. Perhaps the duke was right. He had been responsible for identifying clans to be given the offer of gold for joining the war party. Perhaps he should stay and see it through to the end with the duke.

He must retrieve the relic, and yet he had a duty to his honor as well. Dragonet closed his eyes and tried to reason through what was most important.

All he saw was Morrigan.

Twenty-Seven

"WE NEED TO STOP THEM BEFORE THEY CONQUER THE entire country. We must gather all our forces and march against them as soon as they cross the border," said Douglas.

Dragonet stood beside his fellow French knights in the crowded meeting tent. He was still unsure of his path, but accompanied his old friends to learn the plans to repel the English.

"Nay," said another man, "if we attack them in the open field, they will destroy us. We canna defeat so many trained English soldiers."

"We must meet them on the field of honor," said an elderly laird.

"And who would lead the charge? Ye?" asked Morrigan.

What was she doing in the meeting? Dragonet craned his neck to see her across the crowded tent. Should she not return home to Andrew?

Silence followed her question.

"What would ye do? Swear allegiance to England? I forgot, yer clan already did that," sneered Ramsey.

"If every clan represented in this room who had ever sworn allegiance to England at some point in their clan's history left the tent, there would be verra few standing," retorted Morrigan.

"Enough!" commanded Douglas. "We need a plan to deal wi' these Sassenach devils."

What followed were several ideas; all appeared to be doomed to failure. The unpleasant truth was they could not defeat the English army.

Dragonet wished he could stand next to Morrigan, but dared not. He was not even sure if she saw him. He actually missed being stuck in the cave, not the accommodations or the freezing temperatures, but the camaraderie he had with her. He swallowed hard. It was over. Their time had passed.

"We need time to prepare our forces," called out another man.

"We have no time. None. The English are upon us," said Douglas. He was looking older than the last time Dragonet saw him.

"Starve them!" All eyes turned to Morrigan. "Dinna try to stop them from coming into Scotland. Let them come, but take every scrap o' food, every cow, pig, and sheep, and give them naught to eat. Let them try to live off the land wi' that many mouths to feed. Take all the wood, burn the houses if you must, but leave them no way to find fuel either. I like my Englishmen cold and hungry."

There were loud, unpleasant grumblings as the assembled crowd considered the idea.

"I like it," pronounced MacLaren, much to the surprise of Dragonet and many in the room. "An army travels on its stomach. Without food they canna go far. But we need time to get all the food and people, out o' harm's way. King Edward winna take kindly to being inconvenienced."

"Send a message saying we wish to concede," said Morrigan. "While one of us negotiates the surrender, the rest scourge the land."

"Nay!" Many voices raised together in protest. "'Tis no' honorable!"

"Do you want your honor, or is it your freedom you wish to retain?" asked Dragonet. "Sometimes, you need to consider the needs of the whole, not simply your own personal honor." He looked at the duke when he spoke. The duke gave him a faint smile in return. Dragonet glanced across the room, and Morrigan gave him the smallest of nods in recognition.

"I will go," stated Douglas. "I will keep King Edward busy negotiating terms, then break it off and run. Much as it pains me, ye need to destroy everything in his path. Let us give him as poor a reception as we are able."

The men continued to talk about plans and strategies, and Dragonet continued to watch Morrigan. She took a keen interest in the proceedings and never again looked at him. Even when someone next to him spoke, she still averted her eyes. It took a lot of effort to give him absolutely no notice.

At last the meeting appeared to break up. Morrigan stomped from the tent and he followed. Why, he could not rightly say. She was a bright flame, and he was but a lowly moth.

Morrigan led him to a deserted area between some

buildings and turned to face him. "What do ye want?" she demanded, her hands on her hips.

"Do you plan to march with the Scots against the English?"

"Aye, o' course."

"But… Andrew."

"I have ne'er been good at tending the sick. I will speak to my messenger when he returns tomorrow to ensure the medicine was delivered and that Andrew is improving."

"I suppose it would be fruitless to beg you to stay home and not march out to war."

"Quite pointless."

"Go home, Morrigan. I beg your pardon, but I will reveal you if I must. I need to know you are safe."

Morrigan crossed her arms over her chest. "Go ahead, tell whoever ye wish. MacLaren already knows it. They will no' be sending me and my men away this time, not when they are desperate for troops. Besides, what is safe about returning to the Highlands? If the English take control o' Scotland, do ye think we would no' suffer? Would ye save me from the quick death of the sword to condemn me to the long suffering o' starvation?"

Dragonet groaned and knew he had lost. "You will be the death of me, you."

"I am sorry to hear it. Do ye wish to say good-bye again?" Morrigan gave him a sly smile.

"No, I shall see you again. I… I will be joining the Duke of Argitaine in the fight against the English."

"Ye will?"

He was? "Yes." Having come to that conclusion a

few seconds before, Dragonet reviewed it and found it to his liking.

Morrigan's eyes narrowed. "Ye are no' going simply because I am, are ye?"

Yes. Dragonet cleared his throat. "It is a matter of honor." It was a true statement. He could not allow the duke to return to the fight, let alone Morrigan, without doing his best to protect them both.

Morrigan stepped easily toward him, but the voices of slightly inebriated men got louder until two stumbled past them between the tents.

"This is no' good-bye," said Morrigan, and was gone.

ം⊸

Morrigan slipped into his tent unseen. It was a poor choice, but she had to know. She had questions she must ask. She found him bent over a map and a candle.

"I wish to ask ye something."

Laird MacLaren stood up, his hand on his long knife. He stilled and glared at her, his mouth curling in disgust. "What are ye about, McNab?"

"Ye spent many years in France, aye?"

"Aye. How does that concern ye?"

"I wish for ye to translate something somebody said to me." She had to know what Dragonet had said to her. Was he staying in the fight because of her? What were his true feelings? It could make no difference... but she must know.

MacLaren raised an eyebrow. "Why me?"

"I believe ye would tell me the truth. Our clans may no' be on friendly terms but I ken ye to be an

honorable man. Ye also dinna care to protect me from
unpleasant news if it is so."

MacLaren gave a curt nod and Morrigan interpreted
it as permission to proceed.

"What does 'ma sherry' mean?"

The corners of MacLaren's mouth twitched up.
"'*Ma chérie*' is 'my dear.'"

"What about 'moan pateet tray shur'?

MacLaren winced. "Yer French is as lacking as yer
choice in clothing. Is this the best yer brother can
clothe ye?"

Morrigan folded her arms across her chest as if to
protect herself from view. "I dinna come for fashion
advice. Translation, please."

"'*Mon petit trésor*' is 'my little treasure.' Do ye have
an admirer?"

Morrigan pretended not to hear him, though her
cheeks burned in evidence to the contrary. Despite
her embarrassment she was determined to know what
Dragonet had said to her that night. The night they
made love. What were his true emotions? Had it been
survival or something more? And why would he join
the war against the English? What could he possibly
hope to gain? She must know.

"What is 'Shuh ta dore. Shuh tem'?

"'I adore ye. I love ye.'"

Morrigan blinked. "Pardon?"

"Nay, no' me. That's what '*Je t'adore. Je t'aime*'
means. Who is speaking this to ye?"

Morrigan shook her head to reject the question.
Dragonet said he loved her? *Love?*

"If Chaumont has said that to ye, I swear I will—"

"Nay, 'twas no' Chaumont. He is in love wi' his wife. Can ye no' see that?"

MacLaren scowled. "He better be."

"What does 'shuhn puh pah veevr sohn twah' mean?"

MacLaren frowned, his eyebrows knit together in a fierce scowl. "'*Je ne peux pas vivre sans toi*'?"

"Aye." Morrigan waited, her hands clenched, her breath stilled. What had Dragonet revealed in the throes of passion?

"Words men utter in a war camp where women are scarce should ne'er be trusted," said MacLaren.

"Aye, I ken," exclaimed Morrigan, her pulse starting to race. "What does it mean?"

"It means, 'I cannot live wi'out ye.'"

Morrigan exhaled. She took a shaky step back with knees that were suddenly weak. Dragonet's words revealed no great secret, except that he was a man who loved her. Except he was a monk. So none of it was simple.

"Who has been plying ye wi' talk of love?"

Morrigan shook her head. "Thank ye. Ye have helped me." She turned to leave.

"Morrigan!" MacLaren commanded, and she turned back. "Where are yer brothers?"

She did not know why he asked, but he had answered her questions, so she felt obliged. "Archie is on pilgrimage and Andrew is recovering from wounds he received at Berwick."

"Have ye no uncles, a man who can care for ye?"

Morrigan glared back at him. "I can take care o' myself."

"Ye should no' trust sweet words from a man. Most

o' the time they only want to lift up yer skirts…" He glanced again at her men's attire. "So to speak."

"I understand. I think he spoke his native tongue because he did no' wish me to know his true feelings."

"A Frenchman, is he?"

"Nay!" she said with too much emphasis.

"If ye want I should have words wi' someone…"

"Nay!" Morrigan stepped forward into the light. "I pray ye would do no such thing. This is what I was trying to avoid. This is why I came to ye. Our clans hate each other, remember?"

"I dinna hate ye, Morrigan. I am a Highlander. Ye are a Highland lass. Ye shoud'na be running about in men's clothing, fending off sweet-talking Frenchman. If yer clan canna protect ye, I will see it done."

Morrigan paused, trying to comprehend his speech. "Ye would protect me? A McNab?"

MacLaren gave a curt nod.

"Ye surprise me," Morrigan said softly. It had been her strongest belief that all decent people despised her and would never lift a finger for her aid. Lady Aila had surprised her, but Morrigan reasoned a few people must be of a saintly disposition. But Laird MacLaren had also offered help, and she could not mistake him for a saint. Her head spun. Perhaps everything she knew about the world was false. "I thank ye for the offer. I will let ye know if I am in need."

Morrigan bowed and left the tent more confused than when she entered.

Twenty-Eight

MORRIGAN'S PLAN HAD WORKED.

Yet it came at a terrible cost. Douglas had negotiated with the English for a week, stalling the invasion before sneaking out of the English camp one morning. When King Edward discovered he had been double-crossed, his anger burned against the Scots quite literally. He invaded Scotland, but no one marched against his massive army. Instead he found abandoned towns and empty granaries. Frustrated by his poor reception and his lack of easy provisions for his army, he put the town to the torch in retaliation.

King Edward marched into Scotland but was hindered by the constant need to find food for his army. The English had nothing for the troops to eat save what they could carry with them. The Scots made sure any hunting party or supply line was harassed sufficiently to be ineffective. Still, Edward pushed into Scotland, burning everything in sight.

Morrigan had seen Dragonet but little in the past few weeks. He stayed with the Duke of Argitaine, she with her clan. Harry and Willy had joined her along with several other men. When it came to setting up an ambush, they had much to teach the other clans. She was glad to be of use, though not to have lived such a dishonorable life.

"If King Edward reaches Edinburgh, he can be resupplied. He must not be allowed to take the town," said Douglas to a group of clan leaders. They huddled around a small brazier in the darkness of the tent.

"We canna win against him in an open fight," said one laird.

"We dinna have to win, but rather prevent the English from marching forward. We must hold them. They are nearing starvation. They will verra soon need to return to England."

Morrigan understood what needed to be done. She did not like it, but the English must be stopped. It was going to be a direct fight, nasty and brutal, the kind where a single soldier of great courage could turn the tide. She could be that soldier.

Morrigan walked slowly back to her tent and told her men the plan. Cold resignation permeated the tent. Everyone knew what was to come, and nobody spoke much. Fear had made them mute. They ate their last meal and turned in early. Sleep was important before a battle, if it would come.

Morrigan lay awake on her cot in her tent, waiting for the right time. Tomorrow's fight loomed heavy and dark in her mind. She was not much for praying, but in consideration of tomorrow's labors, she prayed for the safety of her clan, for Andrew, for Archie... and for Dragonet. She did not have the gall to pray for herself, but ever since finding the shroud she wondered if perhaps she too could find forgiveness. It seemed impossible. She knew all too well the darkness in her soul.

She needed to do something to gain forgiveness, something big—a large sacrifice that could win her the absolution. Tomorrow would be her chance. Tomorrow she would show her courage and help deliver Scotland from the English. If she sacrificed herself on the battlefield, surely she could save herself from the fires of hell.

Unless, of course, God sided with the English. Morrigan considered that idea but rejected it. God simply could not be an Englishman… and if he was, she would not care for heaven overmuch.

Morrigan slipped off of her cozy cot, the cold almost forcing her back into the warm blankets. Her muscles moaned their complaint, but Morrigan ignored it. Tomorrow would be about sacrifice, but tonight was for herself.

It was her last chance for love.

Morrigan dressed quickly and tugged on her boots. She wrapped herself in a wool blanket and a bearskin cloak. Creeping out of her tent, she hustled across the camp. She didn't need to fear anyone seeing her. The cold and the dark had driven everyone into their tents for the night.

She paused outside the tent. Was she truly going to do it? Wind blew hard, whipping stinging sleet against her cheek. She pulled back the tent flap and slipped inside. Total darkness surrounded her. She walked slowly, her hands in front of her.

Bumping into her quarry was not part of her plan.

"Ow!" said Morrigan, tripping over a large object. The large object in question grabbed her throat and throttled her to the floor.

"Name yourself!" growled Dragonet.

"Morrigan," she rasped.

Dragonet released her at once. "Morrigan? Wh-what are ye doing here? You gave me a fright."

"I gave *ye* a fright!"

"Did I hurt you? I thought you were trying to attack me."

"No, I came to… well, I wanted to… oh hell, this isna the way it was supposed to happen." Morrigan sat up on the floor of the tent which, considering the mass of blankets, had formed Dragonet's bed.

"Why are you here?" asked Dragonet. She could not see him in the inky blackness, but his voice was close.

"Are we alone?"

"Yes."

"I thought you would be. The duke and his knights are staying in the farmhouse down the way."

"Yes, they have found for themselves better accommodations."

"And left ye here alone."

"I chose it."

"Aye, I know. I gave away my last piece of gingerbread to discover it, and I decided to come here and see you and spend the rest of the night with you because I talked to MacLaren and I know what you said, and I feel the same way; even though I know we canna be together forever, at least we can be together tonight." Morrigan spoke in a great rush of words.

Everything was silent for a moment, and Morrigan held her breath waiting for Dragonet's response. She had practiced seductive things to say, but everything spilled out in the most tumble-down way. She wondered if he would notice if she just snuck out.

"You gave away your last gingerbread?"

"Aye."

"You gave away the gingerbread Alys sent?"

"How did you know Alys sent me gingerbread?"

"She sent some to me too."

Morrigan reached for him in the darkness. "Do you have any left?"

"Living with three other knights? It was gone before the sun rose the next day."

"Pity."

"Yes."

Silence again.

"You did not sneak in here to steal my gingerbread, I think," said Dragonet.

"Nay."

"You came because you spoke to MacLaren?"

"Shuh tem."

"I beg your pardon?"

"Ye said it to me, when we... the last time... in the cave. Ye said it."

"Ah, *je t'aime*," said Dragonet. "Did I say it?"

"Aye. At the end. Ye said a lot of words in French. MacLaren translated it for me."

"You told *MacLaren* about us?"

"Nay, only had him translate."

"Why did you not ask me?"

"I was afraid ye would not tell me the truth. What

you said about loving me, did ye mean it?" Morrigan held her breath. Silence again filled the darkness.

"Yes," said Dragonet finally. "I meant it."

"Truly?" Morrigan wished her voice had not squeaked when she said it. She was trying hard to be a sophisticated lady of the world who boldly went to her lover's tent. Squeaking could hardly be part of that.

"And you. What are your feelings?" Dragonet's voice was soft.

"I am here. That should tell ye everything ye need to know." Morrigan reached toward him and found a thigh. She ran her hand up his leg.

"It does not." He grabbed her hand and held it fast. "*Je t'aime. J'adore.* It means I love and adore you. It cannot change anything between us, but I would like to know how you feel about me."

"I love you more than I have words to express. I would not be here otherwise. What I truly want is a life wi' ye. Since that canna be, I choose to have one night."

"Forgive me, but did we not already have one night?"

"I would like a night that is not about saving my life. One where I can actually feel my fingers, and the pain of my thawing toes doesna ruin all else. I think what we shared has enough merit to repeat. Dammit, if I am going to be punished for the sin at least I'd like to actually feel what I've done."

Morrigan reached out and put her hand on his chest. His breathing was shallow and quick. "I do no' think ye are immune to my charms, such as they are."

"No, I am not immune. And yes, your charms are considerable. In truth I have wanted you in my bed since before we... er... kept warm in the cave. I tell you the truth, you have ruined celibacy for me."

"Should I apologize? That must be verra hard."

"Quite."

"Ye shall no' see me after this. Tonight will be our good-bye." Morrigan wrapped her arms around his neck and drew closer so she was almost in his lap. He was wearing a linen nightshirt against the cold, but his skin was hot.

"Morrigan, I want you." He pressed her closer. "You can feel how much I want you. But I took a vow not to do this."

"Ye were only twelve."

"It does not matter. Also, I do not wish..." He held her closer, so close she could hardly draw breath. "I want you so much. I have dreamed of this so many times. But I do not wish to leave you in the same state my father left my mother."

"You will not—"

"I do not wish to leave you, but I must. It is not in my power to ask for your hand in marriage. If we were to conceive a child, I would be no better than my father. I cannot do this to you. As much as I love you and as much as I want you, I cannot hurt you." He tried to push her away, but she was determined not to be repelled.

Morrigan laid her head against his shoulder. "Ye winna hurt me. I promise ye."

"How can you be sure?"

"Tonight is all I have. Tomorrow is war." Morrigan sighed. She unpinned her cloak and removed her boots.

"Are you removing your clothes?" asked Dragonet in a tight voice.

"Aye. I'm cold. I am going to join ye under the covers."

"I do not think…"

"Good. Dinna think. Better for both of us."

"Morrigan, this is a very poor idea. I should probably ask you to leave. I… what are you wearing?"

"Nothing." Morrigan snuggled beside him under the mountain of blankets. "Why are ye wearing a nightshirt?"

"It is freezing tonight."

"Ye dinna feel cold anymore." Morrigan snaked her hand under his nightshirt. His resistance was easily overcome.

"No. But, Morrigan—"

"Stop thinking. I want just one night. That is all I ask."

"Please, do not turn me into someone that I would despise. If I lay with you tonight, then I am no better than the father who spawned me and rejected me, even as he used me. I would leave knowing that if I had truly loved you, I could not have acted in a way to cause you pain. Do not rob me of this love… sometimes it is all I have left." Dragonet's voice cracked in the darkness.

Morrigan stilled and put her hand over his heart. "Do not worrit over the future for me. Tomorrow I face the English and I… I expect to be dead by tomorrow eve."

"No!"

"I have done a lot of thinking. I even tried praying. I

am at peace with this. Fighting is the one thing I know how to do. Everything else I've attempted in my life has been a failure. But taking up a sword, charging into battle, those are things I know I can do. Maybe I can turn the tide. Maybe I can save my people from English rule. Maybe I canna do it, but I know I must try."

"You must not sacrifice yourself."

"But that is the best part. If I do sacrifice myself and die for a worthy cause, mayhap God would look favorably upon me and I could even find forgiveness."

"No, Morrigan—"

"Listen, I have it all worked out. I want to have, well to go to bed with ye like husband and wife. I know that is a sin since we canna marry and ye're a monk and all, but if I sacrifice myself tomorrow maybe I can win forgiveness for this and all the other nasty things I've done in my life. And it winna be yer fault, because I am seducing ye. See, is it not a goodly plan?"

"Morrigan—"

"I mean, not a good plan, since I am trying to get away wi' sin, but it works, no?"

"Morrigan, your forgiveness is not dependent on you, it is dependent on God's son. Remember the burial cloth we found? What more can you add to redemption than the death of God's own son?"

Morrigan shook her head in the darkness. She could not believe anyone, let alone God's son, would die for her. It was not possible. "No, not me. I do not deserve saving, not in the least."

"He took the punishment of the damned. He died for the forgiveness of sinners."

Morrigan lay beside him considering his words. She

could not imagine a more gruesome death than what Jesus suffered on the cross. What more could she add to that? Nothing.

Nothing.

She breathed deep. "I will need to see a priest early tomorrow morn. I will have much to confess." Perhaps she could be forgiven. Morrigan smiled. It was a happy thought.

"Then you will return home now?"

"Nay. I shall still fight and die. I dinna fear death now. Never thought I'd go to heaven. 'Tis a nice place, I warrant."

Dragonet propped himself up on an elbow and gave her shoulder a small shake. "Morrigan. You cannot throw away your life."

"I am no' throwing it away. I am living to the full. Fighting is all I am good for. It is all I have. Without it, I am nothing. I can use it to help my clan, all the clans. This is what I was born to do."

"Please Morrigan. Please take your men and go home. Please."

Morrigan put her hand on his chest, feeling the solid beating of his heart. "I must stay. There is naught for me at home. I am sorry, Dragonet… Jacques. I hope ye can understand. This is all I have. I must join the fight."

"Morrigan…" Dragonet put a hand to her cheek and stroked up to her head.

"Careful o' my hair pin. Ye dinna want to prick yerself."

"Almost forgot." He snatched his hand away. "I cannot let you die. You cannot ask this of me."

"What I ask is for one night wi' ye, as if we were husband and wife. I ken it can never be, but I would wish it—"

"Me also."

"Being wi' ye, I feel alive. Ye save me from… me. I need ye tonight. I need ye to save me."

"To save your life I would do anything."

"Save me."

Dragonet wrapped his arms around her as his lips found hers. He pulled her beside him and kissed her until her toes curled with delight. When he finally allowed her to gasp for breath, she pulled his nightshirt up, running her fingers over his trim, muscular stomach. He had a body that made her hot inside. He stopped kissing her neck for a moment and allowed her to lift his shirt over his head and away. He rolled back and pulled her on top of him.

She moaned softly at the pleasure of having so much of her touch so much of him. Unlike before, when much of her body had been numb from cold, this time she could feel everything. He was warm and, in certain places, undeniably hot. She would have no need to encourage any response this time.

She had a sudden desire to take him right then. She could straddle him and ride him like… she blushed in the dark at her own thoughts and grew suddenly shy. Neither being a common state for her.

"I dinna ken what I am doing," she confessed.

"It is working for me."

"Aye, I can feel this thing attacking my stomach."

"It is not after your stomach."

Morrigan laughed, giggled actually, though she

would never admit to such an undignified sound. "What do I do now?"

"My only experience, it has been you."

"Ye're no help."

"Sorry. What if I did this?" He moved his hands down her back until he cupped her backside. He massaged her with strong hands, working slowly toward her inner thighs.

"Yes. Yes, that might work. That might… oh!"

He stopped. "Oh? Oh bad or oh good?"

"Oh good. Dinna stop, do that again."

"Um… what did I do? That?"

"No."

"This?"

"Oh, definitely not."

"I am sorry, but it is dark and this is unfamiliar territory. I am not sure I can—"

"YES!"

"Right, this here?"

"Yes, oh yes."

Inspired by the sensations he was building in her, she began to move her hips against him. She allowed the sensations building inside to take control. Her breathing was fast, and her heart raced along with determination. She was chasing something. She needed release.

"Morrigan," he rasped. "I need you. I need you now."

She sat up and angled herself to accept him. Slowly she eased herself down. "Is this… good?"

He made an odd sound with a strained voice.

She could not see him in the dark. "Ye dinna like?"

"*Je t'adore…*" He began speaking in rapid French, and Morrigan decided it was a happy tirade.

Slowly at first, then with increasing speed and intensity, she chased after the building sensation of pure power. With a rush of hot pleasure, she grasped his shoulders and cried out, even as he shuddered beneath her. Waves of joy swept through her, rippling through to her core.

"Oh, I… oh…" She collapsed on top of him.

He rolled her over onto her back and lay on his side next to her, an arm and a leg holding her tight. "I love you too."

"Aye, love, that is what I meant," mumbled Morrigan. Every muscle in her body was so relaxed she doubted she could ever move again. She would be happy to lie in bed with him forever.

"I would do anything for you. Anything. You know that."

"Aye, I ken."

He wrapped his fingers into her hair, massaging her head.

"Careful," she mumbled.

"Yes, I am. To save your life I would do anything. Forgive me, Morrigan, but…"

Morrigan opened a sleepy eye. What was he talking about? She felt a tiny pin prick on her shoulder. "No!" she cried with the instant realization of what he had done.

She fought against the spreading numbness and lost. Succumbing to the poison, she drifted swiftly into nothingness.

Twenty-Nine

ARCHIE MCNAB BREATHED THE FRESH AIR OF SCOTLAND. He was home, or closer to it than he had been in months. He had been to France and Italy. He had been to Rome and stayed with a man who actually had an audience with the pope. He had given his testimony before cardinals. He was not the same man.

"'Ere ye go, sir," said a stable lad, handing him a fresh mount. Archie had returned from abroad with the bishop of Glasgow and some new friends, or at least traveling companions. His pleasant overtures had been largely rebuffed by the group of black-robed men who joined them on the return trip to Scotland. Archie did not take it personally. The bishop said men of the Inquisition were often like that.

Archie swung up in the saddle and spurred his fresh mount forward. The wind blew cold, stinging slush onto his face. It felt like home. He urged his horse faster through the slop. It was unfortunate conditions for a man who wanted speed, forcing him to stop frequently to clear the poor beast's shoes from the packed snow and ice.

They had returned to St. Margaret's two days before and learned of the final offensive of the English toward Edinburgh and of the Scots' desperate attempt to stop them. McNab rushed to join the campaign, determined to be part of the mix. He wanted to defend Scotland against the English as much as any Highlander, perhaps more since he had broader perspectives.

Fortunately for his timing, the snow turned to rain and he was able to ride across the still-frozen ground with considerable speed. As he neared Edinburgh, he hit the fog, thick and cold on his exposed face. He pushed ahead more slowly, making sure he did not miss the road.

Ahead he heard the shouts of men and clash of swords. He started to spur his horse into the melee, but reconsidered and eased up, taking a more careful approach. He emerged on a slight rise. Below him, English and Scots fought hard. Some were mounted, some not. It was difficult to see the full extent of the battle in the thick mist. Archie considered drawing his sword and charging, but reached for his bow instead.

Twang! His shot hit home and an Englishman fell to the ground. The Scot who had been fighting the now-dead Englishman looked around, confused. Archie smiled; in the fog he was nearly invisible, a decidedly good thing when fighting a war one hopes to survive. He shot a few more English with similar effect.

"Hold 'em lads!" roared a familiar voice. MacLaren emerged from the curtain of mist. The muscles in Archie's stomach clenched at the sight of him. MacLaren hated him with a passion. Admittedly with good reason, but still, the man was determined to make Archie's already difficult life even harder.

MacLaren fought two attackers with his massive sword. Archie hated the man. He had everything Archie wanted. He *was* everything Archie wanted. MacLaren got the girl, the inheritance, the respect, the honor. Archie got nothing but derision and disregard.

A third joined in the attack on the massive man. MacLaren was good, but no man could hold his own forever. Sir Chaumont came into view, always at MacLaren's right hand. He was also hard-pressed and unable to help MacLaren. It was inevitable; with so many against him the big man was going down.

Archie pulled back on his bowstring. He was a careful shot, and he knew how to aim for the gaps in a man's armor.

Twang!

His target fell to the ground.

⁂

Morrigan awoke naked, covered by a mass of blankets. She was having the most pleasant dream involving Dragonet, herself, and several pounds of gingerbread. She opened an unwilling eye, still groggy. She was actually hot under so many layers, but that was not what woke her. Her pounding head, that's what woke her.

"Ow!" She sat up slowly. Her head hurt like blazes, and much to her disappointment there was neither Dragonet nor gingerbread in the tent. Which she could see perfectly because... it was the middle of the day!

"Damnation!" She was late for the war.

Morrigan flung the covers aside to get dressed, ignoring the shock of cold that stung her skin. Rummaging around on the floor and bed, she could not readily find her clothes, and so she cursed again, which did nothing to improve her situation. Forcing herself to slow down, she looked through every blanket, taking one to wrap around herself against the frigid temperatures as she searched.

Where were her clothes? Why had Dragonet not woken her when he left? Memories both sweet and disturbing came flooding back. He had tricked her! He had bedded her with the purpose of getting her to lower her guard so he could prick her with her own poisoned hair pin. And he had taken her clothes to prevent her from joining the battle, the French bastard.

"Hell and blazes!" Morrigan cursed. When she found that rat bastard, she was going to make him pay. She was going to make him suffer. She was… ideas more sensual than sadistic warmed her cold skin. She cursed again, flinging the traitorous thoughts from her weak brain.

If he thought he could keep her in the tent by taking her clothes, he had underestimated her resolve. She marched to the door flap of the tent. She could fight in a blanket just as well as anything.

She took one step barefoot into the slushy snow and retreated into the tent. Boots. She could fight in a blanket if she had boots. Morrigan sat back down on the pile of blankets.

"Where did ye put my boots, ye double-crossing bastard?" Morrigan put her elbows on her knees and propped up her head with her hands. Dragonet did not want her to go to war, that much was clear. He was trying to save her, not play a prank. He would not wish her to go outside without clothes, but he would want to slow her down, which meant her clothes must be somewhere in the tent.

Morrigan began a careful search of the tent. The tent itself was large, intended for many people. A canvas divider separated the tent into two rooms. She had only traveled as far as the first room, where Dragonet had laid sleeping. Beyond that was a second section of the tent, filled with many comforts a traveling duke may find to be essential. There were several more elevated cots for sleeping, blankets, a table and chairs with dishes and goblets. A chest was in one corner, a wooden, boxed chess set on top. She took a deep breath and began her search.

She found her tunic first. It had been stuffed high on a tent pole. Her breeches were in the chess box. One boot was in a chest; the other was hidden under a cot. Her woolen hose she found stuffed into a mug... She pitied the man who would drink from it next. With careful searching, she located each article of clothing until she finally found her cloak rolled up in a pillowcase.

Dragonet must have taken a long time hiding her clothes in the dark. He was the most devious, kindest man she had ever met. No one, not even her brothers, had gone to such lengths to try to save her. Everyone else was either afraid of her or did not care. He cared and was not afraid of her wrath.

For one stunning moment she considered not

leaving the tent, but rather waiting for him to return. Perhaps in much the same condition as when he left. She could devise a sweet torture to punish him for his crimes. Morrigan smiled but shook her head to dispel the notion. It was not in her nature to sit and wait for others to do the work. Besides, Dragonet may need her help. The thought got her moving.

Morrigan ran from the tent. She must collect her armor and, more importantly, her weapons. The snow had begun to melt, turning it into several inches of freezing slop. Thick fog had rolled in, making it difficult to find her way in the maze of tents and the slick conditions. She wondered what her men must have thought when they awoke to find her gone. Her absence was going to be difficult to explain. After a few wrong turns, she found her desired tent and burst inside.

"Harry! Willie!" Her men were all still in the tent. "What are ye doing here?"

"Waiting for ye, like he told us to!" said Harry.

"Like he what?" Morrigan was genuinely confused.

"Sir Dragonet came and said ye had taken ill in the night and we were to wait for word about ye here. He said we must take ye back to St. Margaret's for ye were so ill. Are ye well, lass?"

"Damn his eyes!" cursed Morrigan.

"We repaired a wagon to take ye back to the convent," said Harry.

"No, I am well enough. Gather the men. We must join the forces against the English."

Neither of the men moved. They exchanged a glance.

"I said get going!" shouted Morrigan.

"Sir Dragonet said ye might say that, but it was all part o' yer illness. He said we was to take ye back to the convent by any means."

Morrigan grabbed her sword and drew the blade, pointing it at Harry. "Ye wish to try?"

"Methinks she has recovered," said Willie.

The men left to gather the others for battle, and Morrigan struggled to quickly pull on her armor. A padded doublet and a studded hauberk, helmet, and gauntlets would have to do. She took more time to ensure she was appropriately armed. Morrigan cursed throughout the process, knowing she was losing precious time. Dragonet had even tried to turn her own men against her. Wicked, wonderful man.

Morrigan mounted her horse and rode toward the battle. Her head cleared a bit with the exercise and brisk, cool air, but it still irritated her with a dull ache. It was late in the day, Dragonet had worked his mischief well, but there may still be time to die gloriously. She was determined to find a way, or at least find Dragonet and show him her full appreciation for sticking her with sleeping potion. He had better be in good condition when she found him or... she urged her mount faster.

She and her men did not travel far down the road to Edinburgh before she came across the first casualties. A few men were driving a cart back to camp holding the injured. Morrigan ran her eyes over each one to make sure Dragonet was not in the mix. It was a gruesome display of blood and gore.

"How goes the battle?" she asked the cart driver.

"Them bastards have no' gained Edinburgh yet,

but our lads are hard pressed. Hard to see in all this bloomin' slop."

Morrigan trotted forward using some caution. It was difficult to see more than a few feet ahead of her in the thick, dense fog. She followed the sounds of clashing steel with more success. She came upon a Scot losing a sword fight with an English soldier and dispatched the soldier before riding on. Again and again she came across small groups of men fighting hand to hand. Apparently the battle lines had become blurred in the blinding mist and groups of soldiers were fighting on the ground. One positive thing about the current conditions was it eliminated the English advantage of the longbow. With no ability to aim in the fog, they could not fire for fear of killing their own soldiers.

Morrigan pressed on, joining the fight every chance she could. Sometimes they came across small groups of Scots resting before going back into the fight. Often they found the dead and dying, evidence of the bloody cost of war.

Through the impenetrable mist floated fragments of French words. Morrigan froze, straining to hear the direction of the voices. Suddenly the voices turned to shouts and the unmistakable clash of metal. Morrigan spurred her mount toward to the commotion, sword drawn.

Breaking through the murky fog, she found the band of Frenchmen on foot surrounded by about thirty English, determined to take the duke hostage. They were attacked hard, some mounted, some on foot. Dragonet and the three knights surrounded their liege, determined to die to protect the duke. From the look of things, dying bravely would soon be their fate.

Morrigan shrieked an unholy battle cry and flew into the fray, swinging a battle-ax, followed by her small band of Scots. The effect of the ghostly figures charging out of the misty shroud was dramatic. Several English ran away, believing they were being overrun, others were startled, giving the French an opportunity to take advantage.

Though still outnumbered, Morrigan attacked with vengeance; all her frustrations, all her anger, all her confusion and shame roared to the surface in blind fury. She attacked without mercy, focusing her energy on the two English soldiers who were attacking Dragonet.

Morrigan raised her ax to crush one of the soldiers, but her arm was jerked back. With a curse Morrigan swung around, trying to dislodge the chain of the mace wrapped around her ax. Her mounted attacker pulled back, and the ax was ripped from her hand. She grabbed for her sword but her opponent was fast, swinging the mace again. She protected her head with her arm, and the mace tore off her right gauntlet.

The man swung back with his mace, but suddenly slumped forward on his horse, a knife thrown through the small gap in the visor of his helm. Morrigan swirled around to see who had thrown the knife. It was Dragonet.

"No!" she screamed as an English soldier swung his sword at Dragonet from behind. Dragonet parried to the side but was still caught in the downswing of the mace. Dragonet went down, and Morrigan could see him no more.

Spurring her horse, she drew her sword and charged the English soldier before he could deliver Dragonet the death blow. She attacked with cold fury and struck him several times before he limped away into the mist.

"Dragonet!" She bashed another attacker on the helm with the hilt of her sword. He staggered back stunned.

"Get up!" Morrigan yelled. Dragonet mumbled something, but did not regain his feet.

Morrigan charged another who tried to take advantage of the French knight on the ground, clashing swords. This Englishman was a knight by his expensive armor and was skilled at the art of swordplay, driving Morrigan back a few steps before she could read his attack and better hold her own. She swung to defend his attack and then struck at his flank, which he blocked. She swung again, but out of the corner of her eye she saw a man charge her with a spear, just as her opponent with the sword attacked. She blocked the sword and cringed for the inevitable impact of the spear, which never came.

Dragonet had struck down the spear with his sword and swung wildly at the man. Morrigan was prevented from assisting by her own attacker, who was proving to be much too persistent. Dragonet's form was not as precise as she remembered, his attack uncontrolled. Morrigan gasped—he was fighting left-handed, his right arm hung limply at his side.

Morrigan focused on her enemy. She needed to dispatch him quickly before Dragonet fell to his opponent. She memorized the English knight's attack, searching for weakness, and swung left as he lunged right, catching him painfully under his arm. He recoiled from the blow and fled back into the dense fog. She let him go to assist Dragonet, but he felled his opponent with a desperate slash.

Morrigan caught him as he stumbled back. "What is hurt?"

"My shoulder." His voice was tight, as if even speaking the words caused him pain.

"Thank you. Thank you," said the duke, joining them. "I owe you a debt of gratitude."

Morrigan realized the English soldiers had either been defeated or ran away. She took a deep breath of cold, damp air. It was over.

"He needs a surgeon," Morrigan said, putting her arm around Dragonet's waist for added support. He did not refuse it, a sure sign that he was badly wounded.

"Yes, yes. We will take him now," said the duke.

The sound of approaching horses drew the attention of all. From the mist appeared none other than MacLaren, Chaumont, and Archie McNab. They had removed their helms and were riding at a comfortable pace.

"Archie!" Morrigan was so surprised she almost dropped her sword.

"Morrigan! I thought I told ye to stay out o' this. Ye should be at home," chastised Archie.

Morrigan ignored his words. "How are ye here? I thought ye were in Rome."

"I have been to Rome and have returned," said Archie as if he had gone to the market.

"Just in time too!" said Chaumont.

Morrigan opened her mouth to say something, but could find no words. Chaumont was happy to see her brother? What kind of world were they in? Perhaps she was still under the influence of the sleeping potion and was actually still asleep in the tent.

"How goes the battle?" asked the duke.

"The day is won," declared MacLaren. "The English have sounded the retreat; they did not break through to Edinburgh."

Morrigan's men and the French knights cheered at the news.

"And we are still alive thanks to our friend McNab," said Chaumont with a broad smile.

"Ye are supposed to hate him!" blurted Morrigan.

"You will forgive me, *mademoiselle*, if I most humbly disagree. We were pinned down, and Archie turned the tide."

Archie shrugged. "'Twas no trouble."

Morrigan shook her head. She would reason it out later. Dragonet leaned more heavily on her.

"I need to get him to a surgeon."

Thirty

MORRIGAN SAT BY DRAGONET'S BEDSIDE, WILLING HIM
to wake. He was sleeping but was so still and pale,
she put her hand on his chest to make sure he still
breathed. Morrigan leaned her head against the cool
wall and waited.

It took two days to get him back to St. Margaret's.
The cart Morrigan's men found proved useful, and
they traveled without ceasing, changing horses and
drivers as they could. By unspoken consensus they
all went, Morrigan and her men, the duke and his
knights; even Archie, Chaumont, and MacLaren
returned with them.

Dragonet lay in the cart and said very little, not
complaining, but also not resisting the plan to take
him to the convent. His shoulder was not his only
injury; he also sported a gash on the back of his thigh
where the armor did not cover and a large bump on
the head.

Dragonet lost a lot of blood, but Mother Enid was
reassuring. He slipped into unconsciousness shortly
after he arrived, and woke only once since. Mother

Enid reported he had asked for Morrigan in the night, and Morrigan was determined to be at his side the next time he woke.

"Is he awake, *mademoiselle*?" asked Chaumont. He strolled into the small cell like he belonged there and leaned his shoulder against the wall in a casual manner.

Morrigan tried to think of a caustic remark, but she was tired, and Chaumont was too agreeable to grouse at for long. "He sleeps still."

"I was talking to the duke. Dragonet's defense was impressive."

"Foolish," said Morrigan. "He should have left the duke and protected himself. He got hurt because he stood in harm's way."

"Ah, I have labored under the false assumption that standing in harm's way was the job of the soldier. I thank thee for the enlightenment." Chaumont's eyes twinkled merrily.

"Piss off." She lacked the energy to devise an articulate retort.

Chaumont laughed heartily.

Dragonet stirred, and Morrigan immediately grabbed his hand.

"Jacques?" she asked. He mumbled something, and Morrigan leaned in closer.

"What does he say?" asked Chaumont, leaning closer too.

"He says he wants ye to go f—"

"Morrigan!" Dragonet rasped.

She stopped mid-sentence. "Aye?"

"Be nice."

"'Tis not in my nature."

"I sincerely disagree." He squeezed her hand and gave her a weak smile.

"Ye're hoping I'll be nice and forget what ye did to me. Dinna think I'll ever forgive ye for leaving me naked the way ye did!" said Morrigan, forgetting they were not alone.

"Well now!" exclaimed Chaumont. "I do believe my breakfast is calling. I'll be back to visit with you later, Brother."

Morrigan winced as he quit the room. "I suppose I could have phrased that better."

Dragonet clapped his hand over his eyes. "So much for discretion."

"I'm sorry, but it is all yer fault. Ye had no right to seduce and poison me!"

"I beg you to acquit me of the charge of seduction, but of the rest I am most certainly guilty."

"Ye bedded me so ye could stick me wi' my own sleeping potion!"

"I do apologize. I know what I did was unpardonable, but you are alive, and that was my only concern."

"Well… well, that was right nice of ye." Morrigan frowned when she said it.

"Anytime."

"Not a chance."

"*Bonjour.*"

Morrigan swirled around at the sound to see a tall man enter the room. He was dressed in black robes embroidered with gold thread. He must be a priest of some sort, but she had never seen one so finely dressed. He was middle aged and rather handsome, though his carriage and slight sneer revealed a cold heart.

Dragonet started at the sight of the man, his eyes open wide. His already pale skin turned white. Never had Morrigan seen Dragonet afraid, but he was. He struggled to sit.

"Who are you?" Morrigan put her hand on her sword hilt.

The man eyed her with contempt. He spoke French to Dragonet, who had managed to sit up in bed.

"He is the bishop of Troyes," said Dragonet in a voice that wavered.

The bishop of… Dragonet's father? It was Morrigan's turn to be astounded. Remembering herself, she bowed low until she could get her expression under control. She must not reveal she knew anything.

The man spoke again, and Dragonet nodded.

"He wishes you to leave us," Dragonet said. His voice was calm again, but Morrigan knew he was distressed. How did such a man get here?

"He just took a sleeping draft," said Morrigan, pushing Dragonet back down to his bed. Dragonet glanced at her, a question in his worried eyes. With a quick flick of her hand, she pulled out her hair pin and stabbed his shoulder as she pretended to pull up the covers. "All's fair," she whispered.

"He is injured. He needs to sleep," she said to the bishop.

The bishop did not speak to her, but rather continued to address Dragonet in French. Dragonet answered in French, but his eyes started to droop.

"He should have no visitors; he has taken a sleeping draft," said Morrigan.

Dragonet said something in French she hoped was

a translation. The bishop glared at her and pointed to the door. Morrigan was a bit surprised at how much she felt compelled to comply, but held her ground.

"He canna speak to ye," said Morrigan. She needed to give Dragonet time to recover from his wounds and time to grow accustomed to the fact that his father the bishop had traveled all the way to Scotland. No good could come from that unexpected visitor. Dragonet needed time.

The bishop spoke louder to Dragonet, but he had already fallen unconscious. He stood over Dragonet, his face a scowl. Morrigan kept her hand on the hilt of her sword, prepared to draw if he displayed the least amount of aggression. Instead he turned to her and raked her with his eyes. He took a step back as if not wanting to sully himself with her presence.

"You will send for me when he wakes," the bishop said in perfect English.

He swept from the room, and Morrigan collapsed back into the chair. What did that man want?

She put her hand on Dragonet's chest, taking comfort in the gentle rise and fall of his breathing. What were they to do?

❧

Morrigan woke to a slight shake of her shoulder.

"Let us get you some rest," said Mother Enid.

Morrigan stood and stretched, her muscles, cold and stiff from sleeping in the chair. "How is he?"

"He sleeps. His color has improved, and there are no signs of fever. Rest is the best thing for him. You also need sleep."

"Nay, I will stay until he wakes."

Mother Enid shook her head. "You must sleep. Come, let me lean on your arm as we walk. I am not as young as once I was. Sister Lucinda will watch over him tonight."

Sister Lucinda, a thin lady with the deep lines of many years etched into her face, glided into the room and sat in the chair that Morrigan vacated. Mother Enid took Morrigan's arm and gently led her to the door. Morrigan tried to think of some argument to stay, but she knew Mother Enid was right. She was tired, and there was nothing she could do watching over a sleeping man.

She allowed Mother Enid to lead her down the long hallway of the convent's guest house. Their pace was slow, and Mother Enid indeed leaned heavily on her arm. Their journey was not a long one, but at the pace they were traveling it would take some time. Morrigan realized it was an opportunity to ask the good nun a question.

"Mother Enid. What must a person do to be forgiven by God?"

"You are concerned about a particular sin, my child?"

Morrigan sighed. Why could nuns not answer a question directly? "Well… aye." She glanced back at Dragonet's room.

"Your young monk is quite handsome, no?"

Morrigan stiffened. "Ye know?"

"He may have said some things in his sleep…" hinted Mother Enid.

"Then ye ken I am a sinner of sinners. I defiled a monk!"

"Ah, to be young again," said Mother Enid with a wistful smile.

It was not the reaction Morrigan expected. "Ye defiled monks too?"

"Oh no, not monks. Dukes!" Mother Enid gave her a conspiratorial smile.

Morrigan stopped and stared at the elderly nun. "Ye and a duke…?"

"I had the body for it many years ago. Do you doubt me?"

"N-no, I…" Was a nun defending her *bad* reputation? "Ye're making my head hurt. Are ye saying what I did wasna a sin?"

"Oh yes, it was quite a sin. Sleeping with the duke was also a sin, and the cost was more than I could bear. I found myself with child and ailing. I cried out to God for mercy, promising to become a nun if I was spared. I lived, as you see, and became a nun."

Morrigan's stomach churned. "Are ye saying I must become a *nun*? Dammit, I knew there was no hope for me. I thought if I died in battle, I might be spared, but a nun? There's no way."

Mother Enid's lips twitched, and she appeared to be fighting against laughter. Morrigan scowled. What was funny about her damnation?

"You could die in battle a thousand times, and you still would not be spared," said the good nun.

"Well, that's lovely. Thank ye."

"Fortunately, it is not necessary. Christ took our sins and our punishment. All we must do is repent and believe, and we will be forgiven."

Morrigan turned back to Mother Enid slowly,

trying to make sense of her words. "So if all ye have to do is believe, why did ye become a nun?"

This time Mother Enid did laugh. "Oh, Morrigan, you are a delight. Here is your room. Go see Father Patrick tomorrow and say your confession. You'll be alright. God loves you, my child."

"Where can I find Father Patrick?"

Five minutes later Morrigan barged into the sleeping cell of Father Patrick. "Get up, old man. I need to say my confession."

"Wh-what is this outrage?" The sleeping man sat up from his pallet, his eyes squinting against the light of Morrigan's offending candle. "I will see ye tomorrow at the appointed time."

"Nay, I have much to confess, probably take all night."

"Go away, ye heathen!"

"That's why I'm here!" Morrigan drew a knife. "Now get up and hear my confession, dammit!"

Thirty-One

"WHY ARE YE DRAGGING ME HERE?" ASKED ARCHIE, walking into Dragonet's sick room. "Why can we no' talk in the main room?"

"Because this is the only place we can talk and be alone," hissed Morrigan, checking the corridor and closing the door.

Her statement was only half true. She did wish to speak with her brother alone, but Dragonet's room was hardly the only place to have privacy. Truth was she did not wish to leave Dragonet alone and unprotected.

"Why are ye concerned wi' him?" Archie's eyes slid to hers. "I spoke to Mother Enid. Ye do ken he's a monk."

"Aye, I ken it," said Morrigan waving her hands as if swatting away a fly. "Tell me, Brother, how does the bishop o' Troyes come to be in Scotland?"

"The bishop o' Troyes? Ye mean the well-dressed French priest?"

"Aye."

"So that's who he is. We testified in Rome against Barrick. We are trying to get him defrocked, ye ken.

Then we went back up through France. About halfway through, several priests from the Inquisition joined us, and this man, the fancy priest, he seemed to be giving the orders. I was told they were verra concerned about the actions of Barrick and were coming to see for themselves. But why would a French bishop care what happens here?"

"I know the answer to that. Remember the treasure ye told me the Templars hid in the cave?"

"Aye."

"We found it, Dragonet and I. There was gold and—"

"Gold! Ye found gold! Where is it?"

"It was taken from us."

"Taken? How? How could ye let gold be stolen from ye?" Archie's voice was far from soft.

"Attend to what I am telling ye, and lower yer voice," hissed Morrigan. "There was also this sheet that looked like a winding cloth. Dragonet thinks it may be the true shroud o' Jesus, or at least the Templars thought it was."

Archie gave a low whistle. "That would be something."

"It would be priceless. Can ye imagine how much power ye would have wi' that? Especially for the Church, they would build a cathedral for it, open it up to pilgrims."

"Where is it? I want to see."

"Barrick stole it from us too. That is what he has been after."

"So the bishop o' Troyes also wants the shroud?"

Morrigan nodded. "He sent Dragonet here to get it. He must have heard o' some o' yer testimony and decided to see for himself."

"So what are ye going to do now? Tell the bishop the abbot has it?"

Morrigan shook her head, "I dinna want either o' them to have it."

"Get Chaumont," said Dragonet in a weak voice, his eyes barely open.

"Ye're awake! Are ye well?" asked Morrigan.

"Felt better. Chaumont."

"Go get him. Quick, man!" Morrigan demanded Archie. "And Mother Enid too." Archie nodded and left.

Morrigan sat back down by the side of Dragonet's bed and took his hand. "How do ye feel?"

"Ow, my head."

"Sorry for my share in it. I dinna ken what else to do. I was so surprised to see yer, that is, the bishop."

Dragonet nodded and slowly moved to a seated position. "We need to get the shroud back."

Morrigan nodded. "And when we do, what will ye do wi' it?" She had no doubts Dragonet would get the shroud.

He shook his head. "I do not know yet."

Morrigan squeezed his hand. She knew one thing for sure: once he recovered the shroud, he would leave.

Mother Enid entered the room and after a quick examination of Dragonet pronounced him much recovered and recommended a week of bed rest, which no one in the room believed would actually occur.

Chaumont came in, and after some exchanges of pleasantries, Dragonet asked him to close the door. Mother Enid excused herself and closed the door behind her.

"You all know about the existence of the Templar shroud. Barrick must not be allowed to keep it. I beg you, my friends, to help me recover the shroud," said Dragonet in a soft but determined voice.

"Do you know where it is?" asked Chaumont.

"I do. We found it in a cave purchased by the Templars and recovered it. Unfortunately it was taken from us by Barrick."

They discussed the problem of how to recover the shroud. They agreed it must be either with Barrick or hidden in his rooms in the abbey. But how would they get him out of the abbey in order for it to be searched? And how would they get past his guards?

A knock at the door brought the conversation to a halt. The Duke of Argitaine walked in. "I came to see if Sir Dragonet has awakened. I see you have much company, and I will not keep you, but allow me to extend my gratitude for your protection, and if there is ever anything I can do in return, I am at your service."

"It is always my pleasure to serve you, Your Grace," said Dragonet.

"You two look alike," commented Morrigan, gesturing at Chaumont and Argitaine.

Chaumont stood next to the duke and people had to acknowledge the resemblance. "Perhaps there is a duke in my unknown parentage," laughed Chaumont.

"Ye do no' ken yer parents?" asked Morrigan.

"Afraid not. I was raised by the Hospitallers, so I suppose my father could be anyone. Even a duke." Chaumont gave Morrigan a wink.

Morrigan wondered if the real duke would be offended, but he merely smiled. "My father was a great lover of all things beautiful. Beautiful art, beautiful wine, beautiful women."

"But Chaumont is from France..." Morrigan dashed from the room. "Be right back!" she called behind her to the surprised men.

She burst into Mother Enid's room. She appeared to be resting on her pallet or maybe saying prayers.

"Are you going to rouse me the way you did poor Father Patrick last night?" asked Mother Enid.

"Och, sorry about that. I was so excited to be forgiven I could no' wait."

"Next time—" began Mother Enid.

"Aye, next time I'll wait. Ye woud'na believe how much penance he gave me! But that's no' why I came. Forgive me, but was yer duke the current Duke the Argitaine?"

"No."

"Oh, I see. Never mind then." Morrigan began to leave the room.

"It was this current duke's father, also the Duke of Argitaine," said Mother Enid with a slow smile.

"What happened to yer child?"

The smile on Mother Enid's face faded, and the light in her eyes dimmed. "I became very ill after I gave birth. I was told the child died."

"Where was the child born?"

"The hospital at St. John's. Why all these questions, my child?"

"I dinna ken for sure..." Morrigan shrugged and ran out of her room down the hall to where Dragonet was staying.

"Chaumont! Where were ye born?"

"Morrigan? Have ye gone daft?" Archie asked.

"Nay! Well, mayhap…" Morrigan gestured with her hands as if pushing aside the question. "Will ye tell me?" she asked Chaumont.

"I was born at St. John's run by the Hospitallers."

"Truly? What year?"

"Aye, she's daft," commented Archie.

"The year was 1323. Is there a purpose to these questions?"

"Are you certain of the year?" asked Mother Enid, who stood in the doorway, her face flushed.

"Yes," said Chaumont slowly.

"In the summer of 1323, I gave birth to a son that I conceived by the Duke of Argitaine, your father," Mother Enid said gesturing to the current duke.

No one spoke or moved or breathed.

Chaumont and Mother Enid stared at each other, blue eyes to blue eyes.

"It was on a feast day I brought my son into the world," said Mother Enid.

"St. John's Eve." Chaumont and Mother Enid spoke as one.

"Well I never," said Archie, his eyes wide. "Ye mean Sir Chaumont is Mother Enid's son?"

"Wheesht!" hushed Morrigan. Her idiot brother was ruining the moment.

"They told me the baby died," whispered Mother Enid. "Barrick and the other Templars who took me from the hospital and brought me here." Her lips began to tremble and a tear ran down her face. "That bastard told me you had died!"

"*Maman!*" Chaumont rushed to embrace Mother Enid.

"I would have never left you," she murmured in French. "Never."

"I was told my mother had died," said Chaumont wiping away his own tears.

"The Templars must have sent them that message," said Mother Enid and cursed in French. Several eyebrows raised in the room. "Forgive me, my children, but I was not always a nun."

Chaumont rose and turned to Argitaine, who held out his hand.

"Greetings, Brother!" said Argitaine with a wide smile. "It is not every day I meet one of my father's children. At least, not in Scotland."

Everyone began talking and congratulating, and there were many hugs and tears shed all around. Mother Enid gave Morrigan a crushing embrace; she was strong for an old woman. Chaumont also embraced her, followed by the duke, who kissed both cheeks.

A warmth spread through Morrigan with the unusual feeling that she had finally done something right. Perhaps since she was confessed and forgiven, she could live a better life. She glanced over at Dragonet and found his eyes on her. She looked away. She might live a better life, but they could never have a happy ending.

"We still need to get the shroud back from Barrick," said Archie.

"Wheesht!" hushed Morrigan again. Her brother could not speak but for saying the wrong thing at the wrong time.

"What shroud?" asked Argitaine.

The room grew silent again.

"They are my family," Chaumont declared. "I trust them." He glanced over at Dragonet, who nodded.

"Mother Enid, you said you believed Barrick and the Templars used your pallet to hide certain treasures they snuck out of France and into Scotland. I believe we have found this treasure." Dragonet continued to explain how they found the shroud and what happened to it.

Mother Enid was amazed and Argitaine skeptical, but everyone agreed Barrick should not be allowed to keep the shroud.

"Too long I have waited patiently for others to deal with Barrick, accepting and forgiving. It is time to act!" declared Mother Enid. "I do not know how I can help. Although… I do know Barrick has a secret entrance into his private solar."

"That is a help," said Morrigan with a slow grin. "I have a plan."

Thirty-Two

THE NEXT DAY THE CONSPIRATORS PUT THEIR PLAN into action. Mother Enid sent a note to Abbot Barrick, saying the Duke of Argitaine was interested in his abbey and might wish to make a donation for its help in the war effort. Dragonet went off to speak to the bishop of Troyes. Morrigan fretted, but he returned unharmed, at least as far as she could see.

The duke played his part admirably; he kept the abbot and his guard busy while Morrigan and Dragonet searched the abbot's rooms, using the secret back entrance. They found nothing and were forced to retreat before being found. It was time to enact the next part of the plan.

"Ye have something I need. I have something ye want," said Morrigan to Abbot Barrick later that day.

"I doubt that," replied Abbot Barrick, taking a sip of wine. He sat behind his ornate desk, a fine spread of food before him. Morrigan stood before him in the room they had previously searched. The room afforded many hiding places, tapestries on the walls, ornately decorated screens, locked chests, but the shroud was in none of those places. Where was it?

"I need the medicine ye have for men who are returning from the battle," said Morrigan.

"One man in particular, I suppose?" Barrick's smile was unkind.

"Aye. I would do anything for him."

"You have already given me everything I need."

"If it is the shroud ye are looking for, then no, ye dinna have the real one we found in the cave."

Barrick frowned. "Speak plainly, I am in no mood for riddles."

"We found two shrouds, one was clearly intended to fool those who did no' ken what to look for. Dragonet explained to me the difference. He gave ye the false one."

Barrick's smile disappeared and in its place snuck a dark look. "How do you know you have the true shroud?"

"There is a way to tell, I'll show ye what Dragonet showed me, but I want to see the medicine first."

"Where is Dragonet? Does he know you have taken this true shroud from him?"

"Dragonet is grievously injured. I need the medicine. Why do ye hoard it when so many men are hurt and injured? Should not the church be helping others?"

"The church will help those who can reciprocate with a sizable donation. This medicine can save a man's life. It will not be given unless a man can give me his life's worth."

"These are the teachings o' the Church?"

"Church teachings are what I say they are. Now do you have the shroud or not?"

"Aye, here it is." Morrigan removed a velvet pouch from the inside of her cloak.

Barrick's eyes bored into the bag as if he could penetrate the cloth to see inside the bag.

"How do you know you have the correct shroud?"

"Show me the one you have and I can show you the difference," said Morrigan.

Barrick glared at her.

"Are ye afeared o' me?" asked Morrigan. "I have already seen both, and I know ye have the one. Ye can keep both o' them; all I want is the medicine."

Slowly Barrick reached into a large pocket of his robes and drew out the velvet pouch. Morrigan's heart beat faster. That was it, the true shroud.

"If you attempt to take this one, you will die a most unhappy death," growled Barrick.

"Ye would kill me the way ye killed Mal?"

"Oh no, I took care that Mal did not suffer. With you I will not be so kind."

Morrigan took a step back from the evil glint in his eye. She did not doubt he meant to kill her. She needed more time. "One thing I dinna understand is why ye wanted Archie to kill the bishop of Glasgow."

"My dear girl, there are many things you do not understand."

"True. But why no' have Mal kill him. Why Archie?"

"McNab was expendable. You are expendable. Do I make myself clear? Show me the shroud!"

Morrigan untied the laces, taking her time, trying to keep Barrick talking. "So ye wanted Archie to do it so ye could blame him afterwards and let him swing for the murder. And what if he said you forced him to do it?"

"No one would believe him, just as no one will believe you."

"But why do ye wish to kill the bishop o' Glasgow at all?"

"The shroud, lass." He stood up from behind his table. "My patience grows thin."

Morrigan removed the linen cloth from the bag, but did not unfold it. "Why do ye want this old thing anyway?"

"You have no idea of its worth," sneered Barrick.

"Is it holy?" asked Morrigan.

"It is power! There are those who would give anything to see it, to touch it. The Church would not build me a cathedral, but they will now, those fools in Rome." Barrick came around the table and snatched the cloth from Morrigan's hand. "For this I will get a castle even bigger than the bishop of Glasgow."

"Ye wanted the bishop's castle so ye thought to kill him and take his position."

"Obviously. Now what is the difference between these?" asked Barrick, laying both folded linens on the table. He walked around the table next to her. Too close.

"Do ye no' care how many people ye kill to get what ye want?" asked Morrigan, resisting the urge to run away.

Barrick turned on her, knife in hand, and pointed it at her throat. "Let me make it perfectly clear to you. I do not care how many people I kill. To get what I want, I will happily kill you, your idiot brother, every member of your clan, the bishop of Glasgow, and the bloody pope himself. Now tell me about the shroud!"

"Enough!" said Dragonet, emerging from behind the curtain, crossbow in hand.

"Guards!" shouted Barrick.

A loud commotion could be heard from outside the doors and Morrigan prayed Argitaine's men could hold off the guards.

Morrigan went to draw her sword, but remembered she had left it behind so as not to appear to be too threatening. In a flash Barrick grabbed her and twisted her in front of him like a shield, his knife to her throat. Morrigan struggled, but the old man held her like a vice, pricking her throat with his knife as a warning.

"Release her," demanded Dragonet.

"Drop your crossbow or I'll slice her throat," roared Barrick.

"Release her or I'll drop you." Dragonet did not lower his weapon.

Morrigan's mind spun, she calculated the angle of the shot; there was not much of Barrick that was an easy target, and one inch off could kill her.

"Do not think I will be merciful. Lower your weapon," shouted Barrick.

Barrick pressed the tip of his knife into her neck, drawing blood. Morrigan gazed at Dragonet's green eyes. If she were to die, she would die looking at the man she loved.

"Argggh!" shouted Barrick, and his grip on her suddenly loosened. Morrigan broke free and ran to Dragonet.

Barrick cursed them freely, Dragonet's bolt sticking

out of his elbow. "I will kill you. I will kill every one you ever cared about or met!"

Two black-robed figures emerged from behind the screen. One walked up to Barrick and put his hand on his shoulder. "Calm yourself, Brother."

"Who are you? What are you doing in my chamber? Guards!"

"I am Father Pierre, this is Father Luke. We have come to help," the man spoke softly but with authority.

"Who? Help... how?"

"We have been given the authority to investigate and arrest you if required," said Father Luke in a calm voice.

"Our investigation has found enough evidence to enact this arrest warrant, signed by the pope," said Father Pierre.

"Whom you threatened to kill," finished Father Luke.

"No, I... who are you?" Barrick looked wildly between the two priests.

"We are the Inquisition."

Barrick's wide eyes bulged from his head. "No! I will not be arrested!" Barrick broke free and ran to the door to find the Duke of Argitaine standing with sword drawn. Barrick spun and ran for the secret escape route, but Archie blocked his escape with drawn sword and a mace.

"I've waited a long time for this, Barrick," said Archie.

"No! You are nothing!" screamed Barrick. "You cannot arrest me, you pathetic worm." Barrick fought back with surprising strength for a man with a bolt in his arm. In the end it was Archie McNab who wrestled him to the ground while Father Pierre and

Father Luke tied his hands securely and dragged him out of the room with Archie and the duke's help.

"Noooooooo!" Barrick's screams could be heard from the hallway.

Father Luke turned back and walked to the table where the two folded sheets of linen still lay. "I will take these," he said to Morrigan, who had moved toward the table in the commotion.

"Aye, do," said Morrigan. "Though to be honest I think they are naught but old bed sheets."

Father Luke inclined his head and gently removed the folded pieces of linen, exiting the room.

In the room, oddly silent after so much commotion, Morrigan met Dragonet's gaze for a moment, then looked away. He could raise her pulse by simply looking at her.

"Nice shot," said Morrigan.

"If you please do not do that to me again. My heart cannot handle so much excitement."

"Naught is wrong wi' yer heart."

"Then why does it pain me?"

Morrigan looked up at Dragonet. He had tears in his eyes. And suddenly she did too. He was everything she could never have.

"Did you get the true shroud?" he asked.

Morrigan nodded and pulled a velvet pouch from a pocket in her cloak.

"Good girl."

"Ye ken that is hardly true."

"What does Father Luke have?"

"Two linen bed sheets from the good sisters at the convent."

Dragonet smiled. "I love… I love you." His voice cracked with emotion.

"Please dinna do this," whispered Morrigan, brushing away a tear that threatened to fall. "Here, take it. I dinna wish it to go to yer father, but ye can do with it what ye will." Morrigan held out the velvet pouch and Dragonet took it, but put it down on the table, choosing instead to wrap his arms around her.

Morrigan returned Dragonet's embrace. "Will ye leave now?"

"I must."

"I canna do this. I canna let ye go."

"I know."

"Please dinna go." Despite years of pushing aside her emotions, Morrigan McNab began to cry.

"My body may go, but my heart remains with you."

"Aye, that's verra sweet, but I rather like yer body too."

Dragonet laughed and sniffed. He looked down at her, the tears falling unchecked down his cheeks. "The monastic life will never be the same for me, now that I know all I am missing. Though I shall not miss the penance you caused me. I am still working through my rosaries."

Morrigan nodded. "Me too!"

"Want to go for more? Mayhap the time, it is right to say our proper farewells." Dragonet kissed her gently, and moved to deepen the kiss, but Morrigan broke away.

"I'm sorry, but I canna kiss ye when ye are going to leave me. It hurts too much." Morrigan, who feared neither death nor pain, wiped more tears from her eyes. Getting stabbed by a spear was nothing compared to that. A shoulder could heal. Her heart never would.

"I could stay a few weeks before returning?" suggested Dragonet.

"Nay, prolonging it only makes it worse."

"I will love you always."

"Please leave. I ne'er wish to see ye again."

Dragonet winced and looked away. He took a deep breath and gently took the velvet pouch from the table. He stood there for a moment not speaking, not moving. Morrigan waited for him to say something, but he shook his head and walked slowly to the door, his shoulders slumped in defeat.

"Dragonet," she called when he reached the door. He stopped but did not turn around. "I will love ye forever." He paused for a moment, nodded, and continued to walk out the door.

Pain and grief racked through her, and Morrigan clung to the table to keep from falling to the floor. She brushed away the tears, but they kept coming. She tried cursing him to blazes, but her heart was not in it. Finally she gathered her strength and stumbled from the room, leaving behind the shattered shards of her heart.

Thirty-Three

DRAGONET WALKED UP THE DARK STAIRS TO HIS father's comfortable chamber at a nearby inn. It was late, but he knew his father would be waiting for him. He slipped in the door without knocking.

"Leave us," commanded his father, and a serving wench darted past Dragonet into the hall.

"Am I disturbing you?" asked Dragonet.

"I am finished with her," said his father, readjusting his robes.

Dragonet looked away, recognizing with displeasure the hypocrisy with which he mentally judged his sire for breaking his vow of celibacy as Dragonet had done too. The difference was he loved Morrigan. But did that truly matter?

"Where is it?" asked his father. "The linen sheets Father Luke and Father Pierre brought were nothing but bed sheets. Barrick swears he had the real shroud, so where is it?"

"What will you do with it?" asked Dragonet, surreptitiously feeling the velvet pouch hidden within the interior pocket of his cloak.

The bishop gave him a cunning look. "Have you seen the cloth, boy?"

Dragonet nodded.

"Is it convincing?"

Dragonet tilted his head. Odd question. His father was not concerned about its authenticity but rather if it appeared to be real. "I am no expert, but it could be the true shroud. I have been looking for this relic for many years. Now that it is found, I want to know why you want it, and what you will do with it."

"You want your share of the reward." His father's eyes narrowed. "It was not enough that I saved you from starvation, saw to your care, ensured your advancement in the knighthood. No, now you want more. So tell me what you want, my lad. What is it you want from me?" His father's icy blue eyes cut through him.

"I want…" Dragonet paused. What did he want from him? For many years his father protected him and saw to his training and advancement, even as he criticized and used him. Dragonet had wished to find the shroud to prove his worth to his father. And yet his father's approval did not hold the power over him it once had. "I want to know what you will do with the shroud."

"You want to share in the glory the shroud will bring. You are no fool. You understand what this could do for the man who holds it."

Dragonet took a deep breath. It was not what he meant. "The shroud, what will it do for you?"

His father's eyes gleamed. "First I will demand a new castle and more land. The shroud must be housed in a grand palace. I will offer monthly viewings to generate the steady revenue pilgrims would bring, and allow more wealthy patrons closer access to the cloth for a greater price. Having the shroud under my control will do great things for me." He rubbed his hands together.

"Your control? So you do not intend to give it to the Church?"

The bishop shrugged. "I am the Church. And with that relic I could be the head of it."

Dragonet pushed his hair out of his eyes in a nervous gesture. "The head of the Church?"

"Why not? This find is extraordinary. Even the Holy Grail cannot compare. With it I should be moved up to the college of cardinals and from there…"

"Pope?"

His father smiled a cheerless grin. "Yes, I will be pope. When I am elevated, I can make you a bishop somewhere nice."

It was an offer he would have taken six months ago, but now the thought turned his stomach. He could not use a relic for selfish gain. Dragonet took a deep breath. He needed to find courage. "I only wanted to be acknowledged as your son."

The bishop of Troyes's blue eyes grew ice cold. "You are not my son. You are a mistake. An itch I needed to scratch."

"The girl who just left, she was an itch to scratch?"

"Who are you to judge me? I have heard the rumors of you and some lad."

"She is a girl dressed in the boys' clothing!" Dragonet felt heat rise.

His father smirked. "Yes, I know. I also know you may well leave her in the same condition that I leave that tavern wench. And neither one of us will ever look back. I took you in when you came to me starving. It is more than most in my position would have done. I deserve your gratitude and devotion."

"I do thank you, my father. But I cannot be your slave any longer."

His father's eyes flashed and he pressed his lips together until they were a thin white line. Silence filled the room, broken only by the steady drip of the rain. His father gave a forced smile that did not meet his eyes. "Let us not argue. Show me the shroud you found. I am anxious to see it for myself."

"I am sorry. I do not have it here for you."

"Then go retrieve it and bring it back."

Dragonet stood still, meeting his father's gaze.

"Dragonet... my son. Go bring your father the shroud." His forced smile turned to a snarl.

Dragonet shook his head. His father only acknowledged him when he wanted something. "No, Father."

The bishop rose from his chair, the smiling mask falling from his face. "What did you say to me?"

"I will not give you the shroud. It is holy. It should be treated with reverence, not used as a pawn in your bid for power."

"If you try to deny me the shroud, I will deny you!" The vein in his father's head bulged. "I have the power to build you up, and I can destroy you! Think carefully about the words you will say next. I will get the shroud, one way or another, but you need to decide whether you will continue to have a home.

You were starving when I first met you, I can put you back there!"

"I wish to do right by this relic."

"I have told you what is right," roared the bishop. "Give me the shroud now, or you are no longer worthy to be called my son."

"You have never been worthy to be called my father."

"You leave me no choice. Father Luke! Father Pierre!" The two priests entered the room and stood on either side of Dragonet. He was trapped.

"You know who these men are?" asked the bishop of Troyes, his face hard.

Dragonet nodded. The Inquisition. To fall into their hands was an unspeakable fate.

"Tell me the truth. Where is the shroud?"

Dragonet paused. "I do not have it."

"Search him!" ordered the bishop.

Dragonet made no attempt to resist and Father Luke found the velvet pouch, hidden in his cloak.

"Open it!" demanded the bishop, his face flushed, his beady eyes wide.

Father Luke gently opened the pouch and paused. "It is empty."

༄

Earlier that day, Dragonet met with Chaumont before the sun rose above the tree tops. Dragonet handed over the shroud, wrapped in parchment and placed in a plain linen pouch. "For the people," said Dragonet, his breath visible in the cool gray of dawn.

"For the people," said Chaumont, accepting the precious package. "There is a knight I know in France who is incorruptible. He will see this cloth is given to those who will share it, not use it for their own gain."

"Who is this knight?"

"He is Geoffroi de Charny, founder of the Order of the Star and the standard bearer for France."

"I have heard of him; in truth what knight has not? He is known for his piety and honor, I am sure he will do what is right." Dragonet leaned closer. "The bishop of Troyes will be determined to get it. I would leave soon and move fast."

Chaumont nodded. "Gavin and I will leave for France at once. You are a good man, Sir Dragonet."

"Few people think so at this point."

Chaumont smiled. "I imagine the bishop will ensure you no longer have a home with the Hospitallers. Will you continue to serve Argitaine?"

"No, he returns to France, and that country can no longer be my home."

"So what will you do now?"

"Now that I have nothing?" Dragonet shook his head. "I do not yet know."

"*Bon chance, mon ami.*"

Dragonet had no money, no home, and no current means to support himself. He was going to need more than luck.

Thirty-Four

MORRIGAN SAT IN THE WINDOW SEAT OF THE SOLAR, the cold stones freezing her rear. Outside the rain started to fall lightly; gray on black, a colorless landscape. The smell of warm gingerbread wafted through the room. She was not hungry. She was not anything anymore.

She had changed from the angry lass who first began her journey many months ago. She knew she could no longer work as a raider, but more than that, something deep within her had shifted. She used to be confident in who she was, a damned sinner. Life was hellish, but easy.

Her old self might have never returned to McNab Hall, choosing instead to go fight somewhere else until someone finally put her out of her misery. But her old self was gone. Something in her was lighter and it refused to give up. She had... hope. And hope is the most dangerous of all emotions.

Unsure who she was, Morrigan retreated into herself and grieved for what could never be. Yet somewhere deep within, a spark of hope burned.

"Gingerbread!" Andrew entered the room and pounced on the plate like a hungry puppy. The medicine had revived him, as had the presence of his wife Cait who had arrived most unexpectedly.

"Dinna eat it all, ye mongrel. Leave a little for me!" demanded Archie, grabbing a handful.

"I'm taking some for Cait," Andrew mumbled, his mouth full.

"Ye best hand it over before ye forget," said Cait, entering the room. Andrew gave her a piece, if somewhat reluctantly. The men settled comfortably in the chairs by the fire, and Cait sat on Andrew's lap in a manner that turned Morrigan's stomach.

"How long is she going to be like that?" hissed Cait in a whisper Morrigan could still hear.

"'Till her heart heals, I suppose. Sir Dragonet was a good man," said Andrew.

"I dinna ken she had a heart," whispered Cait.

Morrigan wished Cait was right. Without a heart it could not have been broken.

"Dinna fret. She will be back to her cheerful self soon enough," said Archie.

"I have ne'er seen her cheerful," said Cait.

"It's that slight smile she gets when causing someone pain."

Cait nodded. "That I've seen."

"I can hear ye!" shouted Morrigan.

"Morrigan!" Alys bustled in the room with a bundle of silk in her arms. "Yer best gown, hurry!"

"I winna put on a gown for naught." Morrigan turned back to the window. More rain. Gray fog. Heavy sigh. Her life was so full.

"But ye must! Archie?" Alys looked to her husband in vain.

"Leave her be. She'll do what she wants anyway."

"Nay. A gown it must be," insisted Alys. "Dragonet is here."

Morrigan's head whipped around so fast she fell off the window seat and stumbled to her feet. "Dragonet? Are ye sure? He is here?"

"Aye he is waiting in the hall."

Morrigan ran for the door, but Alys blocked it with determination, both hands on her hips.

"Ye will put on this gown, Morrigan McNab, or so help me ye'll wish ye were ne'er born."

Archie, Andrew, and Cait all stared with open mouths. Alys had never spoken to anyone in such a manner. Even Morrigan stopped short.

"I am familiar wi' that wish," Morrigan said quietly.

Alys turned to Archie. "Go downstairs if ye will. Sir Dragonet has come to speak to ye."

"To Archie? Why?" demanded Morrigan.

"Ye will put on this gown if I have to wrestle it on ye myself!"

Archie, Andrew, and Cait slipped out the door.

"Ye told me to put on a gown before and it all came to naught," grumbled Morrigan.

"Please, Morrigan."

"Be quick about it!"

Alys worked fast and laced her into her blue silk gown with great speed. Morrigan's hair was let down and covered by a lace veil. All the while anxiety and questions bubbled within Morrigan. Why was Dragonet here? Why did he wish to see

Archie? Had the shroud been stolen again? Did he need her help?

By the time she raced down the spiral stairs, she was so tense her stomach hurt. What was she going to say to him? Why did he come here? How could she be expected to say good-bye again?

Dragonet stood by the central hearth in the great hall speaking quietly with Archie. When she approached, Archie gave a signal and everyone left the great hall. Morrigan was immediately suspicious. Dragonet was dressed in a fine tunic, hose, and surcoat, with polished black leather boots. The clothes appeared to be new, and she had never seen him so handsomely attired. Her heart beat faster, as it did every time she saw him. This time, it hurt.

"What is wrong? Why did ye come?" she asked.

"I have something for you," he spoke in a soft, low voice.

"What?"

He held out a scroll, which she took. Opening it, she found writing in Latin.

"What is it?" she asked. "Explain yerself. Why are ye here and no' in France?"

"It is a decree from the bishop of Troyes. I have been excommunicated from the brotherhood."

"Excommunicated! But why? Did ye no' give him everything he asked?"

"I did not give him the shroud. I gave it to Chaumont to take to France to give it to a noble knight who will allow everyone to look upon it, not keep it as a secret relic or use it to gain power like my father."

"So he was angry at ye."

"Quite."

"But excommunicated! Can he do that?"

"I have been expelled from the brotherhood, not the Church."

"I dinna ken…"

"I am no longer a monk." A slow smile crept onto Dragonet's face.

Morrigan sucked in a great gasp of air. Not a monk? *Not a monk!*

"I took the books and scrolls we found in the cave and sold them to the abbey," he continued. "I used some of them to purchase back from the Church a certain section of land purchased by the Templars, whose deed was inherited by Barrick and then given to the Church."

"Our farmland," Morrigan's voice wavered as a tremor of raw emotion coursed through her.

"In exchange for the illuminated Bible I was also given this." He reached down to a bag by the hearth and pulled out the silver box.

Morrigan gasped again. "The box we found?"

Dragonet nodded.

"Is it still full of treasure?"

Dragonet nodded again.

"For me?"

"Given certain conditions."

"Which are?"

Dragonet set the box down and took her hands in his. "I love you, Morrigan McNab. I have not much, but what I have, I give to you. If you would consent to be my wife, I shall be happy for the rest of my days."

Morrigan began to shake with emotion. "I thought

ye were lost to me. I thought we could ne'er be together. I thought…" Her words were choked silent by a half sob.

He drew her close and wrapped his arms around her. Morrigan held tight as her knees gave way. She was where she belonged. She was finally home.

"Do you… do you mean to say yes or no?" asked Dragonet, his voice constrained.

"Aye! Yes! I will marry ye."

"Yes!" Dragonet hugged her close and lifted her off the ground, spinning her around once. "I feared you would say no."

"Why would I do a fool thing like that?"

"The last time you saw me, you said you never wished to see me again."

"Because I loved ye so terrible bad, it hurt."

"I love you too, Morrigan. But sometimes… often you do not do as I wish. I wanted to make a proposal you could not resist."

"Shame on ye for thinking ye could buy my affection. Ye can bring me no better gift than yerself. All I need is ye."

"So… am I to wish ye felicitations?" Archie's head peeked into the doorway.

"Yes, thank you," said Dragonet with a great smile.

"Why did ye wish to speak to my brother?" asked Morrigan.

"To get my blessing on his asking ye to marry him," announced Archie, clapping Dragonet on the shoulder.

"I would have wed ye even if Archie said no," murmured Morrigan. "And Archie would have married me off to any man who could draw breath."

Archie laughed. "Verra true! Come in everyone! 'Tis time to celebrate!"

"I ken how I wish to celebrate," whispered Morrigan to Dragonet. Her body came alive when touching his. Colors were vibrant, sounds were like music, and his physical closeness sent ripples of excitement coursing through her. "We need to find a priest before the sun sets."

"Did I mention how much I love you?" Dragonet kissed her sweetly on her smiling mouth, then pulled her close to do more serious work.

"Andrew!" called Archie. "Go find that hermit we got lying around and tell him m'sister needs to get herself wed before she is utterly debauched on the floor o' the hall."

"At least the floor is clean, dear," said Alys, wiping a tear from her eye.

"No' quite what I was worrit about, but good to know nonetheless," said Archie.

Morrigan heard very little of the rest, focusing instead on the growing desire Dragonet was building inside her. Unfortunately the hermit, who was sometimes called upon to do the work of a priest, could not be found until after supper. An eternity to wait for the anxious lovers.

Finally, the hermit was able to hear their vows. Admittedly he was not a formal priest, but one was not required by Scottish law to wed. One did not need a hermit either, but it was tradition for the McNabs, and added a nice touch of formality to the proceedings.

"I do," said Sir Dragonet with great sincerity.

"I do, too! Be quick, man!"

"I now pronounce ye—"

Morrigan grabbed Dragonet and locked her lips to his. Dragonet swept her into his arms and carried her to the stairs without breaking the kiss. By the time they reached the fourth floor, Dragonet was breathing hard but Morrigan was still in his arms. He staggered over the threshold and into Morrigan's chamber, slamming the door closed behind him with his foot and collapsing onto the bed with Morrigan.

"I hope ye have not worn yerself out," laughed Morrigan. "I have a busy night planned for ye."

"I am yours to command!"

Morrigan lay on her side next to Dragonet, who was stretched out on his back. "I canna believe that for once being in bed wi' ye is where I am supposed to be."

"I hope that does not lessen the appeal."

Morrigan looked over his muscular lean body, his full lips, the promising bulge in his breeches. "Not at all."

"Good. For as a wedded couple we have a certain mandate we must follow."

"And what is that?"

"We shall become the one flesh, as it says in the Bible, and never deny the other the... er... benefits of the flesh."

"I defer to yer superior wisdom of the Scriptures, and I am prepared to do my wifely duty."

Dragonet smiled. "God is good."

"Indeed! Now let's get these breeches off ye." Morrigan jumped up and pulled off Dragonet's boots. She unbuttoned his surcoat, winning herself a lazy smile from Dragonet.

He slowly sat up, removed his surcoat and tunic and turned her around to undo her laces. After several minutes Morrigan began to curse. "Take a bloody knife to it! Get me out of this thing!"

"And incur the wrath of Alys? I think not. Patience, my love." He slipped one hand down her bodice, which kept her happy for several more minutes until he could undo her properly. She took out her hair pins, placing her poisoned pin far from reach, and removed the gauzy veil, much to his appreciation. In a few moments they both stood before the other in the same condition in which they entered the world.

"You are beautiful."

She shook her head. "Nay, no' me."

"I say you are, and as you can plainly see, I get two votes."

Morrigan giggled. He put his hands on her waist and lay her down in the bed. She cuddled up to him, her head on his chest, her thigh over that second vote he claimed for himself.

He made a happy groaning sound and ran his hand down her back and squeezed her backside. He rolled her over and kissed her until she saw stars. She watched them circle about as he worked his way down her neck to her breast. She arched her back to him, giving herself wholly to the experience, saving nothing. She was where she was meant to be. He was her lover, her husband, her home.

"Speak to me in French," she purred.

"*Je t'adore.*" He shifted attention to her other breast.

"I adore you too."

"*Qu'est-ce que je ferais sans toi?*"

"Hmmm?"

"What would I do without you?"

"Be miserable I suppose." Morrigan ran her hands up and down his back. She could feel the rough edges of the scars his father had given him, yet another reason to be pleased he had not given that bastard the relic.

"*Je ne peux pas vivre sans toi.* I cannot live without you."

"Good we are married, then."

Dragonet lifted his head to look at her. "I cannot believe we are truly the man and wife. I feel as if I should stop now and run for the hills before your brother finds us."

"I swear if ye stop now…" She wrapped her legs around him and held him tight.

"Not a chance, *mon cœur*, my heart." He kissed her lips, her neck, her dangerous earlobes, sending tingling sensations swirling through her.

"More," she breathed.

"*Oui, mon poulet.*"

"Did ye just call me a chicken?"

He moved forward and claimed her for his own. Her breath caught with pleasure, and she forgot all about French. He moved slowly, building sweet tension.

"More!" she demanded.

"*Je vis d'amour et d'eau douce.* I live on love and fresh water."

"Why are ye speaking nonsense? Move faster. I want more!"

"*Tu me rends fou,*" he growled, but moved faster until their bodies took over all reason. She closed her eyes, lost in the sensation until something exploded within her, and she clutched him, screaming her release. He drove into her with much force, shuddered, and collapsed on top of her, panting hard.

"Canna... breathe..."

"Sorry." He rolled off her and onto his side, still holding her close. "*Je t'aime.*"

Morrigan breathed deep. She did not need that one translated to know he said he loved her. She was exactly where she was meant to be. She was loved. For the first time she could recall, everything was how it should be. It was good. Except... "What did ye say?"

"I love you," he murmured sleepily.

"Nay, before that. Ye said 'too muh ron foo.'"

Dragonet chuckled. "You make me daft."

"What? And I thought it was a term of endearment."

"It was. It is."

"Doesna sound like it."

He drew her closer. "Get some sleep. In about an hour I may call on you again to perform your wifely duty."

Morrigan closed her eyes with a smile. After lying awake for a few moments, she nudged her husband.

"Has it been an hour yet?"

Author's Note

One of the things I enjoy about writing historical novels is doing the research. I often discover things I never knew. For example, in the middle of the fourteenth century, France sent a contingent of knights to Scotland and paid the clans to attack England, essentially to distract England from France (which was busy losing the Hundred Years War). When I discovered French knights were running around Scotland, I knew I had the setting for my next novel.

In *True Highland Spirit*, I tried to stay true to what is known about the war. During the year of 1355, the French/Scot army took Nisbet and the important town of Berwick, but were unable to take the castle. King Edward III of England quickly withdrew from France and marched to Berwick's rescue with eighty thousand experienced and well-trained troops. Knowing they could not withstand a direct attack from the English troops, and growing tired of the rustic charm of the Scots, the French troops abandoned the Scots to their fate.

King Edward was then determined to take the whole of Scotland. Early in 1356, King Edward declared himself the king of Scotland and marched north to take control. The Scots adopted a defensive posture and used a little trickery. They sent the Earl of Douglas to negotiate their surrender and gained ten days of a truce. When Edward finally marched into Scotland, he found it devoid of any food for his troops. The army had to rely on supply lines from England, which were routinely ambushed by the Scots.

King Edward was enraged and marched into Scotland, burning and destroying everything in his wake. Even the beautiful abbey at Haddington, called the Lamp of Lothian, was burnt down and utterly destroyed. This initiative was later known as Burnt Candlemas (so named because it occurred during celebration of Candlemas). Unable to supply his troops, King Edward was forced to retreat, and Scotland was once again saved from being conquered by its more powerful neighbor.

Though I have Morrigan fight in these battles, I must concede it would have been highly unusual for a woman to fight as a knight. Even more unlikely, however, is the story of a French teenage peasant girl who somehow convinced the king of France to let her lead his armies—and won. So if it could happen for Joan of Arc later in the Hundred Years War, I figured it was plausible for Morrigan... and because it is fiction, I was able to give Morrigan a much happier ending!

Another important component of this book is the Templar treasure—doesn't every good medieval novel need a little Templar treasure? Religious relics were big business in medieval times, and churches actively sought valuable relics for the prestige and income from pilgrims they would bring. In this story, the relic in question is a shroud, now known as the Shroud of Turin.

The Shroud of Turin contains the image of a man who appears to have wounds consistent with crucifixion. The origin and meaning of this shroud has been the subject of heated debate for hundreds of years. Some say it is the true burial cloth of Jesus Christ; others contend it is a medieval forgery.

The actual history of the Shroud of Turin before the fifteenth century is a bit nebulous. One theory contends that it was taken from the Holy Land by the Templar knights during the Crusades and later revealed in France by the surviving nephew of one of those knights. Some historical evidence indicates the shroud was in the hands of the French knight Geoffroi de Charny, in the town of Lirey during the 1350s. Interestingly, a Templar knight with a similar name was burned at the stake in 1314, leading some to draw a connection between these two knights and the shroud. According to some accounts, the shroud was displayed in Lirey and declared as a fake by the bishop of Troyes.

For the purposes of this story, I have embraced the Templar theory (though I acknowledge there are many others). While there is no evidence to suggest the shroud was ever in Scotland, we do know that some of the Templars fled to Scotland to avoid persecution… so hey—it's possible!

The Shroud of Turin continues to spark debate. Although many theories exist, no one has been able to definitively determine how the markings found on the shroud were made. Whether or not this cloth has any connection with the historical Jesus of Nazareth may never be known. Regardless of the shroud's authenticity, many believers view the image as a representation of the sufferings of Christ who died for the forgiveness of sins and the promise of eternal life. Here's wishing you the peace of Christ and that most dangerous of all emotions… hope.

READ ON FOR EXCERPTS FROM
AMANDA FORESTER'S HIGHLANDER SERIES:

THE HIGHLANDER'S HEART

THE HIGHLANDER'S SWORD

TRUE HIGHLAND SPIRIT

NOW AVAILABLE FROM
SOURCEBOOKS CASABLANCA

From *The Highlander's Sword*

❧

Gascony, France, 1346

IF THEY CAUGHT HIM, HE WOULD HANG. OR PERHAPS, he mused with the detached calm born of shock, he would be eviscerated first, then hung. Best not to find out. Sir Padyn MacLaren ran through a throng of shocked ladies-in-waiting to the tower stairs before his fiancée screamed in fury. Or rather his ex-fiancée, since the lovely Countess Marguerite had just made it clear she intended to marry Gerard de Marsan. The same de Marsan who had tried to slit MacLaren's throat and now lay on the floor—dead.

Soldiers from the floor below rushed up the stairs to their lady's aid. MacLaren wiped the blood from his eyes. The slash down his face was bleeding something fierce, but he gave it no mind. He needed to get past the guards, or his bloodied face would be the least of his troubles.

"Hurry!" MacLaren said to the first man up the stairs. "Gerard de Marsan has attacked the countess. To her, quick! I will fetch the surgeon." The guards ran past him, and he dashed out the inner gate before the alarm sounded and soldiers poured from their barracks. MacLaren raced toward the outer gate, but the portcullis crashed down before him. Turning toward the stone staircase that led to the wall walk, he ran to a young guard who looked at him, unsure.

"Who attacks us?" MacLaren asked the young man, who stammered in response.

"Go ask your captain. I'll keep watch." MacLaren ran past the guard up the stairs to the battlement. Without stopping to think or break his stride, he ran through the battlements over the embrasure and into the air. For a moment he was suspended in time, free without the ground beneath him, then he plunged down the sheer drop to the moat below. The shock of cold water and muck robbed him of breath, and he struggled to the other side. MacLaren scrambled up the embankment and crawled into the brush, bolts flying toward him from the castle walls. Rushing through the thicket to the road, he pulled a surprised merchant from his horse and rode for cover.

MacLaren raced from Montois castle without looking back. Along the road, a dusty figure of a knight rode toward him. MacLaren drew his sword and charged. The knight reined in and threw up his visor. It was Chaumont, his second in command.

"Marguerite has betrayed us to the English," Chaumont called.

"She told me that herself," growled MacLaren, pointing to his cut face. "We need to get to camp and warn the men, or they will all be put to the sword."

Chaumont nodded. "I got word of her betrayal shortly after you rode for Montois and commanded the men to pull back to Agen."

"Ye've done well." MacLaren exhaled.

"Indeed I have. Nice of you to notice."

The thundering riders approaching cut short their conversation. They abandoned the road in favor of an overland route through dense forested terrain in which they hoped to lose the pursuing soldiers. They traveled many hours into the night, until they finally felt safe enough to stop by the shores of a small black lake.

"You need tending, my friend," said Chaumont.

"Have ye a needle?" MacLaren asked grimly.

MacLaren stood without flinching while Chaumont stitched the gash on his face. MacLaren focused on the dark water before him, unbidden memories of the day's events washing over him. He had faced the English to protect Marguerite before they could reach her castle at Montois. The hard-fought victory had been won, but his closest kin had been lost.

"Patrick died for nothing." MacLaren's voice shook as he struggled with the words. "What an utter fool I was, trusting that deceitful wench. I should be dead on that field, not him." MacLaren clenched his jaw, holding back emotion. "There is nothing left for me here. 'Tis time I take my men and go back where I belong."

"What is it like, this land of your birth?" asked Chaumont, finishing his work.

MacLaren closed his eyes, remembering. "Balquidder. 'Tis a wild place, full of wind and rain. It can be a hard life at times, but I'm never more alive than when I'm in the Highlands." He turned to the young French knight. "Your friendship is the only thing I will regret to leave behind."

Chaumont looked at him intently. "Take me with you."

"Your place is here."

Chaumont shook his head. "If you had not given me a chance, I would still be some rich man's squire, polishing his armor and servicing his wife. I have served you in times of war, and I will serve you still, if you will have me."

"It would be an honor." MacLaren clasped his hand to the Frenchman's shoulder. They embraced the way men do, slapping each other hard on the back.

"Urgh!" Chaumont made a face. "You smell like the devil's arse."

"I swam through the moat to escape the castle. Now I know exactly where the garderobes empty into." MacLaren turned back to look over the lake. "That water was like Marguerite, a beautiful exterior, but underneath, naught but a filthy sewer."

The words were barely out of his mouth before he was pushed hard and he fell gracelessly into the cold clean lake. He came up sputtering, only to hear the Frenchman's laughter. MacLaren bathed in the cold water and emerged the better for it. He pulled himself swiftly up the bank and tossed Chaumont into the water for good measure. It was time to go home.

"Step along now," MacLaren called to his soggy companion. "Come to the Highlands, my friend, and we shall feast like heroes."

෴

Balquidder, Scotland

Shrouded in the winding cloth of the dense mist, a shadowy apparition of a horse and rider stood on the high peak of the Braes of Balquidder. Built into the side of the craggy rock, Creag an Turic, the abandoned tower house of the MacLarens, loomed stark and black against the pre-dawn sky. Below, the small village of Balquidder slept by the shores of Loch Voil. The MacLaren fields lay mostly fallow, brown and grey in the early morning gloom. Without its laird, misfortune and neglect had befallen the clan, leaving it vulnerable to raids from its neighbors. Few clansmen remained, scraping out a living as best they could.

In the valley below, a young boy stood in the doorway of a farmhouse. He gaped up at the ghostly figure and blinked—horse and rider were gone.

"Mama! I seen the ghost!"

"Come away from there, sweetling. What do ye ken about such things?"

"I seen him looking down on us. Do ye think it be an ill omen?"

Mary Patrick sighed. Having your nine-year-old son tell you there is a ghost at the door before you even got your boots on in the morning couldn't be a good sign. She silently said a quick prayer to a few saints for protection and one to the Holy Mother for good measure.

"'Twas the Bruce," whispered Gavin, his eyes gleaming.

"Robert the Bruce is no' riding these hills," said Mary to Gavin's skeptical face. "And even if he is, he's no' going to help ye wi' yer chores. Now off wi' ye. We've much to do if we want food in our bellies."

Somewhere in the ethereal mist, the cloaked figure raced at an inhuman pace... straight for Dundaff Castle.

FROM *THE HIGHLANDER'S HEART*

❧

Northumbria, England
Late spring, 1355

ONE THING WAS PERFECTLY CLEAR; IT WAS TIME TO GET rid of her husband. Isabelle, Countess of Tynsdale, tightened her grasp on the saddle and continued to plot ways to end her marriage, for if she ever was returned to her husband, she would die.

Unfortunately for her train of thought, her tall mount moved with a swaying motion Isabelle found disconcerting. She had imagined riding a horse would be delightful, but now, perched on top of the stiff, boxlike saddle, Isabelle was reevaluating her opinion of horses.

"You must not let him take you back," said Marjorie, Isabelle's former nursemaid and companion who rode next to Isabelle on the dusty road. It was an unnecessary reminder. Other than trying not to fall off her horse, Isabelle could think of little else but escaping her husband, the Lord Tynsdale.

"I am not going to sit idly by whilst that husband of yours murders you," continued Marjorie. "I have raised you since you were naught but a bundle of swaddling clothes, and I will not be having that old worm take you with him to perdition."

"I have no intention of being my husband's fourth deceased wife. I had hoped to be a widow," said Isabelle with a wistful sigh.

"It would be most considerate of him if he was to keel over dead, but I warrant we cannot expect kindness from the likes of him."

"No, not him," replied Isabelle in a soft voice. She had been married five years ago when she was sixteen, and Tynsdale carried more years than anyone cared to count. She spent one violent night with him before fleeing back to her uncle at Alnsworth Castle. Isabelle rubbed the scar on her temple, the one visible reminder of that dreadful night.

"'Tis a shame having a rat bastard for a husband is not grounds for divorce," Marjorie sniffed.

Isabelle smiled at Marjorie. "Indeed, quite so."

"I hesitate to suggest it, but maybe you could do something to cause your husband to divorce you, like take up with another man?"

Isabelle laughed but shook her head. "I could present Lord Tynsdale with a dozen illegitimate babes and he would never dissolve the marriage. Not when he stands to gain all of Alnsworth. The castle is too great a prize."

"I wish your uncle could have clung to life a little longer."

"I wish I had not inherited Alnsworth." Isabelle shuddered to think of what would happen if Tynsdale ever became lord of Alnsworth. Her uncle had protected her from Tynsdale for the past five years, which had sparked a bloody feud between the two barons. If Tynsdale took control of Alnsworth, his revenge would be felt by all. A heavy mantle of fear wrapped around her shoulders, but Isabelle resisted giving in to the seductive draw of despair.

"I must convince King Edward to dissolve this union," Isabelle said brightly, shaking off her fear. They had left Alnsworth that morning to travel to the court of the king of England. Isabelle smiled at the prospect of going to court and meeting King Edward II. For five years Alnsworth Castle had been a safe refuge, but Isabelle longed for freedom.

Isabelle took a deep breath of fresh air, untainted by the smells of castle life. Granted, the smell of horses figured prominently, but the aroma was at least different, if not completely fresh.

The procession of horses was unexpectedly called to halt. On the road ahead, her entourage had been stopped by a group of soldiers riding toward them. It was a bright, sunny day and the hard-packed dirt road bordered a grassy field to her right and a tall forest to her left.

Her captain of the guard rode forward to meet with the lead rider. After a short exchange, both men dismounted and continued to speak with each other. Small in stature, the stranger was as wide as he was tall, a contrast to Captain Corbett, a tall, broad-shouldered man with a thick mustache.

"What is this about?" asked Marjorie.

"I have no idea," answered Isabelle. Captain Corbett turned toward her with a grim expression. "But I fear it is not in my favor."

Rounding the bend, the rest of the approaching party came into view. Mounted guards were followed by a small troop of foot soldiers. Their banner waved bright blue and gold in the sun. Isabelle's stomach churned. They were Tynsdale's men.

"Isabelle!" Marjorie's eyes went wide. Isabelle knew what she was thinking. If she was given to those soldiers she would never get another chance to escape. The small man and her captain walked toward her. She needed to do something—fast.

"Tell them I had the sudden need for privacy. I'll go yonder across the field. Tell Captain Corbett I'll meet him later at the church at Bewcastle. Only…" Isabelle's eyes met Marjorie's. "I do not wish to make trouble for you."

"Nonsense, Isabelle, if they catch you it could mean all our lives." Marjorie leaned toward her, speaking in a fierce whisper. "You are a clever girl, keep your wits and you will do well. Now make haste!"

Marjorie slapped the rump of Isabelle's horse. Isabelle swung the reins and dug in her heels, something she had never before attempted. Her horse jumped and skittered sideways, then bolted into the field. Isabelle hung on for dear life, thrilling in the speed and her newfound freedom. She risked a backward glance. The guards were speaking heatedly with Marjorie and Captain Corbett but had not yet given chase. She had a head start. Isabelle bounced across the field relishing her swift mount, the sun on her face and her last-minute reprieve.

Without breaking his stride, her horse bolted into the thick forest on the other side of the field. Isabelle shrieked and ducked to avoid a low-hanging branch. She abandoned the reins in favor of holding onto the saddle with both hands.

"Ease up!" she called to her errant mount. Despite her desire to put distance between herself and Tynsdale's men, she did not care for being splattered against a tree. "Stop, oh stop, you vile creature."

The vile creature in question did not stop and, being a sturdy mount with fresh legs, continued to run. Isabelle grabbed at the horse's mane and screamed at the horse to no avail. If anything, her mount gained speed. Isabelle closed her eyes and gripped the pommel, hoping the horse would not stumble or collide with a tree.

After what seemed like an eternity, her well-conditioned horse began to break his stride and settled into a jarring trot. Isabelle gritted her teeth, sure the wretched beast had chosen this pace to cause her the most discomfort.

Thick foliage brushed against her, scratching her face, arms, and legs. The road where she had last seen Tynsdale's men was now miles behind her. Her reins were caught on the bridle, and she leaned forward to reclaim them. The horse, sensing her movement, broke into a run, heading straight for a stream. Galloping closer, Isabelle realized the stream was a wide river, swollen from the spring rains.

"Stop! Oh, why will you not stop? Can you not see there's a—" Isabelle's words were stolen with her breath as the horse plunged into the icy water. She clung with desperation to the saddle. The horse splashed forward into the swiftly moving waters. When the horse began to swim, Isabelle feared for her life. It would be so disappointing to escape certain death, only to be killed later that same day by one's own horse. Isabelle clung tighter with icy fingers and fiery determination.

They were swept downstream a good ways before the horse struggled to the far shore and fought its way up the bank. Isabelle hugged the neck of her horse as her mount continued to trot along. Afraid to reach again for the reins, Isabelle contented herself to watch the scenery until her mount finally stopped and put down his head for a bite of grass.

"Oh, finally," Isabelle muttered and slid down the side of the horse, landing in an undignified heap. Isabelle collapsed in the grass, reveling in the wondrous feeling of being on solid ground again. Taking a deep breath, she regained her feet. Tugging at the ties of her wet, wool cloak, she pulled it off and tossed it over the saddle.

"You are a very ill-mannered beast," she reprimanded her mount. "When we get to wherever we are going, I shall ask their cook to serve me some horseflesh stew for supper." The bay horse looked up from his meal. "I shall have your tail made into a flyswatter and your hooves carved into ink wells." The horse turned his head and looked at her with big, brown eyes framed with long, black lashes. Too late, Isabelle noted a flash of intelligence.

"Nooooo!" Isabelle shouted as the horse trotted away. "I didn't mean it. I would never do anything like that." Isabelle ran after her mount. "Come back, oh, please don't leave me. I lost my temper, but it has been a trying day. Oh, please do come back!"

Isabelle ran until every gulp of air burned and her sides stung. Unable to continue, Isabelle doubled over panting, her hands on her hips, watching her horse's disappearing backside. She collapsed on a large rock and evaluated her situation. She was lost somewhere along the border between England and Scotland. Her horse was gone. She had no provisions, not even her cloak, and she was still damp from the river. Not good.

On the bright side, she had escaped her husband's guards, and if she could survive this minor mishap she would no doubt live a long, happy, and prosperous life. She smiled to herself and decided not to let a little thing like being lost, alone, wet, and hungry bother her in the slightest.

Isabelle stood tall, shoulders back, chin high, to march back to the river and from there to the nearest town. From there she could arrange transport to Bewcastle... with her coin purse that was in the pocket of her cloak. She twisted her signet rings, trying to think of what to do. Her rings were her only material possessions now, one on each hand. Tynsdale was on her left and Alnsworth on her right. Her two worlds at war. Twisting off her rings she deposited them safely in the pocket of her gown. It would not do to lose them.

Isabelle marched forward in the direction she thought was the river, ignoring the unpleasant way her wet chemise clung and chaffed her legs. After two hours walking and no river in sight, even she had to admit she was lost. All the trees looked exactly the same. A buzzing sensation in her stomach told her that either she was hungry or starting to panic. She gulped down fear, chose a new direction and strode boldly, telling herself that this was surely the correct path.

Isabelle marched on through the day, trying to find any sort of human habitation. Clinging to the hope that help was near, she pushed her way through thick brush and bramble until shafts of sunlight were no longer filtering down through the trees, a sure sign the sun was low in the sky. Through the fading light she kept moving, hoping that somehow her luck would take a dramatic shift in her favor.

Isabelle's feet were sore and blistered, her gown ripped and tattered, and her long, black hair hung loose, having long since lost her headdress. Her thin veneer of optimism had been scraped away by a thousand clutching branches, and even she had to admit her situation was growing dire. She wanted nothing more than to stop and rest, but feared if she lay down she may never again get up, so she forced her legs to keep moving.

She tore through one more bush and stumbled out onto a wide, empty path. Exhausted, it took her a moment to recognize what she had found—a road. She collapsed to her knees and ran her hands along the hard-packed dirt. The road was rutted and narrow, dense forest on either side, but Isabelle was overjoyed for such a lovely sight. On impulse, she leaned down and kissed the ground.

"There now, what do we have 'ere?"

Isabelle whirled around and stood up so fast her head spun and she stumbled on shaky legs. Three raggedy men were walking down the road toward her.

"Why 'tis naught but a dirty wench," said a thin man in a red cap.

"Looks an ill-used whore at that. Must have been

dropped by her last sport," said a portly man with the remnants of his porridge still in evidence on his shirt.

"Been too long for me," said a third man with large forearms and no front teeth. "I dinna care how used she is. I thinks I'll have me a tickle."

Isabelle gasped. Her heart pounded in her chest and she glanced around for her guard to put a swift end to these insolent men. All she saw was uncaring trees. She considered fleeing, but the brush was thick, and her legs were barely holding her up. She straightened her shoulders and tried to appear severe and forbidding.

"You will come no farther if you please. My guard surrounds you. I command you to leave at once."

The three men stopped short, looking around her suspiciously.

"She be English," whispered Red Cap, loud enough for all to hear.

"Yes, English," said Isabelle, hoping that would be a deterrent. Were these ruffians Scots? What were they doing on English soil? "My patience is not without end. If you value your lives you will leave without delay."

The men stopped walking toward her, but they did not leave. Suddenly, No Teeth pushed Red Cap forward, knocking him into her. She struggled to keep upright, and he jumped back from her immediately. The men drew their knives and watched the bushes, waiting for attack. When nothing happened, Isabelle knew her bluff had been called.

"Well now, lassie," smiled No Teeth, "looks to me no one will mind if we enjoy yer company a bit."

"Leave me alone," said Isabelle, wishing her voice had not wavered when she said it.

No Teeth, Red Cap, and Porridge Shirt crept toward her, their knives still drawn. She backed down the road away from her assailants.

"I am not a... a whore," said Isabelle, hating the way the word sounded on her tongue, but not knowing how else to convey the meaning.

"Aye, ye'd only be a whore if we paid ye," snarled No Teeth, "and we dinna plan to pay."

Isabelle faced her attackers and screamed for all her worth. No Teeth leapt for her and she turned and ran with another ear-piercing screech. She was pushed to the ground with such force it knocked the scream from her lungs. Hands grabbed all over her. She spun on the ground and kicked with ferocity, gaining some satisfaction on hitting something solid and seeing Porridge Shirt doubled over in pain.

"There now, hold her lads, while I gets me turn."

Isabelle shut her eyes and screamed again. Her voice sounded much louder and more ferocious than she expected. Surprised, she opened her eyes to find her three assailants had vanished. She closed her mouth, but the horrible noise continued. A cloaked figure rushed past her, nothing but a blur of fury, his battle cry blasting through the trees.

He disappeared into the brush after her assailants and the forest sank into an unnatural silence. Isabelle sat on the dirt road, unable to scream, unable to move. She strained to hear what was happening, yet all was still. Suddenly, a barbarian emerged from the forest before her like some fey creature. Isabelle gasped and covered her mouth with her hands. He was a monstrous beast holding a long sword with both hands, his face obscured in shadow.

And he was half-naked.

Acknowledgments

I greatly appreciate all the support and encouragement I have received from my family, my local RWA chapters, and my fellow Casablanca authors. Thanks to my editor, Deb Werksman, who has taught me much, and my agent, Barbara Poelle, who is a wellspring of motivation and knowledge. Thanks to Andre Tapp, who ensured my French hero spoke something resembling French. Many thanks to Laurie Maus, who served as my beta reader, and my husband, who helped with edits and walked that dangerous, fine line between encouragement and critique—you are one brave man!

About the Author

Amanda Forester holds a PhD in psychology and worked for many years in academia before discovering that writing historical novels was way more fun. She lives in the Pacific Northwest with her husband and two energetic children. *True Highland Spirit* is the third novel in her Highlander series. Her previous novels include *The Highlander's Sword* and *The Highlander's Heart*. You can visit her at www.amandaforester.com.

A *Booklist* Top 10 Romance Fiction of 2011

The Return of Black Douglas

by Elaine Coffman

He'll help a woman in need, no matter where she came from...

Alysandir Mackinnon rules his clan with a fair but iron fist. He has no time for softness or, as he sees it, weakness. But when he encounters a bewitching young beauty who may or may not be a dangerous spy, but is surely in mortal danger, he's compelled to help...

She's always wondered if she was born in the wrong time...

Thrown back in time to the tumultuous, dangerous Scottish Highlands of the sixteenth century, Isobella Douglas has a lot to learn about her ancestors, herself, and her place in the world. Especially when she encounters a Highland laird who puts modern men to shame...

Each one has secrets to keep, until they begin to strike a chord in each other's hearts that's never been touched before...

For more Elaine Coffman, visit:

www.sourcebooks.com

Highland Heat

by Mary Wine

❦

As brave as she is impulsive, Deirdre Chattan's tendency to follow her heart and not her head has finally tarnished her reputation beyond repair. But when powerful Highland Laird Quinton Cameron finds her, he doesn't care about her past—it's her future he's about to change...

From the moment Quinton sets eyes on Deirdre, rational thought vanishes. For in her eyes he sees a fiery spirit that matches his own, and he'll be damned if he'll let such a wild Scottish rose wither under the weight of a nun's habit...

With nothing to lose, Deirdre and Quinton band together to protect king and country. But what they can accomplish alone is nothing compared to what they can build with their passion for each other...

❦

"Dramatic and vivid...Scorching love scenes threaten to set the sheets aflame."—*Publishers Weekly* starred review

"A lively and exciting adventure."—*Booklist*

For more Mary Wine books, visit:

www.sourcebooks.com